CONSUMED

P9-DDR-758

CONSUMED

REBECCA ZANETTI

LYRICAL PRESS
Kensington Publishing Corp.
www.kensingtonbooks.com

LYRICAL PRESS BOOKS are published by

Kensington Publishing Corp.
119 West 40th Street
New York, NY 10018

Copyright © 2012 Rebecca Zanetti

All rights reserved. No part of this book may be reproduced in any form or by any means without the prior written consent of the publisher, excepting brief quotes used in reviews.

All Kensington titles, imprints, and distributed lines are available at special quantity discounts for bulk purchases for sales promotions, premiums, fund-raising, educational, or institutional use.

Special book excerpts or customized printings can also be created to fit specific needs. For details, write or phone the office of the Kensington special sales manager: Kensington Publishing Corp., 119 West 40th Street, New York, NY 10018, attn: Special Sales Department; phone: 1-800-221-2647.

LYRICAL PRESS and the Lyrical Press logo are trademarks of the Kensington Publishing Corp.

ISBN-13: 978-1-61650-775-6
ISBN-10: 1-61650-775-6

First edition: July 2012

10 9 8 7 6 5 4 3 2 1

Printed in the United States of America

Also available in an electronic edition:

ISBN-13: 978-1-60183-013-5
ISBN-10: 1-60183-013-0

To celebrate Brandie Chapman's 40th birthday,
a group of twenty gals headed to Vegas in February of 2012.
This book is dedicated to this incredibly energetic group—may
all stories stay in Vegas, and thank God we made it home.

ACKNOWLEDGMENTS

So many people work in so many different ways to make a book come together. I have several people to thank for help with this book and sincerely apologize for anyone I've forgotten.

Thank you to Tony, Gabe, and Karly Zanetti, my very patient family, for giving me time and space to write, as well as support and love . . . and chocolate;

Thank you to my amazing editor, Megan Records, whose hard work, dedication, and sheer enjoyment in the romance genre make this journey all the more rewarding;

Thank you to my incredibly talented agent, Caitlin Blasdell, whose ability to see the deeper layer for characters and arcs never fails to amaze me, and who works so very hard within this challenging industry;

Thank you to all the folks at both Kensington Publishing and Liza Dawson Associates who work many long hours for their authors;

Thank you to my critique partners, Sayde Grace and Jennifer Dorough—you two rock;

Thanks also to my constant support system: Gail and Jim English, Debbie and Travis Smith, Stephanie and Don West, Brandie and Mike Chapman, Jessica and Jonah Namson, and Kathy and Herb Zanetti.

Prologue

Thirty years ago

Katie tried to sink into the dented kitchen cupboard, her bare feet digging into cracks in the faded linoleum floor. Fear hurt her tummy. Jim Bob was mad again, yelling at foster mom Wanda about the soup being cold.

Wasn't soup always cold?

She'd only been at this foster home for a week. Yesterday she'd turned four years old and nobody remembered. That was okay. Her mama and daddy lived in heaven, and they probably remembered. She wished she remembered what they looked like.

Jim Bob yelled louder, grabbing a wooden spoon to throw against the peeling wallpaper of old roses. His face got really red, and the fat under his chin jiggled. Stains covered his big belly and ripped pants, but he didn't care about clothes.

He cared about soup.

Wanda grabbed the spoon off the floor and threw it back at him. Dirt flew through the air along with chunks of noodles. She was skinny in her ugly blue dress, but she could throw. A cigarette hung out of her cracked lips, dropping ashes on her scuffed shoes. She pointed her finger at Katie, yelling that having a foster kid meant too much work no matter how much money she brought in, especially since the stupid kid didn't even do the dishes earlier.

Jim Bob whirled on Katie, his eyes a mean brown.

She bit her lip to keep from crying, her legs shaking. The dishes were too high on the counter for her to reach. Fear made her lungs ache. Panic had her eying the door for an escape. The wild forest outside wasn't as scary as Jim Bob.

Then a tingling started in her cold feet. Shudders swept through her arms. She hurt. A lot.

Crying out, she dropped to her knees. Jagged edges of the linoleum cut into her skin. Black covered her vision. What was happening? She hadn't been bad. All her bones popped and something ripped. Her dress?

Shaking her head, she tried to look past the black. Colors. So many colors danced on the dust mites. A million different pinks swirled around. A zillion different blues. And smells—she could even smell the pine trees outside along with stinky Jim Bob. He stunk like wet dirt. She opened her mouth and a meow came out.

Paws. She had paws.

What had happened? Did she do something wrong? Girls didn't have paws. Fear had her shaking so hard her teeth rattled.

Terror had her lifting her head to see Jim Bob and Wanda staring at her with their mouths wide open.

Wanda started screaming. "It's the work of the devil. Kill her!"

Jim Bob shouted and jumped toward his shotgun in the corner. His beefy hand wrapped around the thick part.

Katie didn't want to die. Where was the devil?

Jim Bob swung the big pointy end toward her.

Run!

She leaped for the doggie door in the screen and rushed into the early night. Seconds later a shotgun blast echoed behind her.

She ran through the forest, her paws slapping the rough trail. How did she have paws? Fear crawled inside her tummy like a mean spider. Nobody told her she was gonna turn into an animal when she got scared now.

Darkness pressed in from the trees on either side of her, but her eyes worked really good. Bugs crawling in the grass. Very cool—so many of them. Different greens shining in the moss. Much prettier than she'd ever seen before. How could she see all the new stuff? Something was wrong with her.

Her panting filled her ears along with the sound of something loud coming. Jim Bob, yelling that she was a monster. He was gonna shoot her.

One smell cut through the rest. Something good. Something safe. She turned and ran harder, toward the smell of cinnamon.

The smell got stronger and stronger until she turned a corner and skidded to a stop. Three super big men stared back at her. They had bows and arrows—were they gonna shoot her, too?

Jim Bob crashed through the brush behind her.

Yowling, she leaped for safety, trying to rush past the people.

Faster than possible, the biggest man snagged her by the fur on her neck. He tucked her into his warm chest.

She struggled, nipping at his hand with her new sharp teeth.

"Shhh." He ran a hand over her head, scratching her ears, leaning in close to sniff her. "We were just looking for you, kitten."

She stilled, allowing his heat to warm her. Her chest

hurt from running so hard. Snuggling closer, the scent of cinnamon and forest surrounded her. She'd smelled the man. How could a person smell like safety?

Jim Bob stood up, his gun pointed at her. "Put that *thing* down."

Her new friend swiveled around until they faced the other way and not the gun. "Noah, please get the shotgun," he said mildly.

Jim Bob yelled and a small fight sounded.

"Got it," a new voice said.

They turned back around. Jim Bob didn't have his gun and he looked really, really mad. His eyes had gone all black and his lips smacked into a tight white line. The lady at the day care Katie went to last year said she wasn't supposed to say "hate," but he looked like hate.

Katie shivered, and the man held her tighter. She tried to talk, but only a *meow* came out.

Jim Bob sputtered, his face turning an ugly red. He hitched his pants up over his big belly, spit flying out of his mouth when he talked. "She's a freak. Foster kid. Turned into . . ." He swept his beefy hand toward her.

Oh no. Now they'd all know she was a freak, whatever that was. Something told her a freak was something bad. She started to struggle again. If the guy would drop her, she might be able to get away. To safety. Even if she was a freak, she didn't wanna die.

He shushed her. "Hold still. Nobody's gonna hurt you, sweetheart. Just hold still for a minute." A gentle hand brushed over her ears again, and she fought the really weird urge to purr. Warmth spread along her neck. The guy stared at Jim Bob. "I'm assuming this is Kathryn Johnson, and you're . . . James Robert Neverly?"

Surprise flashed hard across Jim Bob's face. "Jim Bob. And yeah, that's Kathryn. She's a foster kid. Monster."

Yeah, she was a monster. Funny that she didn't feel

scared anymore. Lifting her chin, she looked at her hero. Long hair slid to his shoulders in lots of colors. Black, brown, blond, maybe even a little red. Pretty. His eyes glowed kinda gold, kinda brown. Right now they weren't nice, but he was looking at Jim Bob, so that was okay. So long as the man didn't look at her like that.

"I'm Jordan Pride," he said. "She's mine now."

Surprise filled Katie. Why would the guy want a cat? She was a cat, right?

Jim Bob took a step back, his gaze swinging from Katie to Jordan. "You don't seem surprised a girl turned into a little cougar."

Jordan's heart beat slow and strong beneath her ear. "Maybe you've had too much to drink. Either way, you're going to forget about her and go on your way," he said.

Jim Bob's eyes began to shine, and he smiled a mean smile, his crooked teeth somehow sharp in the night. His beefy hands rubbed together. "I'm sure we can come to an arrangement."

The smell of burning bushes tickled her nose and came from Jordan. Something told her it was the smell of being mad. How weird to find out "mad" had a smell. Maybe all cats smelled feelings.

He tightened his hold. "Don't you want to know what I'm going to do with her?"

"Not if you make silence worth my while." Jim Bob wasn't even looking at her anymore. "And considering I've just stumbled across a huge-assed secret . . . you'd better make it worth my while."

Jordan's chest rumbled in a snarl. "Noah, Baye, take this guy back to his home, and I'll be along shortly. If he gives you any trouble, kill him—which is always a possibility when one discovers a huge-assed secret."

Jim Bob's eyes widened. The other two men nodded and each grabbed one of Jim Bob's arms. They had cool hair just like Jordan, and their eyes were different colors of green. Both of them gave her a smile before turning to drag Jim Bob away. They had nice smiles.

Katie began to shiver. Her legs hurt again. Oh no. Was she going to turn back into a girl? Then Jordan would know for sure she was a monster. Girls didn't turn into cats. Plus, she'd left her dress back in the kitchen. She would be naked. A low whimper fell out of her mouth.

Jordan looked down at her. "Ah." Shifting her to one arm, he yanked his shirt over his head. Quick motions had the soft cotton over her fur, her paws trapped inside.

Warmth and cinnamon surrounded her. With a loud *pop,* she turned back into a girl.

Jordan smiled, his eyes crinkling. "There you are." He helped shove her arms into the sleeves. "Bet that hurt."

She nodded solemnly. "I'm a monster."

He laughed softly, his eyes turning to magic. "No, you're a mountain lion shifter. Very tough cougar."

The way he said it made it seem okay.

"Are you gonna kill me?" She could still run.

"Nope." He began walking. "I'm going to find you a good home where you don't have to run."

A real home sounded nice. "Are you gonna kill Jim Bob?"

Jordan's chest stiffened. "No. I'm not going to kill him, little one. But he'll never bother you again. I promise."

She believed him. If anybody could make Jim Bob go away, Jordan could. Just like Superman. "Okay."

He sighed. "I knew your parents and just found out they'd died—which took much longer than it should have. We learned of your location and were on the way to find you. I'm sorry about your parents."

Careful hope warmed her chest. "You knew my mama and daddy?"

"Yes."

She took a deep breath. "Um, did they like me?" Please, let them have liked her.

"I'm sure they loved you." He peered down at her. "In fact, you're the perfect image of your mama. She was pretty, too."

He called her pretty. Katie giggled. "Did they like you?"

"Yes. We were friends. They left the pride to travel and live in different cities for a while. They would've come back home eventually."

The idea of a real home made Katie's heart kinda hurt. "What's a pride?"

"Mountain lion shifters live in a pride. You're a member of my pride."

That was too good to be true. "Where are we goin'?"

"To a lady named Millie Smith. She loves little girls and little cougars . . . and makes the best apple pie in the world." Jordan kissed Katie softly on the head. "You'll want protein first and then we'll have some apple pie."

"What's protein?" Her eyelids drooped and she snuggled into safety.

"Meat. You need to eat meat after you shift so your muscles stay strong."

"What's 'muscles'?" she mumbled, trying to stay awake. Her eyelids got so heavy they closed.

"I'll explain later—sleep now." Jordan tucked her closer. "Welcome home, kitten."

Chapter 1

Last week

As nights went, it wasn't a bad one to die. Jordan Pride ducked behind a tree in the West Virginia forest, his footsteps silent and deadly, not sure how he'd suddenly become prey. As a lion shifter, as the leader of the feline nation, he was usually more of a predator than he liked to admit.

The force surrounding him edged closer, altering the atmospheric pressure enough to flood adrenaline through his veins. Clouds blanketed the sky, keeping the meager moon hidden. Good thing he could see in the dark. He considered shifting into a lion, but for now, he wanted the clear thinking he had only in human form. Once he let the animal free, instinct overcame intellect. For now, he needed to think this through.

He gave a barely perceptible nod to his enforcer, Mac. Mac's eyes burned a harsh emerald through the dusk, the soldier seriously pissed someone had breached the security on shifter headquarters. Not someone—the Kurjans. The enemy smelled of sulfur, a smell Jordan had always associated with evil.

The air stank with sulfur.

The Kurjans were an evil vampire race unable to venture into the sun without getting fried. Unlike the true vampires who were Jordan's allies—who enjoyed a day at the beach. Nighttime created excellent opportunities to attack, and the Kurjans had waited for a good one. Dark and deadly.

Mac's brother, Noah, flanked his other side, looking even angrier than Mac, if that were possible. In fact, Noah had been pissed for the last ten years—since they'd moved to the mountains of West Virginia—since they'd forced their people into caverns and caves. Anything to avoid the Kurjan-created virus that destroyed their DNA and turned them into monsters.

Apparently the Kurjans had found them. Well. It had taken the bastards a decade.

Though ten years of war had depleted Jordan's forces and been incredibly difficult for his people. His soldiers were battered and bruised . . . if not dead.

Jordan's canines elongated . . . the beast within wanting to spring free. Not quite yet. He shot a triumphant grin at Noah. They'd hidden long enough to protect the children, the future. And yeah, for the most part, female shifters were hidden as well.

Well, everyone but the one female he'd give his left arm to protect. No. Katie had to be on the front lines, searching out the few remaining infected shifters. Unfortunately, once infected with the virus, male shifters became were-wolves—true beasts that had to be put down for good.

A snarl lifted his lips.

The battle plan had just changed—thanks to the force around him returning to war against shifters. For the last decade, the Kurjans had directed their energy to taking out the vampires. Apparently they'd now switched tactics.

If he survived the night, he'd call Katie home tomorrow. The thought of her, the image of those stunning bourbon-colored eyes filtered through his memory and shot him into true lion form.

His bones cracked, his muscles shifted, and he landed on all fours. Graceful and deadly.

He ran toward the stench, knowing the enemy waited. Yet they probably hadn't expected him to jump high, sailing right for the throat of the closest scout. While most mountain lions weighed about a hundred and fifty pounds, shifters weighed twice that. His canines aimed true, slicing through cartilage and bone like warm toffee. Blood sprayed as he flung the Kurjan's pasty white head into the dark recesses of the forest with a low snarl.

Jordan may be the leader of the feline world—through circumstances that still kept him awake at night—but at heart, he was a soldier. Fate had always planned for him to die in battle. Alone, as he deserved.

A whistle of wind sounded, then sharp pains impacted his body from every direction. Startled, he dropped to all fours.

Arrows? The bastards were using arrows?

Rage ripped through him and he shook wildly, ripping the missiles from his flesh to go flying.

His hiss came out more of a growl as he spotted another Kurjan. Red-haired with black tips, the freak had swirling purple eyes. Medals decorated his left breast—a high-up soldier. He smiled, revealing sharp yellow canines.

Jordan snarled back. Whatever the Kurjans were doing, it was going to backfire. Letting the animal fully take over, Jordan descended into the primal being he usually kept at bay. The Kurjan pointed a green gun at him and fired.

He dodged, then sprung.

Time to kill.

Present day—one week later

Katie Smith smelled him before she saw him. His natural scent of cinnamon and oak mixed with an edge of anger, choking the oxygen from the room. She shut the door to her apartment, schooled her face, and turned toward the threat. "Hello, Jordan. Forget how to knock?"

His rangy body sprawled in the leather chair she and her roommate, Maggie, had spent three days haggling for. While she and Maggie both chased werewolves, they also worked other jobs for money. During the war, pride funds had dried up.

Jordan raised an eyebrow, arrogant and pissed. "I sent orders for you to move to Realm Headquarters after the attack on our headquarters last week."

She inhaled deep, her gaze meeting tawny eyes. God, she'd missed him the last ten years. Even now, angry enough to smack him, she'd give almost anything to run her hands through the thick hair falling to his shoulders. Blond, brown, a hint of black, the multitude of raw colors proving beyond doubt his base nature was that of a mountain lion. Like her. "I haven't followed your orders in a decade. Now you need to leave."

She flung her car keys into the merino glass bowl on the table by the door. Next to the glass sat a stack of files— names and faces of known infected shifters. She should file those . . . the werewolves had all been found and killed.

Jordan stood. Long, lean, and rangy. Nearly a foot taller than her own five foot six. Her living room shrank. He'd worn his customary faded jeans, dark T-shirt, and cowboy boots. The outfit was as formal as Jordan ever dressed—if anything, he might have a nicer pair of boots for a special occasion. "Who exactly do you think you and the boys answer to, Kate?"

The urge to step back pissed her off. He was going to

pull rank on her. On all of them. "Listen, I know you're the leader of the feline clans—"

"Disobeying me was never an option for you."

She swallowed hard and put her hands on her hips. Seeing him in her apartment wasn't coming close to the fantasies she'd had of the moment. The man would never view her as an adult. As a woman. She shoved the pain down. "Wrong. I understand you're older than dirt, Jordan, but I'm modern and choose to live my own life."

Like the lion hidden just under his human surface, he stalked past the leather sofa, his eyes darkening to topaz, steady on his prey. "Ah, sweetheart. This is an incredibly bad time to mess with me."

Her breath caught hard in her chest while desire slammed into her abdomen. Something feral lit his eyes . . . something new. Deadly and deep. The wildness made something kick to life inside her. "What the fuck's going on?"

He stopped moving a foot away. "I believe I taught you not to swear at me. True?"

She cleared her throat. "I'm not six years old anymore."

His lips tipped in almost a smile. "I know. And I guarantee when I spank you now, the end result will be much different than you throwing a stuffed pig at me and pouting for a week."

She forgot how to breathe. What was he saying? No. Just words—he was just using words. Was he teasing her? Flirting? She struggled to focus. "Jordan, the moon will be full in less than a week, and I have work to do."

He shook his head. "I've given you a decade to work this out of your system. You're done."

Out of her system? True surprise mingled with a rapidly growing anger inside her. "*This,* as you so moronically put it, is not exactly a choice in vocation. I was infected with a virus that makes it possible for me to track werewolves."

The air changed. His eyes darkened to burnt gold and a

tension swirled toward her. "No. You were infected with a virus that makes it impossible, *for now,* for you to shift from human to cougar." Danger and fury rode each word. He reached out to manacle one burning hand around her bicep. "Then . . . not trusting the scientists enough to cure you, you *purposefully* infected yourself with the catalyst to speed the virus up."

Yeah, she had. The catalyst was supposed to increase the potency of the virus so the illness ran its course sooner . . . either killing the subject or dying out. Probably. She'd expected the virus to allow her to shift again, and had gone against all protocol and injected the weapon into her bloodstream.

Apparently the shifter remained pissed about her attempt, too. "I thought my body would fight the virus so I could shift again," she whispered. That's what had happened to her roommate, Maggie . . . who now shifted into a wolf once a month during the full moon. Katie would've done anything to keep the possibility of being with Jordan open—to recapture her ability to shift.

"Yet that didn't happen, did it?"

"No." Instead, she'd been gifted with the ability to feel the monsters roaming around them . . . to get into their heads and find the beasts. Those who had once been shifters and now were werewolves. Damn the Kurjans for creating the biological weapon. Of course, the bug only affected shifters, with their twenty-eight chromosomal pairs, and vampire mates, who had twenty-seven pairs. No one knew about witches. They protected their own, and no witch had been infected. Yet. Katie sighed. "I'm good at this, Jordan."

His lip twisted. "Which is why you're going under the king's protection. To safety."

More danger was coming? Fear slammed into her abdomen. Had he found out about her special project? The one monster she couldn't quite catch? "We've pretty much eradicated werewolves in the south. What new danger?"

Regret twisted his lips. "I'm sorry, Katie—the three wolves on the Bane's Council have decided to consolidate—they want to return to taking care of all werewolf threats without the outlying squads."

"They can't do that."

"The Council has dealt with all werewolf threats for eons by itself, and it can do as it chooses. All outlying squads are being decommissioned by the end of next month."

Something flickered in Jordan's eyes. Was he lying?

"There are still too many threats." Katie took a deep breath. "The Bane's Council of three wolves can't cover the entire world anymore. Also, while I can't shift, I can still sense the werewolves." So far a unique gift . . . just for her.

Jordan scrubbed a hand over his face. "I wish the scientists would figure out why Maggie is the only infected female shifter able to shift. The rest of you . . ."

Yeah. The rest of them stayed in human form all the time. Feline, canine, or multi . . . no females could shift after being infected with the virus. Only Maggie. "I guess it's better than the alternative." All the infected males shifted into werewolves—true animals, created to hunt and kill.

"The members of the Bane's Council are killers—that's what they do." Jordan's voice softened. "I'll give you the night to pack, Katie. Tomorrow morning we leave."

She frowned. For ten years she'd hunted monsters. She'd fought. Yet, here he stood, not seeing her. Just seeing the child of the past. Just one more reason why it was never going to happen between them.

"My job is here." There was no hiding for Katie Smith. She'd made a good life, one with purpose, and if she couldn't have Jordan, she'd keep what she'd created. Besides, the monster she couldn't catch kept getting stronger . . . bolder. She had to take him down during the coming full moon. "I already told Janie Kayrs I wouldn't make it to her sixteenth birthday party next week." Katie's refusal had nothing to do with wanting to avoid seeing Jordan at the party. She'd tried to convince herself the decade apart had lessened her feelings for the lion leader. Silly cougar—she shouldn't lie to herself.

"Janie will be relieved you've changed your mind." His face hardened into something unrecognizable. A tension emanated from him, a vibration of energy. A new energy. "I'll have movers get your furnishings—Dage and I've decided Maggie will be based out of Oregon as well."

"I don't work for either you or Dage." The jury was out on whether she worked for the Bane's Council, actually. The council's three wolves had spent lifetimes hunting down infected humans who became werewolves. While the poor human souls only lived a few months, they wreaked serious damage during that time. The council members hunted and destroyed them.

Once Virus-27 created infected shifters, werewolves became a different species—one that lived forever as monsters. The council had needed help, thus creating the outlying squads. The squads were still needed.

She fought to remain calm. "During the last ten years, we've caught and killed nearly two hundred werewolves . . . saving so many human lives I can't even count that high." If the beasts had remained alive, they would've taken out more human populations than the plague. "In addition, we're closer to finding the Kurjan headquarters." Every shifter harbored the fear that the Kurjan Virus-27 would go airborne someday. The Kurjans needed to be taken out first. She straightened her shoulders, facing a different man than the one she'd always known. War during the last decade had been hard on him . . . maybe too hard. "Go home, Jordan."

In a burst of power, he moved, lifting her against the wall. Way too fast. He leaned in close enough for his gaze to burn her face. "It wasn't a request."

While the man had always been stronger than most . . . this was unreal. Surprise and distress kept Katie immobile. "What's really going on?" The heat from his grip combined with his scent and softened her thighs.

Shock crossed his face. In slow motion, he glanced down at his hands holding her aloft. As if surprised they belonged to him. "I, uh, I'm sorry."

He was finally holding her. Desire pebbled her nipples. Her core heated.

Symmetrical nostrils flared when he inhaled. A dark flush cut across his high cheekbones. "Jesus, Kate."

The damn shifter could smell her. Embarrassment at her arousal dried the spit in her mouth. Until he moved forward, pressing a rock-hard erection between her legs.

Mouth to thighs, she flooded.

The wall cooled her back while the man heated her entire front as he held her aloft. So easily. Too easily.

Focus. She needed to focus. Was this really happening? Her fantasies didn't come close to this heat—to this need. The breath caught in her throat and she held still. So still maybe he wouldn't stop. Maybe he'd finally kiss her. "Jordan."

He blinked. Once. Twice. "I'm sorry, Kate. I shouldn't have grabbed you."

Even so, he settled deeper into the vee between her legs.

Nothing in the world would make her look away. She held his gaze, mesmerized by the multitude of colors combining into topaz. "I'm a big girl." They'd never be able to mate. She knew that. The man ruled the entire feline world—he couldn't mate with an infected lioness unable to shift. With someone who might pass on the genetic mutation.

Resulting freedom brought the moment into sharp focus. Pain, too. But also . . . freedom with the clear knowledge they'd never go anywhere spread through her like a swarm of hungry bees. Her chin lifted—along with her thighs.

He stilled.

Throwing challenge into her smile, she clasped her ankles at the small of his back, sliding along the prominent line of his erection. Her hands clenched his shoulders. "So. I've been waiting a long time for this."

Dreams died. She knew that firsthand. She'd also learned—the rough way—to take the good and ride it hard.

"Kate." Her name came out more of a groan. His tongue wet his lips.

Elation mingled with an odd despair inside her to result in determination. What the hell. She had nothing to lose. "You want me, Jordan." Proof of his desire pulsed against her, even through her jeans. Every ounce of strength she had went into keeping the amazement off her face. He actually *wanted* her. "There's no way we can go back to living near each other—not going to work."

His gaze dropped to her lips. One broad hand threaded through her hair, tangling at the nape. "I'm dropping you off—going to fight."

The words were simple, the tone final. A good-bye of sorts? "You've fought before." Panic bit her words off. It would be just like Jordan to squire her to safety if he were about to fight to the death. To get his affairs in order. What wasn't he telling her? She began to struggle.

He quickly, easily, immobilized her—pressing her body into the wall. "Stop moving. Please, God . . . *stop moving.*"

He tugged her head back. Erotic tingles jerked along her scalp. Her breasts pressed against his chest, forcing a groan from her. So hard. So male. The need echoed her heartbeat between her ears. "Please, Jordan."

"Ah, Kate." Sadness filtered through his amazing eyes. His hold tightened. Regret and inevitability exhaled on his sigh. Better than any dream, his head lowered toward hers.

Then his lips found hers, and she forgot all about sadness and dreams.

Fire, promise, despair, all comingled in his kiss, his lips firm, his tongue gentle. So much softness. The shoulders under her hands went rigid with restraint, a vibration of control as he kept himself in check.

Slowly, too damn slowly, he halted the kiss, levering back. Desire and apology cut hard into the lines of his face.

Oh, hell no.

Swift as the cat she'd once been, she clutched both hands in his thick hair, yanking his mouth back down. Wild, nearly desperate, she slid her tongue inside, pressing her entire body along his length. Demand had her rubbing against him, need had her taking what she wanted. What she needed.

For almost two seconds, he held back.

The first growl came from down deep. He pivoted away from the wall, one hand in her hair, the other cupping her ass. Holding her aloft—taking control. He wrenched her head to the side, stealing her balance, destroying her equilibrium.

His tongue thrust deep, his lips demanding, his mouth scorching hot. The snapping of his control almost made a sound . . . the sound of warning.

She met it with a sound of longing.

He reacted as if time stood against them, taking three steps and dropping her to the sofa, following her down, his mouth busy on hers the entire time.

Buttons scattered as he ripped her shirt open. Kisses, hot and wild, peppered her jaw, neck, and collarbone until he reached her breasts. "No bra," he rumbled against her flesh before taking one aching nipple in his mouth.

She arched, crying out. Splinters of red-hot pleasure whipped from her breast to her begging clit. Then he nipped.

A ringing set up between her ears. She shoved the sound back, lost in the amazing sensation of Jordan's mouth on her. Finally. His body trapping hers. Desire flowing around them.

He lifted his head. "Phone."

Oh. The ringing. "Ignore it." Her hands flattened out across his broad back, not even coming close to spanning the masculine width. The muscles shifted, vibrating beneath her palms. So much strength.

The machine clicked on. A male voice. "Hi, Kate. I have a new set of files and should be there in a minute. Um, we need to talk." The message stopped.

Jordan drew in a harsh breath.

Shit, shit, shit. "That was Baye—he can see you tomorrow." Katie's mind spun. "Let me call him back."

"No." Gently, Jordan tugged her shirt back into place. The mood was certainly broken. "His brother will be calling him tonight to return to the ranch—we've had to relocate headquarters. I'll see him after I get you to safety."

Baye and his two brothers had served as Jordan's enforcers for about a century. When Katie had ventured out on her own, Jordan had sent Baye with her. He'd swiftly become her confidant, often joining her and Maggie for a drink after work. While cats and wolves didn't usually get along well, Maggie seemed like one of them. Wolf or not.

Katie dropped her hands from Jordan's shoulders, not willing to beg. The harsh expression on his face promised it wasn't going to happen. Ever. "Jordan—"

"I have a meeting, too." He levered to his feet. Regret flashed bright through his dark eyes. "I, this, we . . . this shouldn't have happened. I'm sorry." His hands shook. "Be ready tomorrow."

His words penetrated her foggy mind. "I can't. Besides my werewolf job, I work hard as a dispatcher for the police force during the day. Just quitting on the spot would be terrible for my coworkers." She enjoyed her job and heard first about any odd animal attacks.

Maggie worked at the hospital during the day shift for the same reason. But she was just part-time, which gave her freedom to travel west for testing every few months.

Of course, the vampires had to work their magic on the computer systems of both the human police force and hospital to circumvent background checks. Maggie had also needed bloodwork to be employed at the hospital. Such tests were easily manipulated by the vampires—more specifically by Kane Kayrs, the smartest guy on the planet.

Jordan's eyes hardened. "Call and quit, Katie. I'm not asking." Three strides and he disappeared out the door.

Damnit. Katie pressed a trembling hand to her burning mouth. Hopefully that huge erection would cause him serious pain. Finally, to have been so close. But no, Jordan had stopped. He didn't want her—at least not badly enough to take a chance. She'd known him almost her entire life. When Jordan wanted something, *nothing* stopped him. Time to face that fact and stop freaking pining.

Katie jumped up, her body humming, aching from remaining unfulfilled. Her heart splintering. She ran into her bedroom and changed her damaged shirt, emerging just as someone knocked on the door.

Her breath caught. It wasn't Jordan. Yet she dashed forward, throwing the oak door open to reveal Baye. All six feet of him—tough-ass feline shifter. Behind him stood Lance, tiger shifter and fighting champion. The three of them made up a squad. Her squad.

Disappointment threatened to choke her. "Hi." She gestured them inside.

Baye didn't move, surveying the room, scenting the air. Symmetrical nostrils flared and he ran a rough hand through his dark, shoulder-length hair. "Lion."

"Yes."

"I know Pride's scent as well as my own." Baye lifted an eyebrow, stepping inside.

Lance followed and quietly, too softly, he shut the door and handed her a file. "We have a new report of an infection."

Of course they did. Now she had to go out and hunt a shifter who had probably been a good man at one time. "Just one, huh?" Taking a deep breath, she returned to the sofa, trying so hard not to think of Jordan pressing her into the soft leather.

Baye leaned against the door. Lance hovered near the couch.

What was their problem? She frowned.

Baye's eyes darkened further. "Open the file."

A tickle set up at the base of her spine. Her lungs compressed. Something whispered she should run. Shrugging her shoulders, she flipped open the file.

Jordan Pride's picture stared back at her.

Chapter 2

Jordan jogged through the alley, cutting a hard right to end up at his hotel. Cobbled stones protested with each beat of his boots. The city of New Orleans didn't agree with him. Too hot, too muggy, too many damn humans. Their merriment wandered on the breeze—carefree and joyful at the constant parade and fun. He'd lived his life alone, and the ever present comraderie in the southern town only made him feel more so.

The breadth of magic mixed with the humid air, coating his skin. He didn't like humidity or water, either. Most cats didn't—which is exactly why he'd assigned Katie to the area. If she found werewolves, they wouldn't be former members of her clan.

Maybe when he turned completely into a werewolf, he'd jump right into the sea. Though he'd be dead before that happened.

What the hell had he been thinking? Touching her? Kissing her? Sure, he'd noticed her as a woman years ago. Had known without a doubt, the pretty shifter deserved better than him. Had also known such knowledge wouldn't have stopped him from taking her. Who knew? Maybe they would've stood some kind of chance.

But not now, not with the beast inside him calling the shots.

Scaling the rickety fire escape to the third floor of his antiquated hotel, he shoved open his window and jumped inside. No need to go through the lobby. Stealth had always been his friend.

A rust-colored shag carpet muffled his steps as he strode past the bed to the scarred table to boot up his laptop. At one time, before war had intruded, he'd been able to afford the best. But all funds had been earmarked for war, safety, and more hospitals. The last ten years had been the most difficult his people had ever faced, considering so many had been lost to the virus. Besides, right at the moment, he needed solitude and peace, and the dive provided quiet.

Connlan Kayrs took shape, his angled face filling the screen. "How did it go?"

"Not good." Jordan dropped into a ripped leather chair the color of a yellow cake Katie had once burned for his birthday. "Exactly what I expected, actually."

Conn's metallic green eyes narrowed. He rubbed his short hair. The ends had recently been singed off when he tried to harness his mate's magic without permission. Moira was an incredibly powerful witch and had apparently set a booby trap, though if anyone tried to ask Conn about it, he hit them in the face. The vampire frowned. "When will Katie be arriving at headquarters?"

"Tomorrow." Jordan scratched his chin. Tired. He was so damn tired. "We both will."

"Does she know?"

"No. Well . . . maybe. Baye was on his way with a file. I'm assuming my face is in it." Jordan had handpicked the assassin to cover Katie's back. Though the enforcer's services were no longer needed. Katie would soon be underground.

Conn leaned forward. "You should've told her yourself."

"Probably." He'd chickened out. Well . . . not exactly true. His mouth had been too busy on her breast to actually talk. "Whatever happens, you'll keep her safe and away from feline headquarters until Noah is secure as the new leader. Keep her away from me, too." The people Jordan trusted in this life were few. Connlan Kayrs sat atop the list.

"I will." Two words—yet an absolute vow from the soldier. "Though I don't think you're giving yourself enough credit. You wouldn't hurt Kate."

Jordan wasn't sure. "The virus . . . I've changed already."

Conn rolled his eyes. "The virus has nothing to do with it. When did you know?"

Irritation had Jordan clenching his hands. "Know what?"

"That she was yours."

Heat slid down his spine. "Never."

"Bullshit." Conn flipped a knife in his hand, the silver coming in view and back out. "When did you turn around and notice she was all grown up?"

Damn his friend. They knew each other too well. "When the Kurjans took her and Talen helped me get her back." Jordan would never forget the sight of her in that hospital bed, so pale, so fragile. "It was like a kick to the gut." Thank the fates she'd recovered perfectly. That time. Before she'd been infected by the virus.

"Yeah," Conn said softly. "You sent her away, Jordan. To fight werewolves."

He'd never been able to tell her no. "She needed to go. To grow and learn . . . not be confused by—"

"By her feelings for you." Conn tucked the knife away. "Been there, done that. It's been ten years for you. I'm thinking the woman has had long enough to decide if she has a childhood crush or something more."

"What's the point?" Jordan shook his head. Yeah, the

woman had kissed him like it was more—definitely more. But he'd spent over three decades protecting her, and he couldn't stop now that he was dying. "She's in every thought—I'll take her, Conn. I can feel it." He'd kill himself before he hurt Katie. He sighed. "A werewolf wouldn't fight the attraction."

"Neither should you."

God spare him from happily mated vampires. "I appreciate you wanting to make my last days on earth full of love and sex, but get a grip." He'd let Katie go a decade ago to find herself . . . to learn to deal with her illness on her own terms. To become strong enough to deal with him. Too bad it couldn't happen now.

Fate truly was a bitch.

Conn raised an eyebrow. Anger flashed across his cheeks, fury had his lips going white. "Did you just tell me to *get a grip?*"

"Yes." His friend had been pissed since the blood tests came back on Jordan. "Let it go—there's nothing we can do."

Silver shot through the green of Conn's eyes. Vampires had a secondary eye color that came through during emotional times. "Stop fucking punishing yourself for what we did."

Jordan didn't need this shit. "I'm not punishing myself. The virus came from arrows shot by the Kurjans—and has nothing to do with my past."

Conn shook his head. "I know you."

Unfortunately, the vampire did know him. "So?"

"So, this lone wolf bullshit has gone on long enough. You deserve to lead and you're an excellent leader. Nobody says you have to do it all alone."

"Did you just call me a wolf?" Jordan forced a smile. What was it with happy vampires? They instantly wanted everyone else to be happy, too. Then if you didn't go along, they tried to beat you up. Vampires were an odd species.

Conn rolled his eyes. "We'll deal with your personal problems later. For now, I'm not giving up on curing you of the virus." He leaned forward. "Maggie has been here for the last month, and I think Kane is close to some sort of antiviral."

Kane was Conn's older brother and the smartest person on the planet. Even so, with less than a week until Jordan turned into a monster, there wasn't time for *close*. "Sounds good. Tell Kane he can experiment on me all he wants during the day." Nighttime, well, nothing kept him from the moon.

"Your acceptance of this is pissing me off." Conn's jaw hardened.

Jordan shrugged. "You can be as angry as you want, so long as you keep your word." They'd fought together during the last war three hundred years ago. Both assassins, close enough to be brothers. Which meant Conn was the only person he trusted to end this right. "When the time comes, you need to kill me."

Conn went still. Even across the country, his tension emanated. His eyes flashed green to vampire silver. "*If* the time comes . . . I will."

Chapter 3

Katie tugged leather gloves on her hands, her boots clomping on the docks of the marina. Jordan had kissed her. *Finally kissed her.* Then he'd apologized. *Fucking apologized.*

Salt coated her skin, breezing in on the muggy wind from pounding waves of Lake Pontchartrain. Darn saltwater lake. After spending hours on the phone until the half moon rose, the truth remained the same. Jordan had been infected with the virus. "The Kayrs lab has a possible cure generated from Maggie's blood." Okay, not exactly what Emma, the Realm queen and chief geneticist, had said, but close enough.

Baye twirled a wicked knife in his hand, his gaze alert on the covered docks toward the south end of the lake. "If Jordan believed he'd be cured, he wouldn't have set my brother up to lead and called me home."

"I know." But Jordan was a good leader and a true planner. He'd cover every contingency. "This is the first time the lab has blood tests from a male shifter *just infected.* That has to be good." Usually the shifter didn't know until the first full moon . . . when he changed into a werewolf. Forever. At least humans got three full moons until turning into beasts for life.

Lance nodded, his gun at ready. "They'll find a cure in time—they have nearly five nights until the full moon. I mean, counting tonight. So four nights." The tiger had joined the New Orleans squad a year ago, his tracking abilities almost as good as Katie's. He'd lost the two other members of his old squad in a werewolf raid and every once in a while suffered panic attacks. Post-traumatic stress disorder didn't only affect humans, unfortunately. But he was a good fighter, and his intense protection of his current squad made sense. He snarled. "Pride is strong. Don't worry."

Katie gave him a grateful smile. Lance was always on her side. He topped out at six feet, long and lean, dangerously quick. Angular tiger features made up his sharp face, his mouth generous with a smile—usually. Better yet, Lance treated her as an adult, while Baye sometimes still saw the child she used to be.

Baye halted, sniffing the air. Shaking his head, he resumed the hunt. "Leave it to Jordan to feel a little weird and instantly order a blood test. Through arrows tipped with the virus. We didn't see that one coming."

"No. To be honest, I figured at some point the bug would go airborne." The idea of the world being infected made her head ache. Only humans, vampires, and demons would survive. And maybe witches. Nobody knew if witches could be infected. Trials attempted in test tubes led to uncertain and odd results.

"All we need is an airborne killer." Lance cracked his knuckles, his body staying tense. His lips turned down, and a dark frown settled between his brows.

Katie glanced at his tight features. "Are you all right?"

"Yes."

This was more than Jordan's news, considering Lance and the lion leader barely knew each other. Katie shoved hair out of her eyes. "Come on. What's wrong? Is it Linda?" He'd been extremely cranky the last week after his girlfriend dumped him.

"I don't want to talk about Linda." He surveyed the boats on either side of the dock.

Katie sighed. She wished he'd snap out of it and be her jovial friend again. "Are you sure?" They'd spent the last week talking about the situation, with the tiger showing up drunk on her doorstep more than once. She'd force-fed him coffee to sober him up. The poor guy had passed out on her sofa several nights in a row, trying to snuggle with her to sleep.

Tigers were known to be good snugglers.

"I'm sure." He flashed a grin. "Though we could get drunk later and hash it out again."

Yeah, unless she was packing. "I feel like I should go with Jordan to the lab." She'd need to cancel two lunch dates and a hair appointment the next week. "Maybe I can get someone to cover for me at work." She'd made a good life with a lot of human friends the last decade. In fact, she was mainly human now. Just disappearing wasn't an option.

Lance nodded. "Well, besides the guy we're chasing, just turned werewolves are few and far between. The shifting clans are doing a good job staying underground, so we could probably handle things here without you for a spell. A very short spell." His cell phone buzzed and he lifted the device to his ear. "When? How bad? Okay." Flipping the phone shut, he smacked his fist into his other hand. "We've had a report of an infected human—guy showed up at the hospital with fur growing all over his body."

Baye frowned. "We haven't had a human infection in a year. What's that about?" He rubbed his chin, surveying the docks. "All right. You head over there to find out if he's really a werewolf or some idiot on meth. Katie and I will keep looking around here—though there's no way a lair is on a boat."

Lance sniffed the air, concern shadowing his eyes. "I sense a werewolf signature . . . one has been here lately." He nudged Katie with his hip. "Why don't you come to the hospital with me?"

She rolled her eyes. Now Lance was getting overprotective, too? Sure, she'd been weaker lately from the virus, but she hadn't thought anyone else had noticed. "I'm fine. I need to track this guy." So far, she was the only one who could actually get into the beast's head . . . or heart . . . or wherever the evil lived. The other shifters only sensed the bastard. "Besides, we never hunt alone."

Baye eyed her. "I'm just surveying the land and trying to find where the werewolf last played—no hunting tonight. Why don't you go with Lance?"

Oh, no way. Her squad was not going to treat her like some fragile human. She settled her stance, glaring at both men. "We. Don't. Hunt. Alone."

They shared a look. Baye shrugged. "Fine."

Lance grimaced. "Fair enough. I'll call you later with answers about the human. Maybe I'll drop by Linda's after the hospital."

"No." Baye hissed out a breath. "Let the woman go. She said it's over."

Katie gave Lance a sympathetic smile. He'd really liked the psychologist. "Either forget her or tell her the truth about yourself. She knows you hide something . . . it's the only chance you have."

Lance shook his head. "I can't tell her about shifters unless I mate her, you know that. And I'm not ready to mate." He tucked his gun in his jeans, the odd glow of his eyes piercing the night.

"Then she's not the right one," Baye muttered.

A slow smile wandered over Lance's chiseled face. "You're the only woman who truly knows me, lioness." He shot Katie a wink and then pivoted, loping slowly out of sight.

Katie stifled a grin. What a flirt.

The breeze picked up, bringing salt and the smell of fish across the dock. She shivered.

Baye leaned over and eyed the still water. "Let's find where this werewolf was, so we can prepare for him coming back."

Katie nodded, opening her senses.

The creak of the dock over water masked their footsteps as they stalked closer to a row of pleasure yachts, white decks shining in the soft moonlight. The lap of water gently rocked them to and fro.

Baye rolled his neck. "I'm so sick of saltwater. Why can't this bastard head inland?"

"Because we hate saltwater." The beast had a brain and a sick sense of fun. Each time a full moon came and went, his strength increased. A sad and newly discovered fact regarding shifters turned werewolves, as was intelligence. The beasts seemed to get smarter the longer they lived— smarter and fully psychotic. The monsters hid for most of the month, waiting until the moon rose high to hunt and kill. For some reason, the rays gave them strength. "We need to find his lair."

Though finding werewolves in lairs had nearly gotten Katie killed numerous times. Of course, that's what she'd signed up for. She wasn't supposed to fight but needed to get close in order to sense the beasts. At that point, fighting became inevitable.

Baye eyed the nearly full moon. "This guy is underground—somewhere close. The full moon isn't for several nights."

"I know. But he comes here when he goes out to play."

A sense of oiliness coated the docks. A psychic footprint only Katie sensed. Sometimes she feared the evil would seep in through her senses and take root. "If we found where, we could have troops waiting."

"Sounds like a great plan." Baye dropped to a crouch, wiping a hand across the faded dock. "Uh, what's going on between you and Lance?"

Katie's head jerked to the side. "Nothing. Why?"

Baye shut his eyes and lifted his head, nostrils flaring. "Just making sure. Emotions get in the way when hunting animals. You know that. We don't date members of our own squad."

She so didn't need the lecture on dating in the workplace. Sometimes Baye forgot she was all grown up. "Lance and I are just friends." Good friends, sure. They'd fought together and she trusted him. "You know how I feel about Jordan." Everybody knew.

Baye sighed, standing and opening his eyes. "I thought maybe you got over that crush." His tone hinted he'd hoped she'd let go of that dream. "Especially now, Kate. Time to move on."

"With Lance?" Humor lifted the corners of her lips.

Baye twisted his neck to see beyond a stack of buoys. "Maybe. If he can get over the damn psychologist."

"I'll think about it. But, really, I'm not taking dating advice from a lion who goes through women like cat treats." In fact, she'd never seen Baye get serious about any woman.

"I'm too young to settle down."

"You're over four hundred years old."

"Exactly."

Katie chuckled. Then, a scent . . . an intent carried in with the breeze. Dark images of death and blood filled her vision. Holy crap. Was the werewolf waiting? Couldn't be. He'd be underground until the full moon. Storing his strength. She pushed the grotesque vision out of her brain.

"I think the werewolf is here." Too bad Lance hadn't stayed.

Baye's shoulders went back. "Werewolves stay hidden until the full moon." Even so, the shifter's stance dropped to fight, his body going deadly still.

"This one's different." The bastard was close—she just knew it. She cupped her hands around her mouth so her voice would reach the rafters. Maybe more than bats and water spiders hung out in the high beams. "Come on out, Snuggles. I know you're there."

Baye snorted. "Snuggles?"

"I got tired of thinking of him as 'sociopathic monster.' So I named him Snuggles." She kept her tone matter-of-fact. In truth, the werewolf scared the crap out of her. She felt him . . . he carried more inside than mere beast. A darkness, oily and evil, slid through the images she gleaned. No way had he been a decent man before turning into a werewolf. Researching him had led nowhere. She had no clue what his name had been—many werewolves didn't have files. Unfortunately.

"He's underground, Kate." Baye's cautious surveying of the area belied his words. "But I do find it interesting he's stayed around town with us taking so many of his kind down."

"No you don't." She reached for the knife along her calf, eyeing an empty berth at the end of the dock. A yacht horn blared lonely and sad in the far distance. Waves lapped up on the shore. "As always, you have a hypothesis."

He shifted his weight, stepping in front of her to inch down the dock. Blocking her. "As a matter of fact, I do."

She hustled to his side, growling when he elbowed her back. "Get out of my way."

"Rules. You sense, you direct . . . you do not fight."

Baye kept his voice low, his gaze forward. "There's some-thing up ahead, I sense some type of animal. Maybe good old Snuggles is living on the water full-time now."

"I'm an excellent fighter." Sure, she'd lost some ability from the incredibly slow progression of the virus. But she could still fight. The fact that part of her wanted to run and hide from the brute forced her shoulders back and her feet into motion. The second she let evil intimidate her, she lost.

"Rules."

"Screw the rules." If Baye had a clue as to the night-mares this werewolf had given her, he'd try to force her out of the field. Could Snuggles actually be near? "We have one night to get this guy before you head home and I go to Oregon." She'd go with Jordan just to get him there for Emma to experiment on. To cure. Then she'd figure out the rest of her life.

A boom echoed behind her. She swiveled, her back smashing into the bow of a pleasure yacht. Bruises cut deep, and she bit her lip to keep from groaning. Feet braced, hair bristling, a seven-foot werewolf stood in the middle of the narrow dock. The stench of unwashed ani-mal assaulted her nostrils. Her eyes actually burned.

Baye shoved her behind him.

Another hairy beast leapt out of the shadows to block her way. She angled around, pressing her shoulders against Baye's back. They both dropped into fighting stances.

Images of death and such pleasure taken in killing al-most dropped Katie to the ground. She yanked mental shields into place. Her chest tightened. Her hands damp-ened. Drawing on years of training, she settled her mind and tilted her head to the side, studying the deep black fur of the monster in front of her. Intelligent yellow eyes glinted in the dim moonlight. Adrenaline shot through her tissues, shooting the night into pinpoint focus. Why wasn't he attacking? "Well now, Snuggles. We finally meet face-to-face." Her voice wavered slightly.

He lifted his long snout, sniffing. "Kaattieee."

Low, mournful, nearly gleeful, his voice spiraled true fear into her gut.

Baye stiffened against her. "Did he just fucking talk?"

"I, uh . . ." Katie gasped out. "No way. Just a weird growl."

The monster flashed sharp, yellowed canines. "Kaattieee. Kaattieee." He sniffed again. "Been watching Kaattieee."

On all that was holy. Werewolves didn't speak.

Baye growled. "Kate, circle to your left. I want to face this asshole."

The werewolf shook his head. Thick fur flew. "No. Kaattieee mine." He bunched his legs. "Now."

Boards creaked. The other werewolf charged, rushing into Baye and sending Katie flying. Right into the arms of the beast. Fur slammed up her nostrils. He grabbed her, lifting up. With a snarl, she shoved her knife into his throat, slamming her head into his nose.

He dropped her, howling in pain. She landed on her ass, bouncing on the wet dock. Hurt shot up her tailbone. Fear caught in her lungs. His claws swiped out, grabbing her by the hair. Blood gushed when he yanked the knife from his neck, throwing the blade into the water.

Pain lanced her scalp as he jerked her up. His other hand shot out, claws scraping down her arm. Agony flared along her nerves, the skin flayed open.

She opened her mouth in a silent scream. Tears clogged her vision.

Baye and the other werewolf tumbled into the lake, teeth flashing and claws emerging. Bubbles shot to the surface. Baye needed to shift.

Jordan's voice slammed into her head. So many lessons in self-defense had been required of her growing up. *Think. Accept the reality . . . and think.* Bending her leg, she kneed the werewolf in the groin.

He howled, releasing her, stepping back. His irises turned red. Then he smiled.

Darting out his long tongue, he licked red off his claws. Blood. Her blood. A low rumble came from deep in his chest. "I . . . find . . . you . . . now . . . Kaattieee."

Nausea swirled in her belly. Taking a step back, she slid a gun from her ankle holster, aiming between his eyes. Silver bullets—they wouldn't kill him, but they'd knock him down long enough so she could remove his head. But first . . . "Who were you? Do you know?"

He licked one claw clean, a low moan filling the night.

She needed to puke. "Who—were—you?"

His paw dropped to his side and he smacked his lips. "Me."

"Yes, you." If he'd evolved, what had happened to the virus? Should she try to keep him alive? Could he be the key to curing it? Would dead blood be as good to Emma as freshly pumping blood?

"Me." He stretched his neck, eyeing the moon. "Not Snuggles."

"No. Not Snuggles." God. She wanted to kill him. But what if the cure ran through his blood? Or at least a mutation of the virus that allowed him to evolve. "What was your name?"

Several berths down, Baye leaped out of the water in cougar form. Oh, he was going to be angry. He hated the water in any form . . . especially cougar. The salt had matted his unusually dark coat, turning his fur nearly black. Seconds later, the werewolf followed, landing on the cat. With a screech of outrage, Baye flipped around and went for the monster's throat.

The werewolf in front of Katie turned, viewed the fight, then shrugged and refocused back on her. Sparks lit his odd eyes. "My name not Jordan."

Everything inside Katie silenced. Stilled. "You know Jordan?"

"Saw Jordan. Visit you." The beast's snout lifted in a fierce snarl. "Jordan baaaad."

The werewolf had been watching her? Her breath began to pant out. So much for hiding out until the full moon. The beasts were evolving into a more dangerous threat to all beings than they'd realized. "Did you know Jordan before?"

"Yeesss."

She'd shoot him in the leg if it would gain his cooperation. More likely, he'd charge and rip her throat out. If she fired, she needed to kill. "One last chance. Who were you?"

A huge splash sounded as Baye and the werewolf fell into the lake again.

The werewolf eyed the gun. "Brrenntt."

"Brent? Your name was Brent?"

"Yeesss. Brrenntt."

The cougar scrambled up the dock, slipping.

Faster than wind, Brent jumped on top of the boat, leaping for the next berth. Fiberglass cracked with a loud protest. Katie yelped and fired, bullets ricocheting off the bow. A second later, the monster disappeared.

The air shimmered and Baye shifted from cougar to wet, pissed-off male. He stalked forward, buck-ass naked. "I smell blood. God, he didn't bite you, did he?"

"No." Werewolves infected humans by biting them . . . the bites had no effect on shifters. Of course, Katie wasn't quite a shifter anymore, so there might be a risk. "I have a nick on my arm." Katie averted her eyes from the sight of a lot of male flesh. "Did you kill the other werewolf?"

"Yes, I bit his throat out, decapitating him." Baye grabbed her wrist, flipping her arm over. "Jesus, Kate. You won't need stitches, but it'll hurt for a while."

That wasn't the half of it. Brent had the taste of her blood. Every instinct she owned screamed he wanted more of it.

Chapter 4

Katie awoke to a warm rain splashing her window an hour before dawn. She'd managed about thirty minutes of sleep—the pain in her arm kept her awake most of the night. Residue remained in her head from the run-in with the werewolf . . . tarlike and painful. All werewolves were monsters, but Brent went beyond animalistic. Truly evil, he needed to be stopped.

Her pink kitten-shaped clock flipped numbers over to reveal the early time. Lance had given her the goofy clock as a joke a few months back, but she kind of liked the color.

A sound caught her attention. Her heart increased in tempo. Someone waited in the living room. A quiet presence. Considering Maggie had been away at the labs for the last month, whoever hovered in there wasn't invited.

Darkness slid inside and a shadow filled her doorway.

Scooting back, sitting up, she reached for the light.

Jordan leaned negligently against the door frame. "Told you to be ready."

Relief relaxed her shoulders. She shoved long, sandy-colored hair away from her face. The pattering rain was failing to dispel the muggy air. "You really need to learn to knock."

"I'll work on it."

Silence stretched out. Even from across the room, she could feel his heat. Male and strong. In her bedroom. Why hadn't she worn the sexy negligee Maggie bought for her last birthday instead of a ratty old T-shirt? Her chest began to ache. She cleared her throat. "I read a file on you earlier."

"I figured."

Something inside her fissured. "How were you infected?"

He glanced around the soft yellow room, interest lighting his eyes. "The Kurjans attacked feline headquarters. Arrows tipped with the virus. Good plan."

She tugged up the deep green bedspread that perfectly matched the one on Jordan's bed. God, hopefully he wouldn't notice the similarity. "Anybody else infected?"

"No." His gaze landed on the pretty desk in the corner he'd carved for her sixteenth birthday.

"So you were the target?" Made sense. Jordan was the most powerful leader in the shifter world—take him out and more chaos would ensue.

"Probably." He straightened his pose and tilted his head toward three watercolors lining the wall. "Those are by Brenna Dunne."

"Yes." The young witch was incredibly talented. "We're friends. When Maggie and I moved here, we asked Brenna to paint us a couple forest scenes." Forest scenes reminding Katie of home. Reminding her of safety, family, and Jordan.

"Hmmm." Jordan shook his head, eyes focusing as he faced her fully. "I have four days to get things in order. We should get going."

Something didn't quite track. If she ended up being confined to headquarters, then she'd rather be at home with her people. Even though she couldn't shift, she was still a shifter, darn it. "Why don't you want me at home?"

"I'm endorsing Noah as leader of the feline nation. Some people won't agree, and it'll be dangerous until he proves himself. I need Baye at home to help Mac cover his back." The three brothers had served as Jordan's enforcers for centuries. The feline nation was a monarchy, and Jordan had no family. Nobody waited to ascend and lead, so there'd be fights until one victor emerged. Jordan ran a rough hand through his tawny hair, leaving it mussed.

Her hands were jealous. "I spoke with Emma earlier."

A genuine smile tipped his lips. Finally. "How is the Queen of the Realm?"

"Good. She said they might have an antiviral for the virus based on both Maggie's blood and the sample you sent right after being infected." After all this time, could they have found a cure?

"That'd be great." Jordan's inflection didn't change. Lightning cracked outside, brightening the room. "Don't get your hopes up. We both know there isn't enough time for me, but maybe for others." He took a step inside, bringing the scent of wild male with him.

An unwelcome hurt chilled her legs. "Why didn't you call me? I mean, when you were infected?"

He stilled, lifting both eyebrows. "I came as soon as I knew the results."

"I could've worried with you while you waited for confirmation." Why couldn't he see her as an adult—as someone he could count on? "You can trust me."

"I do trust you."

No, he didn't. In fact, Jordan didn't really trust anybody. "You don't have to be so all alone all the time." Ruling a nation took a strong hand, and Jordan held strength in bulk. But Dage ruled with family around . . . with friends being a part of his life. Why couldn't Jordan?

Irritation cut lines to the sides of his mouth. "Let's discuss my leadership issues another day. I don't suppose you've packed?"

"No."

"We can do this my way, Katie . . . or my way." Then his head lifted. His eyes darkened.. "I smell blood."

Shit. "I, ah, cut my arm. No big deal."

Two strides and he sat on the bed, reaching for her bandaged arm, zeroing right in. "What cut you?" His voice lowered to deadly.

She shivered in her thin T-shirt. "Ah, well, a werewolf?"

He ran his fingers along the side of the bandage. "Tonight?" Puzzlement combined with anger in his frown. "The moon isn't full. Did you find a lair?"

"No." She trembled but not from the cold. The contrast in Jordan's gentle touch and dangerous tone caused a warming in her belly. A tingling in her thighs. Man, she needed to concentrate. "Baye and I went looking for the place we think he'll go when the moon is full . . . at the marina . . . and he was, uh, there tonight. He's evolved, Jordan. Actually spoke to me." Kind of.

Jordan straightened. Doubt filled his eyes. "A werewolf *spoke* to you?"

"Yes. He said his name was Brent, and he knew you. Didn't like you much."

"Brent? Couldn't be." Jordan frowned, gently setting her arm on the bedspread. For two seconds, he didn't move enough to even breathe. Then he exhaled, his jaw hardening. "I have calls to make." He stood, crossing the room in three strides, lifting his cell phone to his ear. "You have an hour to pack."

Glass shattered.

Shards flew from the window to cover her bedspread.

Fur shone in the moonlight, and a low growl vibrated

as a werewolf leaped inside, landing solidly on two feet. He sniffed, straightening to his full height.

Jordan pivoted, snapping the phone shut.

Oh God. Katie scooted farther back against the headboard, her heart slamming behind her ribs. Her mental shields dropped into place, protecting her from evil. The smell of wet dog made her cough. Calm. She needed to stay calm to think. "Jordan, meet Brent."

The two studied each other. Rain splashed inside, droplets glimmering on her polished oak floors.

Weird. This was too weird. The werewolf should be going for their throats, not staring at Jordan with an amused glint in his yellow eyes.

She had a gun in the nightstand. Slowly, casually, she reached for the drawer.

"No," Brent growled, keeping his gaze on Jordan. "No, Kaattiieee."

"Jesus." Jordan shoved his phone in his pocket. "When did you evolve enough to talk?" He eyed Katie and the beast, anger darkening his smooth skin.

Yeah. The bed lay between Jordan and Brent. Not a good place to be in her flimsy shirt without any weapons.

Jordan moved toward the bed.

"Stop." Brent flashed yellow teeth in a parody of a smile. "I talk. I think. I hunt." He jerked his head toward Katie. "Miiiine."

"You couldn't be more wrong. Kate, get out of bed and come here." Jordan's skin shimmered. A growl, deadlier than the one issued by Brent, rumbled from his twisted lips. "You said you know me?"

"Yeesss." Brent moved his hairy body closer to the bed. "Brennnt Bowwmn."

Jordan snarled.

Katie froze. Animalistic tension swirled through the room, raising the hair on the back of her neck. As a smart woman, she knew her limitations from the damn virus—getting between two shifted animals trying to kill each other would end badly. Hopefully Jordan wouldn't shift.

Jordan took another step toward her, his hands clenching into fists. "I thought I killed you. Three hundred years ago."

Brent shrugged a massive shoulder, sending fur rolling down his body. "No. Almooossst. You left tennndon attached in neck. I had to diiiig out of graaaave."

"That's unfortunate," Jordan said, his voice a low tenor Katie had never heard. "How long you been a werewolf?"

"Ten yearrrsss."

Jordan kicked off his boots.

Brent licked his lips.

Katie bunched her muscles to attack.

Brent settled his stance, fur rippling. "The Pride issss mine, coussssssin."

Cousin? Katie frowned. Jordan had family?

"Kaattieee one of us." Brent slid another foot closer to the bed.

Jordan ducked his head and charged. He hit the werewolf dead center, throwing them across the room and through the window. The window frame cracked down the middle, leaving a gash in the wall. They disappeared from sight. Air exploded as he must have shifted. Snarls and growls filled the night as they fell three stories.

Katie rushed to the window, her hands clutching the jagged sill. Rain slammed into her face.

In a tangle of limbs, the duo landed, werewolf solidly on top of cougar. Brent must've twisted them midflight. He rolled away, gasping, teeth flashing as Jordan's head thunked hard on the cobbled alley.

Panic caught Katie's breath in her throat. She rushed back to the drawer, reaching for the gun and swinging around. Her foot caught on the bedspread and she went

sprawling across the floor. Pain ripped across her knees.
She tightened her hold on the weapon. With a sob, she
scrambled to her feet, leaping back to the window.

Down below, Brent backed away from Jordan. The
massive cougar, much larger than any true animal,
sprawled on the wet bricks. Blood cascaded from a cut
above his left ear. He didn't move.

The angle of the fire escape kept her from getting a
clean sight. Frustration caught in her throat. Determination straightened Katie's spine. She aimed the barrel for
Brent's neck. He bunched to attack.

She fired.

The shot ricocheted off the metal fire escape. He
paused.

Both Jordan and Brent looked up, eyes wild, fur standing on end.

Jordan jumped to his feet with a high-pitched snarl.

Katie's hand trembled, and she slapped both hands
around the gun. The cougar and werewolf circled each
other, jaws wide, teeth flashing. Blood flowed from the
cut along the top of Jordan's head, dying his fur a dark red,
even with the rain pelting down.

She tried to aim, but the animals moved too quickly.
Toeing on her tennis shoes, she gingerly stepped over the
jagged glass to the fire escape. The wind blew water into
her face . . . even then a heavy mugginess assaulted her
lungs. She had to get closer to aim for Brent's legs. Too
bad she didn't have a tranquilizer gun.

Grabbing the slippery rail, she maneuvered down the
wet steps, her gaze on the fight. Jordan jumped Brent,
sinking his canines into the werewolf's neck. Brent howled
in anger.

Chills ripped down Katie's spine. Her arm ached, a dull,
thick pain, pounding with her rapid heartbeat.

Brent swung, connecting with Jordan's chest. The lion

flew across the alley to land hard against the building. Brick shattered, sending chips flying.

Jordan rolled, landing on all fours, teeth bared to kill. He took a step and halted, his wet ears going back. Rage filled his eyes when he turned his head and looked up. The snarl he gave at seeing her made her step back.

Brent hissed, shooting farther into the alley, his feet pounding and sending cobblestones flying. With a yowl sounding as if it came from a churning hell, Jordan bunched and followed him into darkness.

"No," Katie whispered, rushing down the remaining steps until splashing in a puddle at the bottom. Dusty water washed up her bare legs. Clutching the gun harder, she hustled after them.

Rain splattered into her eyes as she ran through the alleys, following the demolished ground. Fear propelled her. She had to reach Jordan—if there was any way to stop Jordan from killing Brent, she needed to do it. Brent's blood might hold hope for them all. They had to take him down, not end him for good.

She slid around a corner to see Brent disappearing over a rooftop, Jordan springing onto a fire escape. "Jordan," she screamed.

He halted, eyeing her and leaping back to the ground. Raw fury folded his lip.

The world stopped moving. The brick on either side of the alley turned a deep black from the rain splattering up from the cobblestones. Darkened windows lined high above, while even higher, two building lights shone down, weak in the murky night. A horn bellowed in the distance. She shoved hair from her face, gulping in air. Muggy and hot, air coated her throat on the way down.

Her lungs heated.

The cougar eyed her, rage in his eyes, fur rising on end down his back.

The need to aim the gun at him made her stomach clench.

The air thickened and he rose to full height, a human male standing in the rain. Nude and enraged.

Katie shivered. His eyes glowed in his angular face, revealing the animal present even in human form. His nose was straight, his cheekbones high and symmetrical, pure-bred lion embedded in every feature. While his chest had always been broad, cut definition enhanced more powerful muscles than she remembered. His narrow waist tapered to...

God. She *would not* look lower.

Jordan's gaze started at her tennis shoes and traveled up her bare legs to the clinging T-shirt. Fury lined every strong contour in his face.

Awareness slammed desire out of the way. She took a step back. Okay, running through alleys wearing only a T-shirt might have been a bad idea. Very bad. Intuition yelled at her to flee. No way in hell could she outrun him. Aiming the gun would be a serious mistake. She knew it . . . yet her hand trembled as she raised the weapon.

His chin lowered. A stalking predator, he strode forward with measured steps, water sluicing off his hard body.

Retreat was her only option. A loose stone tripped her, and she dodged to the side, her back flush to a building. Thank God the weapon hadn't gone off. A second later he trapped her, his abs square against the barrel of the gun, his gaze primal.

Something inside her hissed. Deep down, beyond humanity, at her very core . . . a lioness stretched.

The breath caught in her throat. She stilled. Searching down deep. Searching for the animal she used to be. The animal that had been silenced ten years ago by the virus. A tingling wandered through her veins, igniting her blood. An animal sense that she'd missed so very much. The slumbering cougar awakening in reaction to a male.

And the male was *pissed*.

He may have shifted to human form, but a primitive tension poured off him that sent her heart beating hard enough to hurt.

Splashing rain counted dangerous seconds as he waited in silent demand, not saying a word.

Sawdust filled her mouth. She tried to swallow, her gaze caught and held by his. Heat flashed in her abdomen. The animal deep down took over, lowering her hand and the gun. Her teeth sunk into her bottom lip, her gaze dropping to his chest. Both shoulders shook with the need to challenge him, but inside, the lioness purred.

Her mind blanked. Was the lioness returning? Finally?

He held out a hand. She faltered before sliding her palm along his. Strong fingers threaded through, and he pivoted to lead her home. "We'll discuss this on the plane."

Chapter 5

Jordan's cell phone rang on the way to the airport. Glancing at the silent woman in the passenger seat of the rented SUV, he shoved away the sense of dread and put the device to his ear. Leather crinkled when he moved. "What?"

"I found a lair," Baye said, birds squawking in the background. "At least, the werewolves have hunkered down around here somewhere. Lance and I need Katie to come sense them."

Irritation heated the air in Jordan's chest. He had enough on his mind at present. "She's busy and we need to meet the plane."

"I know. But it has to be Brent, and this might be our only chance to find him."

Jordan fought a growl. Brent's survival was on his head, and if possible, he needed to end the evil bastard. He eyed his watch. They did have enough time to do one last mission. Plus, he'd never seen Katie in action with her team. He glanced at the quiet woman, wondering what was going to happen when all the outlying squads were taken out of service. With werewolves becoming more intelligent, would they be able to find more shifters to infect easier than the Kurjans did? He shook his head and shoved frustration down. "All right. But we need to make it fast."

Signaling, he moved into the right lane. Dawn had arrived not long before, and the interstate was mainly empty. "Give me directions."

Katie waited until he'd clicked off. "Baye?"

"Yes. Lair." Jordan took the next exit, his mind humming. "We need you to find it."

"Finding lairs is my job." She turned to look out the window, her voice distracted. "What part of the area?"

Why did the local trees fascinate her so much? "Salvador Wildlife Management Area."

"Interesting. We'll need a boat to get to the inner marshes." She didn't really sound interested.

He eyed her, trying to figure out what was wrong. The woman had dressed in faded jeans and a yellow top reminding him of her mama's tulips. Millie Smith had the prettiest garden of anyone in town.

He grinned, remembering when Katie had to pull weeds for an entire summer after trying to sneak out of the house when sixteen. Not much got past Millie. He cleared his throat. "Um, you're probably wondering about Brent. About us being cousins."

Katie tilted her head. "Oh yeah."

Well, apparently she hadn't been wondering. What in the world was the woman thinking about? "Brent's father led our people about three hundred years ago. The Kurjans massacred his parents, my parents, the Kayrs rulers, and many others." A brilliant trap had been set into place, and the Kurjans had changed the dynamics of the world. The war had instantly started.

Katie rubbed her chin, turning to face him. "I'm sorry about your parents, Jordan."

Figured the woman would offer comfort instead of

condemnation for his never telling her the story. Something cut deep in his solar plexus. "Well, Brent disappeared and I stepped up to rule in a time of war." In a time of blood and death.

Jordan held his breath as he awaited her reaction. The woman's IQ reached genius level. She'd know Brent didn't just disappear.

But apparently her mind was focused elsewhere. She nodded and turned back toward the window.

His frown hurt the bruises on his face left by Brent. With a shrug, Jordan followed the directions, heading south until he couldn't stand the silence any longer. "You're awfully quiet." Maybe she was pouting since he was forcing her home. She'd been quiet since returning to her apartment and packing, not giving him any grief, even as they'd loaded up his rented Jeep. Not arguing at all. "What's wrong?"

"Nothing."

Now that was a lie. "Are you upset I kissed you?"

She started, facing him and flashing a surprised smile. "Ah, no. Not even close."

Well, now. The woman might at least be thinking about the kiss. Their first kiss. The damn moment had rocked his world. His hands tightened around the steering wheel. He should be happy Katie wasn't obsessing about one kiss, especially since they had no future. But hell, she could at least be sad about that. "Then what has you in such deep thought?"

Several expressions crossed her face, but he couldn't read any of them. Finally, she shrugged. "Just looking forward to seeing the queen." Katie turned back to the rushing forest and weak sunshine outside.

There was a time Katie would've told him anything—shared everything. Something in his gut suddenly ached. Anger followed ache. "How's your strength?"

"Same as a human, pretty much." No inflection rode her tone.

"What's it like? I mean, living as a human?"

"It sucks. Makes me sorry for them. I mean, I empathize with humans but sure don't want to be one. Lacking normal shifter strength makes life difficult."

He blinked twice, forcing down anger and sorrow. "When we find the lair, you stay back. The rules have been clear from day one."

"Fine."

Her easy acceptance pissed him off more. He wanted to argue with her. Wanted to see her flushed, angry, passionate, and not so . . . uncaring. "You're really pissing me off."

She faced him again, a frown between her fine brows. "Why?"

The fact he couldn't answer that question ticked him off even more. The sight of Baye angled to the side up ahead, leaning against an SUV, brought more relief than it should. Jordan pulled over and then cut the engine. Cypress trees lined both sides of the road, the wind throwing their leaves about. "Just do your job."

"Always." She jumped from the vehicle, her boots making imprints in the wet mud as she made her way toward Baye.

Jordan followed suit, his gaze on the most frustrating female he'd ever met. The faded jeans hugged her ass in a way that had his jeans feeling too tight. What the hell was wrong with him? She reached the vehicle, turning to stomp her boots clean.

Her hair had darkened a tiny shade the last decade, turning more sandy blond than golden. Feline cheekbones had sharpened, her pink lips had rounded the slightest bit. But those bourbon-colored eyes had remained the same. She truly was the sexiest woman he'd ever seen—and he'd lived more than three hundred years.

Shaking off the thought, he glared at Baye, taking note of a fat lip and swollen jaw. The fight the previous night must've been rough. "Where's the lair?"

The enforcer studied him, a fathomless expression in his light eyes. "Somewhere close. One of our scouts called with information about a bunch of dead, gutted animals around here. Lance already shifted and is sniffing the best path." Baye snarled and then winced, finger going to the cut in his lip. "Also, Lance had to kill a human turned werewolf last night."

Jordan frowned. "That's new. We haven't seen a human convert in quite some time."

Baye scratched his chin. "Maybe not. But they do pop up once in a while. Some werewolf must've gotten close to the human population and bitten the poor guy." Baye tugged Katie's hair. "I have a sweatshirt in my car as I figured you'd forget yours."

Jordan swallowed hard to keep the snarl in his gut.

Katie chuckled. "Ah, yeah, considering I thought I was heading to the airport." She opened the back door and yanked out a faded New Orleans Saints sweatshirt.

Baye lifted an eyebrow.

Jordan met his gaze squarely, possessiveness nearly choking him. There had better be nothing going on between his old friend and his . . . Jesus. Katie wasn't his. He shook his head, turning toward the swamp. "We need to get moving." The sooner he dropped Katie at headquarters and headed off to fight, the better.

Katie drew the sweatshirt tighter around her, trying to clear her mind. Two guns sat at her waist, three knives were strapped to her legs. Cold from the marshboat seat slid from her thighs to her spine. They traveled a narrow path, sweeps of branches high above hiding the sky. The

ness and cold still ruled. A flash of orange came through
the trees from Lance running along the bank in tiger form.

Baye sat in front of her, Jordan behind her, both keeping an eye on the marshy land while they rowed the small
craft.

Her only thought was of the lioness inside. She'd felt the
lioness awaken. How had it happened? Could the virus be
running its course? Was she going to be able to shift again?
Reality and hope fought for dominance inside her. When
she'd faced Jordan in the alley, for the first time in a
decade, she'd sensed the animal within her pores.

Katie dug down deep to find her again, but nothing. No
feeling of the animal within. Regret and frustration had
her clenching her hands.

Lance gave a sharp yowl from the bank. Birds protested,
wings flapping as they flew for safety.

Katie yanked her attention back to werewolves. She'd
have to worry about the lioness later. Right now she
needed to hunt.

Cattail and bull tongue plants lined the banks, along
with the timber stands. A muskrat raccoon swam by lazily,
seemingly unafraid of the abundant alligators hiding below.
Brave little animal.

The soft splash of the oars was broken only by an occa-
sional cry of a bald eagle high above. Dark and murky, the
swamp hid treasures and wildlife. A lonely breeze swept
her hair, chilling her skin and bringing the scent of decay-
ing moss.

The shifter in front of her was on guard, the shifter behind her pissed off. Jordan must be irritated he had to
stop and fight werewolves instead of heading straight to
Oregon.

She was irritated, too. Baye and Lance were good

friends, the best, and Jordan hadn't even given her a chance to say good-bye. If Baye hadn't found the lair, she'd be on her way to Realm Headquarters right now.

Her spine tingled. An ache centered at the base of her skull. Darkness swam over her vision, and she tightened her hold on the side of the boat. The energy signature sent out by the beasts caused pain as well as disorientation. At least for her. "We're getting closer. They're to the right."

She swallowed, the taste of dead animal permeating her saliva. Yeah, they were close.

Baye steered to the bank, jumping out to drag the boat up the mossy embankment. He lifted his head, scanning the area. "I get a general sense of maybe three werewolves but can't get a direction."

Jordan leapt out, reaching a hand to help her. She paused. For ten years she'd been treated as one of the guys by her squad. Well, kind of—they still protected her during battle. The gentlemanly gesture from Jordan, so natural, set flutters alive in her abdomen. "Oh, for goodness sakes," she muttered, taking his hand and sliding out of the boat. She didn't have time for this crap.

Releasing him, she stomped up the bank toward the trees. The pounding in her skull increased in power. Squinting, she pointed at a narrow trail. "That way."

Jordan nodded, taking the lead. "Stay between me and Baye."

"This isn't my first hunt, Jordan." What the hell did the lion leader think she'd been doing the last ten years? Charging into danger like a dumbass blonde in a slasher movie? She fully understood her limitations from the virus. In strength and speed, she was nowhere near where she used to be as a lioness. For now.

Baye cocked a gun, the only sound behind her as they tromped through the wilderness. "It's still morning . . . they may be asleep."

Lance appeared at her side, his massive head reaching her rib cage. He head-butted her.

"Knock it off." She tried to bite back a smile. The shifter would kill to have his ears scratched, even in the middle of werewolf territory. He huffed and then took up a flanking position, large paws silent on the rocky ground.

They trudged through maybe five acres, scrambling over rocks and through brush. Katie smacked a mosquito off her arm. The air began to turn muggy. Thunder rolled high above, promising a break in air pressure.

Jordan paused in front of her, sliding brush out of the way. "I can feel them now."

Katie nodded, sidling up beside him. Even with her mental shields in place, a dull, dark ache pounded in her head.

She studied the lodging. A dilapidated porch covered the front, hanging drunkenly off one side. Two windows had been roughly boarded up. The roof sagged in the middle. "Weird. They usually try to go underground." A chill having nothing to do with the weather shook her arms. If any humans had lived there, they hadn't survived the werewolves moving in.

A punch of pure evil hit her between the eyes.

She stepped back, hand going to her throat. "I sense Brent." Nothing on earth could make her think of him as "Snuggles" ever again. "Muted, but a sense." Maybe the beast hid in a basement. Though, in a swamp? This wasn't a place to have a basement.

Lance snarled, the striped fur along his spine standing up.

"Katie, stand back. Lance, cover her . . . don't come unless I yell." Jordan took a green gun from his waist. "Baye, you go through the rear door."

"On it." Baye jogged around the perimeter of the small clearing, disappearing silently.

"I'll try to stay in human form—I'd like to just shoot

them and end this quickly." Jordan gave her one last hard look. "Be careful." Then he turned, charging for the front door. If the werewolves were awake, they'd smell the shifters, so stealth was unnecessary.

Katie settled her back against a tree, taking aim at the entrance. Lance stood in front of her, teeth bared, concentration absolute on the shack.

Jordan hit the entrance, splintering the rotten wood in two, crashing inside. A furious roar bellowed forth. Snarls, growls, and loud thunks echoed back. Something impacted the nearest wall. Boards on the front of the house broke outward. Splinters of wood flew across the sad porch.

Fear slammed into Katie. What if more than three werewolves lived in the shack? She maneuvered closer and to the side for a better angle.

Jordan flew out, spinning head over heels, followed by an enraged beast. A seven-foot, huge-assed, hairy werewolf the color of a gray sheepdog. Deadly fangs flashed low, dripping with saliva. The monster advanced on Jordan, eyes a swirling yellow, three-inch claws swiping furiously. The fur stood up along its back.

Hitting the ground, Jordan rolled, landing on his feet with his gun firing.

Katie joined in, aiming for the beast's chest. She used both hands to aim the gun. The recoil jerked her arms each time. An ache set up in her shoulder blades, yet she shoved the pain away and kept firing.

The animal fell to one knee, roaring in fury.

Lance circled to the side, teeth bared, claws out.

Jordan settled his stance, shooting the monster between the eyes. The werewolf fell back, an odd moaning escaping. No expression covered Jordan's face, but his eyes flared with emotion. He yanked a knife from his boot.

Stalking forward, he straddled the werewolf, plunging the blade into its neck.

Blood sprayed across Jordan's throat and chest. Grunting, fighting, and using both hands, he slashed hard to the right. Then the left. Finally, the monster's head rolled away from the body.

"I'm sorry," Jordan whispered.

Lance eyed Jordan, nodded at Katie, and ran full bore into the house to help Baye, clearing the porch in a graceful leap.

Standing up, Jordan turned toward her. Savagery slashed into very lines of his chiseled face. Sorrow cut deeper in his eyes. "I should never have allowed you to be part of this."

Understanding and sympathy slid through her. It wasn't the killing. The pain lay in the fact that the shifter had probably once been a good man. "This is on the Kurjans, Jordan. Not us."

"Is it?" He glanced at Baye, who carried out the head of another werewolf—this one a dark brown.

Baye threw the head toward the trees. "Only two werewolves. Neither were Brent." A long scratch marred his left cheek, and blood covered his torso. "You're gonna want to see this." He disappeared back inside.

Katie hurried forward, clutching Jordan's arm. "You are not responsible for the evil brought by the Kurjans."

His bicep flexed. "How can I not be?" He stared at the blood now covering his cowboy boots. "I thought I'd be the best choice to lead. I made sure I was the only choice." He shook his head, fury vibrating from his strong body. "Maybe I was wrong."

She dug her nails in. "Stop it." What the heck was going on? "I have a sense of Brent. The guy is pure evil—he would've destroyed the feline nation. You did the right thing. And now, you're doing your job by chasing monsters."

"When you chase monsters, you're really chasing yourself." Jordan grabbed her hand, striding toward the building. "Watch your step on the stairs."

Wow. They were definitely going to discuss his family tree later. Katie gingerly stepped over a damaged board, crossing the destroyed porch and entering the dark dwelling. The stench of wet dog hit her immediately. Her stomach rolled. She took an involuntary step away. A warm hand settled on her back, providing comfort. Somehow Jordan had always known how to calm her.

She gathered courage and looked around. Dead and half-eaten animals covered the kitchen counters to the left, a ripped sofa perched against the wall to the right. Different colors of fur were embedded in the old cushions. No bathroom appeared visible, but Baye stood next to the one interior doorway, anger on his face.

He kept her gaze.

Icy fingers danced down her spine. "What?"

"Look inside the bedroom." He tilted his head inside the doorway.

The air thickened. A familiar oiliness covered her skin. Evil. "Brent's bedroom?" She walked inside and stopped short. The room was devoid of furniture except for a filthy mattress on the floor. The window had been boarded up, but enough light shone through the gaps to highlight the walls. Lance sat on his back haunches, ears twitching.

Jordan swore from behind her, brushing past to go closer to the photographs lining the wall. Pictures of her. In front of her building, at a movie theater with Maggie, at the grocery store. He whirled on her, fury lifting his lip. "Explain this."

She stepped back. "I . . . I . . . can't." A picture from last week when she'd met a friend in a bar caught her eye.

Maggie had arranged her first date with Mitch. The guy had been a football player more interested in talking about shoes than football. She hadn't noticed anybody taking pictures, or even taking an interest in them. How was this possible?

"Werewolves don't fucking take pictures." Jordan swept an arm out. "Somebody got close enough to you, several times, to take your picture." He pivoted and peered at the neatly arranged collage, walking along the wall. Finally, he turned toward Baye. "You and Lance aren't in any—these were taken when you two weren't around."

"Which means the photographer was probably shifter, demon, or vampire," Baye growled. "We would've sensed them."

Katie shoved hair out of her eyes. "My senses aren't as good as they used to be, but still . . ." Why hadn't she noticed someone taking so many pictures? Maggie hadn't noticed, either.

Jordan glanced at Baye over her head. "You know what this means, right?"

"Yes. Brent has a friend." Baye stared at the photographs. "Unbelievable."

Lance padded all four legs forward, tiger gaze on one photograph. The one taken during her date. He snarled.

Jordan frowned, ripping the picture off the wall. "What?"

Katie peered over his shoulder. "That's Mitch Meyers. He's a football player I went on a date with last week." She ignored the sudden stiffening of Jordan's entire body.

Baye exhaled. "Shit. That's the name of the human-turned-werewolf Lance went to the hospital to research last night."

Dread had Katie freezing in place. "Mitch was turned into a werewolf?"

"Yes." Fury spun red through Baye's feline features.

"Lance kidnapped him from the hospital last night and, well, took him down."

Lance butted her thigh in support and apology. Absently, she reached down and scratched his ears. A human couldn't survive a werewolf bite . . . Lance had to kill Mitch.

Her gaze remained on the picture of the tall football player, a smile on his face, a beer in his hand. She bit her lip, fear slamming through her. Mitch was dead. All because he'd bought her a drink.

Somebody was working *with* a werewolf.

Somebody who had been watching her.

Chapter 6

Katie paced back and forth by the kitchen table, her mind whirling. She and the men had all showered and cleaned up quickly. For once the calm tones of her apartment failed to provide comfort. Even the handmade tablecloth lovingly stitched by her mother appeared odd with the pictures spread all over the lace. Thank God her mother was safely away on a cruise right then. Millie would be furious somebody was stalking her daughter—and would turn all feline and protective—probably insisting Katie hide while she hunted the threat. For now, Katie would protect her mother and keep her away from danger.

Katie turned toward her friend. "Frank is dead, too?"

Lance nodded, hanging up the phone. He frowned, his tone gentling. "Car accident two months ago. The police report said there was alcohol involved."

She bit back a sob, dropping into the chair next to Baye. "Frank didn't drink. Said he had an allergy to alcohol." The accountant was a nice guy she went on two dates with. Once to a movie and the other time to a festival in the French Quarter. Unfortunately, they'd spent most of the time talking about his ex-girlfriend until they both realized he should go win the woman back. Now, because he'd hung out with Katie, he was dead.

Jordan leaned against the refrigerator, a scowl on his face. "That makes three."

The third man, a police detective from up north, had died on the job two weeks previous. They'd only gone on one date. Lance had promised to investigate further to see if that was what really happened. Katie knew deep down the cop died because of her, too.

Lance rubbed his chin, blue eyes flashing. Most tigers had green eyes, but not Lance. Bluer than blue, the color had made many a woman sigh when the squad had been out enjoying a drink after work. Or rather, before work while they waited for the moon to rise. He shook his head. "I'm not doubting your abilities or trying to diminish your strength. But I think we should get you out of town until we figure this out. Just like we would if someone stalked Baye."

"Baloney." Katie ran her finger along a picture taken of her shopping for apples. First Brent, and now Lance. Somehow she had to conceal her panic and fear from her friends. If they had any clue how badly she wanted to go and hide under the bed, all three men would try to shield her. While she might be ill, for now, she was still a warrior. She *needed* to be a warrior. "Baye wouldn't hide from a stalker. Neither will I."

"I didn't mean hide. Just move to an undisclosed location." Frustration lined Lance's face. "We'll come up with a plan, find this guy, and destroy him. Together."

Jordan smoothed the photographs into a pile. "No. Call it hiding, call it moving . . . either way, you're flying to headquarters in an hour."

Anger heated Katie's ears. Her squad understood her . . . they trusted her. Jordan wanted her to run without even discussing the matter. "I'm not afraid of this guy." She kept her tone level as she told the lie.

"Don't care. Until the next full moon, I'm your Alpha,

and I'm ordering you to Realm Headquarters." Jordan tossed her a notepad and pen. "Write down anyone you've spent time with the last few years. Mainly men, but we don't want to rule out women. This stalker might not be selective."

His absolute refusal to listen wiped away the anger, leaving hurt. Yet she still owed him, and would go to Realm Headquarters in an effort to help him find a way to beat the moon. Then she'd return to hunting down werewolves until not one remained. "A werewolf stalker." She shook her head. "How is it possible Brent killed these people? I mean, how could he have gotten to the cop?"

Lance flipped open his phone to read. "Police report. Says there was a firefight in a northern bayou, bodies fell into the marsh. Animals tore up the detective pretty good by the time the authorities found him and fished him out."

Bile rose in Katie's throat. She gagged and swallowed repeatedly. Torn up by animals? Damn Brent. "I don't believe this."

Fury lifted Jordan's lip. "Either Brent or his picture-taking buddy has to be responsible." The lion gestured to the neatly stacked pile of photographs. "All three men who died are in those pictures."

As were several other people. Katie sucked in a deep breath to keep from puking.

Lance eyed the photographs. "Realm Headquarters is too obvious. We need to get you somewhere off the grid while we figure this out."

Jordan kept his gaze on the photos as if by staring the answers would come clear. "No. Headquarters is secure . . . and we need more blood tests. Katie goes with me."

"You mean the headquarters in *Oregon*? Not exactly a big secret." Lance reached to pat her hand, his palm warm and comforting. "Besides, the virus in your blood makes you unstable, Jordan."

Jordan pushed off the fridge, his lids lowering.

Panic swept down Katie's throat. "Jordan's fine. Emma will cure him and that'll be the end of the virus."

"Right." Lance tightened his hold. "We've fought together, Katie. We're a team. Baye and I can keep you safe."

Jordan snarled. "You and Baye didn't even know she was being followed, much less stalked and photographed. How the hell can you keep her safe?" His hand swept the photographs, sending several flying.

Katie swallowed. Lance had saved her butt, more than once. They were a good team. For the first time, indecision regarding her path had her faltering. She was a good hunter. But she'd wanted Jordan her entire life. If nothing else, she owed him and would try to help him survive the virus.

Baye watched the interplay, no expression on his face.

Lance released her, standing to glare at Jordan. "How safe is she with you?"

Jordan's nostrils flared. "I won't hurt her."

Disbelief had the tiger's brows lifting. "Really? Why do I find that hard to believe?"

Jordan charged, hands fisting in Lance's shirt and shoving the man against the wall.

Face-to-face, furious, both males snarled low. Raw energy and power vibrated around the apartment. Panic rushed to Katie's legs.

She jumped toward them, slapping a hand on the biceps of the deadly cats. "You knock it off, right now." That was all she needed. The men in her life coming to blows. There were too many Alpha males in her business. Damn heroes thought they could control the world and keep her safe. She cast a frustrated glare at the one not involved. "Do something."

Baye shrugged. "Let them fight it out." He yanked a beer off the counter and took a deep swallow. "They both want to protect you, and neither has figured out they have the same goal."

Sometimes he was such an asshole.

She tightened her hold on the vibrating muscles beneath her palms. "Please stop. Lance, I appreciate you're trying to protect me, but I need to go to headquarters. Jordan, release my friend."

For two beats, nobody moved. Then Jordan un-clenched his hands, backing away.

Lance straightened his shirt, his gaze on the lion. But he directed his words to her. "Are you sure?"

"Yes. I'll call when we get there." She'd miss her friends. But she had a plan.

Lance nodded, finally turning to face her. "We'll trace the rest of these people, Kate. And we'll go after Brent at the same time. The bastard only has four nights until the full moon, and we'll be ready. Trust me."

"I do." Fear welled up in her along with the bile. If any-thing happened to Baye or Lance, she didn't know what she'd do. They'd bonded in fear, fight, and survival. "I'll miss you."

Jordan cleared his throat. "Time to go."

Katie clutched the armrests of the small private plane, her heart beating so fast her breath caught. After a tearful good-bye with both Lance and Baye, she'd silently headed to the airport with Jordan. Guilt from the deaths kept her quiet. Logically, she knew her dates' deaths weren't her fault.

Guilt defied logic.

Jordan lifted an eyebrow across from her. He had no problem facing backward as they rose into the air. "You still hate flying?"

"Cats shouldn't fly." No way would she land on her feet if they dropped from the sky. Not this far. Attempting to force a smile, she tried to relax her shoulders from solid rock to liquid cement . . . without success. "I'm surprised you're okay with flying considering what a control freak you are."

"How many men have you dated the last ten years, anyway?" He grimaced after saying the words, as if he hadn't meant to let them out.

"Enough," she said softly. She'd compared every single man to Jordan, and not one had come close to being what she wanted. "Of course, I hadn't thought dating me would be a death sentence."

"Not your fault." He'd tied his thick hair back at the neck after his shower, and her fingers had the oddest urge to yank the strands free. "Date any shifters? Or just humans?"

The conversation made her twitchy. "Both."

"Get serious with anybody?"

"Does it matter?"

He sighed. "Yes. I don't want your dating life to matter to me, but it does."

She blew out a breath. "Is it just me, or was that a, 'Gee, your ass doesn't look as big as usual in those jeans,' kind of compliment?"

He grinned. "Sorry. You know what I mean."

Actually, she didn't. Not really. But she nodded anyway. "I dated my History of Warfare professor for quite a while last year." She'd graduated from the university with a knowledge necessary for her squad. Even if she couldn't fight like a healthy shifter, the battle plans she created bordered on brilliant, according to Baye.

Jordan quirked a lip. "I hope you got an A."

"Of course." They hadn't started dating until after the class had concluded, but Jordan didn't need to know the details. "I also took a cooking class."

Humor flirted with Jordan's full lips. "Did you ace the cooking class?"

"No." In fact, she'd been asked to leave after she'd set the kitchen on fire for the third time. She and the professor agreed she'd take a C and never return.

"I'm not, er, surprised." Jordan glanced at the clouds whirling by outside the small windows.

"Maggie took classes at the same time and majored in philosophy."

"Does she help fight?" Jordan cracked his neck.

"Not usually." Someday maybe Maggie would be well enough to fight, but that day hadn't arrived.

Katie's head settled against the back of her chair, and she studied Jordan from half-closed lids. Concentrating on his symmetrical face was a lot better than imagining herself dropping a zillion feet to hit concrete. A slight purple bruise from the fight with Brent covered the right side of Jordan's jaw, emphasizing strength and muscle. The cords of his neck were all male, so masculine she'd imagined running her mouth along the firmness many times. In fact, she'd like to take a bite right where his prominent jaw met the sweet spot under his ear.

As if he could read her mind, his eyes flared with heat. "What are you thinking about?"

"The kiss in my apartment." The moment hadn't left her thoughts much. And now she wanted to think about anything but the trail of death she'd left in New Orleans.

He licked his lips in thought. She fought a groan in response. Desire began to shove fear of flying out of her consciousness.

The plane leveled off.

"Yeah. The kiss was probably a mistake." He met her gaze squarely, his stunning eyes devoid of expression.

She'd known Jordan most of her life. When he lacked

expression, it wasn't lack of interest. He often made a calculated effort to hide his current thoughts or feelings. Interesting. Her fingers found the clasp of the seat belt, and she freed herself.

He lifted his chin. "What are you doing?"

"Relaxing."

He settled into his chair. "Kate?" His voice held bite this time. "Have you been sleeping with Lance?"

The question jerked her head back. How could he think she'd sleep with someone in her squad? She and Lance were friends—the best of friends. The cat had saved her life numerous times, and she kept him safe, too. Jordan had no right to question her about the tiger. "None of your business."

"Oh, I think it is," he said softly. Too softly.

Temper stretched awake inside her. "Well, I wouldn't call what we do *sleeping*. Especially when Baye joins in."

Jordan blinked. Then a slow grin spread across his face. "Into ménage now, are you?"

"Yep." She lifted her chin. "Especially since Baye always brings bullwhips. I do love a good bullwhip."

Jordan threw back his head and laughed. "That's a good one. Okay. You've made your point. I'm sorry for questioning you. I shouldn't have."

She wished he had the right to question her—that he wanted the right. "What about you? Have you been dating anyone?" Her shoulders stiffened for the blow.

"No."

"Why not?" Now her voice lowered to a soft tone.

His grin hinted at sin. "Dating isn't as much fun since you're not there to sabotage me."

The breath strangled in her throat. "I don't know what you're talking about." Crap. Had he known? She'd messed with his dates the second she became a teenager, once even spilling ice cream down a panther shifter's silk dress to make her leave a party.

"You weren't exactly subtle." Jordan grinned again.

"Well," Katie sniffed, "you've had terrible taste in women, anyway."

His gaze swept her, head to foot, leaving a flash of awareness along every nerve. "I'd say my taste has improved."

Heat filled her cheeks. Before she could respond, lightning cracked. The plane bumped, shimmying to the side. Panic prickled the skin on her neck. She clutched her nails into the leather armrests, and the muscles in her legs tightened until becoming painful.

Jordan leaned forward, tugging her hands free. "You're okay. Turbulence is normal and no big deal." His thumbs caressed her knuckles in soothing circles.

Her eyes widened, and she shook her head.

The craft lurched again.

Darn it. Many people took sedatives to fly. She should've gotten a prescription. Well, she would've if she'd had any warning she'd be flying. The plane dipped, quickly righting. A soft whimper escaped her.

Jordan yanked her toward him, settling her on his lap. She tucked her face into his neck.

He held her tight. "Just hold on, kitten. We'll be through the storm soon."

Her body coiled. She closed her eyes, breathing in his familiar scent. Minutes passed. His warm hand caressed her spine. More bumps had her panting, tensing as she waited for each lurch. Finally, as the way stayed calm, her body relaxed.

Exhausted, frightened, she dropped into an uneasy sleep.

Hours later, a slight change in cabin pressure filtered through her dreams. Slowly, awareness had her eyes opening. They were descending . . . going to land. Then she

came fully awake. Her butt perched on incredibly hard
thighs. A warm chest cradled her in safety. Jordan's heart
beat steady and strong beneath her palm.

She'd slept on his lap for the entire flight.

Giving in to temptation, she wandered her mouth up
his jugular to behind his ear.

He stiffened. "What are you doing?" He sounded
sleepy. Maybe he'd slept, too.

For answer, she nipped his jaw.

"Katie—" His voice came out hoarse. The low timber
danced down her spine as if he'd traced her vertebrae with
his tongue.

She leaned back. "What?" They had so many issues to
deal with—from trust to death. Yet she wanted another
kiss from the lion. Just one more before all hell broke
loose. Before the plane landed and reality slapped her in
the face.

Maybe she was still dreaming.

Smooth, slow, she slid her hands up his neck to tangle
in his thick hair. The sleep cleared from his eyes. They
narrowed, but he didn't stop her. She tightened her hold.
Moving forward, her lips wandered against his.

The lion's sharp intake of breath made her smile. She
flicked her tongue along his lower lip, a soft sigh escaping her.

The tension in his body increased.

"Jordan. Kiss me back. Just one more time." They had
a few minutes until the plane touched down. A few more
minutes to pretend.

Denial was blinked away in his eyes. Frustration and a
glimmer of anger replaced it. Finally, want. Maybe even
need.

His mouth slanted over hers. Taking, giving, his lips
firm and demanding.

She'd been kissed before. Jordan didn't kiss. He consumed. Sliding into arousal wasn't an option. Her body shot from slow burn to inferno in a heartbeat.

He cupped the back of her head, holding her in place. His talented tongue slid past her lips and he explored her mouth as if every crevice was his and his alone. As if he had every right to do so . . . as if she were his.

The kiss declared possession. Demanded submission. He tangled her hair in his fist, plunging deeper. She whimpered against him. Needing more. Needing everything. Her nipples pebbled to true pain. Her sex softened in absolute demand.

Wheels touched down with a small bump. The brakes engaged with a hiss.

Jordan tore away, his five o'clock shadow scratching her face. Desire burned hot and bright in his eyes. He took a deep breath. "I need you, Kate."

She nodded. Even after the kiss, she knew what he meant. "I know."

"Be strong. Help me figure out how to keep the nation together." Pain and absolute determination settled across his face. "Help me leave you whole. I have to know you're going to be okay if I—"

"I'm not giving up." There had to be a way to cure him—to keep him from turning.

Desperation curled his lip. "Okay. But I need you prepared. I need you to be okay."

She wouldn't be. No way would she be whole if he died. She forced a smile, trying to keep her lips from trembling. "I'm strong, Jordan. You made sure of it." For so many years, he'd trained her. "I'll be fine." She didn't bat an eyelash as she told the biggest lie of her life.

Chapter 7

A bulletproof SUV manned by a too silent vampires met them at the airport, squiring them to Realm Headquarters. The area appeared more like an upscale gated community, complete with checkpoints with armed guards along the way. The houses were for peacetime, while the surrounding cliffs and mountains held underground levels of safety.

Arriving at the main building, she smiled at the sprawling ocean extending so far. Even as a lioness, she'd always enjoyed looking at the sea. Upon entering the cedar-sided lodge, she'd been instantly sent to the queen to draw blood.

An hour later, safely being poked by needles in the large lab at the above-ground Realm Headquarters, she awaited the queen's diagnosis, fidgeting on the examination table and wrinkling the paper. Lemon cleanser and the queen's strawberry shampoo mingled in the air. The king's mate worked impossible hours, every day, trying to cure the virus.

While Katie had given more blood during the last ten years than she could count, the above-ground lab was her favorite place to be tested. Wide windows showcased the stunning ocean spreading as far as she could see. "Well? What happened in the alley? I swear, I felt like—"

"Your blood is the same." Emma Kayrs, looking nothing like pampered royalty, scribbled notes in a file, her black hair clipped at the nape. She leaned back against a granite counter lined with test tubes and humming machines. One blinked green lights, spitting out data. "Your chromosomal pairs are holding steady at twenty-five pairs. Even without medication." She tapped her pen on the paper. "Maggie's are back up to twenty-six after a quick dive to twenty-four, which gives me great hope. Male shifters drop to twenty-four pairs, turning them into werewolves. Female shifters seem to stop unraveling at twenty-five, which makes you nearly human but not quite."

Emma flashed a sympathetic smile. "As far as we know, only Maggie dropped to twenty-four pairs, probably because of the experiments conducted on her by the Kurjans that we don't really know about. We don't even know how long they kept her captive. Either way, I just can't figure out why she's different from all the other affected female shifters. Why are her chromosomal pairs back up to twenty-six? Is the cure somehow in her blood?"

"What about Cara's chromosomal pairs?" Emma's sister Cara had been human with twenty-three chromosomal pairs until she mated Talen Kayrs, shooting her pairs up to twenty-seven. Before she contracted the virus.

"She is back up to twenty-six pairs, which also gives me great hope. But no matter what I do or try, or what Talen tries, we can't get her pairs back up to the twenty-seven of a mate."

Katie shook her head. "For the first time in ten years, I *felt* like me. Like the shifter inside had returned." Before getting on the plane, she'd tried to shift. Repeatedly and with no luck. But if the lioness had returned, she might beat the virus. Maybe the cure lived in Katie's blood.

Emma slapped the file closed, her lips pinched. "I don't know. Maybe being close to Jordan after so long did it—

the cougar inside you recognized a potential mate in Jordan and woke up. Or perhaps"—she took a deep breath—"the lioness recognized the virus in Jordan—the same one you have."

Perhaps she'd returned to say good-bye to the only man Katie would ever love. She shoved the thought away. "What about this antiviral you've been working on from Maggie's blood?"

Emma's blue eyes darkened. "We've had some success in test tubes, but it's nowhere near ready to use."

"There isn't a choice." Jordan would be a monster within a few days.

"I know."

"What about," Katie cleared her throat, rolling her shoulders, "if we, I mean, what if we—"

"Mated?" Amusement lifted the queen's lips. "I truly don't know." She lost her smile. "Mating might work, might halt Jordan's virus like it is in you . . . or might turn you both into werewolves. When a shifter bites a mate, their physiology is altered, as you know. Forever. Who knows what would happen in this case."

Katie would take the risk.

Voices echoed down the hallway, and Cara Kayrs swept into the room. "I think you're being ridiculous."

Her husband and mate, Talen, stalked in behind her, a scowl on his broad face. "She's too young to date."

Cara rushed forward and enveloped Katie in a hug. "I've missed you." She leaned back, studying her. "It's been too long."

Katie smiled at her friend. "You look well." Actually, Cara had been unnaturally pale since contracting the virus, but her blue eyes were clear, so that had to be a good thing. As sisters, she and Emma shared the same eye color, but her hair was a much lighter auburn. "What is the cranky vampire growling about now?" Katie gave Talen a grin.

"Hi, monster." He leaned in and tugged her hair. "It has been way too long."

Warmth flushed through her. The dangerous soldier had been calling her *monster* since she dumped a soda on him during a picnic thirty years before. She'd only been four, for goodness sakes. The Kayrs men had been family her entire life. "I'm a grown-up now—you shouldn't call me names."

"You look sixteen." He scowled at his wife. "Too young to date."

"Nuh-uh," Katie countered. Geez. She might look twenty, but she'd lived thirty-four years, and after a moment in his presence, she felt four years old again. "I look my age." Right. If her genes cooperated, she'd always look twenty-five.

Cara sighed, shoving curls off her face. Her dark jeans and simple white T-shirt held splotches of dirt. The woman had probably been gardening, which was a favorite hobby. She gave her husband a glare. "The grumpy vampire is irritated his daughter wants to go to a movie with a panther shifter next week."

"She's too young." Talen crossed his massive arms. His eyes were a deep gold, his features rugged and powerful. Not many people challenged the head of all military strategy for the Realm. "That panther . . . he looks at her funny."

Emma snorted. "You're such a dork."

Katie jumped off the table. "I suppose you'd rather Janie dated a vampire?"

"Hell, no." Talen lifted Cara and set her down gently on the table. "I'd rather she didn't date at all. In fact, she's too young. Period."

Emma grabbed another file. "I think it's good she wants to go on a date with someone, anyone, instead of pining for that Zane."

Cara nodded, rolling up her sleeve. "Yeah. I have to admit, I was seriously relieved when he stopped visiting her dreams about five years ago."

Katie inched toward the door. Something told her Zane hadn't disappeared for all time . . . just while Janie grew up. No need to tell the overprotective parents, however. "Speaking of Janie, I'm supposed to meet her in the game room. See you all later." She turned and ran smack into a hard chest.

"Aunt Katie." Strong hands steadied her, and she looked up an inch into metallic gray eyes.

When had he grown so tall? "Garrett." She enveloped him in a huge hug. She loved that he'd given her the honorary title of "Aunt." Very cool. The kid definitely had his father's size, though gangly was an understatement. "What are you, about twenty years old?"

He returned the hug, large hands patting her shoulder awkwardly. "Funny. You know I just turned ten." Humungous feet shuffled as he stepped back, a dimple flashing in his already handsome face. Good humor lifted his smile, but a clear predator lumbered beneath the surface of that sharp face. There was no question Garrett was his father's son. "Dad? The panther called again. Thought you should know."

Talen growled low. "That kid needs to be relocated somewhere else."

Garrett nodded. "Yeah. He looks at Janie funny."

"See?" Talen gestured wildly. "Even he sees it."

"In fact"—a mischievous light entered Garrett's odd eyes—"Uncle Dage thinks I should go to the movies with them next week."

A smile crossed Talen's rugged face. "Now that's a fine idea."

"No," Cara said.

Talen and his son shared a look.

"We'll see about that," Talen said.

Chuckling, Katie maneuvered around Garrett and strolled by windows showcasing a tumultuous Pacific Ocean on her way to the game room. She found Janie chalking a pool stick in front of the only pool table, the balls already racked. Several dartboards adorned the side, while a huge, fully stocked bar lined one entire wall.

"Katie." Janie hustled past an air hockey game, giving a strong hug.

Katie leaned back, taking a good look at the gorgeous teenager. Intelligent blue eyes set in a heart-shaped face with her mama's delicate features. Her hair had deepened to a light sable. "You forgot to grow."

The grin was all imp. "I know, right? Stupid Garrett is almost four inches taller than me already." She shook her head. "He picks me up just for fun sometimes. But . . . I can still kick his butt."

Probably because the hulking vamp didn't want to hurt his big sister. "Of course you can. We women are tough." God, she hoped Janie mated a vampire or shifter someday so she'd be immortal. The girl was human and had been adopted by Talen when he'd married her mother. Katie grabbed a pool stick.

Movement by the doorway caught her eye.

Maggie dodged inside. "Hey, I found some grape energy drinks." She grinned, her brown curls bobbing and dark eyes dancing. "The king didn't hide these very well." Hustling forward, she plunked the cans on the bar and grabbed Katie in a hug. "I'm glad to see you."

Katie returned the shorter woman's hug. "Our apartment has been way too quiet since you left." When Jordan had rescued Katie from the Kurjan research facility, he'd rescued Maggie as well. The two women had been the best of friends since. Maggie had only been gone a few weeks, but it had been a lonely few weeks without the wolf shifter.

"Kane and Emma have been using me as a pincushion." Maggie hopped onto a bar stool, reaching for a drink. "Though, if my blood will somehow help Jordan . . ." She lost her smile. "I'm sorry he was infected."

"Me, too, though I'm sure Emma will find a cure." Katie chalked her cue. Shrugging off the pain, she forced a smile. "How are the panic attacks? Any better?" Maggie had suffered from terrible anxiety attacks since being rescued from the Kurjans, and not much helped ward them off.

Maggie grimaced. "No. Kane has been trying to hypnotize me and teach me how to meditate, but so far, I really suck at searching for the calm within."

Katie wrinkled her nose. "I don't think many wolves are able to meditate." Something in their wild natures kept them from relaxing enough. She took in Maggie's sad face. Time to lighten the mood. So Katie focused on Janie. "Rumor has it you're dating a shifter."

Janie grinned, lifting a shoulder. "Just a friend. We're going to the movies next week." She pursed her lips. "Though I may kiss him."

"God. Don't let your dad hear that." Katie leaned over, aimed, and shot the break. A striped ball fell into the corner pocket. She lined up the next shot and missed. It had been a while since she'd played.

"I won't." Janie surveyed the table, leaning over and easily making a bank shot. "I miss Uncle Jase—he's the best pool player here."

"What am I? A clumsy wolf?" Maggie swung her legs back and forth.

"Yes." Janie sent her a grin. "Everyone knows wolves can't play pool worth beans."

Katie fought back a snort. Wolves were notoriously bad at pool. "Where is Jase?" She eyed the table. If the youngest Kayrs brother had taught Janie, then Katie needed to get serious.

"Off on some mission." Janie frowned. "Something about demons. I get visions, but nothing concrete."

There was nothing concrete when it came to demons. Katie forced a smile. "So, about that shifter . . ."

"I'm not serious or anything."

"Because of Zane." Concern had Katie concentrating to keep her voice light.

"Yeah. Someday I'll see him again." Janie missed the next shot and straightened up. "But, well, I can see why Zane stopped visiting my dream world as a teenager. I mean, with the six plus-year differences in our ages."

"Yeah. It'd be creepy for a twenty-two-year-old man to visit your dreams, sweetheart."

"Jordan is three hundred years older than you, Katie." Janie flipped curly brown hair over her shoulder. "Like, that's old."

"I'm not with Jordan." Besides, it wasn't like shifters aged. Geez. She missed an easy bank shot, her mind on the lion.

Janie snorted. "Please. You are *so* with Jordan."

Katie smiled. "The older we get, the more complicated life gets." She frowned as Janie cleared the table. "And yes, that sounds like a cop-out, even to me."

Maggie set down the grape soda, stretching her neck. "You want to be with Jordan. Mr. tall, feline, and solo watches you exclusively whenever you're in the same vicinity. What's his deal, anyway?"

Katie shrugged. "I always figured leading made him kind of solitary, like Dage but without brothers. But . . ."

"But what?" Maggie and Janie said in unison.

"The werewolf, Brent. He called Jordan 'cousin'."

"Interesting." Maggie rubbed her chin.

"Yeah. I didn't even know he had family." Sure, she knew his parents had died in the last Kurjan uprising, but had figured they were Jordan's only relatives. What else hadn't the lion leader shared with her?

Janie sighed. "I've been having bad visions lately of something dark pursuing you, but I can't get a full picture."

"Oh, I've had the picture. Probably." Katie exchanged pool sticks with another one in the holder on the wall. "Brent has a serious . . . ah . . . interest in me."

"It's more than one werewolf." Janie smoothed the triangle along the table, neatly lining up the balls.

"Great." A chill swept down her spine even as Katie found the right pool stick. "Sometimes I want to shift back to cougar so badly I think I can make it happen. I need the ability to fight what's coming. Somehow I just know that."

"I wish I could shift." Janie stepped away, tilting her head for Katie to break.

Katie leaned over, aimed, and shot. Balls went smoothly rolling, but not one sank. "I miss feeling the change from human to pure animal, so much." She sidled out of the way so Janie could shoot.

Maggie sighed. "I can shift, but only once a month when the moon is full. Each time I feel a little stronger, so I keep hoping I'll go back to normal someday. I mean, whatever normal used to be. It's not like I remember."

"That totally sucks." Katie gave her a sympathetic smile. Whatever the Kurjans had done to Maggie had destroyed her memories.

Janie lined up a shot and dropped a colored ball. "You're stripes." She aimed again. One shaking hand rubbed her forehead.

"What's wrong?" Concern had Katie pausing.

"Vision about Jase, somewhere near a sea. Scotland, I think. I've tried to get him to come home, but he won't come." Janie leaned over to concentrate on her next shot. Aiming carefully, she cleared the table, straightening with a tight smile. "I've been practicing."

Obviously. Katie slid the stick back into the wall holder. "Maybe you should tell Dage about Jase."

"I have. He nods, but says Jase needs to get a line on the demons before they attack. We've both seen the attacks coming. It's bad."

Demon attacks might rip the Realm apart. "Like we don't have enough to worry about with the Kurjans."

"It's difficult keeping everyone safe." Maggie sighed. "Where is your mom now, anyway?"

"Alaskan cruise." Millie Smith loved to travel with her mah-jongg group. "She should be returning home next month." Maybe. If everything went to hell and Noah had to take over, he'd probably extend the cruise, considering his mama was on it, too. Of course, the new antiviral would work and Jordan would be saved, so Noah wouldn't have to step up. Katie smiled at Janie. "She said to tell you happy birthday next week."

"She sent me a hand-knitted blanket with cougars on it—I love it." Janie brushed curls off her face. "Her note said something about you learning to knit . . . and I tried really hard not to laugh."

"Very funny." Katie flashed a grin. "Mom has tried to teach me so many times, but I'm all thumbs." Of course, she kept trying because her attempts amused her mother. For Millie's last birthday, Katie had actually completed a blanket featuring a bald eagle. Well, the bird looked more like a bald buzzard, but she'd tried her best. Millie had proudly placed the blanket over her sofa in the formal living room like it was a work of art.

"Your mom is pretty cool." Maggie eyed another grape soda.

So true. Katie had been inviting Maggie home with her, and Millie had taken the wounded wolf into the family immediately. "She loves you, too."

If nothing else, Katie would always owe Jordan for rescuing her from Jim Bob and taking her to Millie. The petite lioness had instantly taken her in, even adopting her within the human court system. God, Katie loved her mom.

Janie cued her pool stick and cleared her throat. "Um, I'm sorry about Jordan getting infected."

"Thanks. Any chance you see the future regarding him?" If the little psychic saw Jordan sometime, anytime, in the future, that'd be awesome.

"No, sorry. But that doesn't mean anything, Katie. I don't usually see the stuff I'm looking for." Janie's eyes clouded over. "So many futures spin through my mind sometimes . . . every move we make changes what will happen."

And yet, she didn't see Jordan at all?

Down the hallway, Jordan leaned against the wall, a small smile playing on his face from the interplay. He'd been eavesdropping all day. Talen's suffering at Janie's impending date tickled him. Jordan had never really thought about having a family, but now that it was too late, a sense of loss centered in his chest. He'd heard the truth earlier in Emma's tone—the antiviral wouldn't work by the time he needed it. Which was now.

Old doubts crowded in. How could Brent be alive? Though, well now, that would be fate's idea of a freakin' joke. Jordan's darkest moment, coming back to haunt him just as death knocked on his door.

The moments before that one . . . they were good. Full

of carefree laughter and way too much juvenile fun. Even then, he and Conn Kayrs had been the best of friends, causing havoc.

Jordan shut his eyes against the last week of his life, memories flooding in. Three centuries ago, the leaders of his pride had relocated them to the mountains of the new country. Away from rumors, away from humans who suspected some people could change into animals, the mountains of what became the United States seemed a safe place to land.

The turn of the century had created a new ample playground for vampires and shifters. Jordan and Conn had committed themselves to exploration. For years, the two of them had wandered, meeting newly arrived folks as well as those who'd lived in the area for so long.

Awakening one morning in a ramshackle barn, straw stuck to his forehead, Jordan had looked for his friend. The vampire had stumbled in, his green eyes bloodshot and a stupid grin on his face. "Where's the lady?"

Jordan groaned, pushing to his feet. He smelled like cow dung and ale. "Probably hurried back to her husband. Lucky fellow."

Conn had snorted. "We might need to leave the area for a bit. Farmers get particular about their daughters."

"Did you finally choose one, then?" Jordan swayed, the ale from the previous night making his head ache. There had been three curvy women vying for Conn's attention at the barn raising across the dusty town.

"Not exactly one."

"Your parents would kill you." Jordan grimaced, as his parents wouldn't be too happy, either. Of course, he and Conn were just in their early twenties and responsibility wouldn't arrive for a century, maybe two. At least Jordan didn't have to worry about ruling his people, like the Kayrs men did.

Conn shrugged. "They should be finishing up at the world symposium brokering deals with the new land in play now that the Kurjans finally want to be part of the Realm. My mum was looking forward to seeing yours again."

"Yes—they'll have a good time together." Even though Jordan's father wasn't the leader of a pride, he was a statistical genius, and often advised his cousin, their ruler. "Well, what do you think about heading west and really exploring? It appears to be all mountains and wildlife. Might be fun."

"I don't know. Civilization appeals to me. All the women and ale, I mean." Conn rubbed his chin. "I wanted Dage to come over and have some fun, but he's so bogged down in duty. It's like he thinks he'll take over soon, rather than a thousand years from now."

A chill swept down Jordan's spine. "The guy is psychic."

Conn laughed. "I know. Which so far has just made him difficult to beat in games. We need to come up for a plan next time we have a vampire/shifter soccer match."

"We will." Jordan smiled at his best friend. Life was fantastic, he had amazing friends, and the world was his. No responsibility for a while, and a whole new continent to explore. "For now, let's go scale mountains."

Conn stiffened.

Tension spiraled through the barn. Jordan pivoted toward the door. Power lay on the other side . . . raw power.

Conn frowned, sliding open the door.

Dage Kayrs stood on the other side, a frown on his face, fury in his silver eyes.

"Dage, you're here." A wide smile covered Conn's face that slowly disappeared as he took in his brother. "How did you find us?"

"I teleported a few towns over and have been looking for you." Dage took a deep breath. "I have bad news."

Jordan shook himself back to the present, not wanting to relive the moment when he discovered the Kurjans had engineered a brilliant massacre, taking out the leaders of the Realm. Taking out his parents.

Keeping his eyes closed, he took several deep breaths.

Pain exploded across his cheekbone. His eyes flashed open to see a fist coming at him again. He ducked, pivoting around to see the threat. "What the fuck?"

Connlan Kayrs settled his stance. "I'm tired of this shit."

"What shit?" The bastard had coldcocked him for no reason. Anger swirled deep in Jordan's gut. He dropped into a fighting stance.

"This . . . I give up . . . I'm gonna be a werewolf . . . bullshit."

Garrett loped into the hallway. "Uh, Uncle Conn? You're supposed to go to the gym next time you wanna hit somebody."

Conn growled low. "You're right. Let's go, cat."

Chapter 8

Kalin relaxed in the newest Kurjan encampment and surveyed the waiting werewolves. Experienced, strangely calm, the twenty killer beasts sat on stumps or rocks in the forest, eating raw meat. Of course, he'd injected the meat with massive amounts of horse tranquilizer, but still. The monsters had gained some self-control during the last decade. Unfortunately, unlike human converts, the shifter-turned-werewolf couldn't be enslaved completely—there was no binding spell with silver and slavery. But with food and pain . . . they'd obey.

Dusk had fallen, and the moon would soon rise, normally sending the beasts into a frenzy. The tranquilizer would control them until the night of the full moon . . . then he'd let them free. Free to hunt and kill, once he sent them in the right direction.

His second in command jogged up, red hair framing a stark white face with amethyst eyes. No wonder people saw the Kurjans as monsters. They were. Of course, Kalin could almost pass for human if he applied facial makeup and wore contacts over his odd green eyes. His black hair was tipped with red—the opposite to most Kurjans—and was easily altered. Even his skin was just pale, not the frightening white paste color of others. "What?"

"The sedative is working. They traveled nearly a hundred miles today without mishap, sir." Milton flashed sharp yellowed fangs. "I'll miss Seattle. The weather agreed with me."

Kalin returned the grin. "Someday we won't fear the sun. My uncle Erik is closer than ever to creating a cure." Erik was actually Kalin's second cousin, but the term *uncle* brought a closeness to Kalin's ascent to the throne that he liked. Erik, a brilliant scientist, had created Virus-27, and he'd create an inoculation against the sun someday. "Think of the women in bikinis we'll someday hunt."

Milton threw back his head and laughed. "Yes, sir."

The acknowledgment of seniority had Kalin's chest swelling. Milton was at least five hundred years old, yet Kalin, in his midtwenties, led all troops. His entire life had been filled with fighting, killing, and planning. Someday, when he killed Erik's brother, Franco, he'd lead all Kurjans. For now, Franco ruled from a remote area of Nova Scotia, leaving the military troops to Kalin.

He gave a curt nod to Milton, irritation sweeping that he had to look up. He'd only reached a height of six feet, six inches tall, which was short. For a Kurjan. He'd still top or meet eye-to-eye with most vampires and shifters.

The breeze picked up, scattering pine needles across his boots. The moon tipped over the far mountains, brightening the scene.

As one, the beasts stopped eating and stilled. Snouts switching, they closed their eyes and lifted their heads. Bliss crossed their furry features. A melodic keening came from them collectively as they worshipped, the sound reminiscent of whale song.

A chill swept across Kalin's neck. Creepy. Every night the same routine. He cleared his throat. "How would you boys like a treat tonight?"

Slowly, languidly, they lowered their heads, opening their yellow eyes. The tallest one stood and shook out his dark coat. He'd taken to standing on two feet, a position most werewolves who'd survived the virus more than seven or eight years preferred. Somewhere, somehow, he'd become the unofficial leader of the group. Kalin had dubbed him Jack. The monster did have a hobby much like Jack the Ripper's.

Speaking of which . . . "Why don't you release our friend?"

Milton nodded, jogging over to a horse trailer and jumping inside. Chains rattled, and he yanked a vampire out. Well, what used to be a vampire. The man stumbled, his gaunt body swimming in the dirty, shredded clothing.

Kalin rubbed his chin. "I think I'm about done with you." Had been for about three months, actually. But torture was so much fun.

A desperate hope lit the vamp's metallic purple eyes. "I've told you everything I know about the Kayrs family."

Which had been just about enough to determine their current location. "You're a lowly soldier from a different country. You don't know the Kayrs family." But his information had checked out.

"I knew enough." He coughed out the words, his throat no doubt dry.

How long had it been since Kalin allowed him food? He shrugged. No matter. "Give him to Jack."

The vampire's eyes widened in his thin face. Bruises still mottled his white skin from the beating the day before. "No." Bruised knuckles grabbed at his chains, yanking away from Milton.

"Yes." Kalin took two steps, wrapping his hand around the vamp's throat. "Catch, Jack." He lifted the prisoner, throwing him one-handed across the clearing.

The vamp landed with a hard thump, denting the dry earth.

The animals leapt for a fresh kill.

His high-pitched scream pierced the peaceful night. Growls and yelps mingled with cries of pain as the beasts ripped limbs from the body . . . digging in with teeth sharp enough to score granite.

Milton cleared his throat. "Do you really think they'll be able to kill the vampire soldiers?"

Kalin nodded. "Sure. They'll kill a few. The Realm forces are weak . . . seriously depleted from the last ten years of war. As depleted as our troops, and they don't have werewolf soldiers fighting their front line like we do. Plus, I just need the vampires busy so I can finally kill Talen Kayrs."

The bastard had killed Kalin's father a decade ago because of a woman. Kalin shook his head. "Such a waste. Two powerful men fighting over a female." Rumor had it the female had given birth to Talen's son a few years back. Kalin should take out the son, too.

He focused on the feeding frenzy.

Blood.

The scent permeated the fresh air, elongating Kalin's teeth. He inhaled deep. How the hell did the vamp have any blood left after all the beatings? Kalin's stomach rumbled, hunger speeding his heart rate.

Male blood didn't appeal to his palate . . . how long had it been since he'd hunted a woman? Too long. Most women didn't provide much challenge, though a shifter he'd found in Atlanta had fought like a warrior. Now, she had been an enjoyable kill. "I might leave you in charge for some time tonight."

The skin around Milton's mouth pinched. "Of course." His voice held no inflection, yet disapproval had his chin lifting.

Too fucking bad. While no doubt Franco had hoped Kalin would give up his nighttime hobby as he aged . . . he hadn't. There had been a moment a decade ago when he'd faced doorways into different futures; he'd chosen one. With a fresh kill of a human girl he'd actually liked. "If you tell my uncle, I'll stake you to the ground an hour before sunrise." There was no question Milton reported back to Franco. They were morons if they thought he remained unaware of such an allegiance.

"Of course." Milton frowned, his gaze on the pile of werewolves. "I would appreciate if you didn't take my son with you this time."

Milton's eighteen-year-old son had an even greater thirst to kill than Kalin. "Roy is a natural." The kid needed training in the thrill of the hunt . . . not just the easy kill. Where was the finesse in just killing a woman? The fear—the fight—the futility at the ending. Now those moments created a worthy pursuit.

There was a time years ago when Kalin had studied death, philosophy, and fate. Anything to harness the urges that rode him so hard.

After much time, he concluded his animalistic nature required the hunt. The pursuit of other beings. Well, women. And it didn't take a psychologist to understand his anger at the mother who'd abandoned him in death. She'd deserted him on purpose because she couldn't handle being a mate to his father.

Most Kurjan mates didn't last long.

So Kalin's need to hunt worthy women and take them down probably had some logic behind it. Not that he truly cared. The pursuit was what mattered.

A pursuit worthy of a predator, not a lowly animal like the werewolves. Of course, the original goal of Virus-27 had had nothing to do with turning shifters into werewolves. The first stroke of the virus was to impact human vampire mates. Mates were special and far between. The new class of werewolves was an unexpected side benefit of the bug.

Wait—what was this?

Jack shoved away from the pack and rose to his full height, finishing swallowing the vampire's cranium with a loud gulp. Blood stained his teeth, matting his fur a motley red. His eyes glowed an eerie jaundiced yellow in the waning light.

Kalin settled his stance. "We're going to need the electric prods."

As one, the devouring beasts stood, turning to face him, death in their eyes.

All former shifters, all former soldiers, they could fight better than any other wild animal. But animals they were . . . and they needed a master.

A young Kurjan soldier hustled up, handing them both tweaked prods. The altered devices emitted enough electricity to shock a werewolf into unconsciousness. Kalin leaned on his, smiling when Jack eyed the weapon. "Don't worry, my friend. You'll kill soon. All you want."

Jack lifted his feral gaze to meet Kalin's directly.

He swept a large hairy hand out, a guttural snort coming from down deep. As one, the remaining werewolves stood down, heads bowed.

Kalin eyed the monster. Very interesting. "I'm the master here, Jack."

The beast smiled.

Chapter 9

Standing next to Conn, Jordan rested a shoulder against the wall in the gym, slowly opening his right hand as the broken fingers mended. Nothing like a sparring session with a friend who had no problem taking your head off. His tennis shoes left deep imprints in the worn grappling mats as he tested his steadiness. He'd fought many times in a Kayrs gym . . . though this was the first time they grappled aboveground in the main lodge. The ocean rolled lazily below, sending salt through the open windows.

He allowed his mind to blank in order for several concussions to heal. The past flashed back with a vengeance. Three hundred years ago, after the Kurjan massacre, peace was impossible.

Still in the new colonies, Jordan shoved the pain somewhere to be dealt with at another time. Sitting in a hastily built meeting room in the middle of thick trees and dark rocks, he glanced out the window at an unfamiliar world. With the death of his family, the world had changed.

Conn sat across the rough-planked table, anger and sorrow cutting new lines into his face. "What do you want to do?" His deep voice echoed in the silent room as the rest of the leaders had taken a break outside.

"I don't know." Jordan needed guidance. He needed his fa-

ther . . . or Kyle Bomant, their former leader. Their deaths were fresh . . . too fresh. "I just don't know."

"You don't have to do anything." Conn leaned forward, ensuring their conversation didn't reach through the holes serving as windows in the pine walls. "Dage said your cousin will arrive later today and is considering allying with the Kurjans. What do you know about him?"

Jordan shook his head. "He's an asshole. Beat the crap out of a girl last year because she didn't respond to him. I can see him backing the Kurjans, considering they just took out half the Realm." Over three hundred years older than Jordan, the other shifter had never grown up.

Conn paled. "If you align with the Kurjans, that makes us . . ."

"Enemies." Jordan met his friend's gaze squarely. "Not only that, both our forces will be depleted and we're at war. Nobody knows if the demons will jump in and if so, which side they'll take."

"Not to mention the damn witches." Conn exhaled, the sound full of anguish. "I've never understood those crazy magic users and hope to God I never have to deal with a witch. Though Dage secured the canine and multi nations as allies, and they're sending troops to fight."

"That's good." Well, that was good if Jordan's people remained allies with the Realm. Otherwise, the wolves would be chasing him. His mind spun, and his gut ached as reality settled hard. "Since Dage has relocated Realm Headquarters to these mountains in the new world, we have the opportunity to take care of business quietly and without a formal challenge to Brent."

Conn lifted his chin, a veil dropping over his eyes. "Are you ready to challenge your cousin for leadership?"

"Yes." The word weighed heavily in the room, and even more solidly in Jordan's stomach. The choice might be out of his hands. His people were too scattered and scared for anyone else to step up, with the exception of Noah Chance. But Noah was a fighter,

one of the best, and they needed him on the front line now more than ever. "I want to meet with Brent first and make sure he's unwilling to align with Dage."

No expression crossed Conn's broad face. "You're a good fighter."

"Thanks." Jordan allowed acceptance of the unspoken words to filter down his back. "But Brent is three hundred years older, is more experienced, and has fought before." Fear at the decision he was considering made Jordan's head pound. "I've never killed anyone."

"Me, either." Emotion broke through the false calmness on Conn's face. "I think that's about to change."

Two weeks ago Jordan's biggest decision had been what woman to woo. The world wasn't the only thing that had changed . . . he and Conn were next. Destiny slammed him right in the face. "If Brent turns against the Realm, there's really no choice."

"What are you saying?"

Jordan studied his friend. Conn knew exactly what Jordan was saying, but sometimes the words had to be spoken. "If necessary, I'll challenge him. If I lose . . . I need you to . . ."

"Kill him." Conn's lids lowered to half mast, and suddenly, he looked like a killer. An unwilling, truly unhappy killer, but a killer nonetheless.

Spikes poked the back of Jordan's eyes. The last thing he ever wanted to do was turn his best friend into a cold-blooded killer. "If there was anybody else to ask . . ."

"I'm just meeting my destiny faster than I'd hoped." Inevitability echoed in Conn's low tone. "From day one of my life, I knew I'd be the soldier in my family. The fighter and the one on the front lines. I just didn't think fate would come calling this soon."

Fate had arrived for them both. Jordan extended his hand across the table. "This goes against everything we've been taught, and everything we believe in."

"War leaves us no choice." Conn *took his hand in a strong grasp. "If we do this, Dage can never know. He has enough on his shoulders with the family and now with the Realm. He shouldn't live with this."*

"No. This is ours." Jordan *released Conn and stood. "Let's go issue the challenge. May God have mercy on us someday."*

Conn *shook his head and stood. "What we do, we do because we have to. Mercy has no place—and neither does God."*

The words sent shards of pure ice down Jordan's spine. Not because they were dismal . . . but because they were the absolute truth. The world had changed, indeed.

Back in the present, Jordan opened his eyes in the large gym, his concussions healed.

"You're stronger." Conn popped his neck, grimacing as the vertebrae probably snapped back into place.

"I know." Every day since being infected, his vision had sharpened, his hearing clarified, and his strength increased. As had the need to fight and kill. "I've been craving raw meat like you wouldn't believe."

Conn lifted a bloody eyebrow. "Ewww."

"You drink blood, asshole." Damn vampires didn't know how gross that really was. "Ah, Brent Bomant is alive."

Conn stilled. The air vibrated. "No, he's not."

"Yes. Apparently I left a tendon attached. And now he's a werewolf. One with intelligence and the ability to speak."

"Speak? A werewolf communicated?"

"Oh yeah. Spoke clearly and remembered his life before turning into a werewolf. Worse yet, he remembered me . . . and what I did."

"Unbelievable." Conn scraped both hands down his face. "We did the right thing, Jordan."

"Did we?" Jordan whispered. "I've always wondered." Was it ambition that had him killing his own family? His own blood. "If we did the right thing, you would've cleared the plan with Dage instead of never saying a word."

"We did our jobs . . . and part of my job was protecting my king, regardless of his being my brother." Conn gave a low growl. "You and I buried this issue three centuries ago. Too late to worry about our decisions now."

Was it? The nape of Jordan's neck began to tingle. "I can't figure out who would be working with Brent. Who'd be taking pictures of Katie to give to him." The whole idea infuriated Jordan to the point he could barely see.

Conn shook his head. "Most werewolves feel the need to kill humans. Well, to kill *everyone*. If Brent has progressed to where he can refrain from killing and actually work with a human, he's even more dangerous than I would've thought."

"That's an understatement." Jordan couldn't talk about the past anymore. "Where's your mate, anyway?"

"Moira is in Ireland meeting with the Council of the Coven Nine." Conn rolled his neck. "The council has some sources in the demon nation that say there's an internal war going on. We're trying to find out if it's true, and if so, what to do about it. Who to align with."

The council ruled the witches and aligned with the Realm. If anybody had spies in the demon nation, it'd be the witches. Though, starting ten years ago, certain shifting clans had begun to work with the demons, so Jordan's informants might be of some help, too. "I have several feelers out right now for information regarding the demons. They're centralizing their power bases in Scotland and somewhere in the southern part of the United States." Which meant they'd be hitting Realm forces sometime soon.

Conn nodded. "Between war with the Kurjans the last

ten years, and your people's problems with the virus killing so many, our troops are depleted." He huffed out a laugh. "Thank God the witches have remained our allies."

"Speaking of witches, when will yours be home?" The little witch always made things interesting, and watching her run Conn in circles would lighten Jordan's mood.

"Next week," the vampire growled, frowning. He rubbed his short hair. "I still owe her for the buzz cut."

Jordan fought a smile. "You're lucky she didn't singe your eyebrows, too."

"*She's* lucky she didn't." Conn grinned, shaking his head. "She got me good this time. I'm trying to figure out a decent payback, but all I can think about is getting her home safely."

The moon began to rise, snapping electricity along Jordan's skin. Ever since he'd been infected, he'd been in tune with the moon. He shook off the unease. "Having your woman fighting . . . the reality is hard, isn't it?"

"Oh yeah. I'd love to lock Moira up in some fortress"— Conn snorted—"but she'd just blow the place to pieces on her way out." All five fingers on his left hand popped as he stretched them out to heal. "She's a fighter, and I like that about her, but it's a lot easier when I'm fighting next to her."

"I get that." His friend would probably head to Ireland after the full moon—after Jordan would need to be put down. "The moon is up—I need to go outside." He hated it. But rabid ants crawled under his skin until he leapt into moonlight when the orb appeared after dusk. The pull rivaled gravity.

A door slammed open in the hallway, and Katie rushed inside, her hair a wild mass around her slim shoulders. "Jordan—"

"I know." He strode toward the door and grasped her

arm. "We need to go outside." He hadn't realized how difficult the last decade must've been for her—craving the moon every night. The demand was like having an addiction with no treatment possibilities.

"No." She tugged away. "Emma found a cure." Strong fingers dug into his arm, yanking him into the hallway. "She used Maggie's blood combined with yours since getting infected combined with a spell created by Moira before she left for Ireland." Katie's voice rose in excitement as she dragged him up a flight of stairs toward the labs. "Emma won't use the concoction on me because the cure hasn't been tested. But you're out of time."

Moira was one of the most powerful witches alive. If anyone could alter the subatomic particles of a liquid cure, it'd be Moira.

Jordan allowed Katie to tug him into the main lab where they almost ran over Kane Kayrs.

He lifted an eyebrow, his metallic violet eyes serious. Dressed in black slacks and silk shirt, the smartest vampire on the planet always looked like he should be vacationing in Rome instead of spending hours after hours in a lab working with the queen. Well, when he wasn't catching werewolves for sport. "Good news travels fast."

Hope. For the first time since the confirmation of Jordan's being infected, hope battled through his despair. "Is there good news?"

Katie hopped in excitement next to him, her boots squeaking on the spotless tiles. She reached down to grip his hand. He leaned a hip against one of the three examination tables, trying to stay calm. Trying not to get too excited about the possibility.

Emma turned from peering through a microscope. "Maybe." She glanced at Katie, concern furrowing her brow. "We managed to attack a sample of Virus-27 in a petri dish . . . not exactly the same environment as a living body."

"But the cure worked?" Katie breathed, her grip tightening.

"Yes. The mixture binds itself around the virus . . . keeping the bug from reproducing."

Katie smiled. "So the virus will stop attacking Jordan's chromosomes and he won't turn into a werewolf."

"Theoretically." Kane reached for a syringe off the wide granite counter. "I prepared an injection for you earlier, Jordan. Just in case." The scientist stalked toward them, somehow menacing even in the comfortable lab.

Jordan held out his arm. With the luck he'd been having lately, the cure would turn him into a monkey. "How soon should we know?"

"With the new equipment, in a couple hours." Kane jabbed the needle in his vein.

Lava poured through Jordan's veins. Hot and angry, the liquid bubbled along with his blood. "Holy shit. What the hell is that?"

Emma pursed her lips. "A whole lot of stuff, including magic." Then she frowned at the long row of equipment lining the counter. "In fact, several of our concoctions could be applied to cure human diseases."

Kane sighed. "Emma, the methodology could be applied, not our results. Our results deal with nonhumans. And we let you send the methodology to the human scientists."

"*Let* me?" The queen lifted her chin. Her pointy shoe tapped several times on the thick tiles. "One of my favorite pastimes is kicking you, Kane Kayrs."

"Talk to your husband about outside communications, not me. My brother controls all information going out . . . you know that." Kane pivoted to the machines, turning his back on them all. "Jordan, I want to do blood tests on the hour, every hour. If you feel anything different, please let me know."

Jordan nodded, a roaring filling his head. "Need to get outside." The moon demanded.

Katie trembled, her face going white. "Me, too. Let's go."

Holding hands, they stumbled in their haste to feel the rays, dodging through corridors until running out the back sliding door into a courtyard that extended to the cliffs. Trees lined both sides, leading to forest land. Below them the ocean churned, as if even the massive body of water gyrated to the moon's command.

Katie released his hand, lifting her chin to the heavens, pure bliss crossing her face.

Soft light cascaded down. Tension eased from Jordan's shoulders. Peace, false and temporary, filled his pores. Even then, the woman's pull beat the moon's. Rays tangled around her, highlighting her exquisite bone structure and stabbing the beast inside him awake. Lion or werewolf, he wasn't sure. Either way, the male at his core wanted the female.

He'd wondered. For more than ten years—he'd tried to keep from thinking about her. He'd known her as a child, a teenager, and now a woman. The crush she'd held came from youth.

But something in him recognized her. Wondered if she'd already be wearing his mark, had the damn Kurjans not messed with fate. Along with biology. The need to sink his teeth into her neck just enough to mark had his incisors lengthening, shifting into lion form while his body remained human.

Salty, the breeze carried her sigh as she lowered her gaze to him. Her pretty brown eyes widened. "Your teeth."

"Yeah." He shoved them back up.

"I miss that."

He struggled for control. "You miss having cougar teeth?"

"Yeah." Her smile surpassed beautiful and grabbed him around the heart to squeeze. "Remember when I first learned how to elongate the teeth only?"

Warmth slammed into his solar plexus. "You bit the crap out of us." He chuckled, feeling humor for the first time in a week. "I thought Noah was going to perform a root canal on you."

She threw back her head and laughed, the sound filling the night with joy. "Remember when I bit Talen because he wouldn't play catch with me?"

"You were a monstrous six-year-old."

Her eyes sparkled, then grew serious. The smile waned. Tremors shook her shoulders. Almost in slow motion, she turned her head to gaze beyond the courtyard to the forest extending into darkness.

"What?" His shoulders went back. Electricity danced up his spine. The breeze whipped a new scent into the area. "Dog." Not just any dog. "How—"

His breath caught as fire lanced through his veins. A tidal force of energy ricocheted inside his muscles. Bones snapped. His teeth sharpened, drawing blood from his lips.

Stubborn will had him fighting the change, fighting what overcame his human side.

Without making a determination—against his will—he shot into lion form.

Katie flew across the courtyard to land on her butt. The energy released when Jordan shifted held an element of something new . . . something she couldn't shield against. Her palms pressed into the soft grass as she levered to her feet, her gaze on the massive western cougar eyeing her like a midnight snack.

Even so, a darker danger stalked closer . . . menace and need winding through the oxygen to clog her lungs. Oily darkness reached out to her, sending a humming through her brain. A shiver rippled down her spine. The hair on her arms stood up. How the hell had he found her?

Roaring a battle cry, Brent leapt over the stone wall to land in the center of the courtyard.

She stepped back, fear turning her knees brittle. "How?"

"Kaattieee. Have blood."

Jesus. He'd tracked her that easily—and traveled across the country during *daytime*? Just because he'd tasted her blood? She'd never be free of him. "Guess you need to die then."

Why hadn't Jordan attacked? She shifted her gaze to the cougar, who remained still, head cocked to the side and studying Brent. Was Jordan's coat darker than usual? Had the changes already begun? "Jordan?"

Brent tilted his head, pivoting. Both animals began to circle, sniffing the air. Brent gave a low howl. "Jordaaan. Like meeee." The furry beast clapped his hands together. "Baaad Jordaaan."

Teeth flashed when Jordan snarled, his gaze going from Brent to Katie. He stilled and sniffed the night.

Damnit. The virus had progressed enough in Jordan to confuse him in relation to Brent. Katie kept her hands harmlessly at her sides. "Jordan. You're the good guy. He's the bad." Simple, but hopefully effective. Though, the men had once been family.

The cat licked his lips. Too dark ears lay back, and he abandoned his vigil of Brent to stalk three steps closer to her.

"Uh, Jordan?" She edged sideways toward the door.

His low-pitched snarl stopped her cold.

Fear settled deep in her gut, sending adrenaline to flood her veins, terror erasing years of combat training. The animal held her in his sights. Jordan was gone. In his place a

creature of primal instinct eyed her like she was dinner. Or
maybe dessert.

She cleared her throat, the sound harsh in the quiet
night. "You're still a cougar, Jordan. Fight this. Please." He
wasn't a werewolf yet—he could still think. Still be her
protector.

His huge head lifted.

Powerful muscles bunched.

Then he leapt.

She screamed. Pivoting, she kicked out, connecting
with his belly, sending him sprawling. Oh, she'd caught
him by surprise, otherwise the move wouldn't have
worked.The cat rolled over in the spongy grass, stretching
to his feet, sharp canines flashing. A quick weave to the
side and he blocked her way to the door.

Brent threw back his furry head and laughed, the sound
grating. He leaned against the hedge, amusement lighten-
ing those yellow eyes to something almost translucent.

Katie fought a whimper, sidling to the entrance. Fear
cut through the night to narrow her vision. The cat's low
snarl stopped her escape.

Her feet froze. A tremor started at her knees and slid
north until even her ears shook. "Jordan?"

He lunged.

Both paws hit her shoulders, knocking her down.

Pain radiated along her neck as she landed on the hard
earth. The air swooshed from her lungs. Her head instantly pounded. Adrenaline slid with fear through her
veins, and she calculated ways to take him down.

There weren't any.

Heated breath brushed her face. Wide paws pressed
down on her shoulders, keeping her in place. Blade-sharp
claws ripped into her shirt, against her skin. His entire
body vibrated.

Terror held her immobile. The cold ground chilled her back. Instinct had her stilling, trying not to breathe. Sharp, deadly teeth flashed in the moonlight. He lowered, scraping their fierce points along her jugular.

She fought her body to keep her hands at her sides, not threatening him. Inside her, a lioness awoke. Stretching, cautiously coming to the surface, instinct emerging in a final effort to stay alive.

A low grumble came from his chest. His teeth retracted and he sniffed her throat, along the jugular to behind her ear. His nose pressed against her skin, wet and flared.

Could she punch him in the throat and roll away? Something told her the move wouldn't work—he was too fast and deadly in this state. Ever since she'd contracted the virus, her reflexes had slowed and her strength ebbed. She couldn't take him like this.

Snarling, his head lowered, his teeth slowly elongating into the flesh where her neck met her shoulder.

Pain ripped through her. Reality smacked her—he wanted to mark her, not kill her. His fangs went deeper. She cried out, quickly silencing herself.

He stilled. His massive head lifted, those teeth leaving her flesh. His eyes swirled from yellow to green.

Three darts impacted his face, throwing him off her. Strong hands grabbed her armpits, dragging her to the entrance. Fresh bruises vibrated in her skin.

Her eyes wide on the cat, she struggled to stand. Conn shoved her partially behind him. His hand stayed steady as he extended the dart gun toward Jordan. With a soft snarl, the cougar lifted his upper lip. Then he swayed, dropping to the grass.

Katie gulped, her gaze spinning to the hedges.

Brent was gone.

Chapter 10

Jordan stretched his legs under the conference table, trying without success to ignore the poison still vibrating through his veins. Conn had used a sedative necessary for taking down large game animals. It was a good move, because Jordan had been more animal than man when he'd bitten Katie. The idea that he'd hurt Kate made his stomach lurch. While he'd had no intention of injuring her, the craving to mark her had nearly destroyed him. And marking her, considering she had lost shifter strength and power, might destroy her.

Dage sat at the head of the table, flanked by Conn. Stunning oil paintings by Brenna Dunne lined three walls, while floor-to-ceiling windows showed the sea waiting for daylight. The central aboveground hub of the Realm was both comfortable and imposing.

Dage tapped a file on the mahogany. "We need to decide if we should move again."

"I got the sense Brent is alone." Anger made Jordan's head spin. "He has Katie's scent, her blood, and he'll find her wherever she goes." What had he been thinking to let her fight werewolves? "I'll take her away from headquarters and set a trap somewhere else for him."

"No." Conn leaned forward, his dark T-shirt shoved up past his elbows. "We stick together."

Jordan closed his eyes briefly when the other men nodded. Thank God. He might pose more danger to Katie than the werewolf did. "I bit her."

Conn exhaled. "She's fine. We secured everyone underground, and Katie's sleeping right now. You didn't do any lasting damage."

But he'd wanted to do something lasting. The beast inside of him had wanted to mark her . . . for all time. "That's good to know." He'd broken skin but the mating process could only happen during a claiming. Right then and there he vowed never to be alone with Katie again. He glanced out the window, counting the remaining dawns until the full moon. Three nights left. "I'll head out to find Brent." It'd be the last thing Jordan did as leader of the feline nation.

"No." Dage rubbed his chin. "I have scouts out now—we'll find him. Unfortunately, we have bigger problems than one werewolf."

"One werewolf who can speak and think." Conn yanked a double-edged knife from his side to twirl through his fingers. "I guess it makes sense the monsters have evolved."

"Not this quickly." Jordan eyed the flash of steel. "Plus, he knew me. Remembered me from before he became a werewolf—he knows who he was—next in line to lead." Brent apparently remembered everything.

Dage stiffened. "Anything you want to tell me?"

"No." Jordan kept his face bland and his gaze away from Conn. What they'd done—they'd done together and with a vow that the king would never know. "I have a sense of this guy. Why do you want me to stay here?"

The king didn't look appeased. A hard glint entered his silver eyes, promising the discussion wasn't over. "Because all hell is about to break loose."

As far as Jordan was concerned, all hell had broken

loose ten years ago when the Kurjans had unleashed the virus. "Again?"

"Yes." Conn snorted. "I say we take the Bane's Council out at the knees."

"They're our allies." Dage's gaze seemed anything but friendly.

"What's going on?" Jordan asked, dread slamming into his gut.

"Terrent Vilks will arrive sometime today and wants to see both you and Maggie," Dage said.

Terrent was the head werewolf hunter on the Bane's Council and the most deadly wolf alive. Adrenaline heated just under Jordan's skin. "Who told him about either one of us?"

"We don't know." Conn flipped the knife faster, a true sign of his agitation. "Not only did he demand to see you both, he knew you were *here*."

Jordan sat back, forcing his claws to stay retracted. "He knew the location of Realm Headquarters?" Lance had been correct—the location wasn't close to a secret. "How?"

"We need to find out." Dage's eyes gleamed, flashing blue within the silver.

"We have a leak." Jordan blew out a breath. "The feline nation has had an uneasy alliance with the canine nation for two hundred years—and I consider Terrent a friend. It sucks he's here to kill me." But that might solve several problems.

"He's the most prolific member of the Bane's Council." While his face remained grim, a thread of respect filtered through Dage's words. "Though I'm not sure why the head of the Bane's Council is making the trip."

Jordan nodded. The Bane's Council consisted of three wolf shifters created for the sole purpose of hunting down and killing werewolves. Before the virus had been unleashed on shifters, werewolves were former humans who didn't live very long anyway. Now that male shifters could become werewolves—it was an entirely new world for them all. "I can't let Terrent kill Maggie."

"The Bane's Council has refrained from killing female shifters infected with the virus—so long as they're receiving treatment from the Realm." Conn tucked the knife in the back of his waist. "Maggie's receiving treatment."

"Maggie can shift." Jordan scrubbed both hands down his face. "No other infected female can shift—the ability makes her a threat. The poor woman doesn't even remember her past." Maggie had been one of the first shifters kidnapped and experimented on by the Kurjans, and she had no memory of her life before being captured.

Dage nodded. "No clan has been looking for her the last ten years. We have to assume she was alone, or part of a clan off the grid. Either could be possible."

"My bet is off the grid." Jordan tried to keep track of all feline, canine, and multiclans not part of the Realm, but it was difficult if they didn't want to be found. "Well, we know Terrent is probably coming to make sure somebody kills me if I turn into a werewolf. But again, there has to be more to his visit than that."

The telephone to Dage's right buzzed and he grabbed the handset. "What?" His gaze shifted to Jordan. "Put him through on screen." Dage hung up and pressed a button to make a screen slide down to cover two of the paintings. Conn moved to the side and out of the way.

Noah appeared on the screen, his catlike gaze zeroing in on Jordan. One of the biggest cougars alive, his stealth and quickness were unmatched. The perfect enforcer. He stood in the main control room of the mountainous headquarters, dark rock surrounding him.

Jordan's shoulders went back. "Noah?" he asked softly.

Noah took in the rest of the room. "We need to talk. Privately."

Logic clicked through Jordan's brain along with the inevitability of his demise during the next full moon—that is, unless Kane's cure actually worked. "We can talk in front of the Kayrs family—they're going to need to know what's going on to back you." He already had Dage's guarantee the Realm would back Noah as the new leader of the feline nation. Secrets would only hinder that support.

Noah nodded, keeping his gaze on Jordan. "David Bomant challenged you as head of the feline nation about an hour ago. The challenge has gone public."

"Bomant?" Conn raised an eyebrow. "As in Brent Bomant—fucking werewolf?"

"We thought Brent was our former Alpha's only offspring." Jordan kept his face expressionless. The situation was turning into more of a disaster than he'd feared. Death awaited him in a couple of moons, and he didn't have time for one more issue.

"The Brent who is now a werewolf," Dage repeated, his gaze cutting to Conn. "Well now. I guess we know who has been helping Brent out by stalking Katie." The king was no dummy.

Conn twisted his head to give Noah his attention. "Who's David?"

"Apparently Brent's daddy got around a bit before mating for life and had a child. Illegitimate, yet a son nonetheless. Possibly."

Jordan fought a snarl. "Accept the challenge—somewhere in Nevada, Colorado, or Utah."

"What if his claim is untrue? What if he's not Kyle's son?" Noah asked.

"Doesn't matter right now." Jordan didn't have time to worry about small details. Any feline shifter could challenge him for leadership. The threat developed only if Jordan lost because many people might reject Noah and follow Bomant out of loyalty to his dead father. "If I lose, then you need to investigate his claim."

"I'm on it." Noah cleared his throat. "Ah, there's more."

"Isn't there always?" Jordan rested his hands on the table.

Noah lifted a shoulder. "The leaders of several feline clans want to have a video conference meeting with you. In an hour."

"Set up a meeting."

"Okay." Noah cut the transmission.

Dage leaned forward. "What does that mean?"

Jordan shrugged. "I assume they want to discuss my being infected, my plans, and now the new challenge. I've accepted the challenge, so we fight to the death. If David is truly a blood relative, he'd take over if I died. Well, until someone challenged him. If someone challenged him."

"So why not wait?" Dage asked. Then he colored. "I mean—"

"I know what you meant." Jordan felt an unwilling smile. He'd made the king blush. "Killing me instead of waiting would cement him as leader—not many would challenge him." Irritation heated in Jordan's lungs. His strength had increased since being infected, but his sharpness in battle had diminished to animalistic instinct. The fight wouldn't be an easy one.

Dage leaned back in his chair. "Am I the only one not seeing a coincidence between Brent's resurfacing and David's challenge?"

"No." Jordan grabbed a band from his jeans pocket and tied back his hair. "It can't be a coincidence. You're right. They've been working together. It's the only conclusion that makes sense." A werewolf working with a shifter . . . what had the world come to?

"We need to alter our view of werewolves." Dage nodded. "If they've evolved, you need to figure Bomant out. What do you remember about him?"

"He was a bad guy. Hated women, loved to fight." Jordan fought to keep his hands loose and relaxed. "Three hundred years ago the Kurjans took out his parents when they killed yours as well as mine, and I truly thought Brent would destroy the feline nation and maybe the Realm. Then he disappeared."

"What really happened?" Dage asked softly.

Jordan's hackles rose. "I just told you. So now we have the Bane's Council, intelligent, full-functioning werewolves, and a challenge to my leadership to deal with."

"That's not all." Kane Kayrs strode into the room, a handful of computer printouts in his hands. "I finished analyzing the blood I took from you earlier this morning."

Hope flared hot and bright in Jordan's chest. "And?"

A frown centered between Kane's brows. "The cure didn't work. In fact, as far as I can tell, the concoction had no impact on the virus in your blood. With the magic involved, we should have concrete results at this time. I'm sorry, Jordan."

His chest deflated, along with his future. "Me, too." He rubbed his chin, glancing at Conn. "Well, let's get to training today because tonight, we hunt."

Katie ground a palm into her exhausted eye, wondering how long the headache would last. She had given up sleep after tossing and turning for an hour. Being underground again sucked.

Dawn had yet to break, yet she refused to return to bed. Her sweats hung loose around her hips—looser than last week. But her bunny slippers still fit perfectly. Flipping on the light of the smallest underground lab, she skirted the one examination table and started opening wide cabinets.

"Kate?" Kane Kayrs strode inside and tossed papers on the small table by the door. Even at the early hour, he lounged in creased black pants and silk shirt.

She pressed harder, trying to force the pain away. "Don't you ever dress down?"

He smiled, transforming his angular face into something that should be selling vodka on billboards. "Well, I don't have bunny slippers." Stalking toward the far wall, he yanked open a drawer and tugged out a small vial. "Aspirin." He poured two into her hand and grabbed a water bottle from a fridge hidden under one counter. "You okay?"

She swallowed the drugs and took a drink of the water. The guy moved more like a panther than a vampire—all fluid grace. Rumors had it he hunted werewolves for sport and by himself. "No, I'm not okay." Hopefully the painkiller would kick in soon. "Are those the latest test results?"

"Yes. No change in Jordan's blood. Or yours. I just came from telling Jordan." Kane jerked his head to the side. "Sorry."

The scientist wasn't a sugarcoating type of guy. Disappointment heated down her esophagus. But she did appreciate him working around the clock to find a cure. She tilted her head in curiosity. "I've known you almost my entire life."

He nodded. "Yes. And so far, it has been a great pleasure."

Smart aleck. Not once, in all the get-togethers, had he ever brought a date. "Are you gay?" Not that she'd care, she only wanted Jordan. But she did know a truly awesome fox shifter who was single—great guy. Really fun loving.

"No." Matter of fact, Kane didn't appear insulted or even interested in the topic. "I like women. Always have."

"So you do date?" What kind of woman did Kane like? Probably someone really, really smart. Rocket scientist smart.

"Sure." He tapped a manila file against his hand. "But I usually screw up. I miss hints, miss clues, don't say the emotional thing at the right time. My last girlfriend was probably the most logical woman I've ever met, and even she got angry when I failed to remember our first month anniversary." Bewilderment quirked his lip. "Relationships always come second to my work, and most women don't understand that. Casual, very casual relationships are a must for me, I think. Especially now since the virus takes all my time."

Katie nodded. "That's cool. Of course, maybe you haven't met the right woman. The one you'd put first, before your work."

"No. My work always comes first. It's life or death."

She sincerely hoped she was around when the methodical Kane Kayrs fell hard for a woman. "If you say so."

"Have we spent enough time distracting you from the coming moon by talking about my love life?"

From anybody else, the question would've been either sarcastic or humorous. Not Kane. He was genuinely serious.

Katie shook her head. For a non-emotional guy, the scientist read people really well. "Yes. I've been wondering, should we try to capture Brent alive? I mean, since he has evolved?"

"No." Kane reached into a different drawer to toss her a candy bar. "He has evolved only because there has been time to do so. In all the werewolves I've tested, the virus hasn't changed. If you get the chance to take him out, do it."

"Okay." Back to Plan A—kill the bastard. Taking Brent alive would've been a huge risk, anyway.

Kane frowned. "Your neck is hurting you. Want a bandage?"

She barely kept from rubbing the ache. "How did you know?"

He reached for the bandages. "I'm observant."

Maybe so, but she hadn't given one clue her neck hurt. "I'm fine. No need for bandages." She wanted to keep the bite from Jordan as long as she could. How freakin' embarrassing was that?

Kane cleared his throat. "Okay."

Curiosity reared up. "What's it like? I mean, being the smartest guy on the planet?"

An elegant shoulder lifted. "It's pretty convenient."

Amusement had her smiling. She'd expected him to be nonchalant or humble, maybe even deny he was so brilliant. "No, really, don't argue with me. You're super smart. Honest."

He rubbed his chin with long, tapered fingers, good humor lighting his eyes. "Well, there are issues. Genius and madness skirt a fine line. Most geniuses go stark raving mad at some point."

"You don't seem worried."

"I'm not. If the voices take over, they take over." He grabbed a bandage from the counter to hand her. "If you change your mind, this has numbing medicine on the pad."

She took the small object. To keep Jordan's bite, even for a short time, she'd live with the pain.

Chapter 11

Alone in the underground bedroom, Janie stretched sleepily in her bed, waiting for daylight to arrive. She loved being inside the earth, which often whispered secrets to her. So many secrets existed right now, and every time Janie tried to see the future, it morphed into different paths. The future distorted daily.

She tugged on the horseshoe necklace around her neck. Zane had given the token to her in a dream when she'd turned five years old. Nobody could explain how she'd carried the gift from her dream into reality. They only met in dreams—and somehow the big world seemed smaller, the monsters less scary when she knew Zane waited to meet her someday.

Hurt slithered down her torso to pool in her abdomen. Sure, there was a six-year age difference between them, but they'd been friends. In fact, for too many years, Zane had been her only friend. How could he abandon her? God, she hoped he wasn't dead. It'd been so long since she'd had a vision concerning him.

Her thoughts in turmoil, her stomach rolling, she drifted back into sleep.

The dream came quickly and she dropped right into it.

Dank and wet, the cave made her shiver. Janie rubbed her hands along chilled arms and stopped moving. Taking in each dark wall, the blistering wind whistling outside, and the smooth damp floor, she surveyed her surroundings, just as her father had taught her.

Realization came with a flash.

Dreaming. She walked in a dream . . . one she hadn't engineered. It had been so long, she'd almost missed the signs.

A low groan echoed from the darkness ahead.

She could leave, or go forth and find out what was going on. In a dream, she was safe. Probably. But regardless, Janie Kayrs had never been a coward.

Three steps forward and a dark wall stood in her way. Shuffling to the side, she discovered the passageway and slid her feet slowly, making sure the ground continued to exist. The smell of damp moss permeated her senses. A sharp turn to the right and she found a room.

One lit by a huge hole in the rock roof.

A man sprawled on the stone floor, his back to a wall, his face turned away. He was as large as Uncle Dage, with a buzz cut and wide shoulders. He'd dressed in black combat gear from flak boots to the bulletproof vest lying by his side next to a bloodied shirt. His bare chest bled from several cuts. Deep ones. The wall cradled his head as he slowly turned toward her, eyes closed. Pain etched lines at the side of his mouth and he groaned again.

The world tilted, then focused with too much speed. Janie stumbled back a step. "Zane?"

His eyes flashed open. Dark and green, they zeroed in on her. "Janie Belle?"

She shook her head against reality. He'd given her the nickname years ago, declaring "Janet Isabella" to be too long. A man's voice, low and deep, had rumbled from what was clearly a man's body. A muscular, adult man's body. Thank God he wasn't dead. "You grew up."

His smile tightened into a grimace. "You didn't grow."

She raised an eyebrow. "So I've heard." Caution kept her at the entrance to the cavern. "How badly are you injured?"

"I'll be fine—just need to catch my breath."

"You're bleeding." So much blood.

He exhaled with a grimace. "What are you doing here?"

"I don't know." Hurt filled her voice, no matter how hard she wanted to hide it. "I fell asleep, and here I am. You must be asleep and for once not blocking me." Unless he'd passed out. He had probably passed out.

He closed his eyes again. For a man, he had dark, thick lashes. She'd known he'd be handsome, but hadn't realized how very much. High cheekbones created manly hollows in his face, rugged and strong. The chin that had once been stubborn had grown into a thick jaw, one with an intriguing cleft in the middle. Barely. But enough of one to pique her curiosity. A scar ran from his right temple to his jaw, making him look dangerous. Deadly even.

In all her visions, in all her dreams, she'd never seen the scar.

A deep exhale sent more blood cascading down his defined abs. Whoever he'd battled had done a good job of injuring him.

No way was she letting Zane die during her dream. Thank God he still breathed. Even though he'd hurt her, she needed him to be alive. "Why did you stop talking to me?"

He sighed. "I'm sorry we had to stop talking."

Anger swirled in her chest. "That's not an answer."

Long, tapered fingers reached for his shirt, which he used to wipe blood off his torso. Inhaling, he stared at the opposite wall, and the wounds slowly began to close. "You need to leave, Janie."

Enough with the orders. She strode into the center of the room. "You've blocked me for years. Apparently you're too in-jured to block now." Another step closer, and she halted. "Do you need blood?" Her heart sped up at the thought.

He started. "No." Sweeping one hand out, he sat straighter, back against the wall. "Stay where you are."

"Or what?" She lifted her chin.

He gave a strangled cough. "You haven't changed a bit."

That hurt. "Yes, I have. I'm almost seventeen."

One dark eyebrow rose. *"You turn sixteen next week."*

Warmth spread through her. He'd remembered her birthday. *"I don't suppose you planned to slip into my dreams and sing 'Happy Birthday.' "*

His gaze dropped to the horseshoe necklace. *"Sorry."*

Desire to hide the necklace had her shoulders going back. They'd been friends and she cherished the token. *"Who are you?"*

"You know who I am." He bent a knee and rose unsteadily.

"No, I don't. All I know is your father belonged to a group of vampires, and when he died, you disappeared." She fought the very strong urge to touch him and help him up. *"We can't find out who you are."* So many times she'd asked Uncle Dage to find Zane, and so many times he said he couldn't. She took in the battle gear, the knife strapped to Zane's leg. *"You're obviously fighting. Who and where?"*

His smile flashed the twin dimples she used to love. *"Here and now."* One hand on the wall flexed impressive muscles as he struggled to stand.

Janie took a step back. Huge. He'd gotten so big. Why couldn't she have gotten taller, darn it? *"Did you stop visiting me because of our age difference?"* Only way to get the truth was to ask the question.

He leaned against the rock, head back, gaze on her under half-closed lids. *"No."*

"Then why?" She'd needed him. No matter how old he was.

"Doesn't matter. We can't be friends who jump into each other's dreams. It isn't safe."

That wasn't an explanation. Who the heck was he? *"Are you part shifter?"* What kind of animal lurked inside her old friend?

"Forget about me, Janie. I'm on the front line, and no way am I going to see my next birthday. You're almost grown up—face reality."

The condescension in the "almost grown up" statement had

her gritting her teeth. "Didn't figure you for such a quitter, Zane." Instant satisfaction welled up in her as his eyes sparked fire. "Apparently you just got your butt kicked. Need some help from the vampires?"

His fangs flashed. "I am a vampire."

Tingles rippled through her skin. "You're not with the Realm."

The deadly points retracted. "Not all vampires are with the Realm."

A true statement, to be sure. But there was something more. "What else, Zane?"

He lowered his chin while his shoulders went back. "You made my childhood bearable, Janie, and I thank you. But this is the last time we're ever going to talk."

For just a moment, she saw the boy she'd loved. Her only friend for those scary years when she'd first learned of the Kurjans. "You need me more than I need you." The statement surprised her, but instinct had her whispering the truth.

His smile brought back more good times. "Take care of yourself, Belle."

With a sweep of his arm, the dream disappeared.

She awoke, sitting up in bed, her hand going to the necklace. Never talk again? That was what he thought. Throwing on sweats, she tied her hair in a band and ran through the underground fortress to Dage's control room.

Knocking, she waited for the door to smoothly slide open. Memories assailed her—she'd always visited her uncle in underground rooms like this, and he'd always let her in. Not once had he denied her entrance to a room most of the world didn't know existed.

Stepping lightly, she maneuvered around a counter of computers that often had several people typing away. Today, it was empty. She continued on to where her uncle sat in his leather chair, sketching in a notebook. His thick black hair was tied at his nape and he wore dark sparring clothes. Many people feared the king of the vampires, yet the massive vampire had always been her soft spot to land. A kindred spirit. "Uncle Dage?"

He turned his head, a forced smile on his face. She'd known him almost her entire life, and she knew his real smile. He'd often gifted her with it. "Have a vision, sweetheart?"

"No. The universe is too unsettled for visions." Such odd words to string together and ones she wouldn't share with many people. But Dage understood. She peered at a partially sketched drawing of Aunt Emma working in the lab. "Pretty."

"Yes. Very pretty." Dage glanced at the paper and sighed. "I just came from a meeting aboveground and thought I'd get some perspective down here."

"By drawing Emma's face?" Janie grinned.

Dage exhaled. "Old habits die hard. I've spent three centuries drawing her face, and I found the exercise relaxes me. Even now."

Sweet, and it made sense. Janie cleared her throat. "I've been trying real hard to see what happens with Jordan, but nothing is clear."

"I'm with you. I've got nothing." Dage leaned to the side and lifted a thick leather chair as if furniture weighed nothing, setting it next to his. "What's going on?"

She exhaled softly, putting on her most beguiling expression. Being the only human toddler around a bunch of dangerous vampires, she'd quickly learned how to charm them. "It's time you started trusting me, Uncle Dage."

His dimples flashed. Good. His real smile. "I do trust you. Stop manipulating me."

She rolled her eyes and gave a small laugh. "Okay. For years you've kept the truth about Zane away from me, and I know you checked him out. Tell me the truth."

The king turned his head to the side, pinning her with a shrewd gaze.

She held it, not turning away. Few people existed who could meet the king in a staring contest. Finally, Janie lifted an eyebrow in a show of boredom.

Dage threw back his head and laughed, deep and hard. "I give up." Reaching for a keyboard, he punched in keys and a screen appeared in the quartz wall. Two seconds later, twelve-year-old Zane filled the space.

Janie gasped. Warmth and an odd hurt centered in her chest. "Zane." He smiled into the shot, green eyes light, hair dark and long. Young and innocent, and seemingly happy. Before the sad and angry glint entered his eyes.

"Zane Kyllwood." Dage clicked a few more keys and an immense man with Zane's eyes came up on the screen. "Here's his father, Dane."

Zane looked just like his daddy from the dark hair to the sharp jaw and large frame. They both had tough faces and kind eyes. "Where is he?"

Dage exhaled. "Dane led a faction of vampires in eastern Australia that didn't belong to the Realm. All former soldiers, all former assassins, they created a coalition and lived off the grid, not giving us any trouble, but protecting their own." Another click of the keys and a smoldering, demolished town came into view. "They were attacked by either Kurjans, rogue shifters, or demons about ten years ago, and I believed no one survived."

"Zane survived. I told you that when he came to me ten years ago and said he was moving to live with his mother's people."

"I know, and I've searched high and wide for him. But whoever his mother is, there's no trace of her."

"I wonder if he's a shifter." Janie pursed her lips. "I've always known he was more than pure vampire."

Dage nodded. "His father was a vampire with a vampire father and shifter mother—wolf shifter. I traced the lineage back and he's related to feline and multi shifters as well—on his paternal grandmother's side. Of course, there are vampires all the way back on his father's side."

It was so weird that vampires only made male babies, no matter who they mated with. "So maybe his mama is a shifter and they're living with a shifter clan off the grid." Fate whispered in Janie's ear that she needed to find her old friend and now. "I saw him in a dream this morning. He was wounded in battle, so you need to find information on all battles occurring yesterday."

Dage nodded. "I'll try. But after ten years of keeping my ear to the ground regarding your dream friend, I've not once found his mother or her people. Don't hold your breath, little one."

"I won't." She'd find Zane through dreams, if necessary. "You're dressed for sparring, Uncle Dage."

Her uncle nodded, a hard light cutting through his eyes. "Yes. We're training with Jordan today—wish me luck."

Something told her Jordan would need the luck.

Chapter 12

Jordan winced as he shoved open the door to his underground quarters, trying not to reopen just closed wounds. The Kayrs brothers hadn't taken it easy on him during training, drawing blood and breaking bones, which he'd already healed. He tried to convince himself they wanted him ready to battle, but in truth, they were all pissed. Maybe not at him, but he was a good outlet.

Her scent hit him as he snapped on the light. Dark spices and wild orchids, all woman. Smoothing his battered face into nonchalant lines, he pivoted away from the living area to the utilitarian kitchen and shut the door.

Katie sat on the oak table, swinging a leg. "I'm here to seduce you."

Amusement and something warmer settled in his chest. For seduction she'd worn ripped jeans, battered tennis shoes, and a frayed T-shirt so old the logo had faded beyond recognition. Her multicolored blond hair was up in a ponytail. No makeup adorned her pretty face.

The truth slammed him so hard he took a step back. The woman was fucking perfect.

Saying a monumental thanks that cats were stubborn, he forced himself to chuckle. "I appreciate the warning."

A clock next to the small fridge ticked away seconds.

Katie glanced past the living room to the open door of

his bedroom. A soft blush wandered up over her sharp cheekbones. "I'm not kidding."

"I know," he said softly. "And I truly appreciate the adult way we're discussing this." When it came to mating, discussion had no place. He'd shielded her too much from the ways of their people if she didn't know that. "I take it you heard Kane's cure didn't work?"

"Yes." The blush receded, leaving Katie pale. "The only chance you have is mating a shifter, and although I'm only half that, I'm offering."

He'd saved her as a cub, and the woman took loyalty seriously. "You don't owe me."

"I know." Fire flashed in her tawny eyes. "I'm not proposing to sacrifice myself here. We're both infected with the virus . . . mating might cure us both."

"Or kill us both." Irritation swirled down his spine at the rational talking going on. "I'm almost a werewolf—I could turn you into one as well."

Her stubborn chin lifted. "I'm willing to take the chance."

The irritation slid to anger. "What exactly do you think happens in a mating, Kate?"

The blush returned, red and bright. "Jesus, Jordan. I know what happens."

"No, you don't." Amazement filled him at her naiveté. "I don't just give you a good fuck and bite your neck, sweetheart."

The blush intensified, along with her scent. Intrigue and lust deepened those amazing eyes. "You think you're that good?"

Ah. Challenging him. Smart woman. "Yes." He shoved the beast inside down. Way down. "I've seen the aftermath of a mating. The female is often lucky if she still has a shoulder." Dark and brutal, even in human form, the males became all animal during a claiming. The woman should know that.

"I've seen the aftermath of a mating, too." She shoved off the table. Toward him. "I can handle it."

No mention of love. No mention of forever or even happiness. That more than the calm discussion shot fury through his veins. "No, you can't. Even when you were . . . healthy . . . it was too much of a danger. If I decided to mate you, you'd no longer be Katie, the little girl I protected. My adult friend. The werewolf hunter. None of those people would you be in that moment."

She tilted her head to the side. "What would I be?"

Low, guttural, the snarl came from down deep. "Mine."

Interest flared hot and bright in her eyes. Only a second of warning hinted in her bunched muscles as she leaped. Straight for him, hard and fast, knocking him down.

His head hit stone. Without thought, he clutched a hand into her hair. Flipping them over, he slammed her to the ground, his mouth on hers. Diving deep, his animal roared as the taste of spice exploded on his tongue.

She arched into him, returning his kiss, matching him.

Lava bubbled through his blood. His cock shoved against his zipper in a flash of pain. A roaring filled his ears. Tethering her head with one hand, he grabbed her ass with the other, yanking her up and trying to dispel some of the hurt. Rubbing against her, need flared into demand.

A pounding on the door jerked him to reality. Hissing, he jumped up and threw her behind him. Her shoes slapped the hard floor—the woman always did land on her feet. "What?"

"Calls are coming in for your video conference," Kane yelled from the corridor outside. "Hurry the hell up." Heavy footsteps echoed down the hallway.

Jordan swiped a hand across his mouth. Without turning to look behind him, he yanked open the door and followed his friend. What had just happened?

Fifteen minutes after he'd taken his hand off Katie's ass, Jordan sat alone at a conference table, a myriad of screens before him. A blank wall stood behind him, and the shades had been drawn to hide the ocean. Kane sat off to the side, manning a telecommunications console probably more intricate than the one used by NASA command. The odd thought hit Jordan that the vampires could probably visit the moon if they wanted. Knowing vamps, they had no interest. Frankly, Jordan had enough problems on this planet.

Faces began taking shape on the different screens. Panthers, cougars, African lions, and tigers—all in human form—spread across the globe.

Gerald Shotlam, a black panther, leaned toward the screen. "I've been somehow elected the spokesperson today, so let's get started. Rumor has it you've been challenged."

"Yes. And you're a good choice of spokesperson *for my people.*" Jordan kept his face blank as he issued the statement.

Gerald sat back and then nodded.

Good. Jordan was still Alpha, and everybody better remember that fact. "I've accepted and will meet David Bomant when he chooses a time and place."

"He's also alleging you murdered his brother, your cousin." Not by one inflection did the panther's voice change, but the question shone bright in his dark eyes. "As I recall, Brent disappeared without a trace when the last war started, and we all figured the Kurjans had gotten to him. Did you kill him?"

"Yes." Jordan rested in his chair, fighting to hide the relief that some of the truth was finally out. Though this might either send the feline nation into civil war, or at the very least, have a few old friends gunning for him.

Gerald sat back, his eyes widening, while a couple of gasps could be heard. "You murdered him?"

"No." Jordan ignored Kane's sudden interest in the conversation. "We'd gone to war, and I challenged Brent. We decided to keep the fight quiet, not let the Kurjans know of our unrest, and whoever won . . . would take over." It was almost the truth, and there was no reason to speculate what would've happened had Jordan not won.

"That's not how we work," Gerald snarled.

"I know." Jordan clasped his hands on the granite table, leaning forward. "Brent and I reached a decision together and did what we thought was right." He made eye contact with the panther as he told the lie.

"Jordan"—Gerald shook his head, wisdom shining in his thousand-year-old eyes—"I know you were young, and you'd both just lost your parents, but you didn't have the right to change our ways in such a manner. Nobody witnessed the challenge or the fight."

"Connlan Kayrs witnessed both." Might as well get the bad news out at once. Panic and dread commingled in Jordan's gut.

Ella Frades, a Bengal, coughed and flipped back her strawberry-blond hair. "So Conn Kayrs, the brother of the king you ended up aligning with, is the sole witness?"

"Yes." This was going south and fast.

"Brent had been talking about withdrawing from the Realm," Ella hissed.

"Which is why I challenged him." Jordan lifted a shoulder. "What's done is done. I'm meeting David to fight, and anyone else who wishes to challenge me can step on up afterward." Enough of this crap. "If I don't survive the virus, which you all know I have, then I'm endorsing Noah Chance as your new leader."

Ella frowned. "I'd heard you'd taken a mate. She'd be first in line."

"I have not taken a mate." And he wouldn't. Taking a mate would put a target on the woman's back the second he died. He had to stay the hell away from Katie.

The tigress smiled. "Good. You know as well as I that our people won't accept a lioness infected with the virus as a leader. Sad, but true."

Jordan met her gaze, not blinking. He kept it, not looking away until Ella blushed and glanced down. He understood the danger to Katie if he mated her . . . but no one was going to get away with threatening his woman.

Gerald glared through the camera. "I say we wait and see the result of the challenge currently before Jordan. If you win"—a snarl curled his lip—"I guarantee you'll be challenged again. We'll decide about Noah Chance if and when that issue becomes relevant." With a nod off-camera, the screen went blank.

After a few more polite good-byes, and good wishes considering he was about to turn into a beast, Jordan stared at empty screens.

Kane finished tapping in keys and sat back. "What exactly did you and Conn do?"

Jordan pivoted to face the brother of his best friend. "You probably don't want to know."

Kane nodded. "Probably not." He grabbed a gold Cross pen, twirling the metal through his fingers. "I figured you did what you had to do in a time of war. Feeling guilty or worrying about the decision now is a waste of time."

"I'm not feeling guilty."

"Bullshit."

Irritation clenched Jordan's hands into fists. "What are you, a mind reader?"

"Nope." Kane stretched his long legs out, his eyes thoughtful, his fingers working the pen into a blur of gold.

"Other minds are closed to me. Thank God." He flipped the pen in the air, catching the device with his other hand and resuming the game. "Saw Katie earlier."

Emotion flushed along Jordan's skin.

Kane chuckled low. "She didn't want to cover up the bite mark you gave her last night."

Pleasure warmed Jordan's chest right before dread shoved the warmth away. "She has a crush, and it'll go away if I turn into a werewolf."

Kane tucked the pen in his pocket. "You're an idiot if you truly believe that."

Jordan frowned. The scientist seemed to have several opinions when it came to emotion. Interesting. "You have a potential mate, Kane? I mean, any little human scientist you have in mind?" So far, Dage and Talen had mated scientists, while Conn mated a witch. Jordan didn't see Kane with a witch.

"Hell, no." Kane stretched to his feet. "I don't have patience for emotion right now—I need to cure you of the virus."

"That'd be nice."

Conn slid into the room. "Your fight has come to you. Suit up, Jordan. Time to kick ass."

Chapter 13

"How did Bomant find us?" An hour after the fiasco of a feline teleconference, Jordan stretched his neck under a cloudy sky. Very weak light tumbled through the darkness from the moon. A rumbling roared in his gut, and he squelched all need.

"You'll have to ask him." Conn yanked a knife from his boot. "At least they set down a mile from headquarters."

"We need to move headquarters." Jordan tightened the band on his hair.

"No. There's nowhere else to go." Conn replaced the blade. "We chose the best defensive place in the country, and we'll protect it even better."

The ocean pounded down below while thick trees obscured the forest in every direction. "Interesting clearing they found." Something creeped Jordan out about the place, but he couldn't figure out what. Normal scrub brush lined the ground, the trees pine, the night cold.

He ignored the warning flaring at the base of his spine and eyed Katie, who stood quietly next to him. "You shouldn't be here." If there was any way to do this without her, he would've thought of it.

She tossed her head, gaze solidly on the three men across the small meadow who hadn't shifted as of yet. "You have no choice."

Duty and tradition made his temples ache. The rules dictated he needed a witness from his pride for the battle, and unfortunately, Katie was the only member within three states right now. He'd broken enough of their rules already—he couldn't get out of this one. "Stay out of the way. If things go south, you head for the helicopter where Max is waiting."

Katie tightened the bulletproof vest around her trim waist. "Don't worry, Jordan. You get in trouble, I'm not saving your ass."

Conn lifted an eyebrow, and Jordan shrugged. Apparently Katie was still pissed about the kiss. He'd warned her—she should've listened. Mating was too dangerous, and he refused to destroy her. Even in lion form, he'd be rough. In lion/werewolf form, he would tear her apart. Hopefully he'd scared her enough she wouldn't challenge him again.

He straightened as the three lions stalked forward to stand in the center of the field. They were lighter colored than Jordan's people—golden hair and flecked eyes. The one in the middle took another step toward him. "I'm David Bomant, and you tried to kill my brother."

Conn settled his stance, gaze on the other shifters.

"Be ready for Brent to show up," Jordan whispered. No way the crazy werewolf would miss his brother challenging Jordan. This meeting was as much a trap to catch Brent as a way to take out a challenger. Raising his voice, he stepped away from Katie. "Is that what Brent told you?" His voice carried across the quiet night.

David flashed sharp canines. "Yes. He told me you and the Kayrs next to you set a trap for him and struck from behind. Like cowards."

"You're an idiot," Katie spat.

The cat turned his golden gaze on her. "Katie Smith— I have to tell you, my brother is looking forward to seeing you again. As far as he's concerned, you're the perfect mate for him, considering you're part werewolf."

"Then he needs to come and find me." Katie's snarl rivaled any lion still breathing. She stepped forward, and Jordan tensed. Ignoring him, she planted her feet. "I suppose you're the asshole who's been following me and snapping pictures?"

"Not exactly, though I did get my hands on them." David grinned. "Although I gave most of the pictures to Brent, I have to admit, I kept a couple for myself. You know, for those lonely moments late at night when I needed inspiration."

"You're disgusting." Katie yanked a knife from her boot. "Maybe after Jordan kills you, I'll remove your tongue."

Jordan eyed the angry woman. She seemed serious. The virus had messed with her temper a bit. Though something in her wildness just plain and simple turned him on.

David nodded to his friends, and they loped to the edge of the clearing. "My father was Kyle Bomant, and I'm here to take his rightful place."

"I don't give a shit who your father was." Jordan stalked forward until only a foot separated them. He needed to keep far enough from Conn and Katie that his shifting wouldn't knock them out. A breeze from the chilly ocean slammed into his face. "I had no clue your brother lived."

"We're aware of that." David's accent made him sound like more of a big city lawyer than a cat. Though he was well over six feet with a broad chest, as broad as Jordan's. "It took nearly one hundred fifty years for him to heal and another hundred to train."

Yeah. Shifters didn't heal like vampires. It was a miracle Brent had survived with one tendon attached in his neck. "Then he got infected by the virus." Jordan eyed the other two shifters. Alert, tense, ready to rumble. Not good. "How exactly did he get infected?" He needed answers before he killed this guy.

David gave a humorous laugh. "We attended the colloquium ten years ago—you didn't notice."

"Ah." Several shifters had been infected that year, Katie being one of them. "Guess that'll teach him to crash a party."

"He's evolved. And he has great plans for the feline and canine nations. We both do. No more bowing to the vampires. We're taking over."

Jordan shook his head. "You're about to die, son."

David flicked his glance toward Katie and back. "No, Jordan. You're going to die. Then my brother and I will share your woman."

Jordan smiled. "That the best you got?" Jesus. The moron might as well be spitting from a playbook for dummies about messing with your opponent's head. He tucked his chin, lowering his voice so only the cat in front of him could hear. "Your brother begged for his life. On his knees." Not true, but what the hell.

David snarled, shifting into lion form in a flash, striking for Jordan's jugular.

Jordan pivoted, throwing the cat across the field. With a hiss, he shifted into a mountain lion, bones cracking, pain ripping through his muscles until he landed on all fours. His roar filled the night.

They lunged at the same time, claws rending, clashing upright like dueling bucks. Jordan swiped down David's face, tearing tissue. Baring his teeth, he gave an Alpha's roar.

The other cat howled in pain and snapped teeth into Jordan's front leg.

Agony rippled up his tendons. He batted David away.

The clouds parted. Moonlight cascaded down. A buzzing set up between Jordan's ears, cotton filtered over his eyes. Warmth.

Closing his eyes, he lifted his head.

"Jordan!" Katie screamed.

A wisp of a thought later, sharp canines latched into his neck.

Instinct had him dropping to the ground and rolling over, throwing the other cat away. Blood flowed freely from the wounds in Jordan's neck.

Confusion had him shaking his head. Moonlight. Safety. Where was he?

Then a scent. Wild orchids. He pivoted and saw her. Katie. His. Snarling, he lowered his head and ran his claws through the earth, his focus on her.

Air whispered along his fur an instant before a hard body collided with him, sending them sprawling. Hissing, he rolled to his feet, gaze on the other lion. Challenge. His female behind him, the threat before him, he reacted like any animal and charged.

Digging his teeth into his opponent's jaw, he kept track of the other two lions, the vampire, and the female. The need to protect her battled with the moon's pull . . . but the female's silent demand won.

Twisting his jaw, he scraped through muscle, cartilage, and bones until reaching the jugular. Warm blood flooded his mouth.

The other cat yelped, slashing wildly with sharp claws and snapping with its teeth.

Jordan felt their intent a second before the other males shifted into cougars.

The vampire roared in protest, the female yelled a warning.

The other two cats bounded across the clearing, circling him while he lay on their struggling leader. The vampire leaped in front of one cat, a wicked blade flashing fast and bright.

The female ran to intercept the other shifter, firing green bullets. The cat roared and leaped toward her, knocking the weapon free. She fell back, hitting the ground, her head and shoulders bouncing.

Rage beyond primal ripped through Jordan.

A force of darkness rushed out of the forest. A werewolf. Jordan knew him but the name wouldn't come. The monster stalked into the clearing, eyes on the female. Katie. The female was Katie. She flipped to her feet, yanking another weapon from her boot.

The other cougar took advantage of Jordan's distraction to jump on his back.

Jordan struggled, his sole focus on the female. Sharp fangs ripped into the back of his neck. Fire lanced through his jaw.

He tightened his hold on the cat below him.

Gunshots echoed behind him, along with a primal roar.

Then suddenly, a helicopter blasted through the sky, setting down hard, shifters jumping out.

Not his people.

As a unit, they shifted from human to lion. Every instinct he owned bellowed for him to protect the female—to fight so she could get away. The forces weren't equal, but he could take several out and give her a chance to seek safety.

The shifters made it halfway across the clearing, five of them, before a second helicopter smashed between them, sending dust flying. Vampires leaped out, weapons ready. Allies.

Katie careened past him, thrown by hairy hands. She bounced twice on the hard ground. The furry beast stalked by, taking a moment to kick him in the ribs. Rage ripped through him.

The cat below him slashed deadly claws along his belly. Jordan hissed, digging his teeth in further.

Another vampire jumped out of the helicopter in his direction, rapidly firing green shots into the werewolf. The creature howled in pain. Katie pivoted and plunged a knife up and into the monster's jugular. The beast staggered away.

The cougar on Jordan's back leaped off to stalk toward Katie.

Allowing the animal inside to roar, Jordan clenched his jaw until his teeth met through David's flesh. Jordan yanked. Tissue, muscle, and bone flung across the clearing. David sagged to the earth, his eyes open in death.

The werewolf stumbled to its feet, lurching toward the tree line. Jordan's legs bunched to go after him. But the other cougar continued to advance on Katie. His female.

The moon called to Jordan. The damn light stole his concentration. Stole his drive. Growling, he shifted back into man to avoid the seductive pull. Pain crackled along his bones and tendons. Stars burst behind his eyes. Lunging, he tackled the other mountain lion, arms circling its body, right as the animal pounced for Katie. He slammed the heel of his hand under the cat's massive jaw. Deadly teeth smashed together.

Man and beast rolled in the dirt. Jordan landed on top, straddling the animal. The cat yowled in protest, legs thrashing, claws seeking purchase.

"Jordan!"

Jordan jerked his head at Conn's yell, sharp reflexes snagging the knife thrown by his friend. Two seconds later he gutted the animal and then cut its jugular. Warm blood covered his legs, washed down his hands.

Shoving the carcass away, he staggered to his feet. Spinning around, he found Katie. She scrambled to stand, her face pale except for a spreading purple bruise on one high cheekbone. He glared, and she took a step back, eyes wide.

Inhaling, he turned and took in the rest of the field. Talen and his men had taken care of the other shifters. Brent was gone. Animal blood scented the air along with the sweetness from the moon. Ironic and disheartening. Jordan popped a tendon back into place. "Good timing."

Talen wiped blood off a knife on the grass. "We kept an eye on the airspace and saw the second helicopter coming—Dage sent reinforcements."

Thank God for friends. Jordan nodded, eyeing his ripped clothing on the field. The wind whipped over his naked body. Cuts and bruises marred his flesh, and his gut was still bleeding. He'd heal. "I need my phone. I'll video the result of the challenge." Maybe the carnage would keep other felines from challenging Noah next week.

But probably not.

Chapter 14

Jordan's body ached. The wounds had healed by the time he broadcast scenes of the bloody clearing, showing the dead shifters. He'd ruled for three centuries with fairness and mercy . . . unless challenged. Then whatever beast was living beneath his chest had roared. Being the last of his line, he'd been challenged more than others, considering there wasn't anyone who could easily step up if he died.

He eased through the underground hallway lined with priceless western oils toward his quarters. Still nighttime, the moon pulled him, causing an itch just under his skin.

During the fight, the animal inside had recognized Katie and wanted her. He'd send her away so she wouldn't see his death, but Realm Headquarters was the safest place for her. Maybe he should just leave like a wounded dog to die alone.

Shoving his door open, he stopped short. "Katie," he sighed. "Enough. Go away." Only the back of her head remained visible. She sat on his couch watching a rerun of *Friends*. Allowing the door to shut behind him, he shuffled toward the refrigerator and yanked out a beer.

"No." Soft, angry, her western twang wrapped around his heart. The television clicked off. The leather protested as she must've stood. "I'm here to finish what we started earlier."

Cool beer calmed his throat as he tipped back his head and emptied the bottle. Setting it on the table, he turned around to face her.

Holy shit.

The woman had come prepared this time. A sheer baby-doll negligée left nothing hidden. High breasts, hard nipples, tiny little waist—all visible through the fabric. He would not look lower. "What are you wearing?" he choked.

Feminine and dangerous, a smile slid across her pretty face. "Not much."

Heat rushed to his groin. His balls tightened, and he hardened in his jeans. The teeth from his zipper were going to be permanently indented on his cock. "This is a bad idea." His voice fucking cracked.

Lifting an eyebrow, she circled the couch. Barefoot, bare legged, he could have her stripped in seconds. Those tan, nicely muscled thighs belonged wrapped around his hips. Temptation swirled through his blood.

Reality smacked him in the face. He'd protected her for decades—he'd do so until he died. Panic had him settling his stance. The sigh he gave came from his soul, truly hating what he had to do. Wiping all expression off his face, he stared her down. "You need to understand. There's never been anything between us."

She lifted an eyebrow, tilting her head to the side. "What do you mean?"

Hurting her would cut out his heart. But it was the only way she'd move on. "I've never felt more for you than friendship, Katie."

Her eyes widened. Something choked in her throat.

He stepped forward, then stilled. Offering comfort wouldn't help.

Gorgeous hair flipped when she threw back her head and . . . laughed? A deep, sensual chuckle that moved her entire body. Tawny eyes filled with mirth, and her focus returned to him. "You're such a complete asshole."

Yeah. He was. Apparently he'd gotten his point across. "You need the truth."

Her stubborn chin lifted. "Then why don't you actually give it to me?"

Irritation warmed his lungs. She wasn't making this easy. "I just did."

The woman snorted. Actually snorted that delicate nose. "Bullshit. You just gave me a cockamamie evasion so I could move on without you. Do you really think I misunderstand your feelings?"

The sudden urge to flee fully pissed him off. "Excuse me?"

"You want me. Have for quite some time, Jordan. Deal with it."

He lowered his chin, taking a good look at the woman. And a woman she was. The little girl he'd saved, the teenager who'd dogged his every step with adoration in her eyes . . . was gone. In place stood a fully confident, courageous as hell warrior with challenge lifting her chin.

His belly warmed. Hell. His cock began to pound. "Well, now."

She slammed her hands on her hips. "You can stop worrying. I'm not going to follow you into the afterlife. I'll move on."

He growled low. "That's nice to hear."

Full lips bowed as she shot a hard smile his way. "In fact, I fully intend to go on. Maybe with Lance. Or Noah, our new leader."

The growl turned to a snarl. Possessiveness clenched his hands into fists. The idea of Katie—his Katie—with any other shifter shot his beast to the surface. "Your point?"

"My point?" She stalked three steps forward, putting herself in range. "I choose my life, Jordan. Stop being a

damn coward and take a chance." Slim fingers jerked the
filmy covering over her head, leaving her in a tiny thong.
"Mark me."

Pert breasts, flat stomach, and toned thighs . . . all covered by skin smoother than silk. Perfect. She was so fucking perfect. His lungs compressed. Heat roared into his
head. Inevitability shuddered down his back. The beast inside him rattled hard against the chains, wanting to leap
and take. The man shoved the animal aside, needing reason. Needing to protect her. "Katie—"

"No." She took the final step forward, her scent of wild
orchids wrapping around his heart and squeezing. "I want
you. Even if this is our only chance . . . our only time . . .
I never want to look back and wish." Both small palms
pressed against his abs, sliding up and over his chest to his
neck, finally reaching his hair.

Even with her height, she had to lever up on her toes
to get ahold of him.

Her grip was determined, sure . . . and meant to keep
him in place. But it was nothing compared to the look in
her amber-colored eyes. Need, fear, total determination.

No force on earth existed strong enough to make him
turn away.

One long shudder moved his shoulders, winding down
his back as he gave in. If they only had one time, he
wanted it, too. She'd always been fragile, even before the
virus took hold of her. Now she was breakable. He'd have
to be so very careful.

Lowering his head, he captured her lips in a kiss meant
to convey everything. Tears pricked the back of his eyes,
shocking the hell out of him. He deepened the kiss, tasting honey and Katie.

All wild woman and desperate promises.

She groaned, pressing against him, her hands lowering
to his shoulders.

Ducking, he released her mouth and grabbed her behind the knees, sweeping her up. Gentle. He needed to be gentle. Long strides had them in the bedroom. She peppered hard kisses along his neck, sending demand straight to his cock.

He laid her down on the plush bed. His utilitarian quarters underground weren't good enough for her. Just a bed and dresser filled the room—no flowers or soft touches for a woman. The thought flew out of his head as he took a moment to look his fill. In his long life, he'd never seen anything as beautiful as this woman, nearly nude, face flushed, waiting for him.

A trembling in his hands surprised him as he yanked his shirt over his head. His jeans soon followed. Her eyes widened a little, and he paused. During the last decade, he'd wondered. Sure, she'd dated. How many men had she accepted as a lover? She'd date again, he was sure. She deserved a good life . . . when he passed. "I want this night, Kate."

"So do I." The smile tipping her full lips promised heat.

Right or wrong, he was taking this moment. Pressing a knee on the bed, he leaned over and ran his mouth along her smooth abdomen. Her breath caught, muscles shifting beneath his lips. The scent of woman and wild orchids shredded his heart.

He traveled a path up her torso, between her breasts until he could nip her chin, his body covering hers. "I'm not going to mark you."

"Yes, you are." Satisfaction filled her topaz eyes. Along with trust and love—yeah, love was there. "We both know it's the only chance you've got to live." Her palms spread over his pecs, her gaze following those clever hands as she caressed him, sliding down his sides to his flanks. "I don't want this life without you, Jordan. Please take the chance."

As if on her command, his incisors lengthened. The lion inside him stretched, howled . . . wanting to sink deep into her flesh. He shoved back, returning his teeth to human size. "The risk isn't mine." If he marked her, she'd never get another mate. Sure, she could find companions, even love, but no mate.

"My risk, my decision."

Then she reached for him, partially encircling him with one smooth palm.

His balls swelled, the base of his spine sparked. The air in his lungs began to burn. "Brave little kitten, aren't you?"

"One of us has to be." She rubbed pinpoint sharp nipples against his chest.

The control he'd tried so hard to keep faltered. He jerked her hand off his dick, pinning it next to her head while he reached for the other one. This was such an incredibly bad idea. But his body had taken over. "I think you've misunderstood the dynamic here."

She arched into him, the scrap of material barely covering her. "Dynamic?"

He lowered his head, scraping his teeth over one nipple. Her gasp of breath and low moan made him smile against her flesh. While he might let the animal out to play, he was still in control—and would remain so. But Katie, on the other hand . . . well now.

Pressing her hands flat, he laved her other nipple. Sweetness and salt exploded on his taste buds. His eyes closed in pure pleasure.

Her fingers entwined with his as surely as she was wrapped around whatever heart he still had. An impressive grip the woman had.

"Jordan, let go of my hands." Husky and soft, her voice caressed his skin.

He'd never heard that tone from her. An instant irritation ripped through him that another man would someday hear the sound. Someday feel her incredible breasts, listen to her soft moans, know her in ways Jordan never would. A snarl rippled up his throat and he quashed the anger. They had this night, and he'd make sure the woman remembered him always.

Faster than cat reflexes had him rolling them both until she perched on his abs, his body flat on the bed. He released her hands and put his behind his head on the pillow. "You want to play, kitten?"

Intrigue and delight lit her pretty eyes. "Yes." Her gaze lowered to his chest.

Slowly, almost hesitantly, she reached out, her fingers curling over his shoulders. A soft sigh escaped as her palms slid over his clavicles and down to his pecs.

Fire licked down his spine in response. His hands shook with the need to grab her and flip her under him, so he interlaced his fingers to keep still. If Katie wanted to play, no way was he going to stop her.

Her full breasts tempted him, so sweet, so feminine.

Wonder filled her smile as she ran her hands back up, caressing the cords in his neck until tangling in his hair. Her reverent touch, as if she'd been waiting for so long, humbled him in ways he hadn't expected.

Then she looked up.

Satisfaction lit her gaze as she met his eyes.

For a brief second, time stopped. He forgot how to breathe. She sat atop him, eyes blazing, blond hair wild and mussed, pink lips swollen from his kiss. "You're beautiful."

Those eyes widened. "So are you."

Then she tightened her hold, lowering her mouth to his. A sigh of contentment whispered along his lips before she increased the pressure, stretching out her lithe body.

A muscle spasmed in his shoulders as he held himself in

check. She lay on top of him, her sex cradling his dick, her long legs smooth against his.

Her teeth sunk into his bottom lip.

A roaring filled his ears.

Tucking her knees up, she rubbed against his aching cock. Heat cascaded from her, tempting him. She pressed openmouthed kisses along his jawline.

Nothing could prevent the low groan that shot from his gut. "Katie. You're making it hard to be gentle, sweetheart."

"Very hard." Her canine nicked his ear. "Besides, who says I want gentle?" Then she bit.

The animal inside him roared alive. Grabbing her hips, he lifted her, reversing their positions. Capturing her against the mattress, he ripped the panties off.

Slow. Damnit. Slow.

Two fingers found her wet and swollen. The surprised mewling she gave made him chuckle against her neck. His canines lowered.

He played, testing her. She bucked against him.

Searching, exploring, learning her, his thumb found her clit. She gave a high-pitched hiss of pleasure.

Then he forced his canines back up and slid down her body to stop between her thighs.

"No." Panic filled her voice. Her legs went rigid. Both hands grabbed his head.

"Yes," he rumbled against her mound. No way in hell would he miss tasting her. His shoulders forced her thighs wide. She started to struggle, to scoot her butt up the bed.

Smiling, he latched both hands onto her buttocks and enclosed her clit with his mouth.

She made a sound between a moan and a whimper. All need. Her fingers loosened their hold on his head. Those amazing thighs trembled.

Slowly, truly enjoying himself, he ran his tongue along her slit. Sweetness and spice. Perfect. A craving to take her roared through him, and he slammed control around the animal within. He licked her again.

She relaxed into the bed, her body softening, a pretty sound of surrender coming from her.

Then he got down to business. Alternating between licks, kisses, and small bites, he brought her to the edge several times. Her entire body trembled, sweat slicked her thighs, and a desperate mewling came from her before he'd decided she'd had enough.

Plunging two fingers into her, he nipped her sweet spot.

Her back arched. She cried out his name, the orgasm rolling through her, muscles shaking. His worked her clit to prolong it.

Finally, she went limp against the mattress with a small groan.

Pleasure lanced him. Levering up on an elbow, he placed a gentle kiss on her mound. Then he maneuvered up, taking time to nip and lick at both breasts until reaching her mouth.

She spread her legs, making room for his hips. Long fingers clutched his hair, and she kissed him. "Jordan." The soft sigh held contentment, happiness, and a low demand.

A demand he'd answer. His entire body vibrated with need. A desperate need that should give him pause. But for now, Katie was all that existed. Grabbing her ass, unable to wait any longer, he plunged into her with one strong stroke.

And stilled, shock chilling the air in his lungs.

Wide eyes met his.

He gasped, his hand on her butt, his gaze on hers, his cock gripped tightly in so much heat he had to blink several times to keep control. The woman had been a virgin. "Katie." Jesus Christ. Why hadn't she told him?

"I, ah . . ." She barely seemed to breathe. Pain scented the air. Both hands pushed against his chest, her lower body struggling.

"God. Stop moving." With each tiny shift, she gripped his shaft harder. The lion inside howled, desperate with the need to plunge, to pound, to take. "Please."

Exhaling, she relaxed into the mattress, her palms smoothing out over his flesh. "Okay."

Thoughts zinged through his mind in disarray. If the woman would stay still, he could concentrate. "Why didn't you say something?"

Vulnerable, completely at his mercy considering he was inside her, she still allowed defiance to lift her eyebrow. "I didn't see it was any of your business."

"You sure about that?" Clutching her butt, he slid out and slammed back in. The raw pleasure of the act had him gasping along with her. She was too tight, too damn hot, for him to keep control long. Her nails bit into his flesh. Too bad he liked the sharp pain. "I know you've dated these last ten years." Baye had reported all her movements.

She shrugged, her nipples scraping along his skin. Jordan bit his lip to keep from snarling. Interest lit her eyes before she lowered her gaze to his mouth. "I've been busy fighting werewolves."

There was more to it than that. The truth, he wasn't sure he wanted to hear the words any more than she wanted to say them. Not with this being their only night together—not with his moving on soon. But they both knew—she'd waited for *him*. His heart filled until his entire body flamed. "I love you, Kate."

Her gaze flew up, her nails retracting. Emotions raced across her face. Finally, sliding on a saucy smile, she lifted both knees and clasped her ankles at his back. "Then you should do something about that." She scooted her butt down a fraction, allowing him to go even deeper.

His grip on reality snapped. He reached around and clasped the back of her shoulder, tethering her to him, his other hand sure to leave bruises as he began to pound. Hard, fast, and out of control.

Blood dropped onto his tongue from his canines shooting down. The flesh of her shoulder beckoned him, right where he'd bitten her the other night. Against his will, his head lowered to scrape along that so fragile skin.

She gasped, arching against him, turning her head and exposing the spot.

Still, he pounded.

Fighting the animal within, he scraped up her neck to the soft spot behind her ear. "Come now, Kate." Low, dominant, his voice gave no quarter.

She cried out, back bowing, the orgasm whipping through her so powerfully her internal muscles clamped down on him. The instant reaction appeased the beast. The fangs retracted without leaving a scratch. His spine tingled, his balls drew tight. Pleasure burst through him so hard he saw stars as he went over the edge with her.

Chapter 15

Janie turned off the massive television screen, sliding off the plush couch, her gaze on the panther shifter replacing pool sticks in the wall rack. "Thanks for helping me clean up."

Charlie nodded, stifling a yawn. "Sure. It was cool of the king to let us stay up all night watching movies."

"Yeah." The quiet of the early morning surrounded them since the rest of the kids had headed off to bed. Janie slid around the sofa and ran her hand along the wide counter holding bowls now emptied of chips. Skirting the air hockey table, she began rolling billiards into the pockets of the pool table. "Uncle Dage feels bad when we have to go underground, so he tries to find some fun for us."

"Being underground is, ah, uncomfortable for shifters." Charlie shoved a hand through his dark brown hair. He'd grown it out to his shoulders when he'd turned sixteen a few months ago, and he looked older, more dangerous, just like Uncle Conn. But he laughed a lot more than Conn, which was one of the reasons Janie liked him.

"Yeah, I noticed you guys seemed irritated during training yesterday morning." Shifter and vampire trainees had worked out on the mats in the underground gym, throwing each other across the room. Many of the males

had discarded their shirts, showcasing new and rather impressive muscles. Janie had watched for fun.

While she'd wanted to join in, considering she'd been
training since kindergarten, the shifters couldn't go all-out
with her. Sometimes it sucked to be human. "I thought
you and your cousin were going to kill each other. I mean,
being underground isn't all bad."

Charlie grinned. "I'm part panther, not gopher, Jane.
Being underground makes my skin itch." He shook his
head. "All of us are off having to hold in so much energy.
Did you see Todd and Suzy going at it over in the love
seat?"

Everyone had seen the two shifters kissing off and on
through the movies. They'd been dating for almost a
month, and Suzy thought she knew all about guys suddenly. Janie grinned. "They were just kissing. Don't tell
me kissing makes you uncomfortable, too."

"No. But when I kiss a girl, we're alone. As far as I'm
concerned, kissing isn't a group sport." He grabbed a couple of darts from the floor to put in the cups lined along
the wall.

A warming filtered through Janie's cheeks. "Who have
you kissed?"

He shrugged, his concentration on the darts. "Nobody
special. Yet."

Was there a hint there? Or maybe she was reading too
much into the words. Why couldn't her psychic visions
lead to important stuff like first kisses? Janie fought a
yawn. Even the idea of kissing Charlie wasn't going to
keep her awake after an all-night popcorn party. "I'm
sorry we didn't make it to the new movie like we'd
planned."

"Well . . . we kind of had a date." Charlie turned toward her, deep brown eyes twinkling.

Good humor lifted Janie's spirit. "Yeah. If you call

watching old horror flicks with a bunch of wolf shifters a date."

"We could end it like a date."

Her face heated. She swallowed. "Um, yeah. We could."

He reached out to cup her chin. His warm palm seemed strong all of a sudden. She had to tilt her head back since he'd sprouted up so much last year. Then he started to lower his face.

Oh God. It was really going to happen. She fluttered her eyes closed. His lips met hers, increasing in pressure until she opened her mouth. He swept his tongue inside.

Tingles wandered through her, along with the thought of how weird it was to have someone else's tongue in her mouth. He tasted like chocolate and popcorn. Charlie gave a low hiss and turned to press her into the wall. She kissed him back, tentatively at first, following his lead. Man, she hoped she was good at this.

The idea of Zane zinged through her head, and she raised her hands to push Charlie away.

But she didn't get the chance.

Charlie was ripped away. She opened her eyes in time to see Charlie fly over the pool table, thrown by Garrett.

"Garrett!" Janie grabbed her brother. "What the heck?"

Charlie landed and rolled, shooting to his feet. Fury lined his face. The air shimmered.

Garrett's eyes went wide. "Don't shift!" He grabbed Janie by the shoulders, tucking around her and dropping down against the wall.

An explosion of air shattered the room.

Janie waited two heartbeats and then shoved Garrett away. He landed on his butt. She stood and surveyed the playroom. The light above the pool table swung drunkenly back and forth. The plasma television hung from one nail, the screen shattered. Shards of colored plastic decorated the carpet from the chip bowls exploding.

And a fully grown, snarling, pissed-off panther crouched ready to attack on the other side of the table. Sable brown fur stood up along his back. His eyes had morphed to a catlike hazel. Fangs dropped low from his mouth.

Garrett jumped up. Green ripped through the gray of his eyes. He growled and leaped for the animal. Janie screamed, grabbing the back of his jeans and trying to yank him down.

He slammed onto the pool table, muscles bunching in his arms. "Lets me go." He stilled, twisting out of her grasp and standing. "Ows."

Janie gasped. Blood dripped from his lips. "Oh my God. You're bleeding."

His eyes widened, returning to metallic gray. Gingerly, he reached up and touched his teeth. "I gots my fangs." His delighted smile flashed sharp, bloody teeth.

The air shimmered, and Charlie shifted back to human, smoothly stretching from four legs to two. Janie averted her eyes from the naked teenager. Mostly.

Conn ran into the room. "I heard a scream." He took in the scene with one hard glance. "What the hell?"

Garrett pivoted. "Uncles Conn, I gots my fangs." He blanched. "Ows."

Conn frowned. "That's early. Good for you. Now shove them back up before you rip off a lip." He yanked off his T-shirt, quickly tugging the material over Charlie's head to cover him to the thighs. "Someone explain."

Garrett wiped blood off his chin. "Mom got up early to work in the lab, and Dad went to train, so I came to find Janie. That cat was mauling her." His fangs dropped low again. "Ows."

Charlie snorted. "Nice fangs."

Janie barely grabbed Garrett in time to stop his next lunge. "Knock it off." She sighed. "Uncle Conn, I kissed

Charlie, and then stupid Garrett threw him over the pool
table."

Garrett gave her a wounded look and then turned a
glare on Charlie. A glare very much like the one their father used when angry. His biceps visibly vibrated. "He deserved it."

Conn scrubbed both hands over his face. "Okay. If I
were a shifter and someone threw me over a pool table, I'd
probably shift." He eyed Garrett with a look promising
there'd be a later discussion. "Which means Garrett gets to
clean up the mess. Charlie, go get some sleep."

Charlie smiled, tugging the T-shirt down farther. "No
worries. And Janie, thanks for covering for me, but I
kissed you."

"A fact I'm sure her father will appreciate knowing,"
Conn said with an answering smile.

Charlie choked and lost the grin. "Ah, see you later."
Grabbing his destroyed clothing, he fled the room.

Garrett slammed his hands on his hips. "Uncle Conn, I
came in here and that jerk had his tongue halfway down
my sister's throat."

Conn groaned. "Shut up, Garrett." He shuffled his feet.
"Ah, Janie, well—"

"No." Her blush actually hurt. With as much dignity as
she could fake, she stomped around the pool table toward
the door. "We don't need to talk, Uncle Conn. I know all
about sex."

Her uncle emitted a sound like a cat getting its tail
caught in a door. "God."

Janie fought a grin, leaving the room. She touched her
lips. Her first kiss.

The wolf arrived at the crack of dawn. Tall, broad
across the shoulders, with eyes the color of dark chocolate,

and shoulder-length black hair with interesting mahogany streaks, Terrent Vilks looked like a wolf. His nose had been broken, maybe a couple of times, resulting not in the look of a street brawler, but of a predator who had probably retaliated. He sat in the plush leather chair, hands clasped on the conference table, focus solely on Maggie.

She swallowed. For ten years she'd trained to fight. After one moment with the leader of the Bane's Council, she knew ten years wasn't enough. Not even close.

The king sat to her right at the head of the table, and she faced the wolf.

Dage cleared his throat. "While I appreciate the Bane's Council's desire to see Maggie taken to your headquarters, we won't force her to go."

Terrent lifted one dark eyebrow. "She's ours. If we say she goes, she goes." Low, arrogant, his voice nevertheless held a hint of humor. A twinkle glimmered in his eyes, but the set of his jaw promised a stubborn nature.

Dage frowned. "You've never forced wolves to live anywhere. Your people are as free as ours."

"True." Terrent leaned back and his chair creaked in protest. "Maggie, you've lived with lions and vampires for a decade. Your memory hasn't returned. Maybe being among your own people will help you." A slow, sexy smile spread across his face. "You must be tired of cats. Really."

Cats and vampires were the closest beings she had to family. His attempt at charm wasn't lost on her. She'd have to be blind and probably in a coma not to recognize the charisma held by the wolf leader. She forced an answering smile. "In the last ten years, with all your contacts, you haven't found a hint of my past, either."

He lost the grin. "True."

She bit the inside of her lip to keep from trembling. "Maybe I was alone. No pack, no family." What else could it be?

"It's possible," Dage said quietly. "There haven't been any missing persons type inquiries from humans, either."

Sadness and an odd fear wandered down her spine. How bad of a person had she been not to have anybody looking for her? She settled her face into smooth lines.

Terrent leaned forward. "There are several reasons people who care about you might not have gone public." His dark gaze pierced her eyes as if trying to see into her memories. Into her past.

She started. The big wolf was trying to reassure her? "Right." The meeting would be a lot more comfortable if she could find either Katie or Jordan. Both shifters had disappeared, which burned curiosity right through Maggie. In fact, even though the wolf seemed intent on either charming or intimidating her, her mind kept going to her friends. Part of her wanted them to have finally gotten together. The other part of her worried about what would happen next considering the moon would soon rise. If Jordan died, how would Katie survive?

Dage cleared his throat. "I'm in the middle of a couple wars and really don't have time for games. Why is the head of the Bane's Council here at my headquarters regarding one little wolf shifter after ten years?"

Terrent's nostrils flared. "There's a hit out on her."

Maggie drew back, a buzzing filling her ears. "Excuse me?"

"The Kurjans have wanted her back since they infected her ten years ago," Dage said calmly. "Your news isn't . . . news."

Terrent's bottom lip turned down, and his gaze remained on her. "Not the Kurjans. My sources in the demon nation confirmed yesterday that the demons want her dead."

Fire heated in Maggie's lungs. Calm. She needed to stay calm. "I don't understand."

"What do the demons want with her?" Dage growled.

Terrent shrugged. "We don't know. Yet. But she's safer with her own people considering the entire world knows she's here with you."

Dage stiffened, tapping his ear communicator. "When?" He shot to his feet, gaze encompassing them both. "I've had an emergency and will be right back." Two steps and he yanked open the door. "There are guards outside the room." The door shut behind him.

Terrent steepled his fingers. "Guards, huh? Apparently the king doesn't trust me to refrain from kidnapping you."

"I can take care of myself." A lame line, but the only thing that sprang to her panicking mind. The king had left her alone with a wolf. With *the* wolf. Little pins pricked the skin on her arms. Her heart began to ache. She swallowed, forcing panic down. No way would she let an anxiety attack take her down in front of Terrent. "I don't know any demons." This didn't make sense.

"The demons sure know you." Terrent's voice stayed level, while his eyes darkened in sympathy. "I'm seeking more information, but all I have right now is that they want you dead. Five million dollars' worth of dead."

She blinked away haze. Why in the world would demons want her dead? Fear had her digging in. "I'm staying here."

"Everyone knows you're here. I can keep you safe—nobody knows our secure locations, even the king is in the dark. Besides, Maggie, you've been living with cats. Don't you want to be among your own people, feel at home, maybe remember what it's like to be a wolf?" He rubbed his jaw. "Have you ever run with another wolf? With a pack?"

"I don't know," she whispered. Her breathing evened out. "If I have, I certainly don't remember."

"Then you should give it a try." Warm, even gentle, his tone wrapped around her.

The guy should bottle the charm and sell it. "You kill

werewolves." She said the words to remind herself as much as him.

"Yes." No apology, no hint of doubt. "I kill werewolves. Every chance I get."

She blinked. "You'd kill me if I turned into a werewolf." Every month of every year, she feared the second the moon rose high, she'd finally lose to the virus and turn into a hairy beast with no conscience.

"In a heartbeat."

That should scare the hell out of her. Yet something in his conviction provided an odd reassurance she quickly squashed. "I may have no memories of my past, but I know my rights. I don't have to go anywhere."

He cocked his head to the side. A smile flirted with his masculine mouth. "What rights?"

For a second, she went blank. "You know, rights." Everyone had them.

"We're not humans, *little wolf*," he drawled.

A southern drawl and masculine lips made for a dangerous and intriguing combination. She needed to get a grip. "I'm aware of that, *big bad wolf*."

Devastating was the only term to describe his sudden full-on smile. "For ten years, we've allowed you to stay where you're comfortable, where the Realm scientists can study the virus and hopefully cure you. Unless there's some sort of breakthrough soon, the patience of the Bane's Council is at an end."

"I've heard *you're* the Bane's Council."

He lifted a shoulder. "I lead the council. You're a wolf, darlin'. As such, you're subject to our laws. Perhaps we've been remiss in explaining that fact to you—especially since you're now in more danger than we'd expected."

"If I belong to an outside clan, I don't follow your laws." She'd studied the hierarchy of the canine world during the last decade . . . just in case.

"Everyone follows our laws."

This was getting nowhere. A roaring began to fill her ears. She blinked several times to keep calm. "I'm staying here." Though the temptation to go with him, to meet other wolves, had doubt clouding her brain.

"I hope you'll give me the chance to change your mind." His tone stayed level, but an undercurrent hinted she'd be changing her mind one way or another. "I'm here until the full moon."

At his timeline, the breath rushed out of her throat. "Oh God. You're here to kill Jordan." That was the other reason Terrent had arrived personally. She would not let that happen. No matter what.

Terrent's face hardened to stone. "My business is none of your concern."

"Bullshit." She leaped to her feet. Jordan had saved her from the Kurjans and offered her a home. Protection. Family. "You'll have to go through me."

Faster than sound, Terrent reached across the table, manacling his hands around her arms. Lifting her over the table and pivoting, he had her against the wall before she could blink. "I don't think that will be much of a problem."

The air swooshed out of her lungs. Shock kept her still. The wolf easily held her off the ground and pressed against the wall. Up close, he was bigger than she'd thought. Probably as big as Dage, and even broader across the chest. She opened her mouth to speak, but nothing came out.

He leaned in close, the scent of wild oak swimming around him. "I'm neither a cat nor a vamp, sugar. You challenge me, and you won't like what you get."

His gaze lacked anger or other hint of emotion. Pure fact, even and reasonable, echoed in his tone. As if they were discussing the weather and he hadn't put his hands on her. Physically and way too easily overpowering her.

Fury zinged through her so fast her ears burned. Instinct had her going limp in surrender.

Satisfaction lit his gaze. His hold relaxed.

With the slightest twist of her hips, she shot her leg up, nailing him right in the balls. Shock covered his face, his mouth opening silently. He released her, leaning over and dropping to one knee. He dented the rock floor.

Panic threatened to blind her. She shoved both hands into his massive shoulders, sending him into the edge of the table. "I guess I'm more of a problem than you thought." Quick steps had her in the hallway. Waiting until she was out of sight of the two guards, she launched into a run. A very fast run so she could get to safety and lock the door. Her breath began to pant out. She might be feisty, but no way was she stupid.

Terrent Vilks would be coming for her.

Chapter 16

Katie sat on the cold wooden bench, her gaze on the too silent sea. Still and gray, the ocean seemed to hold its breath. The stone entrance to the underground headquarters stood behind her. Pine trees and dark forest spread out on either side and she tuned in to listen. No images, no hint of predators arrived on the soft breeze. The werewolves hid far away, probably waiting for the full moon.

She shivered, clutching her parka closer around her.

A woman's irritated muttering echoed behind her. Light footsteps sounded as Cara made her way into the small courtyard to slide onto the bench. "Hi."

"Why are you muttering?" Katie kept her gaze on the sea.

"Emma kicked me out of the lab. Something about chemicals I shouldn't be exposed to since I have the virus." Cara stomped a boot on the damp grass.

"How did you get outside?"

Cara tucked her hair into her jacket. "Talen did a full sweep and there's no one near. Which is how I assume you got outside."

"There are at least seven snipers in the trees on either side of us." She sensed them and could probably guess their locations. "If Brent has healed enough to attack, it won't be until the full moon so he's at his strongest." But truly, she didn't care. A sigh escaped her. She and Cara had become close friends while training together to fight the Kurjans when they'd both stayed at Jordan's ranch a decade in the past. Right now, Katie needed a friend. "I slept with Jordan."

Cara coughed. "Wow. Did he, I mean, did you—"

"No. We didn't mate."

"Oh." Cara tucked her hands in her thick coat. "I'm an empath, you know."

"I know."

"What's wrong, then?" Cara grew stiller. "Oh God. It wasn't . . . *bad* . . . was it?"

Katie snorted. "No, it wasn't bad. Sex with Jordan was hot, fun, and I had three orgasms. Four if you count this morning before he left to train." She kicked a pebble, watching it roll over the cliff. "He was very gentle."

Cara gasped. "Oh no. Not *gentle*." Sympathy coated her words. "In perfect control, determined to keep you safe?"

Katie turned to face her friend. "Yeah."

"Oh honey." Cara absently rubbed a permanent bite in the side of her neck. "Talen was like that after I had Garrett, and we weren't sure if I could survive having the virus in my blood without a vampire baby inside me to counteract it."

"What did you do?"

Cara's smile held definite menace. "I challenged him. All those guys are pure Alpha—you challenge and they can't help but respond." She bit her lip. "He has even tried to mate me a couple of times."

Yeah, Katie had discussed the issue with Emma in wondering if mating would cure her. But maybe Cara's attempts were secret. "Really?"

"Yes. The brand is always on his palm now, and sometimes, during really . . . ah . . . energetic sex, the mark transfers to me again." Cara blushed, and then sobered. "But the marking doesn't stay. Never lasts. The virus is too strong."

"Fucking virus."

"Amen, sister."

Katie stomped wet grass off her shoes. "Well, I guess I'll need to challenge the big lion leader."

Cara chuckled. "Up to you. But make sure you want what you'll get. You let a guy like Jordan claim you, and there's no going back."

"I know." Katie sighed, turning toward the dismal ocean.

"What else is wrong?"

Damn empath. Katie ground her heels in the grass. "For so long, all I wanted was Jordan. I don't know if it's been fighting werewolves for a decade, or if I've grown up, but . . ."

"Ah. That when you got the guy it'd be happily ever after, holding hands, dancing through the tulips?"

Katie chuckled "Yeah. You know. Be the first lady of the feline nation . . . throw parties, support my husband."

"Being in the background isn't your thing, huh?"

"Jordan is awesome. He's enough to make anybody happy." Katie bit her lip.

"There's nothing wrong with wanting more. With wanting to make your own mark . . . and have the man of your dreams." Cara nudged her with a shoulder. "Fight for what you want, Katie. It's all you can do."

Now Jordan might turn into a hairy beast she'd have to kill. If they could somehow save him, she still didn't want to be in the background. She had a job to do.

One battle at a time. Even if they only had two nights together, Katie wanted all of him. "I want to mate him."

"Then do it."

Boots stomped on the ground behind them. They turned around to see Janie zip up her coat. "Mom? Stupid Garrett got all mad and threw Charlie across the room. He's all bloody now from fangs."

Cara jumped to her feet. "Who's bloody?"

Janie rolled her eyes. "Garrett cut his mouth with his new fangs. Charlie is fine but will probably never kiss me again."

Cara shook her head, clearly trying to make sense of the conversation. "You kissed Charlie?"

"Yeah. And Garrett's fangs came in. Dork."

Cara hustled toward the door. "Does your father know you kissed a panther?"

Janie snorted. "Considering Charlie is still alive . . . no."

Cara chortled, a small grin playing on her face. "We may need a tranquilizer gun. I'll take care of it."

"Funny." Janie grinned.

Katie wasn't so sure Cara had been joking. A dart gun seemed like a wise move.

Cara sobered. "I'm checking on your brother, and then we're having a talk." Muttering to herself, she disappeared from view.

Janie huffed out a breath, gliding forward to sit on the bench. "Great. Another sex talk."

Katie laughed, sliding an arm around the girl. "So, your first kiss, huh?"

Janie blushed. "Yeah. The kiss was nice . . . but I kept thinking of Zane."

"Been there, done that, girlfriend." If Katie could spare Janie from the Zane-crush, she'd do so in a heartbeat. "Don't let a guy you may never see again ruin your happiness right now."

"I'm psychic. I don't know how, I don't know when, but I will see him someday."

The words sent a chill down Katie's spine. "Things very rarely work out the way you think they will, sweetheart. Psychic or not. You know the future changes daily."

"Yep." Janie snuggled closer. "So, you and Jordan, huh?"

Katie stiffened. What? Could the girl smell Jordan on her? Wait a minute. Janie wasn't a shifter, she couldn't—

"Man, stop thinking so hard. You're hurting my head." Janie giggled. "Sometimes I just know stuff, remember? I mean, I don't get images or pictures in my head, so don't worry about that."

Katie gave a strangled cough.

Janie kicked out her feet. "Though now I've seen a naked shifter, I kinda wonder if they all look so good."

"What?" Katie froze. "I mean . . . what?"

Janie rubbed her nose. "Charlie shifted when Garrett attacked him. Shredded his clothes. I gotta say, great body . . . but penises are weird."

Katie's left eye began to spasm. "Uh-huh."

"Can I ask you a question?"

Only if it had nothing to do with penises. "Sure."

"What's it like when the guy you *really* like . . . actually likes you back?"

Katie bit back the sarcastic jibe about Jordan. Janie had so much longing in her young voice, Katie had to be truthful. "Well, at first you don't believe it because it's too good to be true. Then you don't want to believe it because it must be a trick. Then you do believe it, but it turns out to be different than you'd always thought."

Janie sighed, turning to the ocean. "Why is life so confusing?"

"Why indeed." With a matching sigh, Katie followed her gaze, but the ocean provided no answers.

Jordan kicked the punching bag, sending it flying across the wide gym. Irritation had him snarling. Even with funds so low from the war, Dage should create a better fucking workout area.

He'd slept with Katie. Pivoting, he slammed a fist into a second bag. Told her he loved her. Jesus. The fact that she didn't say the words back wasn't lost on him. Another kick, and the second bag tore in two.

"Stop breaking things." Conn strode into the room, hands in his faded jeans.

"Facilities suck." Jordan grabbed a towel off the thick mat to wipe his forehead.

"Want to talk about it?"

Jesus, no. "Why don't you go get your mate so you have something to do?"

"My mate has work to do in Ireland. I have work to do here." Conn's voice stayed even.

Guilt swamped Jordan. His shoulders slumped. Conn remained behind so he could either save him or kill him. "I'm sorry."

Conn shrugged and leaned back against the wall, keeping his flak boots off the mats. "Right now you're the least of my worries. Any chance the shifter headquarters in Western Virginia needs a visit from Talen?"

"We want to get rid of Talen?"

"A shifter kissed Janie."

Jordan jerked his head. "She's too young to kiss."

Irritation swirled in Conn's eyes. "She'll be sixteen in a week. When did I become the voice of reason around here?" He kicked a medicine ball. The heavy leather crashed against the far wall and returned, zinging by Jordan's head.

Jordan cracked a smile. "Reason suits you. Tell me the guy wasn't a wolf shifter."

"Nope. Feline. Panther."

"Well, that's okay then." Jordan eyed his friend. His best friend. Tension lines cut into Conn's face, his shoulders seemed stiff. The guy could use a brawl. Jordan opened his mouth to offer when Dage's voice came over the speaker in the far wall.

"Conn, Jordan, get to control room one. Now."

They didn't pause. Loping into a jog, Jordan followed Conn through corridors and down three flights of stairs, deeper in the earth. If the king wanted to meet in his private control room, something was very, very wrong.

They arrived in unison with Kane, Talen, and Max, who had been Dage's primary bodyguard until taking over Janie's protection. The door shut, locks sliding soundly into place.

Tension and power filled the small room. A large table sat abandoned to the side, but nobody moved toward the various chairs. They stood by the control panel near the entrance. Jordan tucked his hands in his sweats, resting against the side wall. Silence pounded around them.

Dage punched in keys on the panel and two men took shape on a large wall screen.

"Jesus," Conn breathed.

Caleb Donovan, a vampire prophet, and Kellach Dunne, a witch enforcer, barely held each other up, leaning against a black stone wall.

Blood cascaded from Caleb's eyes and nose. It flowed out his ears to mat in his long brown hair. He opened his mouth to speak. Blood poured out. He staggered, and Kell shoved them both against the wall.

Kell's head swiveled. The flesh on his face flayed open from inside, veins and shards of bone sticking out through the flowing blood. His black eyes were a mottled red.

Caleb spit out blood. "Demons attacked. We lost—" He bent over, a rattling cough shaking his huge chest. Kell held on to him, then helped him to straighten.

Nausea rolled in Jordan's gut. The demons fought with mind control—misfiring neurons in the brain until the victim bled out or went stark raving mad. They could also force horrible images inside until the person couldn't distinguish between reality and illusion. It was a miracle the two men were still functioning.

Caleb coughed blood. "Jase."

Talen and Conn stepped forward as one, concern for their youngest brother obvious. "Where is he?"

"Demons." Caleb fell to the ground.

Kellach swayed, blood pouring from his hairline and down his face. "I'm sorry." Then he dropped out of range.

Jordan tried to stamp his temper down. Harsh breathing filled the control room around him. The men stared at the stone wall in the screen, and nobody moved.

Finally, an angry female voice echoed. "What the hell are they doing in here? Get them back to the infirmary, now."

Rioting red curls and sparking green eyes came into view. Moira Kayrs, Conn's petite mate and tough witch, took a deep breath. "The demons attacked a settlement outside of Durness in Scotland where Caleb, Kell, and Jase were providing support. We heard of the attack and arrived in time for these two, but Jase was gone. We're going after him in an hour."

"The fuck you are." Conn stepped toward the screen. "Stay where you are until I arrive."

Moira shook her head. "They hurt an enforcer, Conn. I'm an enforcer, too, as you well know." She straightened her shoulders. "Have your people had any luck in finding a demon destroyer? Or five?"

Conn stepped closer to the camera. "No. My guess is they've all died out. The demons probably took care of anybody who could combat their mind games years ago."

Moira bit her lip. "That doesn't work with my idea of the world. There has to be an enhanced human somewhere who can beat the demons."

Jordan had had his people searching the globe for a demon destroyer since the damn demons had entered the war. Enhanced females lived on earth with psychic, empathic, and other abilities . . . women who could mate with immortals. One such group could actually mind battle demons. While he wished a person existed who could counter the demons' cruelty, he was with Conn. The demons had taken them all out.

Moira sighed, turning her attention to Dage. "Ah, king. I guess I should give you the rest of the bad news."

"Which is?" Dage's tone remained even, but a sense of raw power cascaded off him.

"We just had our first confirmation of a Virus-27 infection in a witch. Female." Irritation pursed Moira's lips. "Conn, stop that growling." She nodded to someone off-camera. "Apparently only vampires and demons with their extra chromosomes are safe from this bugger."

Dage shook his head. "I figured since there hasn't been an infection in your people in ten years, you were safe."

Green power began to dance along Moira's exposed skin. "We've kept very strong protocols in place—anyone who has followed them has remained safe. This woman, girl really, didn't follow them. Somehow the Kurjans gained access to infect her. I'll find out how." Sorrow filled her eyes. "For now, I'll go find your brother."

"Dailtín"—Conn's voice dropped to pure warning—"what is the constant reality we live by?"

Moira frowned, and then her green eyes warmed. "I do love it when you call me 'brat.' " She sighed. "The world starts with the two of us . . . and spirals out." A pretty grin lit her face. "We're a pair, Conn."

He nodded. "So you'll wait for me before heading into battle."

She lifted her chin, the grin widening. "Then you'd better hurry, mate." The screen went blank.

Dage yanked a gun out of his waist to toss on the table. Two knives followed. "Conn, I'll teleport you to Moira right now. Talen, you take the jet—go directly to Durness." He focused on Kane.

Kane settled his stance. "I'm going. Emma can handle the lab work here—there isn't anything else I can do."

Dage frowned.

"I'm going. I'll sense him before any of you do—as you well know." Kane's voice stayed calm, but a hard core of determination echoed in the tone.

Jordan scratched his head. Most vampires had special powers, and he'd never wondered about Kane. Being the smartest person on the planet seemed special enough. Guess not. There was more to the scientist than he'd figured.

Dage nodded. "Fine. You go with Talen on the jet. Max, you're in charge until I get back." He turned toward Jordan. "I need you to protect headquarters and keep from turning into a werewolf."

"I'll do my best." Jordan lifted an eyebrow at Max.

The massive vampire crossed his arms and nodded, his light brown eyes somber. He'd kill Jordan if necessary.

A chill swept down Jordan's spine. Hopefully the protector would make sure Jordan was actually a werewolf before beheading him. "I'll send for backup. We have soldiers we can call on."

"Good." Conn cleared his throat. "Jordan—"

"Me, too." Jordan nodded. The right words to say good-bye to a lifelong friend didn't truly exist. "Go. I'll be here when you get back."

"I know." Emotion shot silver through Conn's green eyes.

Dage reached for Conn. "Let's go." The two disappeared.

Kane retrieved the discarded weapons. "We need to hurry. Transporting Conn will seriously weaken Dage."

Talen nodded and clapped Jordan on the back. "Good luck."

"You, too." God, he hoped they found Jase. The idea of the fun-loving brother being tortured by demons made Jordan's head pound. And he hoped he'd beat the moon and see his friend again. Something told him it wasn't going to be that easy.

Chapter 17

At yet another Kurjan encampment miles south of the last one, Kalin leaned against a pine tree and out of the rain. Night had arrived quietly. Clouds filled the sky, so the werewolves were easier to handle. Even so, they tilted their heads up, wailing softly as if they knew the celestial light hid out of reach.

Except for Jack.

Jack sat on a fallen tree, his legs extended, the rain matting his fur. He kept his yellow gaze on the trees to the north, ears up.

Interesting. Intense focus had ridden the werewolf all day. Well, from Kalin's vantage point in the secure building, it had seemed Jack had been preoccupied. When was Kalin's uncle going to find the cure for sunlight? He was so tired of living in darkness.

Though he and Roy had found some fun before dawn. A group of women they'd stalked and terrorized through a town to the east. Unfortunately, the sun had begun to rise, so they had to end the game and head home.

He kept his gaze on the creature, welcoming the cold bite of wind carrying rain.

Jack sprang to his feet. Hair bristled all down his back. Emitting a growl, he took a step toward a stand of silent Douglas firs.

Kalin settled his hand around the top of the electric prod. Movement filtered through the thick trees. He sidled away from the pine, searching the recesses of the forest.

A werewolf limped into the clearing. Broad across the chest, taller than Jack, the brute bled from his neck and shoulder. His yellow eyes took in the werewolves on the ground, Jack, and finally Kalin.

Jack growled, muscles bunching.

"Stop." Kalin sidled into the wet brush, keeping Jack between him and the newcomer. Rain smashed into his face. "Fall in!"

The werewolves scrambled into position behind Jack. After years of torture, starvation, and rewards, the beasts had finally learned the score. They deserved to have some fun. Kalin waited for the new werewolf to attack.

Yet the monster kept his gaze on Kalin. The werewolf angled his head to the side, sniffing the air. "Kurrrrjaaaaan."

Kalin froze. He exhaled. "Say that again."

The animal curled its upper lip. "Kurrrrjaaaaan. You. Kurrrrjaaaaan."

So, this was new. Kalin rubbed his chin. "Yes. Apparently you can speak." Made sense. Jack had evolved in the short time Kalin had been training him. Evolution included speech. The new creature must've been infected years ago. "You have a name?"

"Brennnt."

Jack shuffled his feet, looking over his shoulder at Kalin. Waiting for the attack command.

Kalin needed to call Erik with the update. The breeze picked up, carrying the scent of wet dog, rain, and . . . shifter. "You been in a fight, Brent?"

"Yesss. Wanted Kaattieee. Vampires got in way." Brent surveyed Jack head to toe. With a shrug of indifference, he turned back to Kalin. "Kaattieee mine. Not Jordan's. Jordan bad. Katie miiiine."

Milton jumped out of the building to the side, and Kalin motioned him to stay still. No need to spook the beast. "Are you talking about Jordan Pride?" Wasn't the infected lioness named Katie? His sources claimed she was Pride's mate. "Pride has been infected by the virus." While Kalin hadn't been there at the time, he'd read the reports. The leader of the lions would soon turn into a hairy beast.

"Yes. Jordan baaaaad." Brent howled, the sound full of pain and anger. "Killed me. Killed my brother. Needs tooooo die."

Kalin clucked his tongue. "Well, we are hitting Realm Headquarters tomorrow. The moon is full soon, you know." They had over a hundred miles to travel in preparation, and he needed the werewolves steady. He tightened his hold on the deadly prod. "But we're only taking the best. You're injured." Tilting his head, he gave Jack a nod.

With a yowl from hell, Jack sprang.

Brent pivoted, much too quickly for an animal, and shot a sidekick into Jack's gut. An actual sidekick.

Kalin frowned. The implications of the beast's development were staggering.

Two more animals rushed Brent, and he clapped their heads together. The sound of melons bursting echoed through the rain. Thunder rumbled in the distance, matching the roar from the monster.

Jack scrambled off the ground, fury turning his eyes red.

Just as he bunched to lunge, Kalin let out a short whistle. All eyes turned to him. "Enough." Jerking his head toward Brent, he let his fangs drop. "You'll do. There's meat coming for you—get your strength back. I have plans for you, friend."

The werewolf shook rain off his fur. "I'll helllpp. But Jordaaaan mine."

"Fair enough." Kalin nodded for Milton to fetch the raw meat. "Talen Kayrs is mine."

His second returned with many Kurjans pushing wheelbarrows of raw meat and blood toward the beasts. Jack grabbed his own and wheeled over to a tree, turning his back on Brent. Kalin fought the urge to roll his eyes. The werewolf was put out.

Wiping rain off his brow, Kalin stalked toward the windowless building where he and the other Kurjans laid low during the day. Quick movements had him inside and down a flight of stairs to his private quarters. A panic room of all panic rooms, no sunlight could get in. Even if fire consumed the first floor, he had a way out.

Locking his door, he stretched his neck and wrung out his black/red hair. He'd dyed the mass all black as a kid, thinking he'd look human. Turned out he didn't want to look human.

Shrugging off his jacket, he dropped to the bunk. The cheap springs protested. Besides the bed, a dingy night table and coat rack adorned the room. Dirt covered the floor, and Sheetrock made up the walls. Well, except for the one area where he could escape if necessary.

After he took out Realm Headquarters, he was heading for luxury. Somewhere he could hunt for days on end—maybe a female shifter or two. Or a witch. He'd love to find a good female witch to hunt and destroy. Now that'd be a worthwhile game. He'd never fucked a witch. Or a demon. Female demons were almost impossible to find considering they were so few and far between. Man, finding and battling one would be a good time.

With a sigh, he reached under the mattress to drag out a battered sketch pad and flip over the cover.

"Hello, Janie." Sketch after sketch of the intriguing female flipped by as he ran through the pages. Janie as a little girl who had let him into her dreams. Janie as a woman—beautiful with such intuition in her blue eyes. He might not have her psychic powers, but the future sometimes granted him a glimpse.

He paused at a page where he'd drawn her as a teenager. Probably what she looked like that very day. Running a finger down her pert nose, he frowned.

The girl was likely at headquarters. Oddly enough, he had no interest in meeting her. Yet.

Kurjan oracles had declared Janet Kayrs the key to the future—the key to the future for them all. If she was at headquarters, he'd have to kidnap her. The question of where to put her had kept him awake for several nights. He wanted nothing to do with a teenaged human girl.

They were destined, and when the time was right, when she reached adulthood and could fight him, then he'd take her.

The idea that he'd have to protect her until then provided an irony that had him clenching his teeth together. As prophesied, she'd be in danger, even from his people, until he made his claim. Something he had no intention of doing until she could provide some challenge. Once she became a woman, she'd have impressive strength and make the battle worth his time.

As a child, she'd tried to be his friend. Even worse, she'd tempted him to be something he wasn't. To be decent. Some days, when his shoulders slumped, when his gut ached from training, when exhaustion made him sway on his feet, he could almost see the road he hadn't taken. Almost wish. For that, she would one day pay.

Dearly.

Chapter 18

Katie jumped into Baye's arms for a huge, feline hug. Seconds later, Lance engulfed her in a quick hug before handing her over to Noah and Mac. Family. They'd arrived to help protect headquarters while the Kayrs brothers had gone after one of their own. She'd rushed out to meet them, squiring them to the room where she, Maggie, and Janie had played pool.

But maybe that had been a mistake. Every time she looked at a pool table, she thought of Jase. She and the vampire had often played billiards when in the same town. Fear and anger swirled down deep in her stomach. Jase Kayrs was a friend, and she'd do anything to get him back. "Let's kick the crap out of this virus, and then we'll go hunting Jase."

Baye nodded. "Ah, we researched your dating history. No more victims than the three men we talked about."

Thank God. Though she'd always feel guilt about those three. "Thanks for researching them. I can't believe Brent and his brother actually killed those poor men."

"I know. I'm sorry I couldn't help Jordan end David." Baye tugged her hair. "Right now we need to meet with Jordan about Noah's, I mean . . ."

Noah frowned, fighting a snarl. He stood taller than his brothers, a century older, and tougher than anybody Katie had ever met. But the shifter had taught her to dance when she was ten, and she had a soft spot for the enforcer. His hair was cool and multicolored, his eyes an odd green. It was a wonder some female hadn't chained him yet.

Katie gave him another hug. She knew, without a doubt, Noah only agreed to lead out of a sense of duty. The powerful lion thrived on the front lines. "I'll show Lance around." The tiger belonged to a different clan, and internal mountain lion matters didn't interest or concern him.

Plus, she didn't want to talk about Jordan moving on.

The brothers took off, leaving her in the playroom with Lance.

He rolled his shoulders. "Let's go outside. Being this close to the ocean makes me twitchy, but I'd like to hear the waves after riding in a plane all day."

She nodded, showing him through the main lodge to the quiet courtyard. Lifting her head, she tuned in her senses. No predators existed nearby. Well, no predators that weren't allies, anyway.

Lance loped toward the cliff, his large hands in faded jeans, tight muscles shifting beneath a Saints T-shirt. "I can smell Pride on you."

The ocean churned gray and restless far below, spraying against jagged rocks. Embarrassment clogged her throat. Katie hunched her shoulders. "We didn't mate."

"I know." Lance eyed her from the corner of his eye, the blue darker than usual. "There's a good chance you'll turn into a werewolf if you mate. The idea of my having to hunt you down makes me sick to my stomach."

She closed her eyes. "I know. But what if mating saves him?"

"Mate me."

Her eyes flipped open. Surprise had her facing the tiger. "What?"

"You have the virus, but for some reason, just can't

shift. I think if you mated a *healthy* shifter, you'd regain your ability." He pivoted toward her, both hands clasping her arms. "When you left, I realized how much I enjoy being around you. I don't want to lose you, Kate."

"But"—shock froze her in place—"you've never, I mean, we've never—"

"Baye and I talked about saving you. He sees you as a kid still. I've only known you as an adult." Lance's sharp cheekbones created interesting hollows below them, giving him the look of a tiger. His gaze wandered her face. A masculine scent of sweet grass and spruce wafted from him. His voice lowered. "I see you as all woman."

Warmth slid down her spine. The guy was still in love with a psychologist and refused to take a chance after everyone he'd lost. She sighed. "I appreciate you and Baye trying to save me, possibly sacrificing yourselves for me, but how is that any different from my trying to help Jordan?" Belonging had her lips lifting in a smile. Lance and Baye were good friends . . . willing to do anything for her. Even mate for life. But they didn't love her.

Lance shook his head. "The virus is different in males, and you know it. I can save you. You mating Jordan will kill you." His hands tightened. "We could be really good together."

God spare her from sweet shifters trying to save her for her own good. "You're still hurting from losing Linda." Katie forced a gentle smile. "You and I don't love each other."

"Love's overrated." Lance's gaze dropped to her lips. "We have friendship, trust, and we're both sexy as hell." His grin lightened his face.

She chuckled. "If you so modestly say so."

"I do." Pain vibrated from him. "When I lost my squad, I almost went crazy. You know that." The breeze lifted his hair, highlighting his feline bone structure. "I can't lose you, too."

She nodded. The war had been hell for them all. "Mating isn't the answer for us, Lance."

"We're a match." He cocked his head to the side. "Haven't you wondered? I mean, even a little?"

Her cheeks heated. Of course she'd wondered. After hunts, after the guys shifted back to human, she'd seen them nude. Powerful and strong . . . and yeah, sexy. "I'm flattered." She spoke the truth. Lance's thick hair slid around his shoulders, making those blue eyes stand out. Tall, broad, and so male, a woman couldn't help but look.

But her heart had belonged to Jordan Pride since he'd rescued her as a cub.

She shook her head. "I'm on my path." Right or wrong, she'd chosen to risk all for the lion leader.

"I can't accept that." Emotion echoed in the tiger's tone. "The world is a better place with you causing havoc in it." He yanked her into a granite-hard body, his mouth sliding down atop hers.

Shock kept her immobile.

Warm, seductive, he wandered his lips across hers. One hand released her arm to slide around her waist, tugging her even closer.

For one second, temptation flirted with her to dive in, to kiss him back. But curiosity wasn't a good enough reason to screw up her future, or to hurt him. So she pushed both hands against his chest, turning her face to the side.

He fought her for two heartbeats, trying to press the issue. Finally, he paused, exhaling loudly. "Are you sure?"

"Yes." She kept her gaze on the grass.

A warm knuckle lifted her chin to face him. He released her arm and grimaced. "Fine. Just promise me you won't turn into a beast."

"I won't." Hopefully. But now she needed to make arrangements for someone else to take her out if she did end up a werewolf. The job couldn't fall to anyone in her family or squad. Especially Lance or Baye. "You kiss well."

"Shut up." His grin banished the rest of her worries. "I'm even better at the other stuff, but now you've blown your chance."

She bit the inside of her lip. "I have no doubt you're amazing at the other stuff." With any luck, she'd still be around when Lance found a mate and had his world rocked for the right reasons and not to erase the pain of the past. Or not because he wanted to sacrifice himself for a friend.

Sure, she was doing the same thing. Love made the difference. It had to.

Lance tucked a friendly arm around her shoulder. "Come on. I'll kick your butt at pool while we wait for Baye to finish his meeting." He cleared his throat. "This didn't happen."

"What didn't?" She grinned, allowing him to lead her back inside.

Jordan had the oddest sense of bringing his prom date home an hour late as he faced the three enforcers across the polished conference table. His three enforcers. The Chance brothers had protected Jordan's back since day one of his becoming leader of the feline clans. All at least a hundred years older than him, they'd followed orders and defended their people using any means necessary. Right now they looked at him with varying degrees of irritation.

He cleared his throat. "I've publicly endorsed Noah as the next leader." Hopefully he wasn't signing the cougar's

death warrant. "Though I can guarantee you'll be challenged. At least once."

Noah shrugged.

The enforcers continued to stare.

On all that was holy. He so didn't need this crap. "Fine.
I didn't mate her. What the hell do you want?"

"Why not?" Baye snarled.

Jordan frowned. They were pissed he hadn't mated
Katie? "Come on. If I mate her, I could kill her. I mean,
the virus might kill her."

"Or save you both," Noah muttered.

Mac pursed his lips. The middle brother, he had lighter
hair and darker eyes than the other two—and was by far
the wildest lion in history. "Though, I get you not wanting to sacrifice her. I mean, it's Katie."

"She can make her own decisions." Baye shoved back in
his chair. "Little Katie is all grown up. I've seen her
fight . . . even with the virus slowing her down, she's
tough. Strong mentally. You're lucky to have her."

"I know she's strong." Jordan took a deep breath. "Listen, tomorrow night isn't going to be good. And I wanted
to say . . . I mean . . . well—"

"Jesus, Jordan. We love you, too." Noah snarled more
than said the words. "You're not going to die. I haven't
followed you for three centuries just to watch you turn
into a beast."

"Why have you?" Shit. It was the absolute last question
Jordan thought he'd ever ask. Deep down, he'd always
wondered. After the way he'd gained leadership, he figured one day Noah would challenge him. Not stick by
him to the end.

Noah growled. Mac frowned. Baye stared. "You're
family," they said in unison, the different timbers of their
voices melding deep.

Air coughed out of his lungs in disbelief. "No, I'm not." He'd lost all his family the day he'd killed Brent Bomant.

Noah got the look he had right before he punched his fist through someone's face.

Jordan tensed just in case he needed to block the blow.

"We became family the day the three of us vowed to be your protectors." Noah spoke slowly, unusual emotion in his deep eyes. "You've done a good job—put our people back together after the last war. Got most feline nations unified under one leadership. Nobody else in the world could've healed our people so completely."

Yeah, but he hadn't ruled with charm and promises. There had been blood and bruises, too. "I didn't do it alone."

"No. And it's good you finally realize that." Baye stood. "I'm going to check on Katie and then meet the king to go over the battle plans. I have faith in you—always have. If there's a way to beat the moon tonight, you'll do it. When you head up to the surface to prepare, I'll meet you." With a nod to Noah, he strode from the room.

Mac followed suit, leaving Jordan with Noah.

Noah leaned back. "So Kane can't cure the virus?"

"No." Jordan fought despair down, setting his jaw. "I may need you to kill me when the time comes." With Conn across the world, he'd rather have Noah do it than Max. Not that Max wasn't capable, Jordan just didn't know the vampire as well as he knew Noah.

Noah's eyes were a deep, catlike green. They darkened with emotion and sorrow. "Not a problem." He ground a palm into his eye. "You're family, Jordan. Always have been. You don't have to do any of this alone."

Jordan studied his friend. He'd kept himself aloof, kept himself alone because he figured that was the price of leading. The price he had to pay. "I know."

"No, you don't." Noah rolled to his feet. "I know what

you did, what you had to do for the good of our people. Let the past go. You'll never keep that lioness, virus or not, if you don't let her in. Even if you only have a short time, isn't every second worth taking?" He paused near the door, his back to Jordan. "I had a woman once. I lost her and would give anything for just one good day. Just one."

Without another word, the feline enforcer slipped out the door.

Jordan sat back in the chair, his mind reeling. How could he not even know the name of the woman Noah missed? He'd kept himself so distant he couldn't even consider himself Noah's friend. The shifter's words echoed in Jordan's head. He closed his eyes, his hands clenching as memories flashed through him so quickly his brain ached.

Three hundred years ago, Jordan had intercepted Brent at the docks, taking him deep into the forest. His cousin had grown even bigger, though some of that was all belly. Apparently Brent had been enjoying a lot of ale, as well.

Jordan cleared his throat as they neared the clearing where his fate would be decided. Pine trees surrounded them, all creatures deadly quiet in their depths. Small prey always sensed predators in their midst, as well as tension and an inevitable battle. "I truly am sorry about your parents, Brent."

Brent had pivoted, his eyes a burnt amber. "And yours. I know Kayrs moved headquarters to the center of, well, nothing . . . but why are we in the forest, Jordan?" Peering down from at least four inches of additional height, the shifter flashed sharp teeth.

"I need to know. What are your plans for the feline nation?" Jordan's breath hitched on the question.

Irritation curled Brent's lip. Tall, broad across the chest, the raw-boned shifter's lumpy features reddened. "If you must know, I plan to sign a treaty with the Kurjans. There is no other choice."

Jordan's foot caught on a root and he stumbled. Fire and anger rippled through his muscles as he righted himself. If that were true, Brent might've arrived to kill Dage. "The Kurjans will turn on you . . . on all of us. We need to align with the Realm."

Brent snarled. "I'm the new leader, and I will bind us as I see fit." He paused at the clearing, anticipation cascading from him. "Unless you plan to challenge me?"

"I hereby issue said challenge." The words hurt to say, but determination welled strong within him. Jordan turned to face the only family he had left on earth. "Just between us."

Brent circled around. "That's new."

"Yes. The nation is in enough turmoil . . . there's no need to show our enemies we're not solid." Jordan casually sniffed the air to see if Conn's scent rode the breeze and just smelled pine and wet moss. Apparently the vampire had set up downwind and far enough away as to be undetectable.

Brent scanned the area. "We fight to the death, then."

"Yes." Jordan would need to get the larger man down to the ground. He'd probably be Brent's size someday, but not for decades, and the ground would level the fight.

"I have no problem killing you." Brent shrugged off his jacket, his gaze piercing. "I want your word that the victor will lead our people. I know you've aligned with the Kayrs family . . . I want your word they won't take me out after I kill you."

Jordan stared Brent right in the eyes during a moment that would change him forever. "You have my word."

The fight was brutal and took hours. They started as men . . . and finished as mountain lions. When it was over, when Brent was dead, Jordan had shifted to human, bloody and hurt.

Conn jogged up, darkness in his eyes. "Sit down. I'll bury him."

"No." Jordan struggled to remain on his feet. The haunted look in his friend's eyes belonged on Jordan's shoulders. While Conn hadn't had to kill Brent, he'd resolved to do so . . . which was something he'd never escape.

Rulers ruled alone . . . or their loved ones got hurt. Jordan would never again make the mistake of involving someone he cared about in business. "I'll bury him. It's my job."

Footsteps outside the conference room yanked Jordan back into the present. Maybe he hadn't needed to isolate himself to such a degree. Either way, it was probably too late to worry about it. His problem remained the same today as it had three hundred years ago.

Brent Bomant had to die.

Katie leaned against the door of the lab, seeking another update. She'd been sure the new cure would work in Jordan's blood . . . it had just needed more time. Her breath caught in her chest as the queen turned around.

Emma scanned the newest results. "There's no change."

Disappointment burned on the way down. Katie tried to breathe. "There's still time."

The queen's eyes dimmed. "Probably not. Anytime we've manipulated a substance with magic, the change has been almost instant. If this concoction worked, we'd already know it. I'm so sorry, Kate."

Katie nodded, pain sliding through her skin like sand in a bottle. So much hurt filled her she forced a smile. "I'll be back later." Pivoting, she walked with measured steps down the hallway.

No cure existed for the werewolf virus.

Everybody had been trying to warn her, but she couldn't let hope die. She found her way to Jordan's quarters and slipped inside. Silence and a sense of emptiness surrounded her. He was probably arranging for one of the Kayrs men to kill him once he turned into a werewolf.

Stumbling past the small table and sofa area, her vision graying, she limped into the bedroom and curled up on the bed. Jordan's scent surrounded her with what could have been. With what might have been.

She wanted to let the tears fall, but her spirit had gone dry.

Cotton failed to soothe as she tucked her body around his pillow.

He'd told her he loved her.

Jordan didn't lie. The man loved her. Yet she hadn't returned the words. The idea of saying them with death so near had caught the truth in her throat. And yeah. He'd surprised her. Dreams didn't have words. Yet he'd found some.

Her dreams had always included him. Even while lying to herself, trying to move on, she'd harbored the hope of their future. Deep down at her core, she'd believed.

Fate smashed hope and belief into splinters of nothingness.

Fear that he'd see her feelings as a silly crush, or worse yet, have pity on her had kept her distant from him for ten years. An entire decade had passed when she could've been with him.

And now, Jordan was accepting fate. He was going to leave her all alone again.

She flashed back to the moment she'd first shifted as a small child, scared beyond belief and running alone in the woods. If anything, the woods and the world were much scarier today than they'd ever been.

And he was going to leave her alone again.

At the thought, fire welled up in her with a strength that had her sitting up. Fuck that. Fuck fate. And fuck Jordan, too.

Katie had absolutely nothing left to lose. She did, however, have one last chance to save him. Sure, it might kill them both. Or anger Jordan to the point that he hated her. She could live with the hate, if it saved him.

With a quick punch to the pillow, she shot to her feet. She could either lie back and let fate decide, or embrace the dark.

Life truly was all or nothing.

Chapter 19

Out of the whipping rain, Katie stood at the entrance of headquarters, peering from under a New Orleans Privateers hat. The clouds shot across the sky, revealing and then hiding the moon, the storm never pausing. She tilted her head for a better sense, nodding when no vibrations came back. Brent and any others of his kind remained too far away to feel.

The safety wouldn't last, of that she was sure. The moon would be full the next night, and if Brent attacked again, he'd strike under its power.

But for tonight, the forest around them remained clear. The snipers had headed indoors after making sure the area was secure. They weren't needed outside tonight in the storm. The folks could sleep peacefully in the earth one more night.

She double-checked her readings. Now that she'd decided on a path, no emotion clouded her mind. "I don't sense anyone."

Jordan lounged against the rock, not touching her. Dressed in a black T-shirt and cargo pants, he looked as impenetrable as the rocks around them. They stood less than a foot apart, but the distance felt like miles. "I'm betting we see some action with the full moon tomorrow."

He peered into the darkness. "Yeah. The woods are safe tonight."

Anticipation and an odd inevitability hinted in his low tone. The man was planning on going out strong, taking out werewolves before losing himself.

That's what he thought. Thunder rolled high and loud. Katie jumped and then cleared her throat. There had to be a way to get through to him. He was the most honest person she knew and wouldn't play coy even if he could figure out how. "Did you mean what you said earlier?"

His eyes darkened. He sucked in air. "Yes."

Her smile came unbidden. "You don't sound happy about that."

"I'm not." He scrubbed both hands down his face. "I have twenty-four hours until I go over completely. Telling you I loved you was a mistake."

At least he didn't call the actual fact of loving her a mistake. "I kissed Lance." Well, Lance had kissed her, but close enough. She wanted a reaction from Jordan, and she'd get it.

Fire shimmered along his skin. "Katie, come on." Then he lifted his head ever so slightly. His nostrils flared.

So far, he was keeping an admirable hold on his impressive temper. She'd need him to unleash for her plan to work. "I want all of you, Jordan." Her voice stayed soft, but the guy had animal hearing.

"You have all of me."

"Bullshit." Something inside of her enjoyed the flash of warning that lit his eyes. He'd always hated when she swore. "While I thought you were a good fuck, you didn't give me all of you."

His chin lowered. "What's your goal here, kitten?"

Leave it to Jordan to cut right to the issue. "What do

you mean?" Unlike the leader of the lions, she had no problem playing coy.

"You're trying to piss me off, and for the world of me, I can't figure out why."

Because Cara had told her to challenge him. "Cowards piss me off."

"You're calling me a coward?" He sounded more be- mused than angry.

Okay, this wasn't going according to plan. Well, if all else failed. "The sex was just fine, Jordan. I know you're not feeling a hundred percent lately."

His eyebrows lifted. "*Just fine?*"

"Well, yeah. I mean you're cranky tonight, obviously, and I figured you might be stressed about what happened between us. It was . . . nice. Really, really nice."

He studied her like she was trapped in a slide under Emma's microscope. "So *nice* you screamed out my name each time. Four times, to be exact."

"I know." She lowered her voice to something sooth- ing. "So stop worrying about it. I mean, you'll move on, and I'll learn the really hot stuff from Lance." She bit her lip. "Or maybe Terrent Vilks. I've heard wolves are crazy wild."

"Katie." Jordan's voice cut like a whip. "Stop it."

"Stop what?"

He rolled his eyes. "Stop trying to make me mad. This isn't going to work."

The clouds chose that moment to part a sliver, allowing the moon to shine through the rain. He lifted his head, a low rumbling spilling from his chest.

Well, if words wouldn't do it, she had one card left to play. Twisting her body, she shot a sidekick to his knee. With a muffled *oof,* he went down, surprise lighting his face. Jumping, she kicked him square in the temple. His head bounced off the rock with a sickening thud.

With a gasp, she ran. She dodged left, then right, having scouted her path earlier.

A shiver wound across her torso to land in her abdomen. She probably had less than a minute until Jordan recovered and came after her. The rain pelted down, soaking her white T-shirt and ripped jeans. Her tennis shoes squished in the mud as she jogged. No sense making this easy on him.

God, she hoped this wasn't a huge mistake.

She yanked the bill of her cap lower to shield her eyes. Thunder complained high and loud. Lightning flashed across the sky, turning the clouds a light gray for the briefest of moments. The ocean churned far below.

Panting, she leaned against a tree, allowing the boughs to protect her somewhat.

Jordan's bellow rose over the storm. Calling her name. Oh yeah. The lion was angry.

Gingerly, quietly, Katie headed deeper into the forest. This was all or nothing. God, she hoped it was something. Using all the training he'd given her, she tried to avoid leaving signs. Rain dripped off her hat. Wet clothes molded to her skin. Wind smashed into her body. She shivered.

The hair on the back of her neck prickled. She turned around only to see dark forest. Pivoting, she hurried the other way. Every instinct she owned clamored she was being stalked.

Several quick turns and she stopped cold. Jordan stood between two trees, clothes plastered to his hard body, his hair long and wild in the wind. But those eyes. Nearly glowing in the dim light, something more than lion.

She hadn't thought about the emerging werewolf inside him. The lion would never hurt her. The werewolf . . . who knew?

Thunder roared, and she jumped.

"Why did you kick me?" Low, guttural, the primal tone cut through the storm.

"Because sniveling, fucking cowards should be put down and out of their misery," she yelled over the increasing wind.

The animal shimmered under his skin. Anger, deep and primal, harnessed and rode the breeze.

She took a step back. Water from her bill dropped onto her nose. This was more than Jordan. Fear caught in her throat. "Jordan, I—"

"One chance, Kathryn." His voice didn't even sound like him. "Turn and go back to headquarters. Now."

Doing so would end any chance she had of mating him. Of saving him. But did she have the courage to face whatever he was becoming? Moonlight slithered down, and he bared his teeth. His tight muscles seemed to vibrate in place as he held himself in check. Barely.

She took a deep breath, fear buzzing in her ears. All or nothing. "Fuck you." Pivoting, she ran in the opposite direction of headquarters.

The howl he gave was much more wolf than lion.

Desperation had her really running, turning, seeking safety. Instinct took over and she forgot her plan. Run, damnit, run.

He caught her by the nape, sending them both sprawling across the drenched trail. She bit her tongue as she landed, hands sliding in the mud. Pain flared along her skin. Flipping over, she slammed her heels into his hips, sending him flying over her head. Leaping to her feet, she bunched to run.

A thick hand banded around her ankle, yanking her down, ripping her shoe off. Panting, nearly sobbing, she kicked him in the face with her other foot. That shoe and both socks sailed through the air to join the first one.

Thick claws shot out of his hands to shred her jeans. She

yelped as he nicked her knee. Swinging wildly, she punched him in the nose. He bellowed, grabbing his face.

Rolling over, she levered to her knees and stood. Claws tore the back of her shirt. Shrugging free, she ran in her bra and underwear, the mud soaking her bare feet.

Oh God, what had she been thinking? Panting, she dodged left and right, trying to keep trees between her and the lumbering force bearing down on her. Sticks and pebbles cut into her feet. Rain beat at her face. Sure, she'd heard true claimings were bloody and brutal. Those damaged shoulders she'd seen on other mates had seemed romantic. Crazy and romantic.

This was neither. But it was real. Desire slammed through her along with fear. An odd combination, animalistic and true. They were animals, and this would happen in the wild.

She ran harder, arms pumping.

Jordan stepped onto the path before her.

She halted, sliding two feet before stopping. The rain battered down on her hat. Panting, she put both filthy hands on her knees, trying to catch her breath.

"This what you wanted, Katie?" His chest seemed broader, the tight muscles in his arms and legs more powerful. The animal shifted beneath his skin, morphing back and forth from something dark to the lion. But the man remained upright, topaz eyes blazing and a red flush high on his face.

Deep inside her, a lioness stretched awake again. Katie stood to her full height, forcing a sneer. Her knees trembled with the instinctive need to flee. Her heart pounded with the storm. But this was their only chance. She wanted all of him, even if some of that was now werewolf. "Is this all you've got?"

"You're about to see what I've got." Silky, low, the husky threat shot straight to her clit.

She edged to the side of the path, her breath panting out.

He stalked nearer, his eyes unblinking and focused solely on her face. Primitive and deadly, hunger shone in his gaze. The edge of darkness that had been shadowing him curled his lip in a snarl of determination. A preternatural stillness surrounded him, screaming *predator*.

Katie trembled. She might only be half a lion, but she deserved it all. "You want me, you take me, Jordan. You fucking *earn* me." Feinting, she lunged the other direction, pivoting to run.

He caught her by the arm, jerking her off her feet. A smack had the hat falling to the ground. Her hair tumbled down around her wet shoulders. He sucked in air. "Stop this."

She truly had no clue which one of them he was talking to. "No."

His mouth slammed down. Hard—forceful—desperate. As if he could kiss the defiance, the challenge out of her. His tongue penetrated her mouth, all male, accepting no resistance. He controlled his fangs, but their sharp points, their deadly ability remained right there.

She groaned, fire boiling through her blood. Locking her hands into his hair, she met his kiss, slamming up against his hard body. His fully clothed body. Decadence and the sense of vulnerability had her head swimming.

Then she bit his bottom lip until she tasted blood.

He shoved her away. Wiping his lip, his eyes morphed to gold. The animal inside him took precedence, rising to the surface. A casual observer wouldn't have noticed the change.

Katie was anything but casual.

She turned and ran, knowing there was no way she was getting out of the forest. Heart racing, adrenaline zipping through her blood, she fled like her life depended on it.

Which it probably did. The inevitable sound of him pursuing spurred her to flee faster.

He took her down hard.

The breath whooshed from her lungs. She stilled, hands sliding, mud splattering her neck. Sucking in air, she tried to lever up on hands and knees just as her bra went flying into the trees. Her underwear followed. Panicking, bucking against him, she fought with the intense training she'd learned over the years.

Countering every move, keeping her on her hands and knees, somehow his pants and shirt flew over her head.

A whisper of warning sounded before he grabbed her hips. His hands were rough, his hold unbreakable, his intention absolute. She struggled, fighting him, fighting the future . . . fighting herself. Tightening his hold, he roughly plunged inside her and yanked her back. Shock filled her at not only the sudden pain, but with awareness that she had been wet and ready. The lioness within roared.

The man behind her slammed into her hard, fast, and relentless. Nothing could stop him. The knowledge, the certainty of that fact had her screaming through an orgasm so powerful her heart may have stopped for a moment. Yet he continued to pound, his hands digging into her hips, his body strong and full. The storm, the pelting rain, all ceased to exist.

Leaning over, his lips enclosed her shoulder.

She tensed, closing her eyes, heart galloping. Finally. Jordan was finally going to mark her.

He struck fast, fangs digging past muscle and tendons to embed in bone.

Agony consumed her. Her cry echoed through the storm. She bowed her back, struggling, fighting against the incredible pain. He held on tighter, pounding harder.

Oh God. The shared, secret, twisted smiles of the female felines who had mated became clear to her. It wasn't the fact that they'd found their mates—it was the fact that they'd survived the damn mating that they wore like a badge of honor. Katie coughed out a sob.

Jordan released her hips, sliding both hands beneath her to cup her breasts. Fire flashed past the pain to her core. She moaned.

He tweaked her nipples, shooting electricity to her sex, his pumping somehow increasing in force. Then he pinched. She exploded. The forest receded as waves of raw pleasure shot through every nerve in her body.

Inside her, he swelled even more. The hold on her shoulder tightened. She closed her eyes, unable to fight the whimper that escaped.

Jordan paid no heed, a lion claiming his mate unequivocally. No mercy, no second thoughts . . . no turning back. Ever.

With his jaw only, he shoved her upper body down on her hands, those sharp fangs remaining locked in place. His strong legs braced hers, keeping her open to him as he gave her everything.

Katie's heart swelled. Humans would never understand it, but the harder he thrust, the more he cemented his claim, the more she loved him. He'd do everything in his power to stay with her, to protect her, to kill and even die for her. A lion mating was absolute.

Harsh pants heated the skin at her shoulder. The hands still on her breasts tweaked, then one slid down to tap her clit.

No way could she come again.

He pinched.

Her scream rivaled the lightning flashing across the sky. The orgasm tore through her more dangerous than any tornado, sending pleasure so intense ecstasy flashed to pain and beyond. Her sex tightened around his shaft. With a howl, he held tight against her, coming hard, his entire body shuddering.

He slowed and then stopped, still inside her, fangs embedded deep. The storm returned, whipping rain into her face. She blinked, dazed and seeking reality.

Jordan didn't move.

The pain in her shoulder screamed for relief. At least she still had a shoulder.

She slowly turned her head to see just his eyes. Hard, determined, lacking any leniency. The vow shone deep and bright. He'd stay there forever.

With a shudder, she gave him what he silently demanded. Her heart beat wild and true. For him. "I love you, Jordan."

He blinked, triumph filling his gaze. The fangs slowly retracted, and he licked the wound, sealing the mark forever.

Her shoulder was on fire. She protested when he withdrew from her body. Grabbing her around the waist, he shot to his feet to cradle her in his arms. Without a word, he headed back toward headquarters.

Chapter 20

Maggie ventured into the storm, wandering toward the edge of the cliff. The almost full moon tried to cut through clouds without much success, every once in a while succeeding enough to pierce the churning gray sea. She'd heard Jordan and Katie return to Jordan's quarters. Had they finally mated? Hopefully they knew what they were doing. As much as she wanted her best friend to be happy, she sure didn't want the virus to kill them both.

Rain cut into her face, matting her hair. Man, she loved a good storm.

"Go back inside." Dark, stealthy, Terrent Vilks appeared at her side.

"Don't make me kick you again." She kept her gaze on the ocean, trying to refrain from smiling.

His chuckle cut through the storm. "Don't worry. I'll know to be on guard next time."

The tone held humor and warning. She responded to both, her smile widening and her shoulders going back. "I have the feeling most people just follow your orders."

"All people follow my orders—even pack Alphas." He yanked a Dodgers hat off his head and plunked the cap over her wet hair. "At least protect your head."

The hat covered her eyes. Reaching for the fastener in

the back, she tightened it and tucked her hair behind her ears. Living in a world where everyone did as you ordered? How could you ever know who to trust? "You seem like an Alpha."

"Yes. But as a member of the Bane's, I don't have my own pack. There isn't time to hunt and also protect a pack." While his tone stayed matter-of-fact, there was an underlying tenor of . . . what was that? Loneliness? "We're honorary members of all packs."

"What about when you retire?"

He threw back his head and laughed. "Well, theoretically, I'd form my own pack."

"Theoretically?"

"Ah, yeah. Members of the Bane's Council don't usually reach retirement." Amusement wrinkled his brow.

Something warmed inside of her. The guy embodied danger, yet once again the humor lurking within his huge form surged forward. A big guy who could laugh—even at death. Intriguing.

Her mind tried to understand the concept of his life. "So, as a roaming Alpha, everyone follows your orders. That must get so boring for you."

"Actually, order makes life smooth." The rain smashed down, turning his hair all wild and dark. Sexy and dangerous.

Maggie had the oddest urge to run her fingers through the thick strands, seeing how long it would take to get entangled. "Smooth is boring."

"No. I insist on smooth." He shook his head, sending droplets spraying. "Females infected with the virus show a more volatile temperament. I'm willing to allow some leeway for your actions the other day."

"That's kind of you," she muttered, rolling her eyes. "I'm thinking I should've kicked you harder."

"I'm glad you said that." He grasped both her hands and

pivoted her to face him. "Why don't you try kicking me now?"

Even the storm seemed to rage around him, leaving him solid and alone. He loomed over her, curiosity and challenge on his hard face. But something else lingered in those too dark eyes. Interest.

Great. Kicking the wolf leader in the sack had gleaned his interest. Just what she needed. "I figure once a week is enough."

"You're awfully brave now that I'm ready for you."

"I bet most people are scared of you." She tilted her head back, allowing the rain to coat her neck in order to see him better.

"They are." He frowned. "You don't seem to be." Puzzlement twisted his lips. "Interesting."

Fantastic. The guy was probably chalking up her lack of fear to her viral infection and ensuing craziness. She sighed, her gaze holding his. The storm stopped raging, mellowing to a soft rainfall. "Believe it or not, you're not the scariest thing I've seen." In fact, after spending who knows how much time in a Kurjan research facility, her anxiety attacks came from the past, not the present. Her nightmares were scary and grounded in reality.

"Well"—he released one arm to run a finger down her wet neck—"you haven't really seen me in action, now have you?"

Desire slid from his finger down to her abdomen as if he'd traced her naked body. Fire flashed hot and bright inside her. "No." Man, she bet he was magnificent in wolf form. "I guess if you try to kill Jordan, I'll see you, huh?" She'd meant what she'd said—if standing in front of the lion would help, she'd do it. Though the idea of actually hurting Terrent, maybe killing him, made something around her heart hurt.

Irritation flashed across Terrent's face. Fire burned deep

in his eyes. "If you think I want to kill one of my oldest friends, you haven't read me right, *Olathe*."

She sighed. "You don't have to kill him. We can find a cure."

"No. There's no cure once someone turns into a were-wolf." Absolute conviction lifted his chin.

"Well. We're at opposing ends, then." Too bad. She would've liked to get to know the wolf better. "What does *Olathe* mean?"

"Beautiful. In the language of your people." Apology filtered along his slight smile. "I'm trying to be accommodating, but you need to understand when the Bane's Council requests your presence, you make yourself available. Whether or not I have to kill my oldest friend tomorrow night."

"You don't want me for an enemy, Terrent." Somehow, she didn't figure the guy would care who his enemies were—he'd just cut them down and move on.

"You're far from my enemy." His hands framed her face, smoothing the rain away. "I appreciate Jordan offering you sanctuary and protection, but you're one of my people and you belong with wolves—especially now that the demons want you dead. I can protect you. Life will be much easier if you come to that conclusion on your own, Maggie."

Tingles set up in her skin from his warm touch. Irritation battled down her spine from the threatening words. Instinct kicked in. Pivoting her hips, she shot a knee up.

And found herself plastered up against an incredibly hard body two feet off the ground. Man, he had fast reflexes.

His smile lacked warmth. "Wolves don't play like kittens, sweetheart." With a dip of his shoulder, she was upside down looking at his ankles as he stalked toward headquarters. "It's been a long night. Get your stuff packed, and we can head out after the full moon tomorrow."

Whistling a cheerful tune, the prolific werewolf killer headed into headquarters with her ass over teakettle.

Katie woke up alone in the big bed, her shoulder a dull ache. She stretched her legs, wincing as bruises flared to life. Jordan had quickly washed them both off in the shower upon returning to headquarters before meeting Emma in the lab. The queen had taken blood, and Jordan had squired Katie to bed.

All in silence.

She'd slept for several hours. The masculine scent of cinnamon and oak filled the room, for once not providing comfort. Scooting over, she wearily yanked on sweats and a T-shirt, searching for socks. Not finding any of hers, she tugged a pair of Jordan's on, rolling the tops over several times.

Who the heck cared how she looked? The full moon was hours away, her friend Jase had been taken by demons, and Jordan hated her.

The last thought had her biting back a sob as she dodged down the hallway toward the lab to find Emma muttering while peering in a microscope. The scent of lemon cleanser and bleach hung heavy in the room.

Katie cleared her throat, fighting an unwilling laugh when Emma started, dropping her pen.

The queen whirled around, blue eyes widening. "You look terrible."

"I was mauled by a lion last night." Katie stretched her neck, wincing as her blazing shoulder protested.

"I know. Try being branded by a vampire king."

Katie had never really thought about it. When the

Kayrs family found their mates, an intricate marking appeared on their palm, transferring during sex. "So much for wine and roses."

Emma ground a palm against her eye. "No kidding. But I figured you'd look better after sleep."

If anything, Katie felt worse. "Are those the test results?"

"Yes." Emma shoved a stray strand of black hair away from her face. "Jordan's results show no change from your mating." Sorrow and irritation mixed in her eyes. "Neither do yours. I'm so sorry."

Desperation had a rock slamming into Katie's gut. The last night couldn't have been for nothing, especially since she might have lost Jordan forever. "But the results could change, right? I mean, it's early."

"Sure." Emma's eyes darkened to match the circles under them. "You really look bad."

"So do you." The king wasn't there to make sure Emma got rest, so she wouldn't rest. Katie bit her lip to keep from crying. "Jordan is mad at me." At least, she assumed he was mad. It wasn't like the guy had been talking to her.

Emma blew out a breath. "Why?"

Katie lifted her good shoulder in a shrug. "I don't know. Maybe because I manipulated him to chase me through the woods and mark me?"

Emma barked out a laugh, wiping a hand over her eyes. "Please tell me you didn't take relationship advice from my sister."

Katie's temples began to pound. "Well, kinda."

Emma shook her head, reaching down to retrieve the pen. "Cara and Talen have their own dynamic." Both dark eyebrows arched in her classic face. "But you got what you wanted, right?"

Did she? If so, why did she feel so crappy? "I guess."

Emma's lab coat swished as she stepped forward and tugged Katie's shirt to the side. "That's not healing very quickly."

Katie twisted her neck to see the back of her shoulder. Jordan's mark flared swollen and sure. "Maybe because he didn't want to bite me." The whine in her voice irritated her even more.

Emma released the material. "Don't be silly. No matter how much you tried to manipulate him, no way would Jordan mark you unwillingly. Whether he admits the truth or not, he wanted to mate you."

Hope caught in Katie's chest. "Maybe." She shoved her hands in her pockets. "Do you need my help in here to-day?"

"No." Emma tilted her head toward the door. "Go find Jordan and make things right."

With a nod, Katie loped out of the room, aiming for the gym. She needed to work some angst out of her system before facing Jordan.

Alone in the massive room, she jumped on a treadmill, trying to relieve the aches in her legs. Unfortunately, the pain came from bruises and not muscles. Five minutes into the run and she couldn't see. It took several seconds for her to realize she was crying, tears streaming down her face.

Reaching for the side bar, she missed it and tripped.

Two loud thumps later and she sat on the ground, hugging her knees, shaking silently with sobs. Now her butt hurt from falling off. The treadmill continued to run next to her. Jordan would never forgive her.

Oh God, what had she done?

She'd finally gotten exactly what she wanted, and she'd never felt so alone. Jordan was her safety net, the one place she could go. Now she needed him and couldn't go there. Her sobs increased.

Several minutes later, air whispered around her, and the

treadmill clicked off. Strong arms lifted her onto a warm lap as Jordan sat down. With a muffled sob, she snuggled into his chest like she had when young, letting his masculine scent surround her.

She flattened her hand against his heart, which beat strong and steady. "I'm sorry I manipulated you."

His sigh parted her hair. "I'm not that easy, kitten. I marked you because I wanted to."

"But you're still mad." She sniffed into his dark T-shirt.

Muscles shifted as he settled her. "Yeah, I'm still mad. But not at you." Tugging her thigh, he moved her to straddle him, lifting her chin with one knuckle. "I'm mad at myself—and the virus—and fate."

She met his gaze through wet lashes. "You talked to Emma."

"Yes." Sorrow and anger mingled in the lion's topaz eyes. "There's no change." He tugged her T-shirt aside, rubbing a finger across his mark.

Fire ripped straight to her core, and she gasped, arching against him.

Dark amusement lifted his lip. "I would've loved to have explored this with you." Leaning down, he ran his tongue over her shoulder and across the bite.

Her entire body went rigid. Electricity shot through every nerve ending. She moaned, fingers clutching into his chest.

He leaned back. "Very nice." Framing her face with both strong hands, he placed such a gentle kiss on her lips that tears spiked behind her eyes again. "I love you, Kate. No matter what happens, every good memory I have is filled with you."

Her nipples peaked while her heart warmed. "I love you, too." Determination straightened her spine. "We're not giving up, Jordan." They had at least twelve hours until the full moon rose high in the sky.

"I know." His gaze hardened. "I had a long talk with Noah and his brothers. You're leaving with them in an hour. I promise I won't give up."

Surprise caught her off guard, followed by heated fury. "I'm not leaving."

"Yes, you are." The gentle tone failed to mask the hard core of determination underneath. "Any shifter will be able to smell me on you from a mile away. Don't you understand the danger this puts you in if I don't make it tonight?"

She swallowed. Truth be told, she hadn't thought beyond the full moon. "We're family now." Happiness caught in her chest.

"Yes." Jordan looked anything but happy. "We are. Which means if I die, you're the next in line to lead." He lowered his head until his gaze captured hers an inch away. "You'll be challenged immediately."

With the virus in her blood, with being unable to shift, she didn't stand a chance. She shook her head. But she wasn't leaving him to face the moon alone. "So, what's your plan? I mean, do you think the mating will kick in soon?"

"No." His smile turned rueful. "I'm going deep underground where the moon can't touch me."

Disbelief had her shoving against his chest. "You're fucking crazy." She started to struggle, to get up, and his hands clamped on her hips. "Your head will blow off." Unfortunately, she wasn't being dramatic. They'd tried to help infected humans centuries ago by hiding them from the moon. The moon still called—loud and strong enough that the infected's brain blew to pieces if they didn't obey her call. "If nothing else, turn into a werewolf."

He jerked his head back. "No."

"Yes." She grabbed both of his shoulders and shook. "Look how Brent has evolved. If you let the moon take you, at least you'll still be alive. We'll have time to fix this." If he fought the moon by hiding, he'd die.

"I'm not turning into a werewolf. No way will I be like Brent." Anger scented the air.

Enough with the secrets. The lion either trusted her or not. "What happened? I mean, with Brent? Years ago?"

Jordan stiffened. Fire flashed in his incredible eyes. "Nothing."

Hurt spiraled down through her chest. "You don't trust me."

"I do." He shut his eyes and exhaled. "You don't need to know that side of me."

She speared both hands in his hair, cupping his head. "I want to know all sides of you. No matter how much time we may or may not have together." Scrambling to make him understand, she tightened her hold. "A public challenge was made, and David made accusations. I need the truth to counter them, Jordan."

"He gave the truth." The lion's jaw hardened. "I killed his brother. At least, I thought I had killed Brent."

She huffed out an irritated laugh. "I know you. And I know Conn. There's no way you two sprang a trap on your cousin and then stabbed him in the back."

"Very *distant* cousin." Jordan jerked his head in almost a nod. "But you're right. The truth should be known. Brent's father was a good guy . . . strong supporter of the Realm, which is one of the reasons the Kurjans took him out."

"Brent didn't support the Realm?"

"No. Brent advocated withdrawal, which would've weakened the feline nation as well as the Realm." Agony cut hard lines into Jordan's sharp face. "Conn was my best friend. Sure, we knew someday we'd be called on to fight, but we never thought it would happen so quickly. So, when war was absolutely declared, at the time, our only solution was . . ."

Katie frowned. Anybody could challenge a feline leader as Alpha. "But you didn't challenge Brent."

"No. Not publicly." Regret twisted Jordan's lip. "I challenged him privately. In the woods that were clean and new, where cubs still play. He wasn't getting out alive."

A shiver wound down Katie's spine. In that moment, she saw the assassin he'd once been. "I'm sure the fight was fair."

Jordan's short laugh lacked humor. "Well, we faced each other and went at it. The fight was bloody . . . and I had to work for it."

"So it was a fair challenge."

"No." Inevitability turned Jordan's face to stone. "Brent was going to die that day—even if I did."

Katie caught her breath. "Conn."

"Yeah, Conn. He waited, just in case, sniper position, ready to take out Brent. If Brent and I both died, then Conn was going to approach Noah to step up."

Katie shook her head. "Does Noah know?"

Jordan shrugged. "We've never talked about it, but Noah doesn't miss much."

"You did what you had to do."

"Yeah, but I changed Conn forever." Regret twisted Jordan's lips.

"Conn would be mad you took responsibility for his decision." Katie sighed. "Enough of that nonsense."

Jordan gave a short nod and kissed the tip of her nose, leaning in to nuzzle her neck. "I love the way you smell." His talented lips wandered up her skin.

Then his entire body went rigid. He leaned back as if she'd kicked him.

His hands wrapped around her biceps. Fire and an odd panic filled his eyes. He sniffed again. "Oh God." Leaping to his feet with her still in his arms, he ran out of the gym.

Katie yelped, trying to get her balance as he hurried through the underground hallway. Paintings and light sconces blurred together. "What are you doing?" He jostled her again, and nausea rose in her throat. "Stop running, damn it."

They swept into the main lab and he dropped her on the examination table.

Emma flipped around, surprise forming her mouth in an O. "What's wrong?"

"Do a pregnancy test," Jordan growled.

Max sauntered into the room, his hand on his gun. "What's going on? Saw you running on the monitor."

Jordan pointed at Katie. "She's pregnant. I can smell the baby."

Max lifted both eyebrows and then closed his eyes, sniffing the air. "Yep. New baby. Just like a brand-new snowfall."

Panic danced large dots in front of Katie's eyes. Pregnant? She couldn't be pregnant. Then joy swamped her so fiercely she swayed. Pregnant. Jordan's baby.

Emma cleared her throat. "Ah, there's no test for a pregnancy this early, Jordan."

Max shrugged massive shoulders. "Don't need a test. Can smell a new baby. She's pregnant." A wide smile split his face. "I have to go tell my mate. Sarah loves babies." Quick strides had him out the door.

Jordan's face lost all color. He swayed, blindly reaching for the counter to balance himself.

Katie frowned. "Jordan, it's okay."

He rounded on her so quickly she shrank back. Anger filled his face, but something else filled his eyes. Seconds passed until she recognized the look. Pure, raw terror. "You don't understand." His voice dropped to a hoarseness that hurt her ears. "It was one thing to have Baye hide you since we mated. But with a baby, *my baby* . . ."

Oh God. Katie slapped a hand over her mouth. Her entire body trembled. Anyone wanting to challenge for leadership of the pride would have to take out the baby. Jordan's heir. She could try to hide, but shifters were hunters at heart. She'd be found.

Jordan yanked the band out of his hair and started pacing. "Okay. I can fix this. We can keep the pregnancy quiet, so nobody knows. But I'm afraid they'll still come looking for you."

Emma stepped out of his way. "We'll keep them here, Jordan. Keep them safe."

His low laugh lacked humanity. "At Realm Headquarters? No. Too public, too known. A challenge will be made, and she'll have no choice but to accept. Or they'll come for her." He ran a rough hand through his thick hair. "You'd end up at war with my people."

He stopped pacing, his gaze on her. A deep sigh escaped him. "Emma, do we have a Realm prophet someplace close?"

Emma scratched her chin. "I think so. I think Lily is in Seattle—we could have her here in a couple of hours." She yanked open a file cabinet and pulled out a thick stack of files. "I have her direct number in here somewhere."

Katie scooted off the table, panic making her hands tremble. "Why do we need a prophet?"

Jordan's expression smoothed out. "So you can marry Noah. He's strong enough to lead and protect you." He nodded at Emma. "Call Lily." Quick strides had him at the door. "I'll find Noah. Right now, I need some air." He disappeared.

Katie put her hands on her hips. Sure, she could marry someone else besides Jordan, could even sleep with someone else, unlike the vampires, who once mated, caused a horrible allergy in anyone else trying to get intimate with them. But she'd only have one mate. "I'm not marrying Noah."

Emma shoved the file back in the drawer. "You had better go talk to Jordan—if that's the only way to keep you and the baby safe, he's not going to back down." She smoothed hair off her face. "I'd hate to have to hide you myself, but I will."

Katie flashed her a grin. "I know." Thank goodness for friends. "I need some air, too." About the middle of the day outside, and she could certainly use some warmth. She hurried from the room.

No small amount of hurt settled in her heart as she jogged through the dark stone hallways. How could Jordan even think of her marrying another shifter? He'd said he loved her. There had to be a way to fix this. She passed all the security places, nodding at guards each time. Nobody tried to stop her.

Finally, she emerged outside into a beautiful fall day. The sun shone bright in the sky, the ocean sparkled an amazing blue, and the one man she'd ever love stood tall, his back to her, studying the sea.

Janie Kayrs sat on a bench, her face tilted up to the sun. Dressed in shorts and a tank top, the girl's nose and arms were freckling. She stood and nodded at Katie, her blue eyes serious. "Wanted to feel the sun on my face—it's safe considering it's the middle of the day." With a sad smile, she headed for the door.

The hair prickled on the back of Katie's neck. Almost in slow motion, as if the air itself worked against her, she turned her head toward the forest.

The werewolves chose high noon to launch their attack.

Chapter 21

The hairy brutes attacked from both sides, fur flying and shining under the sun. They must've somehow taken out the perimeter guards.

"Run!" Jordan bellowed, shifting into a massive cougar, sending clothes scattering.

Fear and shock kept Katie frozen for two beats. Awareness slammed home, and she accepted reality. The werewolves were attacking in daylight.

She leapt for Janie, colliding with seven feet of muscle and fur. She bounced back, landing on the soft grass. Pain shot up her tailbone. A breeze lifted her hair, carrying ocean salt and the smell of dirty dog. Scrambling to her feet, she ignored Brent and tried to reach Janie.

The teenager faced a beige werewolf as it advanced on her, teeth flashing. With a sharp cry, Janie executed a perfect jump kick, nailing the beast in the face.

Blood spurted from the monster's nose. He roared, sweeping a beefy paw out and swiping Janie in the temple. The girl smashed into the rock. A loud clunk sounded as her head impacted.

Fear narrowed the day, and Katie yelled. She shot toward Janie.

Brent intercepted Katie, grabbing her by the waist and lifting her high in the air. Smelly animal and evil coated her throat. She struggled, kicking and reaching for his face. With a low growl, the monster threw her to the ground.

Her shoulders hit first, bouncing before the rest of her body followed. The air shot from her lungs. Pain burst in her skull and back. Stunned, she blinked blackness away.

Brent turned his head. "Leave girllll alone."

Growls and snarls echoed through the air as vampires and shifters exploded out of headquarters. They were outnumbered three to one.

Katie took advantage of Brent's distraction, rolling over and crouching in front of Janie. The werewolf advanced, evil gleaming in his bizarre eyes. Feinting to the left, Katie dodged back to the right and nailed the bastard in the balls.

He shrieked in fury, stepping back, eyes going wide.

Katie pivoted to grab Janie and began to tug her inside.

Claws ripped into her elbows, yanking her away from the girl. Katie reached desperate arms out to her friend, struggling against the beast.

Relief filtered through Katie's buzzing brain as Max lifted the unconscious Janie and whisked her out of sight. God, she hoped the girl was all right. She dropped to her knees, flipping around.

Focusing, Katie scissored her legs, catching the werewolf by the ankles.

He jumped out of her hold. Leaning down, he raked devastating claws down her arms, digging in and lifting. "Myyyy Kaattieee."

Agony tore through her. Nerve endings fired, and her entire nervous system flared to life, sending an alert to flee. Brent dug his claws in harder. Katie's stomach rolled, and black dots covered her vision.

He threw her, and she bounced off a rock, darkness falling over her eyes.

Jordan roared, the sound full of fury.

Brent pivoted and jumped into the group trying to kill the lion ruler.

Katie staggered to her feet. She wasn't finished yet. Yelling, she tried to pull Brent's attention away from Jordan. The beast turned his head, and Jordan was on him, teeth flashing as he dropped the werewolf to the ground.

But the other big brown monster roared to the sky. With a dark smile, he lumbered toward her.

She took a step back.

Insanity lit the werewolf's eyes a translucent yellow. "I'm Jaaaack."

Jesus Christ. Another fucking werewolf who could speak. Had Brent taught him? Katie dropped her stance, waiting until the monster was in range. With a howl, she shot a sidekick to its knee.

The beast went down, swinging hard.

She'd underestimated his arm span. He caught her by the wrist, yanking her into his matted fur. His claws dug deep into her flesh.

Her head swaying, she tried to focus and found Jordan. Three werewolves were on him, Brent taking the lead. The lion bled from several areas along his back and flanks.

The lioness within Katie snarled deep. Images whipped inside her head. Jordan mating her. The baby within her. So much hope. Desperation popped like firecrackers through her veins.

Fear and instinct had her struggling for freedom.

The cries and clashes of battle destroyed the day.

Jordan bellowed, the yell full of fury and pain.

Power cascaded through her like lava hurling from a volcano. Smooth, fiery, deadly. Opening her mouth to scream, her jaw kept widening. Fangs dropped low and sharp.

Snarling, she let out a primal roar.

The fighting ceased. For the briefest of seconds, every animal and beast in the clearing paused. All male, all reacting to the sound of an Alpha female.

She shifted completely into a mountain lion, a sonic boom shattering the air and sending Jack flying past bodies. The fight erupted again, shifters attacking with renewed purpose.

Sharp claws dug into the earth as she dropped to all fours. Electricity ignited her blood. Stunned ecstasy caught her off guard. She'd *shifted*.

The animal took over, recognizing the danger. Vaulting over a downed beast, she landed on the back of a werewolf threatening her mate. Blood spurted into her mouth when she cut deadly teeth into its neck. Twisting her head, she yanked while slashing her claws down its vertebrae.

The beast fell, landing hard and bouncing. Holding its back down with her paws, she ripped its spine out. The monster went limp in death.

Bulky hands grabbed her, claws digging into her fur and throwing her across the clearing.

She landed on her side, quickly rolling to her feet, her gaze on Jack.

Colors flashed into her pupils, blood and rage assailed her nostrils, too many sounds pummeled her ears. After ten years of being human, her extra senses threatened to shut her down.

The werewolf advanced, a hard glint in his hungry eyes.

Cries of pain and death swirled in her head. Agony rippled on the breeze. Shoving those away, she focused on the threat, acutely aware of the cub nestled safely inside her. A maternal snarl hissed past her lips.

Even through the confusion, an awareness grounded

her. Different. She was different from before. More powerful, more deadly . . . either from the werewolf virus or from mating Jordan. Maybe from both.

Jack held a paw up, growling and allowing his claws to elongate. Sharper, much longer than any claws she'd ever seen. Although he'd inflicted damage already, he'd been keeping them sheathed. Smiling, he followed suit with the other paw. Make those hands. Furry hands with claws deadlier than any hunting knife.

Fear kept her gaze on the killer.

Out of nowhere, satisfaction coursed through her. She lifted her ears in question. The feeling belonged to Jordan. He'd dispatched one werewolf and was gaining ground on Brent. Intriguing to be inside his heart, privy to his thoughts.

Jack charged.

Training and instinct kicked in. Katie lowered her head, shooting forward and between his legs. Bounding around, she leapt onto his back. Her claws dug deep, her jaws snapping to gain hold.

With a roar, Jack reached back, grabbed her by the scruff of the neck and yanked her over his head.

The world blurred as she crashed to the ground, rolling to the side to protect the cub.

For two seconds she was a child again, scared and running from a bully. But this time Jordan couldn't come to her rescue.

Desperation had her mind blanking. Her shoulder pounded where Jordan had placed his mark. Her mate. She'd run from him . . . and being part animal, he'd had no choice but to chase.

Snarling, she flashed her teeth at Jack. Dodging to the side, she ran.

All furious animal, Jack howled, his claws scraping down her flanks.

Panting, her heart racing, she ran around a vampire decapitating a werewolf, past Lance and Baye as they battled several beasts, past fighting vampire soldiers and away from the entrance to headquarters. Toward the cliffs leading so far down to the sparkling ocean.

Jack lumbered after her, howling.

Her paws slipped on the wet grass, and she went sprawling. So many years had passed since she'd run in lion form.

Jack gave a gleeful yowl and pounced.

She turned onto her back, her hind legs catching him at the hips and thrusting him over her head.

His arms spiraled. He hollered in anger as he went pummeling through the air.

Katie jumped to all fours, turning around. Jack staggered to his feet, arms windmilling to regain balance. Roaring a battle cry, Katie lunged for him, hitting him solidly in the chest and bouncing back. Jack disappeared over the edge of the cliff. His holler turned to a high-pitched scream, echoing up as he fell. Finally, silence.

She flipped around, surveying the area.

Jordan snarled, fangs flashing, and tore the head off a werewolf. Jerking to the side, he threw the head over the cliff. Brent gave a howl of outrage. The remaining werewolves echoed his bellow. Glancing at the empty cliff, Brent and the still standing beasts shot back into the forest. Several vampires took off in pursuit.

Jordan lowered his head, stalking toward her, his eyes primitive and gold. Sniffing her neck, he gave a short, satisfied growl. Moving closer, he nuzzled her jaw, wandering to the bite in her shoulder, which he nipped.

Warmth flushed through her. Her mate.

One by one, the remaining feline shifters stalked toward her. Forming a line, Noah bowed his head. His brothers and then the rest of the lions followed.

A vow of allegiance from their soldiers to their Alpha

female. A promise to follow and protect her, regardless of what happened to Jordan.

Jordan nodded in approval.

The shifters turned and bounded in pursuit after the werewolves.

Then Jordan stretched his neck, turning to survey the sun lowering in the sky.

A cold chill shoved away the warmth in Katie.

The moon was coming.

Chapter 22

Katie shifted back to human with a series of sharp pops. Aches vibrated along her bones as they re-formed.

Jordan shifted and instantly had her in his arms. "You shifted."

She leaned back, joy filling every pore. "I know. The mating must've changed me." Hope flared hotter than the joy. "You, too! Marking me would've altered your physiology, too." Her excitement dimmed. Hopefully Jordan had changed enough he wouldn't turn into a werewolf. "We should go after Brent."

"No. Let Noah get the bastard."

A sudden thought made her gasp. "Janie was hurt."

Jordan nodded, stepping back to survey the cuts, bruises, and gashes marring Katie's flanks. Gentle hands brushed along her hip. He leaned over to place a soft kiss above a bruise. "You need bandages." He grabbed Katie's hand and strode into headquarters. "Let's hit the infirmary."

After stopping for Jordan to yank on jeans, and Katie to throw a loose cotton dress over her head, they limped down several flights of stairs. Opening the door at the medical level, Jordan held both hands up in surrender, keeping Katie behind him. "The fight is over."

Katie elbowed him, sidling to view the small vestibule. Max and Garrett flanked the single doorway cut into rock,

guns in hand, stances set to shoot. Stone-cold determination sat comfortably on Max's wide face. Anger and
youthful bewilderment filled Garrett's eyes. But his hold
remained steady on the gun, and a hard line of conviction
angled his jaw. The kid wouldn't hesitate to shoot.

Jordan stepped forward. "The werewolves are gone—
soldiers are pursuing them north."

Max nodded. "I sent my mate, all the kids and non-
soldiers, as well as the injured to the level ten secured
section. We needed to bring Janie here." His expression
remained the same, but a low hitch caught on his words.
"Dage and Talen should be teleporting home any minute."

Fear rolled in Katie's stomach. With a nod, she shoved
open the door to the small room better equipped than any
big city hospital. Five beds lined the far wall, and Janie lay
motionless in the farthest one, attached to several beeping
machines. Cara held her hand from the far side of the bed
while Emma checked her pulse, her gaze on the watch
adorning her wrist.

Katie's steps slowed on the spotless tile as she approached
the bed. Janie's cheeks lacked any color, her skin pasty and
her lips blue. A devastating purple bruise marred her left
temple to her jaw. The air around her seemed . . . heavy.

Cara glanced up, tears shining in her dazed blue eyes.

Emma gently placed Janie's arm back on the bed. "Her
pulse is way too slow." Pressing several buttons on the
nearest machine, she shook her head. "I can't get any brain
readings." She bit her lip, an obvious struggle not to cry
on her face.

Garrett hovered closer. "Janie? Wake up." The protector
was gone, and a scared brother stood in his place. "Please."

Katie slid an arm around his waist. He burrowed as
close as he could get, his body trembling.

Male voices echoed outside, and then Talen Kayrs
stalked into the room followed by the king. Dressed in

black combat gear, a dark scowl covered Talen's dangerous face. The massive vampire hurried toward the bed, stopping cold in the center of the room.

Then he blinked. Twice. Metallic green shot through the normal gold of his eyes.

"Janie?" He held a hand toward the bed, hesitantly moving forward. Once reaching his daughter, he dropped to his knees. "Janie?" Hoarseness lowered his voice to something guttural and full of pain.

Tears filled Katie's eyes. She held Garrett tighter even as Jordan hugged them from behind. Fear had her shoulders shaking. The boy's entire body stiffened, terror cascading off him in scents of sulfur and grass.

"Janie?" Talen smoothed a stray curl off the girl's face. "Baby, wake up." The entreaty, the desperate plea from a father for his child, had Katie swallowing a loud sob.

Dage moved closer to his mate. Dark circles lined under his eyes. Teleporting his brothers twice in one day had obviously taken a toll. "Emma?" The king took in the beeping machines with a glance.

Emma shook her head, leaning into the king's large body. "She's in a coma. Pulse slow, immeasurable brain activity." The queen swayed, her face as pale as Janie's.

Talen covered Cara's hand with his free one. "What about blood?"

Emma closed her eyes, her hand to her head. "I don't know. Vampire blood for a human teenager might kill her. Mates can take blood, but I just don't know about a girl Janie's age."

Vampire blood was magical and full of healing power for their mates. But the thick liquid could be deadly for other races. Uncertainty kept Katie grounded in place. Too bad shifter blood didn't help humans.

Garrett shrugged free. "We share a parent—similar genetics. What about my blood?"

Dage rubbed his chin on top of Emma's head. "His blood would be safer than any of ours."

Uncertainty wrinkled Emma's brow. "Yes. But he's still a vampire, and Janie is human. Plus, even though the kids share a mother, Cara's genetic makeup had begun to alter when she became pregnant with Garrett. We don't know . . ."

Cara bit her lip. "I can't get anything from her. No feelings, no thoughts . . . nothing."

As an empath, the girl's mother should be able to feel something. Katie shuffled her feet, denial slamming hard into her brain. Janie would be okay. She had to be.

Talen kept one hand on his wife, the other on his daughter. He turned toward Cara. "Mate?"

Cara's lips trembled. She eyed her mate and glanced past him to their son. "Are you sure, Garrett?"

"Yes." Garrett yanked up his sleeve. "Losing a little blood is no big deal. And I've been eating healthy lately." Hope and determination rode the boy's words, and his teeth dropped low and sharp.

"No." Dage grabbed his arm. "You'll take off your wrist with those things."

Emma nodded, reaching for a syringe. "We want to inject her." She rolled Garrett's sleeve up past the elbow and swabbed his vein before sliding in the needle. Filling the shot, she pivoted toward Janie. Dage slapped a bandage on the inside of his elbow.

Talen turned his daughter's arm over, exposing her vein and flattening his hand over her small palm. "Not too much."

Emma nodded. Seconds later, she'd injected about half the contents into Janie. "That's enough for now." Smooth movements had a bandage covering the wound. She exhaled. "Now we wait." Tossing the needle into the garbage, she turned toward Katie and Jordan. "You both need medical attention."

Right around dinnertime, Katie handed a green gun to Lance in the fully stocked armory. "How many werewolves survived earlier?"

The shifter passed the weapon to Dage. "Several. And they may not have attacked with their full force today." He tugged down an almost see-through T-shirt. The shifters wouldn't remain dressed for long, so the easier it was to tear clothing, the better. "The Chance brothers are scouting the area as we speak . . . checking out defensive positions. Where's Jordan?"

"He went to check on Janie." Katie fought the sick rage burning in her gut. "Last I heard, there was no change." The girl's death would cripple the Kayrs family. The Realm.

Dage nodded. Fury and despair swirled bright blue throughout his silver eyes. "I'm going to recheck the secured areas down below. We have three hours until the moon rises, until the werewolves are at full power." He frowned. "Do you think they'll wait until the moon is high or hit early?"

Katie shrugged. "Waiting would be smart, but they're ruled by blood and death, so instinct may take over." But there was no doubt the monsters would be hitting and soon.

Dage slipped from the room.

Lance sighed. "Is there any way I can talk you into protecting the kids in the lower levels? You just shifted for the first time—being on the front line, especially where that jerk Brent wants you to be, is a bad idea."

"I'm not going to the front line." She settled her stance.

"What?" Lance rounded on her, fury lighting his stunning eyes. "You're not saying what I think you're saying."

"I am." She didn't have time to convince her friends she knew what she was doing.

"No." Lance reached for a green gun, his hands trembling as he checked the clip. "You can't possibly be considering staying with Jordan while he shifts into a werewolf. He'll kill you—I won't let another one of my friends die. Don't make me fight you on this."

The mating could still save Jordan. Katie had to have faith in the possibility. "He won't hurt me. And if his brain begins to explode, I have to shove him under the moon."

Lance took a step back, shock crossing his face. "You'll allow him to turn into a werewolf?"

"If that's the only way to keep him alive."

Lance's head shook wildly. "Well, if that isn't the fucking worst plan I've heard in my entire life, I don't know what is."

Anger narrowed Katie's eyes and shoved doubt to the cellar. "I know what I'm doing."

The smile sliding across Lance's handsome face contained darkness and raw fury. "You don't know shit." He took a step toward her, gun aimed at her abdomen. "I really wanted to wait until you were forced to kill Jordan, but that's not going to happen, is it?"

Shock kept her immobile. Then fury slammed her hand against the gun, swiping the barrel away. "Wait for what?"

He shot a hand into her hair, tangling and yanking. Pivoting, he hauled her back against his front, the gun pressed into her rib cage. "You're being awfully slow here."

She struggled, surprise causing her mind to blank. This didn't make sense.

Pain flared along her ribs as he shoved the gun harder. "Stop fighting me."

She stilled. Fear flared bright. The baby. "What are you doing?" Her mind fought with reality. This was a terrible mistake.

The hand in her hair tugged to the side, exposing her neck. He ran his mouth over her jugular, teeth scraping just enough to draw blood. "The scent of your blood covers the stench of Jordan on you. Barely." Lance bit. "I guess you'll be bleeding a lot in the future."

A strong inhale centered her. She allowed acceptance to arrive. "Say the words, Lance. I need to know the truth." She needed to believe the truth.

"Sure." He straightened up, releasing her and turning her around, the gun pointed at her stomach. "I love you."

She blinked. How could she get through to him? "No. You're confused. You're hurt because you lost your squad . . . and because you lost Linda."

His eyes swirled a maniacal blue and he snarled. "No. That bitch was a pleasant diversion. Smart, though. She figured out rather quickly my feelings for you." The smile he flashed was one Katie had never seen on the tiger. "It was more fun killing her than the assholes you dated, I have to tell you."

Katie stumbled back a step. "You killed them?"

"Sure." Lance exhaled. "I couldn't have you with another man."

She shook her head. "What about Mitch? He didn't turn into a werewolf?"

"No." Lance snorted. "I just said that so I could go hunt him down. He died well, if that helps."

Nausea rippled through her stomach. "You killed them because of me?"

"Yes. So we could be together. We need to be together. To live and get away from this war. I can't let them kill you. I thought we'd mate. Though, now, well . . . you fucked that up."

She'd mated Jordan. "Right. So . . . there's no chance for us." The guy was crazy. She eyed the nearest gun.

Lance growled. "You move, and I'll shoot the baby. Jordan's baby." Lance's voice promised he'd do exactly that. "I want you to like me, and I know if I take out the baby, you probably won't. So I'll let you have him, but that's all you're getting from me."

"We can't mate, Lance." She spoke slowly, rationally. Where the hell was her friend? How had she read him so wrong?

He shook her. "I know. But we can still be together. And you're gonna watch me kill Jordan after he turns into a werewolf. Well, if his brain doesn't explode first." Anticipation had Lance licking his lips.

She shook her head. Denial wasn't going to get her out of this. Betrayal ate away the haziness. "Did you take the pictures? I mean, the ones from stalking me?"

"Yeah." Arrogance lifted his chin. "You never noticed, not once. But"—he frowned—"I thought the photographs were for David. I had no clue he was working with Brent the werewolf, had no clue they were related. I figured David would challenge Jordan if somehow Jordan survived the moon."

She tried to clear her mind. "That makes no sense. Why would you take pictures and give them to David?"

Lance sighed. "I'm starting to doubt your intelligence."

"I'm right there with you," she snapped back. How stupid was she to have missed this?

"Okay." He exhaled, irritation curling his lip. "David paid me money, a lot of it, to get those pictures of you. I thought he had a hard-on for you . . . and figured I'd take the money and deal with him later. One time he let loose he was going to challenge Jordan. So I figured I'd let them fight, then take out whoever survived. Simple plan."

The guy was nuttier than a cobbler. "When did you find out David knew Brent?"

"Same time you did—when we saw the pictures in that

crappy shack." Lance grimaced. "I'm sorry. I should've protected you better, and I will from now on. I promise."

She wrapped her arms around her middle. Flesh and bones wouldn't protect the baby from a bullet, but she couldn't help herself. Tears pricked the back of her eyes. "I thought we were friends." Trust didn't come easily to her, and she'd given it to the tiger. They'd fought together and had protected each other's backs.

"We are." He frowned. "How can you not see everything I've done has been for you? You're everything."

Even now, with a gun pointed at her and his eyes a crazy blue, she expected him to snap out of it. "Then why are you doing this? I'm asking you to stop."

He shook his head sadly. "You don't know what you want . . . what you need. I can't let you sacrifice yourself with Jordan—he's a dead man before midnight. Even if you won't protect yourself, as your future, I will."

"Lance, I care about you. A lot." There had to be some way to reason with him. "But I don't love you or want to be with you. Please stop."

Indulgence quirked his lips. Amazing reflexes had his hand around her arm, and her back in the same position as before, facing the open doorway. Lance had always been quicker than most cats—he'd moved before she could draw a breath. "We need to go."

"Go where?" Panic had her fighting to stay still.

"This is no longer our fight." His forward step moved her right along with him. "I have transportation waiting outside. Do what I tell you, and I won't shoot you."

Jordan suddenly appeared in the corridor. His tawny gaze took in the situation. "This isn't good."

Chapter 23

Katie breathed out, the gun inhibiting a full exhale. Jordan kept his hands at his sides, his face placid, his stance relaxed. But fear and fury burned hot and bright in his eyes. She went lax against Lance. "We seem to have a situation."

Jordan eyed the weapon. "Did you kill Linda, Lance?"

The tiger stiffened. "Sure. She was a threat to my future with Katie. How do you know about Linda?"

"I've been investigating you since you threw the tantrum when I took Katie from New Orleans." The lion lifted his gaze to Katie's eyes, talking to Lance, but watching her. "Just got off the phone with an informant. My timing sucks."

"Yeah, well"—the tiger shrugged, his large chest knocking into Katie's head—"I figure your timing is excellent. You turn into a werewolf, your people kill you, and I get the girl." His voice was almost . . . cheerful.

Jordan had been in several fights, been injured, and the moon would soon start to call. Lance was definitely in fighting shape. Katie glanced down the empty corridor. Where was everybody?

Jordan snarled. "I'm rather pissed at the girl."

Katie's mouth dropped open. He had better be trying to distract Lance. "Excuse me?"

One arrogant eyebrow lifted. "There's no excuse. Apparently, while you've been off fighting on your own, you've had not one, not two, but three fucking stalkers you haven't noticed. When we're finished with this guy, you're going through training again. *If* I let you out of the house."

Irritation had her chin lifting, knocking her skull against Lance's chin. "There's a gun in my ribs, Jordan. Do you think you could concentrate on that and not on being a complete asshole?"

Lance's breath warmed her ear when he lowered his head. "See why I'm a better choice for you?"

Fear swirled in her gut. "You killed Linda?" He was in love with the woman. How could this have happened?

"Sure. Nothing is as important as keeping my squad safe. As keeping you safe. Linda was a threat to our future, and she had to go." Lance's voice stayed calm with conviction.

Katie shook her head. There was no reasoning with him. Every move flitting through her head resulted in the gun going off. She needed the weapon away from her abdomen. "You're hurting me, Lance."

A low growl hitched Jordan's chest.

Lance merely tightened his hold. "Move back, Jordan. I'm done talking."

The lion leader took a step back, hands out, gaze on the gun. "There has to be something we can work out here. How about you take Katie underground, and we wait until tomorrow morning to worry about the situation? I mean, chances are I'll be dead."

Lance's muscles vibrated down her back. "And give the Chance brothers opportunity to take me out? No thanks. You know Baye will try to stop me from taking her. She's mine, Jordan. You should've realized that fact before screwing her."

Hearing her mating reduced to a vulgarity shot heat straight to Katie's head. If she could just get Lance to loosen his hold—

Jordan shot forward, his hand sliding between the gun and her ribs, his palm cupping the barrel. Pushing her to the side, he shoved Lance against the door frame.

The gun went off.

Katie screamed.

Jordan hissed in pain, clutching his wounded hand. The scent of blood whipped through the oxygen.

Lance smiled, raising the gun toward Jordan's head.

Noise faded away, as did fear. Katie dropped into a slide across the smooth rock, hitting Lance in the ankles. Her hip pounded in pain. She connected with a loud *pop*. An ache ripped up her shin. He fell, and she rolled away.

Jordan was on him that fast. The gun went spinning down the hallway. The punches were too fast to track, fury behind them. Lance's head knocked against the rock wall, bouncing twice, and his eyes fluttered closed. Quick and deadly, Jordan's fangs dropped and pierced Lance's jugular. There was nothing like an Alpha protecting his family.

"No!" Katie grabbed his shoulders, trying to shove him off the unconscious tiger. "Don't kill him."

Jordan eyed her, his dangerous fangs still embedded deep in Lance's neck. A couple of furious slashes, and he'd decapitate the tiger.

Katie calmed her voice. "He's sick, Jordan. Since he lost his squad." She'd had no clue how sick he was. "Please don't kill him." She tried to reach her mate, but chances weren't good. Alphas took care of threats to their families with a quick death.

His eyes morphed into an animal, while his body remained human.

"Please, Jordan. He has saved me before." Yes, Lance

had killed. And he'd answer for those crimes when he was well enough to do so.

Jordan retracted his fangs and stood, blood sliding down his chin, his eyes calming. "We'll secure him in the cells on the ninth floor. I'll let him live . . . for now."

Katie sighed in relief. Then she stared at horror at the hole in his hand. "You need a bandage."

Talen Kayrs held his mate's hand while they kept vigil at their daughter's bed. How could he have allowed her to be injured? What if her head didn't heal? A helplessness flushed through him that had his eyes heating. His family was his life.

Cara tightened her hold, her tiny hand encased by his. She smiled, her gaze on their daughter. "She's strong, Talen. Trust me."

His breath caught in wonder at the strength of the woman. So small, so delicate, yet she held strength unmatched by any warrior he'd ever fought. So he allowed her to shoulder the burden, to comfort him. "I believe you." And for the moment, he did.

The injured girl's eyes fluttered, then her breathing smoothed out.

Janie wandered along warm sand, the ocean rolling, the sun shining, and an excruciating pain pulsating her face. She tucked her hands in her linen pants. Linen, huh? The material wrinkled like crazy, and was quite worthless when training to fight. Odd that in her dream she wore it.

Not that this was a normal dream.

The breeze lifted her hair, wandering along the bruises in her face. Werewolves hit hard. Though she'd nailed the jerk in the nose first. As soon as Uncle Jase got home, she hoped she could tell him all about the fight. He'd promised she'd like using the jumping front kick if she ever needed to defend herself.

Hopefully she'd see Uncle Jase again. At this point, the future wasn't looking good. For either Jase or her.

Interesting that she'd never seen this ending in visions. An outcropping of rocks rose ahead and she slowly climbed, using her hands against the rough ridges and finding a nice seat where she could view the ocean. Dazzling and blue, the water shimmered with a world of life she couldn't see. The rock warmed her, providing a smooth surface for her to lean back.

Endorphins kept fear at bay but failed to erase the pain in her face and head. Odd to be actually dying. Even as she sat, the blood slowed in her veins.

A figure stood farther down the rock cropping, tall and broad, white face reflecting the sun. Janie tilted her head to the side.

Catching sight of her, the figure straightened and then sauntered her direction. Agile limbs had him climbing the outcropping to pause and take a seat. His greenish eyes flashed. "Janet Isabella Kayrs."

She'd smile, but her lip hurt. "Kalin the Kurjan. Do you have a last name?"

"No."

Too bad. She loved hers. Surveying him, her mind in a daze, she struggled to concentrate. "You grew up."

He rubbed his prominent jaw. "I thought you'd end up taller."

"Yeah. I get that a lot." She should be afraid. Instead, cotton surrounded her, safe and warm. Haze fluttered over her vision, yet she tried to study him. Well over six feet, his long hair was black with bloodred tips. His shoulders had broadened out, and his features had turned from teenager to man. Well, Kurjan. Kind of handsome in a totally creepy way. He wore a Kurjan soldier uniform. "You're a soldier."

"Yes." Puzzlement wrinkled his light eyebrows. "What happened to your face?"

"Werewolf attack." She shrugged, then winced as bruises flared to life.

"Oh." *Anger burned bright in his eyes. "I'm so very sorry to hear that." He shook his head. "But you need to dig deep and get better. Now."*

Somehow she'd never figured Kalin would be giving her "dig deep" pep talks. "So you're sleeping now, and I can't block you. Since I'm dying." She'd never figured to spend her last minutes with Kalin. They'd almost been friends once.

"You're not dying." Fury danced on his angled face. "You can't die. You're the future."

"The future changes by the second. You should know that." She swayed, his face melting a little bit. "Besides, you don't like me."

"That's irrelevant."

Yeah, somewhere deep that kinda hurt. "Whatever."

Clouds, dark and full, rolled in from the ocean. The sea churned and turned gray. Thunder rumbled directly above. The wind cut hard and cold.

Kalin's hair lifted and he growled. "Stop that."

"Not me." Janie actually enjoyed the rain. Would there be rain in Heaven? Was she even going to heaven?

Movement caught her eye. Strong, powerful, and obviously angry, Zane's long strides ate up the beach toward them. His expression darker than the sudden storm, his eyes turned a deep green, and the scar on his jaw held prominence.

It was fitting her life would end with all three of them together in a dream.

Zane bounded up the slab. A swift growl and he tackled Kalin, tumbling them both down the jagged rocks to the ocean.

The sky fissured.

Panic finally shot through Janie's daze. She jumped to her feet, leaning over the rock where Kalin had sat. "Stop it!" she yelled. Wind whipped her hair into her face, and she shoved curls back to see.

The two men battled below, punches throwing, kicks impacting hard.

*The sky spread, showing a red ball of fire on the other side.
Oh God. They would all die.*

*Scrambling down, she lost her footing and fell on the rocks.
Pain lanced across her hip. Pebbles cut into her hands as she
stood, staggering down to the beach.*

*Sand swirled around her legs. She struggled to balance. "Stop
fighting!"*

*Zane shot a roundhouse kick to Kalin's gut, sending the Kur-
jan back three feet.*

*Janie jumped between them. "Stop fighting or we all die." She
pointed to the swirling mass of red pain beyond the tumultuous
sky. Fighting in the odd dream world they'd created could only
lead to disaster.*

*The men paused, both looking up and then back down at her.
Wind whistled around them.*

*Kalin flashed sharp fangs so much bigger than they used to be.
"That's my cue. I do see some of the future, Janie. You're in
mine." With a wisp of sound, he disappeared.*

*Zane growled, dark gaze focused on her face. "What hap-
pened?"*

*"Werewolves." She swallowed. Although the wind beat against
her, she no longer felt its bite. "I told you we'd see each other
again. Though this is the last time." Her brain hurt. Comfort
existed past the dream if she could just let go. Maybe she should
let go.*

Zane grabbed her arms, giving a strong shake. "How bad?"

*"Bad." She forced a smile, lifting her head to see his eyes. For
so long, they were all she thought about. "Thank you for being
my friend as a kid."*

*"You're still a kid," he growled, the sound cutting through the
storm.*

*She swayed. "They hurt my brain. I need it." Her eyes flut-
tered closed. "I had such hopeful plans for us. For the world. I'm
sorry, Zane."*

"Janie Belle!" His bellow shook the dream beach.

A small smile warmed her face. How fitting the last words she'd hear would be Zane's nickname for her.

The world tilted. Something warm and bubbly slid into her mouth. Fire licked down her throat. Her blood bubbled and veins pounded. Healing and hot, the liquid surrounded her brain. Awareness drifted in just as pain exploded behind her eyeballs.

Zane had given her blood.

Janie sat up in the hospital bed with a sharp gasp. Her father instantly enveloped her in a strong hug before her mother pushed him aside to frame her face. "Janie?"

She sucked in air. The pain in her head ebbed. "Hi, Mom."

Chapter 24

Katie stared in shock at the queen, forcing her sharp canines to stay up. "That's impossible."

Worry filled Emma's eyes along with an apology. "I can't explain it." She tapped her clipboard on her hand, leaning against the orange counter in the small third-level lab. Various machines buzzed near two microscopes behind her. "Your chromosomal pairs have already reached a normal twenty-eight for a shifter. So quickly, too." A frown marred the queen's pale skin. "But there's no change whatsoever in Jordan's blood."

The lion lounged against the door frame, no expression on his battered face, a bandage wrapped around his wounded hand. "I don't feel any different."

Katie jumped off the examination table, crinkling the protective paper. "This doesn't make any sense." She yanked the neck of her shirt away to reveal the marking. Her tennis shoes slapped the tile, and she shoved the scent of bleach and cleanser away. "We *mated*."

"Yes. Apparently that mating worked for you." Emma frowned. "But not for Jordan. The virus impacts males differently than females, which we all knew."

Anger and fear spiraled up from Katie's stomach, almost choking her. The virus screwed everything up, even matings. "What are we going to do?" she whispered.

Jordan scrubbed both hands down his face. "I've set up a room where I can lock myself in—it's the best chance I have." He dropped his arms, eyes glowing an odd topaz. "Dage insisted the room be on the top floor—if my head begins to implode, I can hustle outside to the moon."

His tone guaranteed he wouldn't follow suit.

"Turning into a werewolf might be your only chance, Jordan." Katie straightened her shoulders.

He shook his head. "No. There's no way I'll let myself become a beast determined to destroy." His gaze cut hard. "I'll destroy everything I once loved, Kate. That means you and our entire pride. You know how werewolves think."

Unfortunately, she did know. They'd lived in her head for a decade. "I'll stay with you."

"No." With a nod at Emma, he grabbed Katie's arm and tugged her from the room. "You just became the leader of the feline nation. That calling comes before me."

She halted, jerking him to a stop. "You're okay with my leading?" Determination had her already planning to lead the nation should Jordan not make it through the full moon. But she hadn't thought he'd agree.

"Yes." Pride settled on his angled face. "You're smart and you're strong."

"I'll be challenged."

"I taught you to fight." His hands rubbed down her arms. "For so long I've worried about you—wanting to keep you safe. You can keep both you and my baby safe. Besides, there's something . . . different about you. I can sense it."

Yeah. The werewolf virus and Jordan's mark had set something to motion within her. Battle forces clashed in her brain, even now. She may be a bit on the crazy side, but she'd lead well. Warmth settled around her heart.

"You trust me." He no longer saw the little cub or the sickly woman. He actually saw her.

"I do." His gaze gentled. "Though, I'm not really happy about Lance getting past all of us."

Sadness wandered through Katie. The tiger had been a friend. One she trusted. "I won't make the same mistake twice."

Jordan cupped her cheek with his good hand. "I know. Make sure you don't isolate yourself from people who care about you—don't make my mistakes. Never be alone, sweetheart."

"I won't." She pressed into his palm, seeking reassurance.

Jordan dropped a kiss on her nose and then released her. "I need to talk to Dage for a few minutes—why don't you check on Janie and meet me in our quarters?"

"Okay." Leaning up to brush a kiss along his lips, her mind scrambled for a way to save him. There had to be something she could do—if nothing else, she'd throw the damn man to the moon to keep him alive.

Her mind continued to make plans as she meandered down to the infirmary. Janie sat in the bed, munching on a taco. Garrett flanked her side, his gaze on his big sister.

Katie forced a smile. "Aren't you supposed to eat Jell-O while in a hospital bed?"

Janie grinned. "Garrett snuck me one of Max's tacos—they're the best."

Garrett nodded, lumbering to stand. "I'll go find a soda for you while Mom and Dad are in the main lab with Aunt Emma." His metallic gray gaze landed on Katie. "You'll stay with her until I get back."

He'd *almost* phrased the sentence as a request. Katie lifted an eyebrow.

The boy shuffled his feet, a blush winding over his high cheekbones. "Please, Aunt Katie?"

There was the kid she adored. She was so not ready for him to turn into a Kayrs male. "Of course, sweetie pie."

Rolling his eyes at the endearment, he loped from the room.

Katie dragged a chair next to the bed. Her injuries had almost healed, even the slashes that had needed stitches. But her limbs felt heavy. "How are you?"

"Good." The terrible bruise along Janie's face had faded to a light purple. Chalk one up for vampire blood. "I saw Zane in my dream."

Great. Just freakin' great. Katie sighed.

Janie finished her taco, licking sauce off her fingers. "He gave me blood so I'd live." A satisfied smile lifted her lips. "In fact, he got in a big fight with that Kurjan soldier, Kalin. Though the dream world almost collapsed." A frown made her wince.

Katie shook her head. "Garrett gave you blood, sweetie. Garrett's blood saved you."

"Okay." Janie smiled, clearly unwilling to debate the issue. "Garrett's being so nice. I wonder how long it will last."

"Probably a couple of days." Katie smoothed the bedcovers. She glanced at the wall clock. Night would fall shortly. The bite mark in her neck started to pound as if trying to tell her something.

Janie eyed the clock. She cleared her throat, adjusting the pillows behind her back. Sadness filled her incredible blue eyes. "I heard Aunt Emma tell Mom Jordan hasn't changed from marking you."

"Yeah. But I think there's still time." If she kept saying the words, they'd come true.

"Me, too." Janie plucked at a thread from her blanket. "I'm sorry I didn't see any of this happening. The visions can't be forced."

"I know." Katie tilted her head. "You can't feel guilty about that, sweetie."

The girl blinked. "Maybe if I tried harder to understand the visions, and to control them, I'd be better at it. What if all of this is my fault?"

Katie slid her hand over Janie's. "None of this is your fault." Her mind reeled with a way to reassure her friend. "Dage gets visions, right?"

"Sure. He's the king."

"Can he control his visions?" Katie smoothed her other hand over the blanket.

Janie wrinkled her nose. "No. But . . . I'm the prophesied girl." A small grin lifted her lips. "Good guys, bad guys, even middle-of-the-road guys . . . they all saw me coming." She kept her voice light, but her shoulders drooped.

Katie sat back. She'd had no idea the burden the girl carried every day. "None of them matter. *You* matter." She tightened her hold. "The world is not on your shoulders."

"Yeah, it is." Wisdom way beyond her years filtered along the girl's battered face. "I see the choices. And I see the results. What I don't see . . . are *which choices* lead to *which results.*" Tears shone in her eyes. "What if I make the wrong choice?"

"Be more specific." Katie frowned. She needed to warn Cara about this.

"Can't."

Okay. Katie could help. "Listen, Janie. Choices are hard. We take chances, and we take risks. Go with your gut . . . with what you've learned from your family and friends." She had to get going but couldn't leave Janie without some wisdom. "My mating Jordan was a huge risk, and I followed my heart. Now I can shift again." The joy had turned bittersweet. Shifting without Jordan around held very little appeal. Though the mating would save Jordan, too. It had to.

"Hmm." Janie pursed her lips. "You made the right choice."

"Yes. And you'll make the right choices as they come along . . . you need faith."

Janie nodded. "Okay, I understand." Her smile curved. "So your teeth came back in."

"Yeah." Katie allowed the sharp points to descend. "Unlike your brother, I can control mine."

"I heard that." Garrett tripped into the room holding a soda. "I raided Uncle Dage's grape energy-drink fridge."

Janie widened her eyes. "I'm not taking the fall for that."

"I think you're safe." Katie stood and leaned over to brush a kiss on the girl's head. "I'll be back."

"Katie? Good luck." Janie's face held an adult look much too old for her age.

Luck? Yeah, that'd be good. They were certainly due some decent luck. With a nod, Katie hurried from the room. She wanted to scream . . . to cry. Instead, she lifted her head like the leader she was about to become, and went in search of her mate.

Shoving open the door to his quarters, she stopped short.

Candles. Thousands of candles covered every surface, their flickering lights casting an ethereal glow over the stark room. Soft music played from a stereo in the counter.

Her breath in her throat, her mind whirling, she stepped into one of her favorite fantasies. The man she'd cast as the hero in every wish stepped out of the bedroom, bruised, battered, and sexier than any man had a right to be. Shirtless, wearing faded jeans and nothing else, even his bare feet were masculine.

She slowly took a step toward him. "You're better than any dream I've ever had."

His smile was slow. Sexy. Devastating. "*You are* every dream I've ever had." He crooked a finger. "Come here."

Her knees trembled. For the briefest of moments, the world narrowed to the two of them. The coming battle, the deadly moon, even the war . . . all disappeared. She moved as if in a trance, reaching him, his scent of cinnamon and oak washing over her. His chest was wide, defined, and incredibly masculine. Those muscles tapered to a narrow waist that led to heaven. "I love you."

His uninjured hand swept hair away from her face and then cupped her jaw. Smooth, warm, his lips wandered over hers as if they had all the time in the world. Leaving her breathless, he leaned back. "I love you."

She looked in wonder at all the candles. "How did you do this?"

He shrugged. "Let's just say the Kayrs women are romantics." His thumb glided along her cheekbone. "I want to make love to you. Just in case."

The words spiraled sorrow through her heart. She shoved sadness out, concentrating on the amazing male before her. "You up to it?"

His grin flashed. "I'll do my best."

She pressed both palms against his chest, sliding down over hard ridges. "I've wanted to touch you for so many years." The idea that this was temporary made the moment hurt. "To be honest, I never really thought this would happen." Dreams didn't really come true. Not in their world.

Her shoulders shook slightly. This was real.

"From the day you turned twenty-one, I hoped this would happen." He skimmed his fingers through her hair, cupping her scalp and lowering his mouth. "I tried not to want. But God, I did." Gently, so gently, he kissed her, so much emotion packed into the touch tears pricked the backs of her eyes.

Flattening her palms, she leaned into him, letting him lead and take. Yet what he gave slid right in and locked around her heart.

Steady and languid, fire slid through her veins. Deeper than imaginable, stronger than possible, desire bloomed in every nerve. He was hers. No matter what happened, he . . . was . . . hers.

He deepened the kiss, his tongue sweeping inside her mouth, taking his time. Sliding her hands up over so much muscle and strength, she wrapped her arms around his neck, holding tight, pressing against him.

He caressed down her side, stroking her ribs, reaching the hem of her T-shirt. Tugging the cotton up, he broke the kiss to slide the shirt over her head. The material fluttered to the floor. All five fingers on his healthy hand spread over her shoulder and collarbone. So hot. His gaze wandered to her plain cotton bra.

Those primal eyes flared.

She sucked in air. Weakness flushed through her, followed by feminine strength. Next to him, beneath his gaze, she felt all female. Strong and beautiful. Whole.

Levering on her toes, lifting her chin, she nipped his jaw . . . and felt his smile. She levered back to see happiness in his eyes. Pleasure in the curve of his mouth.

He leaned down, nuzzling the tops of her breasts over the cotton. She gasped. Need turned to demand. Yanking the band from his hair, she plunged both hands in, tangling in the thick strands. "I love your hair." From day one, the myriad of colors had intrigued her.

The bra slid open with a flick of his fingers. "I love . . . these." With a chuckle, he lowered his head, taking one nipple in his mouth. His good hand caressed down her hip, following the angle of her body.

She gave a strangled sigh at the scalding heat. Her knees buckled.

Jordan caught her, standing and swinging her into his arms as smooth as any dance. His mouth found hers as he strode toward the bedroom, passing through to gently place her on the bed. He tugged off her boots and socks before unsnapping her jeans. They disappeared along with her thong. His jeans followed suit.

More candles lined the sparse furniture, their soft light flickering over the hard planes of his face.

The idea that he'd spent so much time on romance sent butterflies winging through her abdomen, and pain through her heart. There had to be a way they could stay together. Her eyes filled.

"No." He gently shook his head, sliding a hand across her ribs. Her muscles shifted, and her skin puckered. "No sadness. Only us."

He placed a soft kiss on her mound, his mouth traveling up her torso to wander around one breast. Playing, exploring, he kissed his way to her collarbone, nipping in several places. So many nerves lived under her skin—she'd had no idea. Her heart filled. She arched against him.

Chuckling, he slid up her jugular to her earlobe, where he bit.

The erotic pain had her eyelids fluttering shut. Then she moaned when he traced the shell of her ear, so lightly, as if memorizing every angle and hollow of her body. Gentle kisses landed on her closed lids, her nose, and her chin.

She opened her eyes to see absolute love, real and lasting, in his eyes. "I love you, Jordan."

Jordan absorbed the words he'd needed to hear, wishing against fate they had more than this one moment. Not even an entire night, just a series of minutes, maybe an hour, to show her how very much she meant to him. Several lifetimes wouldn't be long enough.

The idea that he could've spent the last ten years with her nearly broke his determination to go slow. For once, he'd show her slow. He'd show her love.

How could he have missed how perfect they were together? For so long, he'd kept himself apart from his people, even from his friends. But not Katie. From day one, she'd seen the man inside, and not the leader. She'd wormed her way right into his heart, into his life. Then when she'd become a woman, she'd become an insightful and caring cat.

She'd become the perfect mate for him. Kind, smart, and stronger than imaginable. She *knew* him. And for some inexplicable reason, she loved him anyway.

The claiming had been brutal. He wouldn't change a second of it, but she deserved more. More than he could give her. But for now, he'd leave her with a memory of being loved, of being everything. Because she was.

He slid up her jaw, marveling at the softness of the skin covering such fine muscle. A delicate warrior, to be sure. Finally, he found her mouth. His woman liked to kiss. Taking her mouth, he plunged deep, exploring her secrets. He had to learn as much as possible before moving on.

A low whimper escaped her.

Light caresses along her inner thigh had his little warrior trembling. Flattening his palm over her leg, he slid up and over her hip bone and back down her side. So much strength in such a delicate package.

Who would protect her?

Sure, she was tough and would make an excellent leader. But she was his woman, his mate. The most important calling he'd ever have would be to protect her and their offspring.

Her tongue swept inside his mouth, slowly learning him. Stealing his control.

The complete perfection of the moment . . . hurt.

His fingers clenched into her butt. Slowly, he slid inside her. God, she was tight. Her body fought him, even as her legs wrapped around him. Taking several seconds, taking his time, he finally shoved all the way home. He released her mouth to lean back and exhale.

Then he stilled. She enclosed him in so much heat, a roaring filled his head. "You're perfect." And she was. Better than even fate could've created. She was something more.

She smiled. All woman, all mystery, so much love in her tawny eyes she took his breath away. Her eyes fluttered closed, and she arched against him.

His low groan drowned out her soft moan. In unison, they began to move. He slid out, and then back in, trying so hard to go slow. To torture them both. To leave her with memories to keep her warm on the cold nights ahead.

He grabbed her hand, pressing it beneath his, feeling a surge of satisfaction when she curled her fingers through his.

Increasing the speed of his thrusts, he watched in fascination as a dark blush stole from her breasts to her classic face. She sobbed his name.

"Open your eyes," he whispered, waiting until she complied, then, "keep them open." More than anything in the world, he wanted to watch her go over. See those amazing eyes glaze over with passion. For him.

Pounding faster, he angled just right.

Her cry shattered the peace, waves rippling through her

body to clutch him. With a hoarse shout, he followed her into pure bliss.

Coming down, he smoothed a kiss over her gasping mouth. "I love you, Katie. Forever."

Chapter 25

Jordan rubbed a hand over the scruff on his jaw. He hadn't showered, and Katie's scent covered him. No way would he shower her off. He'd left her sleeping, making sure not to awaken her—making sure she couldn't follow him. Deep down, he was almost disappointed he would miss her explosion of temper.

"Don't shave on my account," Talen muttered as he eyed the far tree line.

Jordan shrugged, his gaze on the cliffs dropping to the ocean. "Considering chances are I'm about to turn into a beast, I figured, why bother." Not the truth, but oh well.

"Right." Talen sniffed the air, rolling his eyes. "Right." Vampires could smell as well as shifters.

Jordan turned, checking out the sniper positions to the south. The sun had disappeared and the moon would make an appearance shortly. His neck itched. The muscles along his spine ached with the need to shift. "I have about an hour before I need to lock myself in a room and hopefully keep my head from exploding. Do you mind if we hurry this up?"

"Sure." Talen surveyed the door beyond the courtyard. "All nonessentials will be in the lower level. Guards on every level. Max and his team will cover the kids, who we've decided to keep in the playroom on the tenth level along with our mates."

"Good move." The playroom would keep the kids busy, and the tenth level was the most secure. "Escape routes?"

"We have tunnels leading from there to land, sea, and air options. If Max needs to retreat with the kids and non-soldiers, he'll make the decision as to direction at that time." Talen checked his weapon. "Kane thinks you'll be able to beat the moon."

"He does?" Surprise lifted Jordan's brows.

"Yes." Talen frowned. "We need another front line—the door isn't secured enough."

"Yes, it is." Even in despair, Jordan felt like grinning. "Kane didn't say I'd survive." Talen was actually using positive reinforcement with him. Probably Cara's idea.

Talen lowered his brows. "The idea makes sense. Mating changed Katie, it'll change you. You just needed more time."

Yeah. In a fairy tale. Jordan nodded, giving his friend what he needed. "I think you're right. I'll be fine."

Dage stalked outside, a digital tablet in his hand. "You're not going to believe this." He punched in buttons. "Your buddy Gerald has aligned with the demons. He's in Scotland and is demanding you step down."

The king flipped the tablet around and a form began to take shape on the screen. Jordan stepped forward, waiting until the panther could be seen clearly. "Gerald. What the fuck are you doing?" The time for diplomacy and manners had long passed.

The panther raised an eyebrow. "Figured you'd be dead by now."

Asshole. "Thanks for the support—I'll keep it in mind." Jordan fought to keep his temper leashed. The closer the moon came to rising, the stronger the beast within fought against its shackles. "If you thought I'd be dead, why are you making stupid demands?"

The panther's nostrils flared. "I don't see what's stupid about the king wanting his brother returned alive."

Dage growled low. "You know where Jase is?"

Menace tinged the panther's smile. "Yes. Kill Jordan and his bitch, and I'll make sure you get your brother back."

How did Gerald already know about Jordan's mating Katie? If he survived the moon, he was hunting the leak. He kept his face placid, his voice bored. "What the hell are you talking about?"

"We know you mated the handicapped shifter." Gerald stepped close to the screen, his features distorting. "We also know the second you die, she will be squired to safety by Noah Chance. I'm not playing hide-and-seek for the next decade until finally killing the lioness." He looked past Jordan. "I know where your brother is. Jordan is going to die anyway, as is Katie. Make it easier on all of us. Kill them both."

Anger swept through Jordan, his bones enlarging, the beasts within fighting to get out. He struggled to contain himself. "I'm going to kill you, Gerald."

Talen grabbed the tablet, shoving his face close. "Where's my brother?"

The panther sighed. "Do you accept my terms or not?"

Rage rippled down Jordan's back. How the hell could Gerald turn against him like this? Not for a second did he think the Kayrs men would kill Katie. He, on the other hand, was probably fair game. Especially since his life expectancy wasn't too great.

"You're asking me to trade one brother for another," Dage hissed. "You don't want to do this."

Surprise grounded Jordan. The Kayrs men considered him family. All of a sudden, the last hundred years of his leading alone, solitary and tough, seemed like a waste. "Take me out, Dage," he whispered. "I'm going to die anyway."

"No."

He shoved Dage out of the way. "You don't want Katie. She can't shift, she can't fight . . . she's no threat to you. But the king will kill me."

"No, I won't," Dage muttered softly. "This won't work."

Gerald chuckled, flashing sharp canines. "Katie has to be taken out, and I promise I'm the guy to do it. Unless, of course, the king wishes to save his youngest brother before the demons turn him into an unrecognizable psychotic."

Jordan struggled to remain in control. If his enemies ever found out about Katie's pregnancy, there wouldn't be a place on earth she could hide. Good thing his woman could fight. His claws shot out, and he kept them away from the tablet. "Prove you know where Jase is."

"All right." Gerald reached behind him, grabbing a man's necklace featuring a silver Celtic knot. "I believe you recognize this."

Neither man next to Jordan twitched a muscle. Their faces gave away nothing. Yet anger popped the oxygen and tension vibrated almost strong enough to see. He recognized the pendant, too. Conn's wife had given the charm to Jase for his birthday about five years ago, first blessing the metal as only a witch could. The youngest Kayrs brother wouldn't give it up willingly.

Anger wasn't going to get Jordan anywhere. "The demons consider shifters to be fun pets. They're using you right now, and they'll continue to do so until they get bored. You're a dead man if you align with them."

The bastard's gaze hardened. "For now, they have the power. Soon I'll take over the feline nation and help the demons finish destroying the Realm . . . and then the

Kurjans. Vampires and Kurjans have existed long enough in this world, and we've waited long enough for you two to finish each other off. Apparently you both stink at war."

"I will find you," Talen growled, "and when I do, you'll wish Jordan had found you first."

Gerald licked his lips. "Your choice."

The screen went blank.

Dage tapped his ear communicator. "Conn? Find Gerald Shotlam—he's aligned with the demons and might know where Jase is." Clicking off and pivoting around, he pierced Jordan with a glare. "Don't fucking die." Without another word, the king disappeared inside.

Jordan clapped Talen on the back. "Remember your promise." He'd gotten vows from all his men as well as the Kayrs family to protect Katie and their cub. "My child."

"My life." Talen gave a short nod.

That was as good as a vow could get. Jordan nodded, wishing he could spend what little time he had left with Katie. Man, she was going to be mad when she awoke. "I need to check out my little room of hell." It was right off the entrance, just in case his brain started to explode and he needed to escape. But his friends didn't know he had no intention of escaping into the moon. Shackles remained under the one cot to keep him in place.

He'd never turn into a beast.

Hustling to the small room, he dropped to sit and catch his breath. While his grand plan included staying underground until his head exploded, he knew with a certainty that Brent would find him.

Their final fight would happen that night.

Chapter 26

Katie snuggled her nose into the pillow, the masculine scents of cinnamon and oak bringing a smile to her face. "Jordan?" She sat up, her breath stilling as her arm caught on metal. In slow motion, she glanced down at the handcuff around her wrist. Confusion had her following the other side to see it secured around the metal bedpost.

Surprise had her glancing back and forth from the post to her hand.

Then anger flashed through her so fast her cheeks burned. He'd handcuffed her to the bed.

Humor, unexpected and absolutely inappropriate, bubbled up from her stomach. She gave one short laugh. He'd actually handcuffed her to the bed. "What a moron."

Stretching, she enjoyed the odd flair of intimate aches. Even making love, even so very gentle, Jordan had left small bruises on her hips. Bruises from the pads of his fingers. Reality smacked her in the face. Spent candles lined every surface in the room. The clock on the wall promised the moon would soon be rising. She needed to get to Jordan and fast.

Biting her lip, she checked out the area. Not much was around. With a shrug, she snarled, shooting her canines down. Pleasure burst through her at the simple act. She'd missed it so much.

Ducking her head, she angled a fang into the lock of the handcuffs. A couple of twists, and the metal released her. How silly of Jordan to have forgotten her fangs. Of course, she hadn't had fangs in a decade.

She yanked up her jeans, quickly yanking on her bra and shirt. What if Jordan didn't survive the moon?

A folded note on the table caught her eye. She grabbed it.

Kate—
I know it probably took you two seconds to unhook the handcuffs. I couldn't help myself. Seeing you cuffed to the bed has been a fantasy of mine for quite some time. Please stay down in safety tonight. It isn't because I don't trust you. I do. You're a fighter, and you'll be an amazing leader to our people. But there's a chance, if the beast gets loose inside me, that I could hurt you and our cub. I'd rather die. In addition, I'd prefer you didn't see me descend into a beast. Please. Remember me as we were tonight. I love you. Always. J.

She took a deep breath. He was trusting her and asking her to understand. Asking her to let him deal with the moon. One last request from her mate.

Choices.

Ten years ago, she would've heeded his wishes. Wanting to please him, to make him happy, to show her trust in his decisions, she would've stayed below.

She wasn't the same woman.

Stronger than even he knew, she'd fight for him. She'd fight with him. Telling Janie to follow her instincts had been the right advice. Katie would follow hers, regardless of the consequences.

Panic had her struggling to focus as she slipped on her shoes. If nothing else, she'd throw him under the moon. If werewolves could evolve, then maybe he'd have a chance.

The scent of spent wax and hopeless dreams filled the living area of the quarters as she dodged around the couch and ran into the hallway, smack into a strong chest.

Bouncing back, she gave Baye her meanest glare. "Making sure I stay inside?"

Lines of stress cut beside his mouth. "Jordan ordered me to guard you. I said you'd make it outside somehow." Baye glanced down the empty corridor. "What's your plan?"

"I'm going to find him . . . hopefully save him." She put both hands on her hips, her lungs compressing. The moon would be rising within the hour.

Baye nodded. "I'm so damn sorry about Lance. I mean, I knew he had a small crush on you, but I had no clue . . ."

"That he's freakin' crazy?"

Apology and sorrow turned down Baye's mouth. "I'm so sorry."

Katie grabbed his arm. "Not your fault, Baye. I didn't see it. Nobody saw how crazy Lance is—though we're gonna need to get him help. We're good." Something to worry about another day. Time was running out. "I need to get to Jordan. Are you and I going to fight?"

"No." Baye grinned, but his eyes stayed somber. "Go for it—I'll head to the armory and finish suiting up. We have a real fight coming."

Talk about an understatement. She began running up the stairs, through the wide underground hallways, searching for her mate.

Instead, she came upon Dage and Talen issuing orders to vampire and shifter troops in the large conference room on the top floor. Dodging to the side, she allowed the soldiers to exit the room before approaching the king. Noah tugged her hair, and Max patted her shoulder as they passed.

Dage gave her a nod. "We got about half of the werewolves earlier when we chased them . . . but not your furry friend. I'm assuming they'll be back during the full moon."

Katie slowly nodded. "Yes. Brent won't be able to help himself. But he's injured, the moon will distract him, and he won't be thinking clearly." As an animal, the bastard would just attack. He wanted her, but he wanted Jordan more. The idea of Jordan going up against Brent while trying to fight the moon made something ache deep in Katie's gut.

Talen unfolded schematics and pointed out vantage points. "I have snipers set up along the perimeter—no fighting, just take them down hard. A second force is along the tree line, and that's all we can spare. Considering we sent ten soldiers to the hospital in Canada . . . and buried ten more, we're spread thin right now."

Hurt smashed into Katie's stomach. Three of those buried had been from her clan. She ignored the pain . . . sorrow would have to wait. "What about flying the kids and nonsoldiers to safety?"

Dage's eyes swirled a pissed-off blue. "There is nowhere safe."

Sad, but true. Katie shuffled her feet. "That's scary."

He nodded. "The contingency plans are in place if Max needs to get them out of here."

Talen rolled up the stack of papers. "This is our head-quarters, and we're better able to stand and defend here. Though I want every trained person over the age of fifteen to be armed and ready—even in the secured sections underground." He sighed. "And Garrett. That kid is young, but he can fight." Obvious pride coated the vampire's words.

Dage nodded. "Janie is well enough to move to level ten." He glanced outside the darkening opening. "At least werewolves will hit hard and fast. No real battle strategy for the beasts."

"Keep in mind the werewolves are getting smarter." Katie had better hustle before the moon began to rise. "Any word on Jase?"

"No." Talen checked his watch. "Kane and Conn should be checking in soon. They'll find our brother."

Hopefully. Katie faked a confident nod. "I'm sure they will." She glanced around the utilitarian conference room. "Where's Jordan?"

"Securing a room toward the entrance." Doubt and anger filtered across Dage's handsome face. "You probably shouldn't be there tonight."

"I'm going to be there tonight." She lifted her chin.

"I figured. I'd give you a dart gun, but . . ."

A tranquilizer would be harmful to Jordan in lion form. He wouldn't be able to think much less fight the moon. "A dart gun would only end up in my being tranqued." Katie flashed a real smile.

The king dropped a quick kiss on her brow. "Good luck, Kate."

"You, too." With a nod to both vampires, she headed out to meet with Maggie, finding her friend preparing in the armory with a dart gun.

Maggie snapped a green dart into place. "I talked Charlie into flying the helicopter."

Katie shook her head. "You charmed a teenaged shifter to do your bidding?"

"No. I asked Janie to charm him and she did." Maggie tucked a smaller dart gun into her boot. "The panther flies like a pro, according to Kane."

Reaching out to grab Maggie's arm, Katie struggled to find the right words. "Thank you for doing this—and thank you for being my friend."

Maggie nodded, brown eyes going serious. "Thank you right back." She patted Katie's hand. "We're all going to make it through tonight—I just know it." Her voice came out bright—too bright—but Katie appreciated the attempt.

"No matter what happens, I've enjoyed the last ten years living with you." Katie forced a smile. Maggie had been a constant support during the last decade of werewolf hunting, virus fighting, and Jordan pining.

"You, too." Maggie shoved back her unruly hair. "And tomorrow, when this is all over, I want full details of the mating in the woods. Full details, girlfriend."

Heat climbed into Katie's face. She'd share, but no way would she tell all. "You got it." Giving Maggie a hug, she ventured in search of her mate.

She found him in a small control room near the west exit. Mere feet away from where the moon would call. Everything had been stripped from the space save for a twin bed bolted to the floor and covered with a wool blanket. A chain with ankle clasp hooked to the left leg of the bed, solid and unyielding. A quick glance down confirmed the ultra-strong dead bolt.

Her hands settled on her hips. "Nice lock."

"I'm not turning into a werewolf." Jordan pivoted, his tawny gaze on her. Tall, broad, so strong, he stood before her better than any fantasy she'd ever had. Faded jeans hugged long legs while a dark T-shirt outlined impressive muscles. Lithe and lean, a true lion.

She settled her stance. "Nice try with the handcuffs."

"Thanks. I can concentrate better on this if I'm not worrying about you."

"I'm not letting you die. If you need to turn into a werewolf to survive, you're going to do so."

"Damn it, Katie. I have Terrent on ready . . . he's coming to kill me no matter what happens." Frustration and an odd acceptance filtered along Jordan's sharp face. "We have no choice here."

That's what he thought. "You're wrong. On so many counts."

His canines flashed. "What if I become all beast?" His eyebrow lifted. "Determined to destroy everything you're about to vow to protect?" Stalking two steps closer to her, he brought cinnamon and oak with him. "Think you could kill me, kitten?"

"In a heartbeat."

His smile rang with pride and something else. Pure, raw lust. "I'm proud of you."

Yeah, well, his pride didn't mean shit if he was dead. "Then you should fight for me."

"I will." He stretched his neck, nostrils flaring. "You need to go—we'll have to postpone this little discussion until later. The moon . . . is coming."

Yeah. Katie could still feel the pull. Maybe the moon would always have a purchase in her soul. But the bitch would only get Jordan as a result. Pivoting, Katie kicked the door shut, reaching to engage the lock.

Irritation curled Jordan's lip. "Open the door and go underground, Kate. Now."

"No." Part one of the plan formulating in her head included keeping him occupied as the moon rose to full height.

Fire flashed in his eyes. "At this moment, I'm still Alpha of this pride, and you'll damn well obey me."

Interesting that he played the Alpha card and not the mate card.

"I'm also your mate. Get your ass downstairs."

Ah. There it was. Katie allowed a small smile to scream challenge across her face. "Make me."

Chapter 27

Jordan stilled. The beast shimmered to the surface, deadly and dark. "How about you don't play games with me right now? I'm not exactly in control here." He twisted his neck, agony exhaling on his sigh. "The moon is coming."

"I know." Duty pulled her in several directions. Their people needed a leader—if she and Jordan both died, chaos would ensue. The cub hidden in her belly needed to survive. But above all, at the very core of everything Katie would want to be, lay Jordan. The people, the baby, and Katie all needed him to survive. All or nothing.

Reaching down, she tugged her shirt off. The cool air hardened her nipples. Goose bumps sprang along her stomach.

Jordan gave a low snarl, his gaze on her breasts.

Licking her lips, she kicked off her shoes and shoved her jeans to the floor. A tiny scrap of lace covered the rest of her. Standing tall, she lifted her head. "I thought I could occupy you."

"That's quite an offer." He tucked his thumbs in his belt loops, heat pouring off him. His eyes captured hers. "Disobedience is a bad move for you."

"Kick off your boots." She reached for the bottom of his shirt to yank over his head. Both hands went to the snap on his jeans. "I never planned to obey you—as either a subject or a mate."

Holding her gaze, he moved, his boots sliding to the side. A lethal smile crossed his lips just before he flipped her around to face the door. Brushing his lips across her neck, he licked her marking.

Her knees went weak. Hunger flashed from his mouth straight to her sex. The feeling was more powerful than any dream. He slid an arm around her waist, tugging her into his hard body. Heat and strength surrounded her, all male, all powerful. He licked her again, his teeth sliding into alignment.

A slight pain echoed, but passion overcame it.

Her mind buzzed with both need and curiosity. The bite didn't hurt, but there was no question his fangs were embedded in her flesh. He growled and slid those deadly points deeper.

She exploded.

The room flashed into nothingness as an orgasm slammed through her so heated her breath caught. Only Jordan's forearm around her rib cage kept her standing. He let her ride out the waves and then slowly retracted his fangs. "Disobedience gets you bitten, little one."

"Damn it, Jordan," she sighed, coming down from a truly amazing orgasm. "You can bite me anytime."

His chuckle dropped dark and low. His hand followed suit, sliding down her abdomen and inside her silk panties. "I wanted our last time to be gentle. This can't be."

She shrugged back against him, her mind still spinning. "I've never wanted gentle."

His fingers parted her, and her knees gave out again. She began to struggle in an effort to turn around. Her fingers tingled with the need to touch him.

In response, he shot them toward the wall, slapping his bandaged hand against the solid rock. "Hold still."

"No." She threw a shoulder back.

Three fingers plunged inside her. She gave a short cry, freezing in place. It was too much.

"I said to hold still." The hard line of his erection dug into her hip, even through his jeans. His bare chest warmed her back. His fingers began to play, sliding through wetness to circle her clit. His other hand abandoned the wall to cup her breast.

Hotter than any sun, his mouth brushed her ear, and one fang nipped her earlobe.

Her mind spun. The quartz wall swam before her eyes. With a soft whimper, she gyrated against his hand.

"Ah, kitten. That's the sweetest sound." His breath panted out at her ear, hot and out of control. "Let's hear it again." He tweaked her nipple.

The next sound was more of a cry than a whimper. "Jordan."

His body shuddered behind her. "The moon is coming."

Katie took advantage of his distraction and flipped around, quickly yanking down his jeans, which were kicked to the side.

His gaze feral, his eyes more midnight than dawn, he lifted her. Plunging forward, he impaled her against the wall. Pain caught her off guard. A cry strangled in her throat, her eyes opening wide.

Hunger dancing on his face, both beasts clearly battling beneath his skin, he yanked her leg up higher in a silent command.

She relaxed against the wall, her body accepting him. Clasping her ankles at the small of his back, she followed the order. Curling her hands around his shoulders, she exhaled softly. "I love you, Jordan."

Triumph lifted his chin. "I love you, too. No matter what." His eyes began to glow an odd light. "While I still can, I have to tell you. You were right. We belong together." His face grimaced as the beasts within him fought for dominance just under his skin. "I shouldn't have locked you downstairs."

She struggled to remain still but ultimately ground against him. The feelings were too powerful to ignore. "We are together."

At her movement, he began to pound. The animal within surged to the surface, no humanity left on his hard face. Digging his fingers into her butt, he thrust into her, holding her in place. A harsh spiraling started deep inside her. Need rippled along every nerve ending. Her teeth slashed down with a craving for his flesh.

Even as he hammered into her, lighting nerves on fire, whispers of thought echoed through her brain. Something there. A thought she needed to capture.

His hands bruised her hips. A snarl lifted his lips. The animals within him shimmered beneath his skin, both fighting to get out. His fangs dropped low.

Their sharp glint shot her into awareness. The idea hit her so hard her head snapped back.

Of course.

With a snarl filled of desperation and determination, she struck his neck, fangs digging past muscle and tissue until planting in bone.

He jerked back, a lion's displeasure roaring through the room. Yet she held on, closing her jaw, making sure her teeth met in the middle. Tightening her legs, digging her ankles into his back and her arms circling his neck, she held on with every ounce of determination she owned.

Pumping faster, he tangled one hand in her hair to yank her head back. She snapped her jaw harder, ignoring the sharp pain.

Fighting her hold, pounding harder than possible, he angled over her clit.

She broke with a scream. The flesh and blood filling her

mouth muffled her cry, but it echoed loudly through her head. An energy traveled throughout her body to flow into the wound she'd created where his neck met his shoulder—strong and pure. Tremors ripped along her veins, flashing stars behind her eyes.

His body went rigid. He shoved her harder against the wall. All animal, he pummeled into her, his teeth striking fast and deep in the marking.

Her orgasm grew in strength, taking over, taking everything. Images flashed inside her brain. Jordan when he'd saved her. Jordan teaching her to fight, Jordan teaching her to survive, Jordan marking her for all time. Finally an image of two identical cubs with Jordan's eyes and her spirit. Twins.

Coming down, facing reality, she could only hold on as he hammered into her. Finally, with a hoarse shout, he came, his entire body shuddering with his release.

She retracted her teeth, sighing in relief as he did the same.

He leaned back, still inside her, his strong body trapping her. "What the hell?"

She exhaled, her skin prickling as the moon called from the other side of the door. "I mated you." But even assuming Maggie was successful in her job, would Katie's mark beat the moon's pull?

Chapter 28

Maggie focused on the sounds of night. Life bustled around in the forest, dark and steady. Okay. She could do this. She had to do this. A backpack weighed heavily across her shoulders, but she held on tight. Survival lay in the worn canvas.

Terrent wandered out the side exit, his gaze taking in the training field. Thick boots covered his feet, while combat pants and shirt covered his frame. He hadn't donned a bulletproof vest yet, but no doubt the protective gear awaited him inside. Not by one whisper had he hidden his plan to kill Jordan that night. One dark eyebrow lifted. "Maggie? Katie told me you wanted to speak with me?"

"Hi." She turned toward him, an itch wandering up her spine. The moon would rise soon. "You know I only shift under the full moon, right?"

Interest lit his dark eyes. "I did know that."

She pivoted to face him fully, adrenaline pumping through her veins. He was so much bigger up close—did she have a chance? She cleared her throat. "Well, I wondered if you wanted to shift with me. This one night I'd like to run with another wolf."

He lifted his chin. Those eyes narrowed to all black, suspicion swirling through. His voice stayed level. "Normally, I'd love to. But since we're expecting a werewolf attack in a couple hours, maybe next time?"

Anger heated her breath. While she'd had no intention of shifting with him, he'd refused far too easily. "You're not worried about werewolves attacking. You're ready to kill Jordan if he changes." How could Terrent consider himself Jordan's friend and still want to kill him when there was even a chance of the virus being cured?

Terrent grabbed her arm, tugging toward the building. Warmth and raw strength flowed from his palm. "We're not discussing this. Now you go underground to safety, and I'll see you later."

Maggie stumbled, reaching for her boot. Quick motions had the gun levered into Terrent's ribs.

"What the hell?" He tried to pull back.

She fired three times.

Shock crossed his features. He released her. Most people tripped, fell, or tried to move away when shot with a tranquilizer. Not the wolf. He stood still, head cocked to the side, a deep frown between his masculine brows. "What did you do?"

The weapon remained steady in her hands as she settled her stance and aimed for his chest. "Just a simple dart—you'll be fine in a couple of hours."

Curiosity lit his eyes while his full mouth grimaced. "You drugged me?"

Well, not yet apparently. "Yes."

Incredulousness flashed bright across his face. "Do you have any idea what I'm going to do to you?"

Fear spiraled deep before being shoved away by determination. "Not much." She fired four more darts into his chest.

He growled low, lunging for her. The air swished. Gigantic hands enclosed her shoulders. They hit the ground together. Three hundred pounds of muscled male landed on top of her, knocking the air from her lungs. Panic zinged through her. She shoved him, but he didn't move. His head dropped to the curve of her shoulder as he went limp.

"Terrent." She tried to struggle beneath him, but he remained motionless. The guy was out.

Her abdomen compressed. The chilly ground ate into her clothing. She had to get him off while she could still breathe. He weighed a freakin' ton. "Charlie," she squeaked. "Charlie, where are you?"

The shifter slid from behind a tree, hustling to shove Terrent off. "Man, he's a big wolf." Doubt wrinkled Charlie's forehead.

"Yeah." Maggie sucked in big lungfuls of air. "Help me drag him to the helicopter."

Charlie scratched his head. His Snoopy T-shirt glowed in the meager light of the emerging moon. He'd worn ripped jeans, tennis shoes, and a black hat for his foray into kidnapping. "I'm thinking this isn't such a great idea."

Yeah, she was thinking the same thing. "Listen. Terrent is a good guy, I know. But his job is to take out Jordan, someone whom Janie loves like an uncle. She asked you to help us and you said yes." Manipulating the teenager wasn't cool, but it was the only chance Maggie had. "You'd be doing the right thing." In the long run, anyway. Short run, they might end up torn apart by a pissed-off wolf. "Trust me."

Charlie groaned, grabbing Terrent by one armpit. "Anyone who tells you to trust them is about to get you in trouble."

Smart kid. Maggie flashed him a grin, latching on to Terrent's other side. For the briefest of seconds, she'd enjoyed being under the wolf. Something to worry about later.

Groaning, moaning, and tugging with all their strength,

they managed to drag the man across the training field to the row of helicopters. His heels left huge divots in the grassy field. Several times his weight became too much, and one of them dropped his shoulder to the ground. His head inevitably followed. The wolf might have a concussion when he awoke. Finally, they reached the tarmac and released his arms. She wiped sweat off her brow. "You're sure you know how to fly one of these things?"

"Yeah." Charlie winced. "Though I don't know how the heck we're gonna get this guy up into one. He's so damn heavy."

Maggie nodded and shook out her hands. Panthers were notoriously good pilots—often learning as young as ten years old to fly. "Okay. Let's just lift him one body part at a time."

Charlie frowned, reaching for Terrent's arm. "This is such an incredibly bad idea." With a youthful shrug, he centered a knee inside the door. "At least he's a wolf and not a panther leader. My Alpha will protect me. Well, probably." With a grunt, he yanked Terrent up.

Maggie shoved. After several thuds and thunks, they had Terrent safe on the floor of the 'copter. His big head clunked loudly on the metal. She fought a wince. They wanted to get the wolf out of the way for the night, not give him brain damage. She jumped in and yanked the door shut. "All right. Let's get out of here—head east and keep on going."

Charlie maneuvered to sit in the pilot's seat and began punching in buttons. "No girl is worth this," he muttered.

Too little, too late, buddy. Maggie settled into a seat, her gaze on the downed wolf. He lay on his back, shoulders taking up the entire floor. Long, dark eyelashes feathered against his bronze cheeks—way too long for a man. In rest, or rather, in a drugged state, he still didn't appear at peace. Even now, the sense of an alert predator danced across the tough features of his face. She wondered who had broken his nose, and if that person still breathed. Somehow, she doubted it.

"I'm sorry," she whispered quietly. So far she'd kneed him in the balls and now knocked him out. A guy most people feared. A sadness chilled her. He was the only wolf she knew, and he really wasn't going to like her now. The guy probably liked quiet, demure, classy women.

She failed on all counts.

Maybe he would've liked who she used to be before losing her memory. But considering nobody else liked her enough to be looking for her, she kind of doubted it. Besides, class was something you either had or didn't have—memory loss wouldn't impact that.

Whoever she used to be, she knew exactly who she was right now. Katie's best friend. And that meant Maggie would do anything to help—even kidnap a killer.

The bird rose into the sky. Maggie clutched onto the seat, her stomach lurching. Man, she hated flying. Most wolves probably hated flying, right? Or maybe she was different in that way, too.

Moonlight glinted off the treetops outside. An urge rippled through her veins. After ten years, she could control the need to shift, but the effort cost her. Her legs moved restlessly, and her heart began to pound.

Needing to preoccupy herself, she studied the wolf. He'd worn a black T-shirt that only emphasized his muscular chest. Was that a six-pack? She glanced at Charlie. The kid concentrated on the night, his gaze out the windshield. Good. Leaning down, Maggie slid Terrent's shirt up.

Oh yeah. Talk about ripped. Hesitantly, she slid her palm over the hard ridges of his abdominal muscles. Heated flesh warmed her skin. Desire flared bright through her. She bit her lip to keep from moaning.

A huge hand slapped over hers.

Oh God. The breath caught in her throat. Lifting her head, she stared into dark brown eyes more wolf than human.

With a tug, he landed her on top of him.

Panic had her struggling.

His other hand palmed her head, slamming her lips onto his. Need shot through her followed by pure, raw lust. He kissed her, tongue delving deep, an obvious erection pressing against her core.

Moaning, her mind whirling, Maggie grabbed the gun from her boot and shot him in the armpit.

He released her, and she levered away, mouth bruised and wanting. Rage rippled through his eyes. A menacing growl hissed from his chest. His eyes fluttered closed and his body went lax.

Holy crap. She scrambled off him, falling into her seat. A quick glance at Charlie showed the kid still concentrating on flying. Thank God.

She pressed a trembling hand to her lips. Her other hand held the dart gun pointed at the wolf. He'd be awake again soon. With a sigh, she yanked open the backpack and tugged out restraints. Imprisoning a wolf in a moving helicopter held so much risk her head began to spin. If he became angry enough, he could rip the entire machine apart.

Still, she secured his legs to metal hooks in each side, and then his arms. The locks she used were new . . . and strong.

The wolf was probably stronger.

Minutes turned into an hour. Then another hour. The moon began to climb bright, beckoning her to jump from the helicopter and race through the woods. The wolf remained secured on the floor. Maybe the combination of darts had finally put him to sleep for the duration.

A third hour passed. His eyelids shot open. No fluttering, no confusion. Alert and ready, he took in the restraints, his head moving only slightly. "You're taking your life into your hands here, little wolf."

Hoarse, his voice wandered down her spine as if he licked her. A shiver vibrated her shoulders. "Stay still, and we all live."

"I wasn't talking about right this moment." Half-lidded, the dark eyes promised retribution.

"Oh." Well, yeah. The scary threat was made all the more frightening by the absolute promise behind the words. She struggled to keep her face stoic. "You're mad, and that's understandable. But you'd do the same thing for a friend."

"No, I wouldn't."

"Maybe." She could reason with him. She had to reason with him. "Aren't you a little glad you don't have to kill Jordan?"

"No." Fire burned hot and bright, turning Terrent's eyes a blazing black. "If Jordan turns, he's going to try to kill Katie. How exactly do you think he'd feel knowing I did nothing to protect his mate and their cub?"

"Katie can take care of herself." Maggie fought the fear and doubt suddenly slamming into her gut.

"Against Jordan? The lion she's loved since she was four?" Terrent's head thunked onto hard metal as he shook it.

"Sometimes you need faith," Maggie whispered.

"Have faith in this"—Terrent levered up, his gaze capturing hers—"you will pay for this. I promise." Powerful muscles bunched in his shoulder as his left wrist tugged against the restraint.

Imaginary needles pricked through her arms. Oh God, not now. The inside of the helicopter began to tilt. She sucked in air, forcing oxygen into her lungs, making her chest expand. A panic attack right now would ruin everything.

Sweat danced on her palm. The dart gun began to slip. Putting both hands around the weapon, she tried to steady her aim. The gun wavered.

With a roar, Terrent yanked one leg free.

The craft rocked, air whizzing by outside.

Charlie shouted, quickly righting the beast. "Whatever you're doing, stop it. We're above mountains and there's nowhere to land."

Maggie fired. The dart went wide, pinging against the metal side and falling harmlessly to the floor.

Chain links blew apart with Terrent's next pull, freeing his other leg. Faster than imaginable, he shot his feet around her, yanking her toward him.

She fell on his hard chest, dots flashing across her vision. The air swished from her lungs. Like a guppy, she opened her mouth, fighting for oxygen. Panic buzzed in her ears. Full-on attack coming.

His hands remained shackled to the sides.

Levering up, she tried to get off him. His thighs clapped hard against her rib cage, trapping her. Pressing the air out of her.

Tears pricked her eyes, and she blinked to clear them. Her startled gaze met the furious one of the man below her.

He tightened his hold. "Drop the gun."

Pain lanced into her ribs. If he pushed any harder, they might break. After ten years of training, she still hadn't realized how thighs could be a weapon. A very effective weapon. Struggling to breathe, struggling to keep calm, she allowed the gun to drop from her hand. The gun hit the floor and bounced.

His hold loosened just enough to allow her to take a shallow breath.

Keeping her gaze, holding her hostage, he yanked one hand free. Chain links zinged around the helicopter, and she ducked to avoid getting smacked in the head. A quick glance to the left relieved her somewhat in that he'd torn the shackle apart, but not the side of the craft.

Her relief died a quick death.

The other wrist shackle gave way without even a protest.

Man, he was strong.

The anxiety attack hit full bore. Her vision wavered. Pinpricks nailed her from every direction, her skin protesting. She began to pant, unable to breathe. A low moan spilled from her chest.

Her eyes opened wide, but she couldn't see. She couldn't breathe. Her shoulders began to convulse.

"What's wrong?" Terrent asked.

She shook her head, her mouth opening and closing. Bile rippled up her throat. A soft moan escaped her.

Strong hands manacled around her biceps. Without warning, the world tilted and she found herself facing away from him, sitting between his dangerous thighs, her butt on the floor of the craft. He palmed the back of her head, lowering her face between her knees. She shut her eyes.

"Breathe." Low, soothing, no hint of anger remained in the wolf's voice. His scorching hot palm rested against her upper back, her entire upper back. Slowly, he slid down to her tailbone and back up. "Deep breaths." He growled low. "Keep flying, kid. I'll deal with you in a minute." He continued the soft caress. "Keep breathing, little wolf. It'll be okay."

For several moments she stayed in place, allowing him

to comfort her. The pain in her skin receded. Her lungs relaxed. Finally, she could breathe.

Still trembling a little, her shoulders straightened. Her eyes opened to see the bottom of the craft. "I'm sorry."

His hand stopped the gentle movements. "For what?"

Well, for the panic attack. She always apologized for some crazy reason. "Um, for kidnapping you?" It was the right answer. Probably.

His hands on her hips flipped her around to face him. Still inside his legs, she felt trapped. Well, and kind of safe. Protected in a totally weird way that made no sense, especially since the anger he'd kept from his voice was stamped all over his strong face.

She tried to move back, and his hands clenched.

"No moving." Turning his head, he focused toward the front. "Turn around and head back to Realm Headquarters. Now."

Charlie glanced over his shoulder, eyes wide.

Maggie swallowed. Then she gave a quick nod. The flight would take another three hours to get back. The fight would be over . . . and either Jordan would be a werewolf, or he wouldn't.

She focused on the wolf. "You would've done the same thing."

He slowly shook his head. "No. You're lucky I have to return to headquarters."

Yeah, so he could maybe kill Jordan. Maggie lifted her chin. "Why is that?"

His eyebrow rose. Anger still swirled in his dark eyes. "Because I'd be taking you to my people, otherwise."

She forced a smile, not quite brave enough to break his hold. "I'll consider myself lucky, then."

His smile almost caused another panic attack. "Oh, this is just a short reprieve, little wolf. We're nowhere near done."

Chapter 29

Katie had made a colossal mistake in foregoing a tranquilizer gun. She eyed the man pacing against the far wall, animals visibly shifting beneath his skin. But she'd had no clue she'd be able to mate him, to force the lion genes back into his blood. With the bite, her plans for the night just reversed completely. She had to keep him *away* from the moon now. Knocking him unconscious right now would be a great idea. They'd both gotten dressed to face the night. "You just need to hang on, Jordan."

He whirled on her, eyes morphing yellow, canines flashing. "I need to get outside." Guttural, his voice sounded like cement being crushed.

The moon had been up for about an hour . . . not high, not in full power. Yet.

But even Katie felt the pull. The need to head outside into the balming rays caused her neck to itch and her head to pound. Fear for him, fear for her, made her muscles vibrate in place. This was going to be the most difficult night of her life.

When he resumed pacing, she eyed the leg iron attached to the bed. How in the world could she get the restraint around Jordan's ankle?

He growled, stretching his neck, increasing his pace. "Don't even think about it."

She started, sliding her shoulders along the wall. "We can survive anything for one night."

Pain and a primal rage rode his strong exhale. "Open the door, go out, and shut it behind you." His gaze stayed on whichever wall he faced while moving. "Now."

If she opened the door, he'd be too tempted to get out. "I'm staying here. To help."

He was on her that fast. Hands manacled her biceps, lifting and slamming her against the door. Hard. Leaning down, his face an inch from hers, he snarled.

She snarled right back. Digging her hands into his thick hair, she yanked his head down. Clasping his mouth, she shot her tongue inside, rubbing her core against his. A wildness rode her, deep and strong.

His groan filled her mouth. His hand dropped to her ass and he pivoted, throwing her to the bed. Two strides and he was on top of her.

Biting his shoulder, she pushed up, shoving him over. Jumping on top of his abs, she ran both hands down his amazing chest. Muscles, man and animal, shifted beneath her palms. So much power.

Flashing a saucy smile, she maneuvered down between his legs, unclasping the button on his jeans.

His breath caught, and interest ripped through his now topaz eyes.

She blew heated air through his jeans and he gave a low groan, shutting his eyes.

Leaning to the floor, she made a quick grab for the restraint, snapping it around his ankle. Then she leapt for the door.

His roar filled the small room. Jumping up, he lunged for her, arms outstretched. The chain jerked him back. Raw fury shot across his face. "What the fuck?"

Fear dried the spit in her mouth. Licking her lips, she tried for a shrug. "You placed the restraints there for a reason. Since I bit you, going outside is the most dangerous move you could make." If she could keep the father of her children from turning into a big hairy monster that wanted to kill them, then she would.

"I would've rather had the blowjob you just hinted at." Deep red covered his high cheekbones. Lust, need, and wildness.

Some of that was for her. "You survive the moon tonight, and I'll blow you every chance I get." The breath panted out of her lungs. Some fear, some desire. Mostly fear.

He coughed out a laugh. "I'll keep that in mind." Buttoning his pants, he dropped to the bed. Sweat soaked through his T-shirt. Ripping off the material, he wiped his chest and brow, throwing the cotton to the ground and revealing a tanned, broad chest. "Of course, we could start now."

Temptation warred with reality. She settled her stance against the door. "I think I'll stay right here."

The lion rippled beneath his skin. "Wise girl."

An oiliness slid down her spine. The taste of burnt char coal briquettes coated her throat. Fear and awareness spun inside her brain, as well as caution. She struggled to keep her face mild. Brent was close—and he wasn't alone.

She exhaled smoothly. Good air in . . . bad air out. Electricity spiraled through her chest. Calm. She needed to at least look calm.

Jordan lifted an eyebrow. "What the hell's wrong with you?"

"Nothing." The need to slash through the door elongated her claws.

He closed his eyes, lifting his chin and inhaling. "I feel them coming. Werewolves." Standing, he focused, the lion's eyes gone. Yellow eyes tinted bloodred stared back at her. "Get out of my way."

"Sure," she breathed out, fighting terror. Sidling along the wall, she kept out of his reach.

Steel rattled when he tried to lunge forward. Confusion lifted his eyebrows. He turned to stare at his captured ankle. Several hard yanks later, and the restraint remained in place. His fangs dropped low. Throwing his head back, he bellowed a howl from hell.

Answering howls echoed in the distance. Muted and low-pitched . . . but strong enough to be heard.

Multiple chills vibrated down Katie's spine.

Fur sprang up along his torso. Black, not lion tan.

Katie gulped in air. "Jordan, fight this. Please fight this." He needed the moon to turn completely, didn't he?

Grabbing his head with both hands, he yowled in agony. Pounding pain vibrated through the oxygen, suffocating the room. His knuckles turned white as he pressed, his entire body shaking. The fur turned lion color and then disappeared. He dropped to one knee, head down.

Tears pricked her eyes. Swallowing several times, she tried to force down the bile that wanted out. A couple of gags escaped her. Tremors shook her hand as she stepped forward and caressed his bare, heaving shoulder. "It's all right." She tried for soothing, but desperate and panting emerged instead.

He grabbed her around the waist, flipping them both onto the bed. The air swooshed from her lungs. All muscle, all male; he landed on her, one hand shoving under her chin, thumb and forefinger digging in.

Her head flew back and she cried out, her muscles tightening in panic. Instinct rose and she thrashed against him.

Strong fingers tightened their hold, cutting off her oxygen.

She froze, eyes widening, body shaking.

The hold lessened. "Unlock me," he growled.

No recognition existed on his face, in his eyes.

The hold didn't allow for her to swallow, but she tried anyway. Tears blurred her vision. "I don't have the key." Crap. Knowing Jordan, there wasn't a key. He wouldn't have left himself an out. "Let me go."

His eyes narrowed. Inhaling, he levered to the side, one claw ripping her T-shirt down the middle.

Oh God. Panic welled up in her chest and she tried to fight, claws digging into his chest. He tightened his hold so she had to tilt her head even more to breathe. She paused, blackness swirling across her eyes.

His hold lessened a fraction. "Hands down."

Trembling, mind scrambling, she retracted her claws and lowered her hands to the rough wool blanket. "Please don't do this." The monster inside him was winning. Should she let him continue? Would allowing him to do whatever he wanted with her keep him alive? Was it worth it? Could she even stop him if she wanted to?

She shut her eyes, relaxing against the bed. All or nothing. A tear leaked out the corner of her eye.

His claw ripped her bra. Two fingers brushed her skin. Metal scraped along her rib cage.

He rolled off her, sitting up.

Shaking her head, confused, she scrambled away from him. He slid the underwire from her bra into the lock at his ankle, twisting viciously.

Red covered her vision. Rage ripped up her spine. Jumping up, she nailed him right in the temple with a leaping sidekick. His head bounced back, a furious cry spilling forth.

Not caring, no longer feeling fear, Katie punched him in the nose.

Blood sprayed.

She hit again. And again. No way was the moon getting him. She'd knock his ass out first.

He jumped up, mouth open in a snarl, fangs glinting.

Pivoting, she kicked him square in the chest. The impact threw him back to land on the bed, which crashed to the floor in a squeal of abused springs.

The earth rumbled a second before a deafening explosion tore through the night. The walls vibrated, rocks tumbling from the ceiling. Katie ducked her head from the pelting missiles and tried to balance herself against the wall. Oh God. A bomb? The werewolves hadn't figured out explosives, as far as the Realm knew. That meant one thing. The Kurjans were with the damn werewolves.

Jordan took full advantage of her retreat. Quick reflexes had the underwire twisted. The lock gave with an ominous *pop*.

Katie backed up, her heart beating too hard, blood rushing through her ears.

Jordan stretched to his feet. Fury glittered in his eyes, deep red covered his cheekbones.

Then he smiled.

The vision erupted in Janie's head like a firecracker. Clear, no static, the image of her father being shoved off a cliff slammed like a rock in her gut. Kalin fought above, his sole goal to kill Talen Kayrs. She had to get to them or her father wouldn't see another sunrise.

Terror shot through her veins. Her gaze darted around the underground playroom at Garret playing pool with one of Charlie's buddies. Like typical guys, they seemed to be the best of friends. Of course, Janie knew where Charlie had gone. Hopefully Maggie could handle Terrent Vilks. Something told Janie nobody handled the huge wolf.

She eyed the area. Several other kids played various games or watched movies.

Her mother sat with her aunt and the other women on the other side of the bar, voices low in talk.

Guards lined the hallway outside as well as along every landing.

But Janie Kayrs knew something they didn't.

Her hand trembled around her soda can, sending fizz flying. Setting the grape drink down, she sidled toward the bathrooms set by the bar against the far wall. Well, the soda bar. A blank rock wall extended from the other end of the bathroom in an odd vestibule, and most people thought the king hadn't gotten around to throwing a game or table inside it.

Janie stepped inside the small area and out of sight from her brother. Taking a deep breath, she swept her hand over the wall, sliding open a keypad. She punched in a six-digit code. A door slid open to Dage's emergency elevator. Well, one of the several emergency elevators most people didn't know about.

The king had always trusted her—she knew all the escape routes.

She hopped inside, pressing a button to shut the door. The rock smoothly slid closed. Man, nobody had even noticed.

Her breath panted out. The image of Talen dying pricked tears behind her eyes. She had to warn him.

He was so going to kill her.

The elevator actually rose to different strategic rooms within the compound. She pressed the button for the main viewing room on the top floor. Nobody would be in there, though guards would be standing at the ready in the hallway, gazes on the locked doors.

The lift jerked to a stop. A dull ache still echoed in her

head from the concussion, but her thoughts remained clear. Her heart pounded so fiercely her ribs actually hurt. Sliding out of the elevator, she paused in the empty room.

Set north of the west entry, the room boasted a full communication panel, two chairs, and a one-way window facing the sea. Anybody looking from outside would just see pure rock. The vampires had technology human militaries would probably love.

Dodging for the panel, Janie opened the shades.

Werewolves, shifters, vampires, and Kurjans fought without mercy outside. Blood sprayed, people died.

She stepped back, gasping. Fear fought with nausea in her stomach. A gag escaped her. Quelling the need to vomit, she took several deep breaths. Where was her father?

Movement by the tree line caught her eye. Talen fought hand-to-hand with a Kurjan, knives flashing, a grim frown of concentration on his face. His reflexes were such that his movements became blurry. Man, he was fast. The Kurjan wasn't one she'd seen before, either in briefings or visions.

An explosion rocked the headquarters. A baseball-sized chunk of rock dropped onto her shoulder. She bit her lip to keep from crying out. Blood welled through her shirt. Shouting filled the hallway outside along with rushing boot steps.

Trying to stay calm, her ears ringing, she scanned the buttons on the control panel. One of those had to open the window, right?

No labels. Colorful buttons, dark knobs, even levers made up the panel. But not a one described its function. The men who usually manned the station didn't need labels. And it was probably better that outsiders couldn't figure out how to use it. But she really needed to open the window. If she tried to go outside the door, guards would stop her. Nothing else mattered besides getting to her father.

Movement outside the window caught her attention. Kalin.

The military leader stood close, head cocked to the side, focus on her. Gasping, she stepped back. Chaos ran rampant around him. He stood tall, moon glinting off medals. Slowly, a smile lifted his bloodred lips.

He could sense her.

Unbelievable. No way could the soldier see inside the rock. Yet somehow, he had a bead on her.

Lifting her chin, drawing on courage, she stepped closer to the window. So long as Kalin concentrated on her, the vision couldn't come true. Her father would remain safe. She could even leave the window shut this way.

A werewolf backed into Kalin. The Kurjan shoved the beast away, his gaze never wavering. Seeing him in Technicolor and not in a dream world lent a surreal sense to the night. Thick black hair fell beneath his shoulders. The red tips seemed even brighter and his skin paler under the moonlight and surrounded by darkness. So different from her—from the vampires.

Even amid the battle, amid her fear, sorrow sank deep. She'd known him as a child. They'd almost been friends.

"I will kill you," she whispered.

His smile widened.

No way had he heard her. No way. Even with the best of hearing, a vampire couldn't have heard her words. But maybe Kurjans had better senses? Or maybe, and the mere thought made her want to hurl, Kalin had a sense of Janie.

She sucked in air. "If you can hear me, you need to leave or you're going to die today."

His smile widened. Damn it, he could hear her. Most Kurjans had sharp, yellow teeth. Not Kalin. Deadly and white, the man had the teeth of a killer shark. He nodded to someone out of range.

Seconds later, the world blew up. The window crashed in. She flew backward, her shoulders hitting the wall right before her head smacked hard. Pain flared and she gasped. Lights flashed full and bright behind her lids. How many concussions could one brain take in a week?

Strong, cold hands wrapped around her arms, yanking her up. Swaying, she forced her eyes to open. Hazy shadows danced across Kalin's face.

She struggled to focus. "You smell like the ocean." Even in dreams, the Kurjan smelled salty.

He eyed her forehead, interest lifting his lip. "You're bleeding."

She shoved against him. "Let go." Dizziness swamped her. She had to get out of there.

His hold tightened. Closing his eyes, he leaned in, breath above her cut. He inhaled, nostrils flaring. "So sweet." With a sigh, he backed away. His lids flipped open, deep green eyes flashing.

Her head pounded. Almost in a daze, she studied him. A dark purple line surrounded his green irises. In the dreams she'd never noticed it. "Let me go."

A Kurjan screeched in pain outside as a werewolf clawed sharp nails down its neck.

Kalin frowned. "Apparently that one needs to die."

Janie shoved against his chest, the metals biting into her fingers. "Let go."

"That's not going to happen." Kalin glanced at the ceiling and around the room. Finally, he focused on the deadly battle outside. "A few more minutes and we should be able to get away to the north."

The fight did seem to be heading toward the cliffs to the west and the forest to the south. Janie opened her mouth to scream.

His hand slapped over her lips. "I'd hate to knock you out." Anger had his arched brows meeting in the middle.

Light brown, nowhere near as dark as his hair. "This doesn't please me any more than you. I had hoped to wait."

Anger and fear slammed away the haziness. She went limp. As he struggled to keep her upright, she slammed a hand into his nose, aiming for his brain stem.

His head jerked back. Blood spurted, burning along her neck.

Shock filled his eyes, and he dropped his hand. Then he smiled again, red coating his teeth, the image more frightening than anything Hollywood could create. "Oh Janet. I'm going to have so much fun with you."

Janie dragged air into her lungs and screamed high and loud.

For two seconds, the fight stopped.

Heartbeats later, glass rippled and rocks flew as her dad and Max leapt into the room, skidding over the huge control panel. With a howl, Talen grabbed Kalin by the neck and shot-putted him back outside. Blood squirted across the wall. With a grim glance at her head, he slapped a knife into her hand. Then he was back through the window.

Max settled his stance in front of her, gun at ready. "Stay behind me."

A pounding started in her temple. Dots danced across her vision. Confusion had her blinking. She pressed a hand against her skin, and it came away sticky. "We have to warn my dad." The words came out slurred.

"About what?"

"That Kalin is here." The vision flared behind her eyes again.

"He knows." Max stiffened when a werewolf flew by the hole in the wall.

Janie shook her head to concentrate. Her vision cleared. Pebbles scattered when she slid to Max's side, her gaze on the monstrous fight outside. Talen and Kalin battled, concentration on their faces, their weapons flashing.

The interior door burst open. Three Kurjans jumped inside, two going for Max. Oh God. They'd breached headquarters. The third grabbed her, swiftly leaping through the gaping outside hole.

Wind bit into her arms. She kicked, shoving the knife in his throat. Blood coated her hand, burning like sparks from a fire.

He dropped her. She stumbled, wildly looking around for a safe place. Screams of the dying penetrated her eardrums.

Her father roared her name.

Turning, Kalin did the same.

A werewolf manacled her by the hair. Pain ripped along her scalp. She tripped, falling to one knee. The beast howled, fangs flashing, eyes morphing to red.

Oh God. He was going to bite her.

Talen started toward her. He'd never make it.

A wisp of sound ripped by her ear as a knife embedded in the werewolf's eye. He released her, yowling, turning away. She slowly lifted her gaze. Kalin stood at the edge of the cliff, having thrown the knife.

The leader of the Kurjan military had just saved her life.

Two werewolves stumbled, one falling right into him. They windmilled, Kalin's eyes widening. Even across the courtyard, the green glint shone bright. He kept her gaze as he went over the cliff.

Max reached her first. Blood covered his torso. Hoisting her around the waist, he ran inside the now open headquarters and down the hall, passing two prone Kurjan bodies. Reaching an elevator, he shoved her inside. "Go to the tenth."

The door slid shut.

Gasping, her mind reeling, she sagged against the far

wall. Kalin had saved her. Then he'd fallen over the cliff. As a Kurjan, he'd be seriously injured but wouldn't die from that. Guilt swamped her at the relief she felt.

She didn't want him to die.

Chapter 30

"You're going to have to go through me to get outside, Jordan." Katie settled her stance on the rock floor of the small room, more than prepared to kick him in the face.

"Not a problem." Energy danced on his skin. Fire lit his eyes.

Somewhere in there was the man she loved. "You go outside, and you lose me. You lose yourself."

He blinked.

The sounds of battle outside filled the night. Screams, gunfire, more explosions. All under the moon. Terror and the urge to fight had her knocking her shoulders against the metal door. "We just need to last a few more hours."

The lion shifted beneath his flesh, strong and powerful, fighting so hard.

Hope filled Katie for the first time that night. "You can beat this."

He exhaled roughly. "I shouldn't shift. If I shift . . ."

She nodded. If he shifted, the animal might take over and heed the moon's call. She just had to keep him out of the moon.

An explosion blasted the night. Rock fissured. Blasting

heat and blinding smoke roiled toward them, throwing Katie hard against the door.

Jordan flew across the room to impact the far wall. He dropped to the rock floor with a sickening thud.

Gasping, heart racing, Katie struggled to breathe. The smoke diminished. A gaping hole remained where the outside wall had been. Shifters, vampires, Kurjans, and werewolves battled hand to hand, using guns and knives in a scene reminiscent of a war movie. All hell had truly broken loose. The ocean spread dark and mysterious into the distance. Light glinted off the dangerous weapons.

Moonlight.

She shook her head, trying to process the scene. The Kurjans were using werewolves. And explosives.

A ruckus sounded in the corridor. Had headquarters been breached?

Another explosion detonated. Sharp rocks pelted from the ceiling and walls. She cried out, flinching as one cut into her neck.

The churning smoke abated, called out to sea.

Brent stood right outside the gaping breach. Tall, furry, blood coating his fangs. His arms swept wide, as if welcoming guests for Christmas dinner. "Kaattieee and Jorrr-daaaan." He rolled his massive head, mewling softly in the pretty moonlight. "Come outttsiiiide."

Katie shivered. "Man, you're creepy."

Jordan launched off the floor toward the beast.

Panic halting the air in her throat, Katie leaped for Jordan in a tackle that threw them onto the sagging mattress. Pain ripped through her ribs when they met his hips. Rolling away, she grabbed him by the hair and tugged toward the far wall. With a growl of outrage, he yanked his head away and stood.

She reached for his belt loop. His strength outmatched

hers by far. She needed to get inside his brain. "The lion is winning, Jordan. Stay the hell away from the court-yard." Then she turned, forcing a smile. "You want us, Brent? Come on in."

Scooting in front of Jordan, fear making her shoulders shake, she shoved her butt into his groin in an effort to make him *move back.*

Brent tilted his head to the side. "Come ouuttt, Kaaa-tiiiieee."

A sharp jab of her hip into Jordan's balls made him hiss out a breath. With an irritated snort, he retreated back against the far wall. He cleared his throat. "Come on in, cousin."

Katie crept to the center where she could intercept ei-ther male if they pounced. Deep breaths. She needed deep breaths. Surveying Jordan from the corner of her eye, a roaring filled her ears. The lion leader stood tall, his face pale, sweat along his brow. His shoulders shook. He looked like a junkie needing a fix. Bad.

Brent licked blood off his lips. A Kurjan went flying by behind him, followed by Talen Kayrs, wicked knives flash-ing. Death rattles echoed from out of sight.

God, she hoped the vampires and shifters were win-ning.

Air whispered. Brent charged her, both paws slamming into her shoulders. With a cry, she shot a knee to his groin, but he pivoted, blocking her kick.

Jordan tackled Brent around the waist. They went sprawling across the hard rock floor, pebbles flying. Inches away from the opening, the two threw punches almost too fast to track. Jordan nailed Brent between the eyes, and the werewolf slid into the night.

Standing to his full height, blood dripping down his face, Jordan took a step forward.

"No!" Katie grabbed him by his jeans, tugging back.

Dage Kayrs slammed into Jordan, sending all three of them sprawling. Katie landed hard, her shoulder popping.

"Sorry." The king tugged them to stand. "Kurjans." He eyed Jordan, turning to view the moon. "Shit."

"Yeah." Jordan wiped blood off his chin.

Sharp claws scraped along the jagged hole in the wall. Brent staggered closer, a gash bleeding from above his right eye. Fur matted an ugly red down his monstrous face.

Two werewolves collided with Talen near the cliff's edge, sending the vampire sprawling. Dage growled and threw a knife at Jordan. "My gun went over the cliff— headquarters breached, need to get to level ten. I'll try to get back."

With a battle cry of all battle cries, the king leapt for his brother.

Jordan twirled the knife in his hand. "Come here, cousin."

Brent smiled. "Neeeed more than a kniiiife."

Shock, fear, and pain all commingled to freeze Katie in place. The night took on a surreal sensation . . . cloudy and confusing.

Brent stalked forward. He feinted toward Jordan and grabbed Katie by the hair. Jerking her before him, he dug claws into her neck.

Pain shot through her nerve endings. The haziness disappeared to be replaced with cold, harsh reality. The beast could decapitate her with little effort. The idea of the babes inside her had her mind scrambling for purchase.

Jordan stiffened, fire lighting his eyes. "Let her go."

"Go outsiiiiide." Brent twisted, dragging Katie through the gap into the night. His claws retracted. Blood slid down her throat. Her heels dragged in the dirt and grass.

The moon beat down, covering her. She fought the urge to sigh and relax right into the rays. Even after the mating, the moon calmed her. Tears filling her eyes, terror filling her heart, she slowly shook her head at Jordan. "Don't come out here."

Soldiers rushed into the main entrance to headquarters. Crap. Had it been breached? Were the kids all right?

Brent slid a furry arm around her neck, lifting her off the ground. She dug both hands into his fur, fighting to breathe, her feet kicking uselessly. Tears filled her eyes. The pressure against her windpipe increased. The beast growled. "Come out."

Jordan's knuckles turned white around the knife handle. He took a step forward.

"No," Katie whispered, the tears blinding her.

Sorrow filled his tawny eyes. "I'm sorry."

Faster than sound, he dropped into a baseball slide, catching Brent at the ankles. The beast released Katie. She landed on Jordan, lungs compressing. He tucked, rolling them backward and into the room. Tossing her to the mattress, he lunged to his feet.

The world spun. Her mind bellowed in pain. Dots danced across her vision, and her entire body went cold.

With a bellow of outrage, Brent charged, hitting the lion square in the chest.

They went down in a tangle of arms, legs, and fangs.

Growling, punching, and kicking, the two fought like rabid animals. Brent clocked Jordan in the temple. The lion roared.

Jordan head-butted Brent. Blood flew out of the beast's nose. Scissoring his legs around the werewolf, Jordan reversed their positions. With a shout of pure, raw fury, Jordan plunged the knife into Brent's neck.

The monster yowled in pain, grabbing onto Jordan's arms.

Rage filling his face, his arms visibly vibrating, Jordan shoved deeper and twisted. Sweat covered his bleeding torso, dark circles lined his eyes, and blood coated his jeans. Grunting, fighting, he decapitated Brent.

The werewolf's head rolled across the floor.

Katie gagged twice, forcing bile down.

Jordan snarled, stretching to his feet. Bruises cascaded across his flesh. Several gashes bled freely, including two in his head. His eyes morphed into a yellowish brown. Not lion, not man, not even werewolf. All animal, though.

The scent of blood, death, and smoke overcame the salty brine from the ocean. Katie used the wall to help her stand.

Jordan slowly pivoted toward the hole in the wall.

The sound of fighting had abated somewhat—at least outside. Katie inched toward the opening. "Unlock the door and let's go check on the kids, Jordan."

"Moon." The rays shone down on dead werewolves and downed vampires, sparkling off weapons. He held a bloodied hand out. "Mooooon."

Oh God. Katie searched the battlefield for help. Anybody left standing had headed inside . . . the kids must be in danger. "Jordan! Headquarters was breached. We have to go check on Janie and the other kids."

He took another step closer, paying her no mind. "Warmth. I'm so cold."

One step and she slid her hand into his. Pain flared along her battered knuckles, and she bit back a wince. "I'm having twins. Girls."

His entire body went rigid. "Twins."

"Girls."

For several long, heavy moments of silence, they stared at the moon spreading over the ocean. Jordan tightened his hand around hers. "Pain. This is unbelievable."

"I know." She tugged him toward the far wall, pushing him down.

He yanked her on top of him to straddle his legs. "Need

to stay here." Tucking her close, he burrowed his face in her neck.

Relief and hope coiled through her. She wrapped her arms around his neck, tightened her thighs against his, and held on. "We're gonna make it."

His palms slid up her back to dig into her shoulders. His body shook with violent tremors. Sweat from his chest soaked the front of her shirt. A low moan escaped him, vibrating against her jugular.

"Should we try to go inside?" She could unlock the door and lead him farther underground.

"No. If I move, I'm jumping outside." His voice trembled.

"Okay. I had a vision of our girls . . . I know it's true. How about we think of names?" she whispered. Anything to keep him in place. A fight might be going on down below, but the biggest fight of her life existed right here. Doubt and fear slithered down her spine. She shook them off.

"Names?" He shuddered against her.

"Yes. For our girls."

He took several deep breaths against her skin. "How about Menace and Mayhem?" His voice came out muffled, but clear.

She gave a low laugh, holding tight. "Those sound perfect for *your* daughters. *My* daughters would be something like Faith and Charity. Or Hope."

"Hmm." His breath panted out, heating her neck "Too much irony there, I think. How about Milly and Molly?"

"Too cutsie." She rocked against him "Kitten and Jackass? After us?"

"Funny." His hold tightened. "Samantha and Sidney? Call 'em Sam and Sid?"

She liked that. "Perfect."

"Though I have no doubt Mayhem and Menace will fit

just fine." He nipped her collarbone. His mouth was hot. Too hot. "You saved me. I mean, by biting me."

"You saved me first. By biting me." The marking on her shoulder pounded in agreement. "We're a team, Jordan. We save each other."

"I know."

"You're not alone anymore. Punishing yourself was a waste of time." She stroked his hair, getting lost in the thick strands.

"Maybe." He groaned. "We did what we had to do . . . for peace. It's over."

The note of acceptance in his voice warmed her throughout. Now they just needed to survive the night. His body shuddered against her, the too hot sweat pouring off him and coating her shirt. Every inch of her body hurt, and her shoulder was probably dislocated. If the lion wanted to get out of the room, no way could she stop him.

The strength required in refusing the moon was nearly impossible to gauge. Ninety-nine percent of creatures couldn't come close. Jordan was the strongest man she knew, but he was battered and depleted. She gentled her voice. "Just a few more hours."

Far in the distance, a wolf howled to the moon.

Chapter 31

The sun rose slowly, out of sight, shoving the remnants of night to oblivion. Katie came awake with a sigh. "Ow." Her entire body pulsed like a deep bruise. She pulled stiff arms from Jordan's neck, lifting away from him. Her shoulder popped back into place. "Ouch."

Stubble lined his stubborn jaw. Dark circles cut above his cheekbones. But his topaz eyes were clear and strong. A smile slid across his full lips. "Mornin'."

Warmth slammed into her abdomen. "Ah, morning." Her face heated.

"That's a pretty blush on you, sugar." He ran both hands down her arms, springing tingles to life. "It's cold. Let's go in."

"How are you feeling?" She pushed off his lap with a groan. Every bone she owned popped as she tried to stand.

"Like myself." He stood, stretching and popping vertebrae. "Let's not sleep on the ground again." Rubbing his jaw, he surveyed the destruction outside the gaping hole. A series of loud boots clomped in the hall. Dage appeared in the courtyard followed by the shifter enforcers and several vampire soldiers.

Dage and Noah approached the room. "Everyone all

right here?" The king surveyed them, sending shards of electricity up Katie's neck.

Jordan snarled. "Get out of my head. We're fine."

Katie frowned. "Seriously. You're not supposed to mind read."

Dark shadows lined the king's eyes. He winced. "Just making sure."

Jordan tugged Katie into the meager sun. A soft breeze wandered across the grass. "Was headquarters breached?"

"Yes." Power and anger danced along Dage's skin. "We'll fix the security problem. Most of the Kurjans are down . . . a couple escaped, including Kalin. We'll need to step up efforts to take him out."

Jordan nodded. "We'll do what we have to do."

Katie smiled. If nothing else, the guy had found peace with his past. Hopefully with their future, too.

Dage frowned. He turned to face her fully, gaze dropping to her stomach and then back up. A smile lifted his lips. His metallic eyes shimmered vampire silver. Then he tossed back his head and laughed, a deep, genuine bellow. Winding down, wiping his eyes, he grinned. "Twins. Girls. This is fantastic."

Jordan grinned, turning the warmth of his smile on her. He tugged her into his battered body. "Yeah, it is." He dropped a gentle kiss on top of her head. "Why don't you go check on Janie and I'll help clean up? Be in soon."

Not one bone in her body wanted to help clean up the dead bodies, whether she was ready to help him lead or not. "Good idea." Squeezing his hand, she shuffled through the main doorway, winding down several flights of stairs and getting caught by the queen.

"Oh, good." Emma pushed unruly black hair off her face. "Come into the lab. I need a blood sample." She all but shoved Katie into the room. "Then I need to get Jordan's. I knew he'd survive the moon. I think his blood will be the key to curing the virus." Excitement flushed her classic face.

Katie dutifully jumped on the examination table. "Is everyone all right?"

"Yep." Emma scratched her chin, reaching for a syringe. "Though Janie had a run-in with a Kurjan. Brave little girl." She sighed. Quick movements had Katie's vein swabbed. Emma took blood, slowly removing the needle and gently placing a bandage over the small wound. "I wish we could end this war now."

A chill swept down Katie's spine. For once, she was very glad she didn't have the queen's psychic abilities. "We'll end the fight, Emma. I know we will." Tucking her arms around her stomach, she reassured both herself and the cubs resting there. "We'll make the world safe."

Nighttime had fallen, bringing a quiet sense of peace to the Realm underground headquarters. Emma Kayrs stretched her legs out on the bed and tossed the stack of papers on the table. Everything had gone fuzzy, her eyes were so tired. "Come to bed, Dage."

The king stood tall, shirtless, staring at a wall screen depicting battle plans. Bruises marred his back from the fight the previous night, but with his abilities, they'd disappear by morning. Their bedroom looked more like a combination of war room and laboratory than an actual place to rest. "The plan is good. Conn and Kane should have Jase home by tomorrow night."

"I know." Emma kept her voice soft, reassuring. "Jase will be all right."

Dage turned, blue emotion shimmering in his silver eyes. "He has to be, though I wish we could find a demon destroyer."

Sounded like a special type of weapon. "Demon destroyer?"

"Yes." The king rubbed his face. "Enhanced female— psychic like you but with the ability to deflect the demon mind powers. Maybe even turn it against them."

Intrigue had Emma sitting up. "Human female?"

Dage shrugged. "Rumor has it. I've never seen one . . . they've probably died out if they ever existed. I'm sure the demons went after them, unless they're just a myth." He growled low. "I should've found the truth about them before sending Jase into danger."

Worry and hurt for her husband mingled with concern for Jase. "He wanted to go on this mission, Dage. He's a soldier, and he was ready."

"He's my brother." Simple words, yet a true indication of what the king faced every day in balancing family and duty.

"You trained him well."

"Aye, we all trained him well." Dage stretched his neck, all powerful male animal. "Jordan is all right?"

Hope caught Emma's breath in her throat. "Yes. I think his blood will give me the cure for the virus. As soon as Kane gets back, we can really get down to business." Though she'd do everything possible before then.

Dage nodded. "Jordan's results show no sign of the virus?"

"Not yet. There are still markers in place, but I'm hoping it'll disappear. Or become irrelevant, like mononucleosis after someone survives infection." Emma stretched, purposefully flashing a bit of leg beneath the shimmering blue negligee. "When Katie bit him, she, in effect, mated him. He's back to the arrogant lion leader we've always known." Emma grinned.

Dage quirked a lip. "Arrogance in a leader? What shall we do? Good thing I lack such baser emotions."

She couldn't help the snort of disbelief. Then she took in the king. Broad chest, wicked tattoo of the Kayrs marking winding over his shoulder to his back, a truly sexy vampire. Long legs, so much power for one man. A slow smile spread across her face. "You seem to have quite a lot of energy although you just fought all last night."

One arrogant eyebrow lifted. "I always have enough energy for you, love." Two steps and he perched a knee on the bed, sliding forward to trap her beneath him.

"Prove it, king."

Several quarters down, Talen Kayrs growled low, his gaze on the food before him. Pressing his elbows into the table, he frowned again.

Cara rolled her eyes, shutting the refrigerator door. "Stop growling. Janie wanted to stay with Maggie tonight, and I figured she needed the normalcy of a girl's night. Well, a fun night, considering Garrett went, too."

"She should be here." Rough, pissed, his voice caressed right down Cara's spine as if his finger traced every vertebrae.

Desire slid through her veins like a good wine. "Our daughter is fine, Talen." Cara flipped around, hands on hips. They'd faced a serious threat the previous night, now finally had a night alone, and the damn vampire wanted to pout? Not on her watch.

"Fine?" Talen shoved away from the table. "Janie has been in a coma, been threatened in a dream, and then threatened in reality by a Kurjan leader who breached my security."

Cara sucked in air, searching for patience. Or maybe a bat. Yeah, she'd clock him on the head with a bat. "Yes. But you saved her from the Kurjan." Pride filled Cara for a moment. "Or rather, our girl was in the process of saving herself. You've trained her well."

Talen scrubbed both hands down his face. "When the werewolf grabbed her . . ."

Cara shot the horrendous images out of her head. "Are you sure Kalin wasn't at the bottom of the cliffs?" More than anything, she wanted the Kurjan leader dead. Dead and gone.

"He survived the fall." Talen's eyes burned a sharp green through the gold, a true sign of a vampire's temper. "We scoured the rocks, the cliffs, even out to sea. Several werewolves were found and we finished them off. But, while no doubt he's injured, Kalin lives."

"I figured." Kurjans were stronger than werewolves. Cara shook her head. "I want him dead, but I can't help but feel sorry for the kid he was. I mean, when his father kidnapped me, I saw evil and crazy up close. Can you imagine being raised by someone like that?"

Talen grimaced. "You can't go feeling sorry for the monster that's coming after your family, mate. No matter how crazy his parent may have been."

"I know." And she'd kill Kalin herself if she ever got the chance. Protecting her babies had been her number-one priority since day one. That would never change. She focused on the one man who could make her forget her worries, even for just a little while. "Why are you so cranky? I thought talking with Conn would ease your mind."

His massive shoulders rolled. "I should be there tomorrow—to get Jase."

"The plan is good, right?"

"Yes." Talen rubbed his chin, his gaze wandering down her form. "He'll be home tomorrow. Hopefully without too much mental damage." The words were calm, but an underlying current of concern lifted the consonants.

"Jase is strong. Smart and strong." Cara kept her own fears out of her voice. "Plus, we're all here for him when he gets back."

Talen scowled. "I know."

"Then quit your tantrum. Everything's fine."

"Tantrum?" He paused, irritation deepening the lines in his face.

Ah, there he was. "Yes. If you're going to be such a big baby, I'm heading for girls' night, too."

"You're not going anywhere."

Heat rippled through her body. Her sex softened. "Oh yeah?" They both needed a distraction, and she knew just what would work. "We'll see about that." She lunged for the door, yelping when he caught her around the waist, lifting her.

Trying to struggle, shoving down gales of laughter, she bit his shoulder as he stalked toward the bedroom.

He chuckled. "Now I'm gonna bite you."

Jordan found Katie in the playroom, shooting pool with Maggie and Janie. Garrett sat in the corner playing an old table of Pac-Man. It seemed the young vamp had decided to dog his sister's every move to keep her safe. The poor thing would never date now.

Katie looked up, a smile spreading across her face.

Warmth settled in his heart, granting peace and a sense of family. Something he'd denied himself far too long. The woman had a strength he'd failed to see for too long, as well. Nobody else on earth could've kept him from jumping in to the moon's warmth the previous night.

He nodded at Janie. "Are you all right?"

She smiled, pretty blue eyes sparkling. "Fantastic. No worries. I don't even have a headache anymore." She turned back to study the billiards on the table.

He cleared his throat, facing Maggie. "Terrent Vilks had to leave on an emergency in Canada but made a formal request for you to meet with the Bane's Council at their headquarters next week."

"No." Katie jumped in front of Maggie. "She's not going."

Jordan had no intention of forcing Maggie anywhere. "I said I'd ask, but it's up to Maggie. At some point, the request will probably turn into an order." He grinned. "Apparently Terrent is rather, ah, irritated with you."

Maggie blushed a deep red. "I couldn't imagine why."

Katie shuffled her feet. "Gee. Me, either."

Jordan forced the smile off his face. "Really? Hmmm. I believe it has something to do with a missing helicopter and a grand scheme set into motion by my mate."

"Don't blame her—it was my fault," Maggie snapped, tapping the bottom of her stick on the floor.

Katie groaned, rolling her eyes. "I was going for complete denial, Mags."

"Oh." Maggie gave a rueful smile. "My bad."

Jordan tried to look stern. The humorous, unapologetic glances from the two female shifters pretty much guaranteed he'd missed the mark.

Dodging forward, he lifted Katie off the ground, cradling her. "We're off to bed, mate of mine." With a nod to Maggie and the kids, he squired his mate out of the room and down the hallway to their quarters. Going inside, he kicked the door shut with one boot. "Helicopter and kidnapping?"

Her tongue darted out to wet her lips, her gaze wandering the line of his neck. "We had to get Terrent out of here in case you turned into a werewolf. You would've done the same for me."

True, and not something he could truly argue against. Now Terrent seemed more determined than ever to get Maggie within reach of the Bane's Council. A fact Jordan would share with Katie on another day. Plus, they truly needed to find out why the demons wanted the little wolf shifter. "Your plan worked, sweetheart."

"Of course our plan worked." She toyed with the neck-line on his T-shirt. Her claws shot out and ripped the cotton down the middle. "Oops."

He shifted her to one arm, tugging her shirt over her head. "Double oops."

Quick as any cat, she moved, straddling his waist. His hands settled on her butt, holding her against his suddenly raging erection. Slowly, with just enough pressure to drive them both insane, he slid her against his length, striding toward the bedroom.

Grabbing his face, she tugged him close and wandered along his lips. "I love you, Jordan. No matter what . . . and I'm keeping you forever."

He took her mouth in a hard kiss, deepening it, giving everything. Drawing back, he captured her tawny gaze. "I love you, too. Welcome home, kitten."

Epilogue

The doorbell pealed. An odd sound, considering Jordan had known his guests had arrived on the ranch the second they'd crossed the first fence, nearly three miles away. The lion leader loped to his feet, deserting his favorite leather chair and his momentary peace.

He leaned down, picking up two pink bunnies and a small tennis shoe on the way to the door. A homey fire crackled in the brick fireplace, while the television played some odd show with a purple dinosaur.

Opening the door, he gave a slow smile. "Welcome to chaos." He tossed the stuffed animals into an overflowing bin by the wall.

Kane Kayrs shook rain from his hair. "Thanks. My neck is itching like you wouldn't believe. How many snipers have their sights trained on me?" He shoved Janie Kayrs inside, using his body as a shield until he could shut the door. Then he relaxed, unconcern on his face.

"How many did you feel?" Someday Jordan would discover Kane's true talents. Probably not today, though. He reached for Janie, enveloping the young woman in a hug.

"Three."

Son of a bitch. "Yep. Three snipers." Jordan released

the little brunette. "It has been a pain, but we wanted to let the girls live at the ranch for a couple of months, aboveground. They need to see life up here. There are roving squads as well as camera feeds all along the perimeter." He and Baye had discussed land mines, but they were just too risky. Plus, money was still incredibly tight. Good thing he had owned the ranch free and clear before war broke out.

Kane nodded. "Yeah, and after the last big battle, the Kurjans have backed off. At least for now."

Jordan gestured toward the leather couch. The pretty pillows Katie had picked last year were strewn about the room. "Have a seat and tell me what you couldn't say on the phone."

The quiet was too good to last. Almost on cue, two whirlwinds ran into the room, blond hair flying. "Unk Kane!" they both shouted, leaping for the vampire.

He caught them easily, swinging both toddlers into the air for noisy kisses. Even as he moved, a sense of restrained gentleness cascaded from him, as if he was a little afraid of the boisterous bundles. "Well, if it isn't Menace and Mayhem."

Katie strode into the room, wiping her hands on a dish towel. "You really have to stop calling them those names. They'll stick."

Jordan hid a smile. The nicknames fit, unfortunately. He winked at his mate, pleased when a pink flush wandered over her high cheekbones. The woman had tried to pin up her blond hair, but the tendrils escaped in wild disarray. In her faded jeans and old T-shirt, she was truly the sexiest thing he'd ever seen.

She gave him the look that told him to knock it off.

He winked again.

With an eye roll, she glided forward to hug Janie.

"Happy birthday, sweetheart. Well, happy birthday last week."

Janie smiled even white teeth. During the last two years, her face had narrowed, her cheekbones becoming more prominent, just like her mama's. "Thanks for the bracelet you sent—I love silver."

The twins abandoned Kane to get hugs and kisses from Janie. With a mischievous glance at each other, they leapt back for the vampire. For some reason, the stoic scientist was an absolute favorite with the imps.

Jordan chucked Janie on the chin. "How in the world did you escape Realm Headquarters?" Although the girl was eighteen, Talen kept her under wraps. Which made sense, considering the Kurjans had stepped up their plans to get ahold of her. It was dangerous for her to leave Oregon and showed incredible trust in Jordan and his people to keep the girl safe.

Janie chuckled. "I asked to visit you for my birthday present." She grimaced. "Though we brought enough guards to start our own army. They're around the perimeter with your guys."

Jordan nodded. "Yeah. I know Noah was looking forward to arm wrestling Max again."

"Dorks." Janie grinned.

Kane cleared his throat, gracefully sitting on the sofa, a giggling blonde in each arm. "Samantha, Sidney, stop pulling my hair."

The giggles deepened as the girls tugged on his ears. The vampire rolled his eyes. "I'm here with good news."

Katie stilled, her gaze cutting to Jordan and back.

Jordan shook his head. Hope slammed into his gut. He and Katie had allowed Kane to poke and prod them for two years . . . trying to figure out how they were both healthy, purebred shifters again lacking any results from the virus. Other male shifters had tried to mate infected females to heal them, and it hadn't worked. Only Jordan's blood, right after being infected but before turning into a werewolf, had worked in fixing Katie. Then her bite had somehow cured him. The scientists had been unable to duplicate the exact interaction. Yet. He sighed. "I don't know what it is."

Janie maneuvered around stuffed animals and tossed pillows to sit on the couch. "Good news, for sure."

Kane cleared his throat. "The cure works and we've created an inoculation for shifters. Virus-27 will never harm your people again."

Katie dropped into the chair Jordan had vacated. "Are you sure?" Tears filled her eyes.

"Yes." Kane smiled, his eyes remaining serious. "Whatever happened with the two of you, when you were both infected but Jordan hadn't turned into a werewolf yet . . . created antibodies for shifters. Emma and I just finished formulating the inoculation. We'll give shots to all shifters."

Jordan struggled to keep from shouting out loud. Finally. A cure for their people . . . a way to balance the forces in the war destroying the world.

Then he frowned as Kane's words sunk home. "Only shifters? What about vampire mates and witches?"

Kane rubbed his chin. "The inoculation only works on shifters. But it's one more step toward curing mates and witches. We're incredibly hopeful at this point."

Jordan lifted Katie from the chair and sat down, repositioning her on his lap. She curled in to him. "Well, this is good news." No more shifters becoming werewolves. The Kurjan fighting forces just decreased. But the first step wasn't enough. Sure, the Realm was on the right path, but everyone needed to be free of the virus.

Katie took a deep breath. "What about people already infected?"

"No help for males already turned into werewolves." Kane's face remained placid, while regret flashed in his eyes. "We think the inoculation will cure infected females as well as any males infected who haven't turned into werewolves yet. Of course, we don't know of any infected males who haven't turned."

"Most werewolves have been finished off by the Bane's Council," Katie murmured. "Keeping Terrent busy the last two years has been . . . beneficial to Maggie. At some point, he's going to request her presence again. And we still haven't figured out what the demons want with her."

Jordan shrugged. "We'll worry about that when it happens." Frankly, he thought Maggie might like to visit a wolf pack and be among her own people. But the woman staunchly refused to meet with Terrent. Wolves were well known for carrying a grudge, and the Alpha wolf was probably no exception.

He snuggled his woman closer. They'd led well together the last two years—her time living with humans had taught her empathy and a way of communicating that'd he lacked. Of course, when it came to blood and fighting, he took the lead, whether his fierce lioness liked it or not. She was the mother of his cubs, after all.

Another change involved his delegating more to the Chance brothers—to trust and not lead alone. So far, the new methods were really working.

He cleared his throat. "Any word on Jase?"

Kane stiffened, shaking his head. "No. Dage gets visions once in a while, and we believe Jase is still alive. In fact, sources in the southwest have reported murmurings of a vampire being brought to the states by the demons. So we think we're getting close to getting him back."

Jordan nodded. "When it's time to go, I want in."

"Of course." Kane gave a short nod. "But for tonight, I think we should celebrate the end of the virus for your people. It's the beginning of the end to the war."

Janie tugged Sidney's braid, turning a sweet smile on them. "What you did, risking your lives, you created a cure for all shifters. A cure that will someday work on mates and save my mother. I can't tell you how much that means to me."

Katie placed her hand over Jordan's heart. "Every risk we took was the right choice."

Jordan covered her hand, kissing her nose. "You were the right choice. Always."

After a commotion-filled dinner with Jordan's family, they'd watched a movie about ponies, and then Janie had headed off to bed. Two years had passed since she'd been in a coma, and her energy had finally returned. But flying all day had tired her out.

She dropped into the dream as she'd planned, wandering down the sandy beach and enjoying the soft spray of waves. With a shrug, she continued down the sand, committing to the path she'd come up with months ago. Her birthday wish held more than a desire to visit Katie and the twins. Leaving home, getting away from the mental power of the vampires and mates surrounding her, allowed her some space to explore. To create a dream and hopefully have enough power to find Zane.

She purposefully created the same ocean scene from when she'd been in the coma. Hopefully the plan would work.

A new fire had lit her veins after waking from the coma, a power she hadn't figured out how to tap. Yet.

Aunt Emma had taken blood, assuring her everything was normal. No extra vampire remnants, either from Garrett or Zane, remained in her human blood.

Emma was wrong.

Janie had tried bending spoons with her mind, punching a bag, imagining the future on demand. So far, whatever new bubbled inside her, hadn't changed her a bit. But she could feel something . . . or rather someone.

Zane lived in her pores more than ever before. Sure, he didn't want to. Whatever or whoever he was, he held serious power. Nobody else in the world could've saved her by giving her blood in a dream. That much she knew.

Either that, or she had a serious crush.

The sand warmed her bare feet. She hadn't meant to be barefoot in the dream, but suddenly, the feeling calmed her. Continuing down the beach, she kept her gaze on the rock outcroppings from last time. The sun shone down, not too hot, just right to enhance the soft breeze.

Zane sat on a rock a few feet up, long legs dangling. The sun glinted off his short black hair that was a couple inches longer than last time she'd seen him. No more buzz cut. Even with the dangerous scar lining his face, his features were beautiful. Masculine, tough, yet symmetrical to the point of perfection.

Yeah. She probably had a crush.

He lifted an eyebrow. "Happy birthday."

Joy filled her so fast she bit her lip to keep from exploding in a smile. "Thanks."

"Did you do anything big?"

She shrugged, going for casual. The six-year difference in their ages didn't seem like such a big deal since she'd turned eighteen. "Party. Like usual." Her hands slid into the pockets of her shorts. "I've tried to seek you out in dreams so many times, but you've been blocking me. So, ah, thanks for saving my life two years ago. For giving me blood."

He rubbed both large hands down the front of his dark jeans. "Sure. I couldn't let you die." The smile was one she remembered from childhood. "Though, well, I don't understand how it worked."

"Yeah." No logic could explain their connection in dreams.

She crinked her neck to peer up at him. "I'm surprised to see you here." Sure, she'd hoped. But he'd gotten so good at blocking.

He rubbed his chin. "I'm surprised to be here. Every time I go to sleep, I put mental blocks in place. Yet, I'm here." Curiosity and caution lit his green eyes.

Satisfaction heated her abdomen. "I'm not at home. I'm away from my uncle's psychic powers, away from the powers of all the people surrounding me." She took another couple steps toward the future. "I thought maybe I could send out a clearer signal . . . maybe yank you here even if you didn't want to come." Of course, since she'd taken his blood, as her powers increased, she might be able to seek him out even at home. She lifted her chin, trying so hard not to be mad he'd ignored her for two more years.

One dark eyebrow lifted. As graceful as any panther, he jumped from the rock. Sand sprayed when his thick boots landed.

Janie took a step back. Man, he'd gotten tall. As tall as Dage.

Both of Zane's eyebrows lifted. "So, let me get this straight. You left the safety of the king's headquarters to enable yourself to become more powerful and force me, willing or not, into this dream?"

Well, since he put her idea like that. She shuffled her feet in the sand. "Pretty much."

"Why?" The sun came from behind him now, leaving his eyes in shadow.

Because she'd missed him. Because she needed him. "I think it's time we begin planning to end this war."

He choked on a laugh. "Just like that, huh, Belle? Let's just end this fucking war."

Irritation began to crawl up her neck. "Yeah. Just fucking like that. We've always known this war will come down to you, me, and Kalin. I'm grown up now . . . it's time."

"Grown up?" Zane breathed out, turning just enough for the sun to highlight high cheekbones. Incredulousness melded with anger on his strong face. "You're not even close. You have no idea

*what war is like. No clue." He scrubbed a hand across his mouth.
"Let's just end this war." He shook his head.*

*So she hadn't fought on the front lines. She'd lost people. A
monstrous vampire race had hunted her since childhood. "I know
exactly what war is like."*

*"No, you don't. God, I hope you never do." He shoved his
hands in his jeans pockets. "Everything is so clear to you. Right,
wrong . . . good, bad . . . friend, enemy. You have no concep-
tion of true war."*

*The day he'd lost his father, his world had crashed. She knew
that and had been there for him as much as he'd let her. Reality
wasn't foreign to her, either. She knew the risks they might face.
If he lived with a shifter clan off the grid, he could be fighting
against her people. Against her family. "I know your father
wasn't part of the Realm, but he was an ally. But where you've
gone, the people you fight for now . . . I don't know. Are we still
allies?"*

*Zane wet his lips, his gaze cutting to the ocean. His impres-
sive chest shifted as he exhaled and yanked his hands free. Focusing back on her, he took one step forward. Light as any breeze,
he ran one knuckle down her cheek. Sadness and an odd longing
swirled in his eyes. "Janie Belle Kayrs."*

*Warmth and something new flared to life in her abdomen. In-
trigue had her stilling. "Zane?"*

*His gaze dropped to her mouth. His thumb followed suit, trac-
ing her bottom lip. "All grown up and in more danger than
ever." Dropping his hand, he sighed. "There are no allies right
now, Belle. Get that through your head . . . and don't trust anybody."*

*She lifted her chin, ignoring the sudden want of her lips. For
the briefest of seconds, she thought he was going to kiss her. A
real kiss. From Zane. "You said we were going to fix the world.
That everything was going to be all right."*

"I was twelve, and I figured we had the same goals for the

world." His jaw firmed. "We probably did. But when my father died—"

"Where are you?" She had to know. If she had all the facts, she could fix this.

"Doesn't matter. What does matter"—*he grabbed her biceps, leaning down, his face intense and two inches from hers*—*"is that I don't know where you are. Ever."*

"Everybody knows where headquarters is." Her uncle and father had made it the safest place in the world for her. They'd discussed moving, but at some point, staying in place and defending made more sense.

"You're not at headquarters right now." Zane gave her a quick shake. The scar along his jaw seemed to deepen. "If I were an enemy, you just gave away too much information."

"Are you?" She met his gaze squarely and without fear. Nothing would ever convince her Zane would harm her. Nothing. "Are you my enemy?"

His nostrils flared. "No, which is why I'm telling you no more. We don't meet. You don't tell me where you are. You take that fantastic brain and do something really great with it. Study, learn . . . do not fight. Get the hell out of the war, as much as you can, for as long as you can."

His hands enclosed her upper arms, so strong, so warm. A step forward and she'd be pressed along his length. Surprise filled her at how much she wanted to take that step. She shook her head. "This war is about me, Zane." Unfortunately, the Kurjans would stop at nothing to get her. "You've known that from day one."

"I know." He blinked twice, his eyes filling with determination when he focused back on her. "But I need you to stay out of it until I can end it."

"But we're supposed to end the war together." In every vision she'd had, while different results were reached, she had always been a player. She, Zane, and Kalin all participated in whatever final act found peace. Unfortunately, she never saw who won.

Zane's hold tightened. "You stay in this war, and you won't like how it ends. I promise, Belle." Drawing back, he released her. "Good-bye."

The dream disappeared. Janie awoke, sitting up in bed. She hadn't gotten the answers she wanted, but she had a lot more information than she'd hoped. Zane wasn't working for the Realm, but he seemed determined to save her. Somehow, she had to figure out a way to get them working together again. In all the visions, in all the endings, if they weren't on the same side, then everything ended.

Everything.

Looking for more of Rebecca Zanetti's Dark Protectors? Please read on for an excerpt from *Shadowed*, available this month.

Chapter One

"**I** won't be used."

"We'll both be used, sweetheart." The endearment mocked them both. "But we'll get what we want."

She stood, no longer able to sit and discuss revenge and forever. "What is it I want, Jase?"

"You want to live." He unfolded his length, standing at least a foot and a half taller than she. Reaching out, he ran his finger down the side of her face. "You used to like me, Brenna Dunne."

The gentle touch slid right under her defenses and zinged around, warming her abdomen. Her breath quickened. Vulnerability and need battled through her at his obvious manipulation. "I don't know you anymore."

His upper lip twisted. "Nobody knows me anymore." The scar stood out, even on his bronze skin. "I won't hurt you."

So much for being over her childhood crush. Deep down, a base part of her awoke with the thought that he wanted to mate her. She didn't want to die, and she'd love to help him regain his gift. Hell, five minutes in his presence and she wanted to jump him. But to mate out of necessity? "I don't know."

He gave a quick nod. "You have time to think about it." Callused fingers slid the shirt off her left shoulder.

Cool air brushed her. Awareness flushed through her, but the chair kept her from stepping back. "What are you doing?" she breathed.

His gaze dropped to her neck. "I'm going to bite you, and then you're going to bite me."

Her lungs seized. She shook her head, dislodging his fingers. "Why?"

"To feel better." His thumb and forefinger grasped her chin, tilting her head back. "My blood will give you temporary strength, but I need to bite you first so your body can take it." The intensity of his gaze slammed awareness through her blood. "If you're going to consider my offer, I'd prefer you remembered how it felt to be at full strength."

Temptation smacked up against caution. Heat flushed through her from the firm hold on her chin. Commanding and strong, Jase tempted her in a frightening, primal way.

Taking his blood once wouldn't create any sort of bond, and the idea of having strength again, even temporarily, swelled her with hope. Curiosity stretched awake. Years ago, when they'd both been healthy and unharmed, she'd had more than one fantasy of his taking her blood. "All right."

His fangs dropped—low and wicked.

Intrigue hummed beneath her skin.

Releasing her chin, he slid his palm down her bicep and around her waist. With ease and deliberation, he lifted her with one muscled arm.

The intrigue shot into desire. His easy strength fluttered need around her body to thrum between her legs.

His free hand tangled in her hair and tugged her head to the side. Her fingers curled over his hard shoulders.

Lowering his head, he enclosed her neck with his mouth. The sharp points slid into her flesh.

Her breath caught. She opened her mouth, her mind swirling. Her nipples pebbled against his chest. Need ripped through her blood as his mouth pulled. Images of his mouth exploring her body in other ways flashed in picture-form through her brain, and she moaned.

Slowly, the deadly points retracted, and he licked the wound. His tongue was slightly abrasive. She shivered.

He set her down. She released his shoulders and glanced up at his face.

Lust shimmered in his eyes, and crimson spiraled across his high cheekbones. His fingers remained tangled in her hair. Keeping her gaze, he lifted his free wrist and slashed with his fangs. Securing her, he slid his bleeding wrist against her lips.

The moment held much more intimacy than she'd expected. Tingles jabbed her mouth. She opened, and the liquid slid in.

Fire.

She drank, and sparkles popped down her throat. Electricity shot inside her veins. It was almost too much. She turned away, and he removed his wrist. Tightening his grip, he tugged her back around to face him.

Her gaze wide on his, her veins flashing with power, she licked the remaining blood off her lips.

His eyes flared. His lids dropped to half-mast.

Then his mouth took hers.

GREAT BOOKS, GREAT SAVINGS!

When You Visit Our Website:
www.kensingtonbooks.com
You Can Save Money Off The Retail Price
Of Any Book You Purchase!

- **All Your Favorite Kensington Authors**
- **New Releases & Timeless Classics**
- **Overnight Shipping Available**
- **eBooks Available For Many Titles**
- **All Major Credit Cards Accepted**

Visit Us Today To Start Saving!
www.kensingtonbooks.com

All Orders Are Subject To Availability.
Shipping and Handling Charges Apply.
Offers and Prices Subject To Change Without Notice.